FIRE IN

Lightning flashed and filled the room with cold brilliance. The candle flickered and went out.

Annie reached out, searching for matches. Her hand encountered a wall of sleek wet flesh.

"Quiet," T'maho said. Then his hands closed over her shoulders, drawing her against him.

It never occurred to Annie to be frightened. She was all alone with a man who was a stranger. The strangest kind of stranger.

So why did it feel as if she had finally come home?

At the warm touch of his breath, she closed her eyes and lifted her face to his. Just as lightning struck again, the last remnant of reason she possessed flickered out like a candle in the wind. . . .

ANNOUNCING THE

TOPAZ FREQUENT READERS CLUB
COMMEMORATING TOPAZ'S
1 YEAR ANNIVERSARY!

THE MORE YOU BUY, THE MORE YOU GET

Redeem coupons found here and in the back of all new Topaz titles for FREE Topaz gifts:

Send in:

 2 coupons for a free TOPAZ novel (choose from the list below);

☐ THE KISSING BANDIT, Margaret Brownley
☐ BY LOVE UNVEILED, Deborah Martin
☐ TOUCH THE DAWN, Chelley Kitzmiller
☐ WILD EMBRACE, Cassie Edwards

 4 coupons for an "I Love the Topaz Man" on-board sign

 6 coupons for a TOPAZ compact mirror

 8 coupons for a Topaz Man T-shirt

Just fill out this certificate and send with original sales receipts to:

TOPAZ FREQUENT READERS CLUB-1ST ANNIVERSARY
Penguin USA • Mass Market Promotion; Dept. H.U.G.
375 Hudson St., NY, NY 10014

Name_____

Address_____

City_____State_____Zip_____

Offer expires 5/31/1995

This certificate must accompany your request. No duplicates accepted. Void where prohibited, taxed or restricted. Allow 4-6 weeks for receipt of merchandise. Offer good only in U.S., its territories, and Canada.

Bedeviled

by

Bronwyn Williams

A TOPAZ BOOK

TOPAZ
Published by the Penguin Group
Penguin Books USA Inc., 375 Hudson Street,
New York, New York 10014, U.S.A.
Penguin Books Ltd, 27 Wrights Lane,
London W8 5TZ, England
Penguin Books Australia Ltd, Ringwood,
Victoria, Australia
Penguin Books Canada Ltd, 10 Alcorn Avenue,
Toronto, Ontario, Canada M4V 3B2
Penguin Books (N.Z.) Ltd, 182–190 Wairau Road,
Auckland 10, New Zealand

Penguin Books Ltd, Registered Offices:
Harmondsworth, Middlesex, England

First published by Topaz, an imprint of Dutton Signet,
a division of Penguin Books USA Inc.

First Printing, March, 1995
10 9 8 7 6 5 4 3 2 1

To the late Ellis Andrew Gray, Sr.,
who first told us about the glade,
and to all the others from Kinnakeet village
and the wonderful stories they shared.

Bedeviled

Chapter 1

September 1830

"Days like this, damned if I don't wish we was a-herdin' woollies," the old man muttered as he flapped his hat and shooed another wild-eyed steer toward the chute. "Git 'im, son! Watch out fer them stickers!"

His warning came too late. The shorthorn caught T'maho just as he leaned down to make the cut, ripping off his sweat-stained headband and laying open an inch of scalp.

Mingo, Eli's herdsman, nimbly sidestepped the flying hooves. T'maho, who had agreed to help out only because the fish wouldn't run again until the wind shifted, swore and mopped the streaming blood from his eyes with a dusty forearm. It wasn't the first injury of the day, nor would it be the last. Earmarking a herd of half-wild cattle was no tea party, even under the best conditions.

Today was hardly that. The air dripped with moisture. Heat hovered in shimmering waves above the sand, and occasionally the sound of thunder could be heard from a squall out over the ocean.

9

The three men had been attempting to finish the job before Eli left to catch the mail boat, which had been spotted heading into Kinnakeet Harbor some little while ago. At first sight of the familiar sails, Eli had ridden back to the house, quickly changed into his go-to-town clothes, and returned.

Now, stepping back from the fray, the old man brushed the dust from his misshapen hat, tugged at the neck of his shirt, and examined the soles of his boots. Earmarking was a dirty, dangerous business, even with two of the best cattlemen on the island to help out.

Mingo was good, but the half-breed, T'maho, was even better. It was said he could whisper into a horse's nostrils and make the beast lie down and roll over. Trouble was, he didn't much like working cattle, and he downright refused to work for any man regular-like.

"You want to go on, Eli, we'll finish up here," said the badly scarred Mingo, cracking a whip above another bony rump. "Hii-yiii! Move in there, you bloody bastard!" Mounted on a shaggy Banker workhorse, he signaled to the tall man balanced on the fence above the chute, then turned to cut another steer from the herd.

"Make damn sure ye slice down far enough," Eli called up to the blood-streaked, dust-coated figure wielding the blade.

Straddling the fence post, T'maho leaned down and grabbed another half-wild shorthorn. One graceful sweep of the wicked blade and the job was done. He pulled the rope that lifted the drawbar, and the steer made a dash for freedom, bawling his indignation.

The next in line moved up. A less skilled man might

have been thrown when the terrified animal tossed his head, but T'maho pivoted easily, his lithe, powerful body compensating for the shorthorn's bucking and twisting.

Catching Mingo's eye, T'maho allowed his feelings to show for a single moment. *Like all white fools, this one insists on putting his mark on all he touches. Be warned, my friend, or he'll own you, too.*

On the other side of the crudely built chute, Mingo grinned and waved in another steer. He had read the message in his friend's eyes, being well aware of T'maho's feelings toward the white man.

Who, after all these years, wasn't?

Someone had once said in Mingo's hearing that of the two men, T'maho was the more scarred, the difference being that Mingo's scars were on the outside for all to see, while T'maho's were hidden away inside.

Mingo had shrugged it off. He had long since come to terms with his own scars. As for T'maho's, only time would tell.

He did know that the money his friend earned this day would help pay for the fine new boat he was buying. A boat built by a white man, to be used in trade with other whites. T'maho resented his own white blood, but he was not fool enough to go back to fishing from a dugout canoe with a vine-woven weir, using beating sticks to drive the fish into his trap.

Mounted on a mouse-gray mule named Jacob, Eli rode over to where the two men worked. "Reck'n I'd best be a-gittin' on down to th' landin'," he called over the noise. "Much obliged for helpin' out today, T'maho."

His words were ignored, which didn't come as any great surprise to Eli. T'maho ignored most white men, and that was the truth with no bark on it. It occurred to Eli that if the arrogant bastard was to come upon a white man going down for the third time, he might haul his ass out of the water, but he wouldn't hand him any rag to dry off with.

Still, he was a good hand with cattle. None better. Had a way with wild horses that was downright spooky. If it hadn't been for the thunder squall offshore that made the herd restless, and if the men hadn't been hurrying to finish up before Eli had to leave, he'd likely have got through the day without a scratch.

Mounted above old Jacob, Eli O'Neal gazed out over the new herd and shook his grizzled red head. When Snell had sent word three weeks ago that he was fixing to ship out a small herd from up Currituck way, Eli had warned him that the land wouldn't take much more grazing. Snell had sent word back that the herd was such a steal he couldn't resist.

Be damned lucky if they didn't all starve.

As an equal partner in the Snell-O'Neal Cattle Concern, Eli's job, aside from providing the land, was to take delivery and oversee the day-to-day operations. Snell, who traveled extensively in his capacity as justice of the peace, took care of the buying and the paperwork, which suited Eli just fine, because Eli had never been much of a traveler, nor much of a hand at paperwork.

When the time came, Snell would handle the selling as well, and they'd both be set up for life.

They had just been getting started earmarking this newest bunch when word had come from Snell for Eli to catch the next boat out and meet him at Tar Landing over on the mainland. Pushed for time, Mingo had called in his friend, T'maho, to help out. Even so, what with the weather being so chancy, it had taken the three men nearly a day and a half to wind up the earmarking, and there were still thirteen bull calves penned up, waiting for the knife.

"Sure you don't want to borrow my horse, Eli?" Mingo called out, his badly scarred face twisted into a grotesque grin. "By the time that old mule of yours makes Kinnakeet, the mail boat'll be come and gone again."

"Don't you worry none about me 'n' old Jacob. He'll git me there before she sails, else he won't find no licorice candy in my pocket when I git back."

"You be gone long?" Mingo asked.

"Two days out, one day there, two days back. I make it about a week."

"I'll see to cutting the calves."

"Much obliged, son. Jacob'll find his way back to the shed before long. 'Preciate it if you'd pitch him a forkful of grass now 'n' again."

Mingo always looked after things when Eli had business on the mainland—not that there was much to see to. He was a good man. Eli had got so he hardly even noticed his face.

Given a choice, he'd have sooner had T'maho working for him, for Eli had a suspicion the man was a sight smarter than he let on. Knew for a fact he could read and write. Some said he'd gone to a regular school over on the mainland, but you'd never know it now.

Eli admired independence as much as the next man. Trouble was, independence was expensive, and damned hard to come by. Plodding across the barren sand toward the narrow glade trail that served as a shortcut to the village, the old man ruminated on the vagaries of mankind. He'd never held it against any man for being born Indian. Hell, Eli himself had been born Irish, and most folks didn't hold that against him. His dear departed wife, Matilda, had come out of Padstow in Cornwall, and she hadn't held his Irish against him.

His little Annie, now, she'd been born right here in North Carolina. One of these days, Eli vowed as he entered the junglelike glade that separated his thirteen-hundred-acre spread from the village of Kinnakeet, he was going to fix up the house and fetch her out here to live with him.

He couldn't honestly say he'd missed the girl, even though it did get a mite lonesome some nights, living out here all alone with nothing to keep him company but a few hundred head of cattle, a dumb old mule, and one ornery rooster.

Still, he'd done what he figured his Tildie would have wanted, putting little Annie in that fancy school with a decent, God-fearing widow to look after her and see that she grew up to be a fine lady, just like her mama.

Eli nodded thoughtfully. Yep. It was time he fixed the

old place up, maybe build on another room. Might even put up a fence so she could have her a garden. After a while he'd see if Mingo could get T'maho to cut her a pretty little pony out of the wild herd that roamed the island and tame her down some so she could come and go to the village whenever she took a notion.

Come to think of it, he didn't even know if the girl could ride, which was just one of the things he didn't know about her.

His own daughter. Eli had laid off to get back to Hillsborough to see her long before now. What with one thing and another, though, the time never seemed right.

Then, too, he had to admit he'd been distracted lately. Most every time he came away from meeting with Snell, he got this aggravating itch in his brain that no amount of head-scratching seemed to cure. Something wasn't setting quite right, but danged if he could put his finger on it.

Still and all, the time had come to do something about Annie. She was bound to be growing up, and a grown girl needed a real home, not a school. Another few years and he might even start looking around for some decent, hardworking gentleman needing a wife who could read and write and be a credit to him. He wouldn't mind seeing a few grandsons before he went to join his Tildie in the Great Hereafter.

Must be the weather that had him so fidgety, Eli told himself. Worrying about Snell, worrying about Annie. He wasn't by nature a worrying man, but lately his conscience had been kicking up a fuss on him, reminding him that in his yearly letters, he might have led Annie to expect something better than he'd had time to build by way of a house.

As for her own letters, they'd gotten so fine and full of fancy words that a man couldn't half make out that, after a while, he'd sort of stopped trying.

First thing when he got back, he thought piously, he was going to take those letters of Annie's to Miz Rachael and get her to read every word until he knew them by heart. Then, just as soon as Snell sold out and Eli had the money in hand, he was going to set about building his little girl the kind of house she deserved.

Shifting his slight weight on the worn-out saddle, Eli thought back to the house she'd been born in. It had belonged to Tildie's folks and was finer than anything he could ever have bought, but he'd kept it in good repair. Right up until he'd sold it.

"Lord, I ain't been a real good pappy to my little Annie," he muttered, lifting his eyes heavenward. "That's the plain truth with no bark on it, but you tell Tildie fer me that I'm a-gonna do better jest as soon's I git back here." Clearing his throat, he tacked on an "Amen," just for good measure.

For some reason, his little Annie seemed closer today than she had in years. Eli set it down to his newly awakened conscience. Lifting his hat, he wiped the sweat off his brow and thought back to the day he had left her at that fancy place with the twisted iron fence and the hand-painted sign naming the house as some old biddy's school for intelligent girls.

It had hurt him right bad to leave her there, but he'd

done it for her own good. Living in the house he'd shared with his Tildie, sleeping in the bed she had died in trying to give him a son, he'd all but forgotten about the poor little mite. Then one day during a rare sober moment, he had taken stock and realized he owed it to Tildie to do something about Annie.

So he'd sold the house and given the money to the high-rumped old turnip who ran the school before he could drink it up, telling himself that his Tildie would have been proud of him for making the sacrifice.

But Lordy, he could see it plain as yesterday—his little Annie bawling her eyes out and begging him not to leave her, and him promising to come for her just as soon as he dried out enough to locate the land grant he'd inherited in some heathen place he'd never even heard of. He figured he could look around and find a buyer for the land, then maybe look around some more and find a decent place to start over where every stick of wood didn't remind him of the sweet woman he'd lost.

And then along came Snell with his proposition, and Eli had come out here to the Banks where the nearest tavern was a day's sail away, telling himself he'd get back and fetch his Annie in a year or two—three or four at the most.

But the years had piled up on him, and he hadn't had chance to think about anything but the everlasting work of tending a mess of stinking, ornery, bawling cattle.

Until today. For some reason his Annie felt real close today.

He put it down to the weather. Breeding weather, they called it. Late, hot summers always bred storms out here on the Banks. Made folks feel touchy, like looking over their shoulders to see what was sneaking up behind them.

Eli figured the mail boat would have long since called off the mail, offloaded any freight, and taken on whatever cargo she was hauling out. Gigging Jacob into stepping it up, he reached the wharf, slid to the ground, and whapped the mule on the rump to send him home again just as the boat was getting set to cast off.

"Hang on there, fellers, I'm a-fixin' to go with ye," he called out, and for twenty-eight cents, he purchased himself a shady spot on deck and a bowlful of whatever the cook had stewed up for supper.

Even as Eli set sail on the battered old shallow-draft schooner that plied the Albemarle, Currituck, and Pamlico sounds, an oxcart was making its slow, deliberate way north along the soundside road, driven by a fisherman smoking a pipe to keep the mosquitoes at bay and carrying Miss Annie O'Neal, spinster lady of some eighteen and a half years, and all her worldly possessions.

Annie jounced up and down on the rough plank seat, wishing not for the first time that she had padded her skinny behind with every garment she possessed, and that on top of a pillow!

Instead, in deference to the heat, she had worn a single chemise, a bandette instead of her zona, and her second-best gown. The gown was only three years old, cut down from one of Mrs. Biddlecomb's cast-offs, with the worn places covered with a panel of chintz from one of the sun-faded drawing room curtains. She had hoped to make a fine impression on her father.

The cart hit a place where tide had cut away the sand. Annie's plumed hat slid down over her face, and she shoved it back with no regard at all for the turkey feathers she had curled over a steaming kettle to replace the ostrich plumes that Mrs. B. had kept for herself.

"Will we be there soon?" she asked for the third time.

"T'reckly."

T'reckly. Which meant directly. Which was what he'd said when they'd first set out from the docks in Kinnakeet.

She wondered about the name, having written it on dozens of letters over the years. It was probably Indian. Goodness knows what, if anything, it meant. Ends of the earth, perhaps. She certainly hadn't seen anything that faintly resembled a real town.

However, going back was not an option, even if she'd wanted to. The school was no longer there. There was nothing for it but to go on and hope for the best.

A few miles, Mr. Gray had said. Shorter through the glade, he'd said—but the glade trail was too boggy and narrow for a cart.

Annie waved away a biting fly that had tangled itself in one of her bedraggled feathers. She swallowed hard and blinked away a film of moisture. *Papa, couldn't you even have come to meet me? Don't you even want me?*

She told herself that perhaps he hadn't gotten her last letter, but her heart whispered that if he'd wanted her with him, he would have come for her years ago. Most girls left the school when they turned sixteen. Annie had stayed on, expecting Eli to come for her most any day. What with her sewing and taking care of the younger girls, she had tried not to feel beholden to Mrs. B., but all the same, it had been hard to keep hoping with no sign of encouragement.

She would simply have to prove to her father that he needed her. She was educated. She was capable. She would just show him that he couldn't get along without her.

The cart hit another rut, and Annie grabbed her bonnet. "How much farther?" she asked.

A short while later, dazed from fifteen days of traveling by stage and schooner, Annie stared in disbelief at the bleak prospect before her. As far as the eye could see there was nothing but sand, water and dead grass, scrubby patches of badly pruned shrubbery, random arrangements of fence enclosing nothing—and in the distance what appeared to be acres of cows, kicking up dust and making the most fearful racket.

"This be it, Miss. Old Eli's place. Yonder's his man, up on that there bay horse. Looks like him and Eli must be workin' that new herd Eli brung in early this week."

Slowly, as if in a daze, Annie shook her head. She

had come to the wrong island. Mr. Gray had brought her to the wrong address. This *couldn't* be Papa's place! Where was the neat little twin-gabled cottage like the one she remembered from her childhood? The only buildings in sight were a three-sided shed with a sagging gate, a rough, weathered shack perched up on top of a few skinny poles, and a privy, which was leaning drunkenly at an angle, as if it had been pruned by the same hand that had pruned all the lopsided shrubbery hugging the low, sandy ridges.

Annie's mouth hung open as she watched a cow wander over to the largest of the three buildings—the one set up on posts—lean against the corner, and move back and forth, scratching.

"But where is the house Papa lives in?" she asked.

With a look that held more than a little sympathy, the man nodded toward the hovel where the cow was now blissfully rubbing her head bald between a pair of short, wicked-looking horns. "That there's the onliest house I know of, Miss. Eli, he built it up off'n the ground to keep the tide from washin' it out to sea. Right smart man, yer paw. Big winders." Annie wondered a little wildly how big "winders" could indicate a man's intelligence. "Yep. Built 'er up over the tide and wide open to the wind. A man lives long enough, he learns that what don't bend is bound to break."

Bending and breaking were the least of her concerns. *This* was the home her papa had promised to build? The neat, gabled house she had visualized, mentally furnished, decorated, and inhabited over the long, empty years when she'd had nothing to cling to but her own dreams and her father's annual letter—lately no more than a few scribbled lines?

Numbly, she waved away a persistent fly. Perhaps she was still dreaming. Perhaps in a little while she'd wake up and find herself back on the third floor of Mrs. B.'s school, sharing a drafty loft with thirteen little girls between the ages of four and fourteen.

And then it hit her all at once. Drowning in shame, Annie told herself that if she was disappointed, imagine how her father felt, having to live this way all these years just so that he could keep her at Mrs. Biddlecomb's.

Well, she was not her father's daughter for nothing! If he could live here in this wretched wilderness, then she could, too. What's more, she could make things better for them both. She might not have learned all that much about housekeeping. Actually, her talents lay in another direction. But when it came to running his business, she could be of inestimable help. Quite aside from her skill with needle and bobbin, she could read and write and cipher as well as any clerk.

Housekeepers could be hired, as could cooks. It might be best, too, to hire someone to see to the milking and the chickens and the garden. It wasn't that Annie was unwilling, it was simply that according to Mrs. B., her true vocation lay anywhere on earth other than the kitchen or the barnyard.

"Well, now," she said brightly, "Mr. Gray, I'm very much obliged to you for bringing me, er—home. I'm sure Papa must be terribly busy or he would have come to meet me himself."

The old man nodded silently, his gaze shifting from the mail boat, which was fast disappearing in the distance, to the dusty ruckus up ahead. If she'd hoped for reassurance, she could just go on hoping. She fingered her worn reticule and wondered if she should offer to pay him for bringing her here in his cart. She had sat on the dock for so long waiting, and he had offered, and she'd been afraid not to accept for fear her father had been delayed.

But she couldn't afford much. It had taken almost every cent she possessed to buy her passage and pay for the skimpy meals and thin, crowded pallets in posting inns along the way.

"If Eli don't have a place fixed up fer ye, Miss, you're welcome to come stay wi' me and Rachael. We've not got much, but you're welcome to share our roof and table."

No, Annie decided, he would not expect payment. Pride stood out all over the man, for all his bent shoulders and work-worn hands. Annie smiled, the warmth of it lending her pale, thin face a rare kind of beauty as she graciously declined the old gentleman's offer.

The ride in the oxcart notwithstanding, she'd had quite enough of charity. She had been all of nine years old before she had learned the meaning of the word *indigent* on the sign in front of Mrs. Biddlecomb's School for Indigent Girls.

From that moment on, she had been determined to earn her way. Gradually she had learned that those who could pay did. Those who couldn't were taken in anyway, for as Mrs. B. was fond of saying, the Lord had blessed her with a big, empty house, and she knew her Christian duty.

There were no idle hands at Mrs. B.'s school to make work for the devil. Tasks were divided according to ages and abilities. By the time she had been there a year, it was commonly accepted that Annie's ability was sewing and looking after babies.

As Annie grew older and more skilled, Mrs. B. began selling her output through a shop in Hillsborough, with Annie receiving twenty-five cents a month and Mrs. B. keeping the rest in exchange for her room, board, and tuition, although Annie had always assumed, when she thought about it at all, that her father was paying her keep.

A handsome woman of uncertain years, Mrs. B. had not tolerated questions about her business practices. She was a devout believer in doing one's duty to the best of one's ability right up until the very day she had run off with a drummer from Philadelphia, leaving behind thirteen students, a leaky ruin of a house that was impossible to heat, and a mountain of debts.

Creditors had moved in like vultures to strip the house of everything of value, and it had been left to Annie as Mrs. B.'s unofficial assistant to track down what few relatives she could, see those girls settled to her satisfaction, and then find decent homes for the rest.

All that had taken her nearly six weeks, during which time she had prayed nightly for an answer to her hasty letters to Papa. When none had come, she had simply done what had to be done. Taking the few articles left by creditors in lieu of her promised, but unpaid, salary—which included one dented kettle, two pots, a chipped porcelain teacup, an egg basket with no handle in which she stored her precious sewing things, and two pairs of sun-rotted brocade draperies—she had made her own arrangements.

And now here she was.

"Be glad to give ye a lift out to where they're a-workin' the herd," Jackariah Gray offered after he had driven the cart up to the hut on stilts and set her things on the ground. Instead of a set of steps, a huge stump had been left in front of the doorway, the top more or less leveled off to provide a platform. Crude, but effective, if one's limbs happened to be five feet long.

"I thank you kindly, but I expect Papa's already seen me. He'll be coming back most any minute, but if he's not here by the time I get my things put away, I might walk out to meet him."

Jackariah looked at the noisy, dusty business going on in the distance. He looked at the trunk and the stack of assorted bundles in the doorway of the miserly shack, his unspoken doubts clear to see.

"I'm sure it looks far better inside than it does from outside," Annie said with forced cheerfulness. She was sure of no such thing, but she would never hurt her father's feelings by turning up her nose at his house. If she'd been expecting more, then that was her failing, not his. Poor Papa, he must have sacrificed dreadfully all these years to keep her in Mrs. Biddlecomb's school.

Wealthy beyond their wildest dreams. That's what he had told her when he'd first written about his business arrangement with Mr. Snell. *Oh, Papa, why didn't you tell me the truth? I never wanted wealth—all I wanted was for us to be a family again!*

But the truth was that if Mr. Snell had not come along at just the right time with his business proposition, her father would have come to no good end. After her mother had died, Eli had done little but grieve and drink. Even at the age of five, Annie had realized that. If he'd been able to find some small measure of happiness out here in this forsaken wilderness, then she could only be glad for him.

When the old fisherman seemed reluctant to go off and leave her there, Annie pretended to a complaisance she was far from feeling. While she was bracing herself to go inside and view her new home, the cow that had been scratching its head wandered around the corner, came up behind her and sniffed suspiciously at her skirt.

Startled, Annie jumped back with a yelp. The cow backed off, bawling a protest, which startled a chicken that had been perched on the rooftop, causing it to fly. Annie felt as if she'd waked up in the middle of a nightmare. None of this was real.

"Are you sure you won't come go home wi' me, Missy?"

"Oh, no, thank you, I—that is, I'd best be getting settled in," she said with a brilliant smile that took almost the last vestige of courage she possessed.

"Eli, he'll likely be home t'reckly. Elsewise, if ye need anything, Mingo'll do fer ye."

Elsewise meaning just what? That Papa might *not be*

home t'reckly? Annie nodded as if it all made perfect sense.

"Mingo, he's yer pa's man. Ain't much fer looks, but he's sound as a juniper bottom."

"Of course he is," Annie murmured, panic threatening to give way to hysteria. Her stomach growled noisily. She had emptied it more than once on the long journey across the sound. And might again.

Perched up on the hard seat of his oxcart, horny hands on the reins, Jackariah heard it and grinned. "Sounds like ye're a mite peckish. Tell Eli to fry ye up a mess o' mullet gizzards, that'll fix ye up good as new. Gittalong home, now, Paris France."

Watching the backside of the cart pulled by an ox with the unlikely name of Paris France, Annie wondered if anything could ever fix her up good as new again.

Mullet gizzards?

Alone at last, she turned to go inside, shoulders drooping. As her eyes adjusted slowly to the dim interior, her dismay increased. Holding her skirts up off the gritty floor, she explored the extent of her new home, which took all of two minutes. There were two rooms, one for sleeping, one for everything else. No parlor, no sitting room. Not a sign of a dining room, nor even a washroom.

As for furnishings, there was one lumpy bed that looked none too clean; one table, crudely built of rough lumber; and three straight chairs, of which only one possessed a back, and that missing two spokes. An arrangement of bricks and rocks in the corner appeared to be some sort of fireplace, if the grease congealed on the hearth was any indication.

Her feeling of dismay increasing at an alarming rate, Annie continued her inventory. There was an iron spider hanging from a nail on the wall. There was also a shelf, which contained a tin of friction matches, a small japanned box—probably holding tea—a wooden trencher, a pewter tankard, and one cracked white mug.

Underneath the shelf were three crocks. One was empty except for a few grains of brown sugar and a trail of fine black ants. One held cornmeal that appeared reasonably fresh to her inexpert eyes.

Curiously, she lifted the lid on the largest crock and then slammed it shut again.

Rotten fish! Merciful saints, why would her father keep a crock of rotten fish in his kitchen? Living alone, a man might slip into slovenly habits, but *rotten fish*?

She would deal with it later. Perhaps it was bait for some sort of trap, although heaven help anything that would be attracted to such a stench.

"Well, now!" she said firmly. Annie had her own way of dealing with what had to be dealt with. Those ways had stood her in good stead all these years, and she was not about to let a little bit of discouragement get in her way now.

First, a cup of tea—if there was any left in the container. She'd have to see if she could get a fire going in that tiny, filthy fireplace. And if she could find Papa's source of fresh water.

Papa's source of fresh water was a rain barrel, slick

with moss and alive with wigglers, under a rickety gutter behind the house. She scooped up a potful, wondering what she could spare to strain it with, and then began gathering up wood from the stack beside the stump.

She dumped the split logs in the fireplace. She had never actually built a fire, which seemed ridiculous for a woman of her advanced age, but the fire in the kitchen at school was never allowed to go out, and Cookie, the housekeeper, took care of the fires in the other rooms. No fire was allowed in the sleeping rooms or classrooms, of course. They simply bundled up.

It couldn't be that difficult. Wood burned, and Papa had plenty of wood. He also had friction matches, as dear as they were. What more could a body need?

She took down the japanned box, hoping the tea was at least reasonably fresh.

Only it wasn't tea. It was letters. Recognizing her own handwriting, Annie picked up the last one of all, the one she had written to tell him about the closing of the school.

It wasn't even opened.

Puzzled, she took out another . . . and then another. After the first few letters, written years ago, when she'd been so proud of her newly acquired skills, not a single one had been opened.

Thinking of all the hours she had spent composing each one—not to mention all the sewing money she had spent to have them posted—Annie lowered her head to the table and wept.

"Well . . . that explains that, at least," she said after

a few minutes had passed. Tears were an indulgence she could ill afford. With fresh resolution, she blotted her eyes, blew her nose, then set out to choose a small corner to claim as her own.

While Annie was gathering her resources to begin the job of settling into her new home, Mingo and T'maho finished earmarking the new herd, then turned reluctantly toward the home paddock behind the shed to castrate the few bull calves Eli had penned up there.

Earmarking was not particularly bloody, not even all that painful, if done quickly with a sure hand. Neither man held with branding, although Mingo, at least, could see the sense of it, with more and more cattle owners using the barrier islands as a natural corral.

But castrating was bad business. There was something downright mean about it, although both knew it was a necessary evil. Any man with a grain of sense would rather ride a gelding than a stallion.

Both men were anxious to wind up the day's work and wash off the grime, sweat, and blood with a long, hard swim. "Squall's moved on offshore," Mingo remarked.

"Good thing, else I'd be dancing with lightning." T'maho waved the flies away from his bloody scalp. He needed a good hard scrub with salt water to keep his scalp from turning bad. If old Etawak found out he'd laid his skin open, she'd tie him down and smear him with one of her potions, which would sure enough do him in.

"Looks like Jackariah's cart yonder, rounding the

point." Mingo nodded toward the rutted track that followed the shore side.

"Come looking for Eli, I reckon. Must've missed each other."

Neither man paid any more attention to the cart disappearing in the distance, their attention focused instead on the unfinished task ahead. "Me, I like beef as well's the next man, and bull don't make good beef, but I swear, 'Maho, I purely hate this job."

Annie had located a broom and was searching for a pail when she heard the ruckus. Propping the broom against the wall, she leaped down from the stump to the ground and set out to investigate. Evidently Papa had come back and was busy out behind the shed. Picking up her skirts, she hurried around to where the noise was coming from.

"Papa, surprise! It's me—Annie!"

Chapter 2

"Y"ou, there! Just what do you think you're doing?" Annie screeched at the two half-naked savages who were trying to steal her father's cows.

Steal them! They were trying to *butcher* them, right before her very eyes! Oh, this was awful! Where was Papa?

She flapped her apron and ran toward the split-pole gate. "You get out of there right this very minute or I'll tell Papa! He'll have you arrested!"

Outraged, she hopped first on one foot, then the other, then tried to rescue a calf that ran past her, bawling its head off. The ungrateful creature knocked her flat on her backside, kicked sand in her face, and dashed past her through the open gate as if the devil were on its heels.

Blinking sand from her eyes, Annie heard swear words. She thought someone yelled "Watch your head," but everything was happening too fast, with calves bellowing and dashing back and forth while she struggled to regain her footing.

Looking dazedly around, she pinned her accusing

glare on the closest of the two men. "Where is my father?" she demanded. "Answer me this minute!"

The two men ignored her as if she weren't even there. Inside the fence the remaining calves were frantically trying to escape, while outside, several big cows milled around, bawling and swinging their sharp, short horns.

Stiff as a ramrod, Annie struggled to control her anger. Neither of the two miscreants was wearing enough clothing to preserve a speck of modesty, and what little they had on was filthy and spattered with blood. Caught redhanded, the bold devils had gone right back to their wickedness, just as if they had every right.

Well, we'll just see about that!

Her fiery red hair wild about her face, shedding sand and hairpins with every determined step, she picked up a length of fence post nearly as long as she was. Staggering under the weight of it, she tightened her grip and marched into battle before she could lose her nerve.

These were her father's cows! Mr. Gray had said so. And if Papa wasn't here to protect them, why, she would just have to do it for him, because, like it or not, Annie told herself grimly, she was in the cattle business now.

She waited her chance and then edged toward the wretch who was struggling to hold down one poor victim. Catching a glimpse of his hideously twisted face, she shuddered. Would he even feel her blow? He was big as an ox, and looked every bit as hardheaded. What if she only stunned him? In his anger, he might turn on her and—

She'd do better to concentrate on the other one. The one with the knife. At least he was tall enough so that one good whack should be sufficient to topple him. Besides, unless someone stopped him, he was going to cut that poor little calf's throat!

Although it wasn't exactly the throat he was aiming for—it was the other end.

At any rate, he had to be stopped. Still reeling from her long sea journey, Annie braced her feet apart in the treacherously soft sand, tightened her grip, closed her eyes, and swung. "There, you wicked thief, that will teach you to murder my papa's cows! Now get away from here, the both of you, before I—"

He didn't topple. Instead, he rocked on his moccasined feet, uttering what sounded like a soft "Ooof!" Then, as Annie stared in horror, he turned slowly to face her, piercing her with a pair of eyes so cold they were like shards of ice. Dirt and what appeared to be dark red paint covered part of his face and streaked down over one broad, muscular shoulder.

War paint? Annie had never before seen a painted Indian, but she'd heard fearful tales of the olden days.

He was supposed to fall down. She'd hit him hard enough. She shivered, feeling cold in spite of the steamy late September heat. They stood as if frozen in time, the tall, pale-eyed savage, muscles glistening in the sun, and the small red-haired woman dressed in a bedraggled gown made of faded drapery material.

It was then, catching its distracted captor by surprise, that the calf flung its head free and kicked out with both hind legs to catch the knife-wielding savage squarely behind the knees.

He buckled instantly. On the way down he struck Annie, and the pair of them tumbled to the ground in a flurry of skirts, petticoats, and profanity. Falling, Annie had a quick glimpse of the man with the scarred face racing off after the escaping calf.

The fiend was laughing!

Before she could utter a word, a leather-hard palm descended over her face, pressing the back of her head into the sand. She tasted salt and blood. Sand gritted against her teeth as she tried to bite the callused hand. Barely able to breathe, she began to struggle.

Frantically, she kicked out, but entangled in layers of skirt, her feet did little damage. She pounded against his shoulders, but the wicked devil was so slippery that her fists slipped off without having the least effect.

She had to have air! Something of her panic must have transmitted itself to the heavy man lying on top of her, for just as her consciousness began to waver, the hand on her face shifted slightly. It still covered her mouth, but at least her nose and eyes were free.

Filling her starved lungs with air, Annie glared up at him through eyes red with tears, the lashes caked with sand. Slowly, he removed his hand from her mouth, his long fingers trailing down her chin to spread over her neck. Stricken, she waited for him to tighten his grip.

And then he did, ever so slightly, staring down at her all the while. Annie opened her mouth to scream and then shut it again and swallowed hard as a rush of conflicting feelings came over her.

Never, not since she was a child, could she recall being so close to any adult, man or woman. He was touching her . . . all over! "Are you going to kill me?" she whispered.

He stared down at her as if she were some sort of oddity. Did he even understand a word she had spoken? Perhaps he didn't speak English. He seemed fascinated by her hair.

And then she thought about that wicked knife of his. Oh, merciful saints. He wanted her scalp!

She began to squirm and managed only to settle him deeper between her limbs. He was making no effort to spare her his full weight, and from the look on his face . . .

His face. Annie had an impression of something oddly out of kilter with his face. Distractedly, she realized that his features were not altogether dreadful. His nose was straight and high-bridged, the nostrils flared. His brow was high, his jaw firm and square, while his mouth—

She stared at the mouth that was mere inches from her own.

How strange. . . . She had never really thought about mouths before.

Shaking herself free of the odd spell that was due, no doubt, to a lack of air, Annie told herself that he was a savage devil, a cattle murderer. He was mean and he was heavy, and the mere scent of his flesh was enough to set her nerves to quivering inside her.

She sniffed again. Leather, wood smoke, musk, and sweat, overlaid with the metallic scent of raw blood.

Did all men smell like this? Papa had smelled of pipe tobacco. The preacher smelled of bay rum. Except for old Charlie, Mrs. B.'s groom and yardman, who smelled of gin and manure, Annie had never been close enough to another man to smell him.

Swallowing another gulp of air, she struggled for composure, an impossible task under the circumstances. Never in her entire life had she been this close to so much unclad flesh.

The wicked devil shifted his limbs then, and Annie felt a surge of hope, but instead of letting her go free, he pressed his belly against hers in a way that was even more unsettling. She trembled. Paralyzed with fear, she stared up into those pale, mesmerizing eyes, pleading silently for him to spare her life.

How odd. She had the strangest impression that he was telling her something—only she didn't know what it was.

And then he moved again, shifting his weight, and his eyes seemed to darken. Eyes couldn't change color. Yet she could have sworn his just did.

He made no move to get up. Suddenly desperate, Annie kicked out, only to have him throw his leg over hers, pinning her down on the soft, warm sand.

He was hard. He was hot. He was heavy.

Annie forgot to breathe. Reality shimmered like a distant mirage.

He was an Indian. A gray-eyed Indian. She had never even seen an Indian up close before, but she was fairly certain they were supposed to have dark eyes. Suddenly coming to her senses, she twisted in an effort to throw him off. "Get . . . *off* me!" she panted. "If you value your life, you'll leave before my Papa comes home and skins you alive!" Grasping the only portion of his half-naked body she could reach, she pinched as hard as she could.

The savage yelped. He bared a set of square white teeth, causing her to wonder if he intended to tear out her throat, but before she could pinch him again, he levered himself up off her body.

Air rushed into her lungs too fast, leaving her dizzy. She started to get up off the ground, but instead of walking away, he planted one foot on either side of her waist.

To her mortification, Annie found herself staring up at that particular portion of a man's anatomy the existence of which no decent woman ever even thought about, much less stared at. It occurred to her that men and women were cut from drastically different patterns. That much was evident even though he was covered from the waist down by a pair of filthy, blood-spattered buckskins.

Annie closed her eyes and moaned. Then, sensing movement, she opened one of them again. Her attacker had stepped back, but he was still watching her. Watching her the way a hawk watched its prey.

Reddening, she jerked her skirts down over her limbs, praying he could not read her thoughts. Lord, her face was going to catch fire from the heat of embarrassment.

Scrambling to her feet, she busied herself by brushing the sand from her clothing and her hair, ignoring the bloodthirsty devil who leaned indolently against the fence, staring at her.

Her heart was still beating a mile a minute. She was angry and she was frightened, but she'd be hanged before she would show it! "Just you wait until I tell Papa," she muttered as she retied the tapes that had come undone on her bodice.

The savage said something in a heathen tongue that sounded extremely profane, and not waiting to retrieve the hairpins that were no doubt lost forever in the sand, Annie turned and fled.

T'maho stared after the ginger-hair, his expression perplexed. He could have sworn what had just happened was impossible. But it could not have been anger, nor even disdain, that had caused his flesh to leap so eagerly at the feel of her woman's thighs.

"Eli will have more bull calves than he had counted on," said Mingo, riding up on his workhorse. He nodded toward the house. "Did you tell her where the old man has gone?"

"She did not ask."

"Damn it all, 'Maho, she thought her papa was out here working with us! Doesn't she even know he's gone across the sound?"

T'maho shrugged. "She'll know soon enough." Tearing his gaze away from the place where the woman had disappeared, he turned to his friend. "Don't make the mistake of moving downwind until we wash the day's filth away."

"Are you sure that's the only reason you wish to plunge into a cold sea?"

"*Yendare yeccau.* I'll race you out to the bar and back."

Mingo laughed, not at all offended at being called a fat old woman. It was their habit after a hard day's work to cool off in the surf. When the sea was rising, they often rode the waves up onto the shore, the swift, exhilarating ride stripping them, if only momentarily, of the cares of the day.

"Come along, then. The girl will keep well enough."

By the time she made her way back inside, Annie was too shaken to think clearly about what had happened, much less what it meant. Papa would deal with the criminals when he came home, she told herself with a shuttering breath. This had been without a doubt the worse day in her entire eighteen and a half years!

Collecting the broom from where she had left it when she'd gone to investigate the noise, she dropped tiredly down onto one of the chairs, staring at the clutter of baggage just inside the door. Dear merciful saints alive! Not only had she felt a man's naked flesh, she had breathed his breath and smelled his scent! According to Mrs. B., men were the devil's handiwork, and a woman forgot it at her own peril.

Annie sighed. Mrs. B. had had rather a lot to say on the subject of men. Annie hadn't understood half of it at the time, nor had she worried overly much about it. But to give the woman her due, she'd been right about that one thing, at least.

She stared at the poor battered trunk that had stood at the foot of her bed all these years, serving as a repository for her few belongings. It looked every bit as tired and forlorn as she was feeling. But tired or not, she would have to unpack the thing, if only to have something to wear to bed.

Which brought up another problem. A bed. A pallet, perhaps—but before she could make a place for herself on the floor, she was going to have to find soap and a basin or a pail, because she refused to close her eyes until she had scrubbed every surface in the entire two rooms right down to the naked grain!

She might not know how to cook—it had been decided early on that Annie O'Neal and kitchens were not compatible. Meat turned tough, butter wouldn't come, and if there was anything that could be spilled, spoiled, or burned, it invariably was.

She might not know much about cows or chickens, because old Charlie took care of those and the two nags the school kept for church and marketing.

She might not even be all that good at marketing, because Mrs. B. generally did that herself when she took Annie's fancy work in to sell.

But any fool could scrub!

It was nearly dark by the time Annie dumped the last bucket of scrub water out the door and stood back with a satisfied look to admire her wet floors. She had washed down the furniture, too, but it would take more than a good scrubbing to turn the rude little hut into a halfway respectable home.

One hand massaging her aching back, she happened to glance out the window to see two men on horseback cresting the low dunes that bordered the ocean.

"Papa?" she whispered hopefully, knowing in her heart that her father would never appear in public dressed in such a scandalous costume.

It was those two wild Indians again. Not content to steal her father's cows, they were coming back to see what further mischief they could get up to.

Well! Not if *she* had anything to say about it!

By the time they reached the house, Annie had pulled in the shutters and barred them. She had slammed the heavy door shut and, lacking a bar, leaned her full weight against it.

Without a light showing, they might think the house was empty. Please God, let them think she had gone into town. Let them think—

"Eli's daughter!" called a voice from the darkness outside.

Ha! So they knew her papa. They'd known all along whose cows they were stealing!

Well, if they thought they could make just as free with Eli's daughter, just because she happened to be alone and unprotected, they would soon learn the error of their ways, Annie thought grimly. A poker brought down hard on the first foot across her threshold should discourage any such foolishness!

Closed up tight, the house was pitch-dark and stifling. For one brief moment while she breathlessly awaited their next move, Annie felt her senses begin to reel. It was the heat, she told herself. And the stench of cattle and worse.

Just on the other side of the rough plank wall, she caught the sound of voices murmuring quietly.

What were they up to now?

But then, after another few minutes, the voices receded. She heard the whicker of a horse from some distance away, and a sense of triumph all out of proportion to her small victory crept in to replace her fear.

Still, it was a long time later before she dared let down her guard enough to open a window, make up a pallet, and change from her filthy gown into a plain, thin nightshift.

After two days, Annie was frantic. Papa had still not come home. She was beginning to think something might have happened to him. What if those two cattle thieves had done him an injury and then left him out there all alone in all that awful, sun-baked, fly-ridden wilderness?

On the point of setting out to search, she considered taking the dusty old musket she'd found propped in a corner under a filthy leather apron, and decided the broom would be safer. At least it should serve to shoo away any cows that got too curious.

Stepping down onto the stump, she shaded her eyes and began to scan the horizon. In one direction lay the thick green wooded area that Mr. Gray had called the glade. Beyond it, she knew, lay the village of Kinnakeet. Except for the glade, the entire island, as far as she could tell, was comprised of beach sand dotted with cow patties, prickly pear cactus, sparse wild grass, and stunted shrubbery. Behind her, the Atlantic Ocean stretched out to infinity. That first morning, she had walked across the hot sand to stand there and marvel at such vastness.

On the other side of the narrow strip of land was the Pamlico Sound, which she had crossed to get here. The two bodies of water were scarcely more than a mile apart, and if what she could see was all there was of the island, Annie wouldn't have been quite so concerned. The trouble was, the land extended to the north with no end in sight, and she had no way of knowing how far south it reached past the village of Kinnakeet.

Everywhere she looked, there were horny-headed cows! At this very moment, two of the beasts were standing hip deep in the sound, right in front of the house, their tails swishing back and forth like big plumed fans.

Morosely, Annie watched, wondering if the water was as cool and refreshing as it looked. She had left off one petticoat this morning and put on her coolest gown, a white dimity with a green overskirt cut from the side panels of one of Mrs. B.'s old gowns.

If it didn't soon turn cooler, she might even leave off her stays. It wasn't as if there was anyone here to know or care if she was properly clad. One of the first lessons Mrs. B.'s girls learned was that maintaining a high standard of grooming was the first step toward a high standard of behavior, but Annie suspected that Mrs. B. herself might loosen a few stays and roll her stockings down about her ankles if she had to exert herself for very long in such an unsalubrious climate.

Squinting against the glare of sunlight on water, she waved her broom as one of the bigger cows began butting the head of a smaller one. "You out there—you stop that!" she cried.

Scanning the monotonous vista once more, she half expected to see her father come riding up. She'd been looking for him for days. If he didn't come soon, she was just going to have to make that ugly old mule in the shed take her to the village.

"Now, stop that, I said! Don't be such a big bully!"

Tossing down the broom, she leaped down off the high stump and trudged through the deep sand toward the shore. By the time she reached the marshy edge of the water, the two cows had stopped butting heads and had waded in closer to shore.

And then, right before her eyes, the big brown one leaped up onto the back of the little black and white one and began beating her about the shoulders with a set of wicked hooves.

Fresh out of patience, Annie flapped her apron and shouted another warning. "Hateful creature! Stop that, do you hear me? You're going to break her back!" Why on earth had she been left in charge of a bunch of stupid animals when she'd never even owned a stuffed dog?

There was supposed to be a herdsman. . . . What was the name Mr. Gray had mentioned? Miller? Milo?

"Mingo! Mr. Mingo!"

The last time Annie had been on any four-legged

creature was the year before her mother had died. One of the neighbors had bought a pony for his son to ride, and Papa had insisted on putting Annie up on his back. She'd slid right off the other side as soon as he'd taken his hand away, but that was then and this was now. She didn't know a whit more about riding than she had then, but at least now her limbs were long enough to wrap far enough around a mule's belly to keep her from sliding off.

She knew a little about bridles, having watched old Charlie a time or two. However, knowing and doing were two different things. At last she managed to get the thing fitted over the mule's head the right way, with everything more or less in the right place.

He didn't bite her, which she considered a distinct mark in her favor. However, he managed to dump her a time or two before she backed him against the far wall, shoved a box up beside him, threatened his life if he so much as twitched an ear, and climbed aboard, hanging on to his short brushy mane while she found her balance.

"All right, sir, you may take me to the village now. I'll leave it to your discretion to find the way, for I'm sure I don't know it. If you're at all intelligent, you'll make this easy on the both of us."

It didn't help matters that the same wretched chicken she had followed for hours, trying to find her nest, was now perched on a rafter under the shed overhang, squawking as if it thought the whole affair one big jest.

The mule seemed inclined to head for the middle of

the glade. Annie recalled hearing Mr. Gray say that a trail there led to the village, but Annie preferred to stick to the road she knew, which followed the shoreline. The last thing she needed now was to get herself lost in the woods. Using a mixture of tugs and kicks, she steered the mule toward the soundside.

It would have been wonderful if she were to meet her father on his way home, but she didn't hold out much hope. If he'd been anywhere nearby, Mr. Gray would have told him she was here, and he'd have come home right away.

Still, as long as she was there, it wouldn't hurt to ask.

But first of all she had to find someone—this Mr. Mingo, if he was available—and get him to make those cows stop trying to kill one another. She had never before realized how vicious animals could be! No wonder the girls had always complained so about having to help old Charlie with the milking.

Even at the mule's plodding pace, the trip in to the village of Kinnakeet seemed far shorter than the trip out to her father's holdings by oxcart. Paris France? If she hadn't been so worried, she might have found the name amusing, but now, as then, Annie had far more serious matters on her mind than the name of Mr. Gray's ox.

The houses were small, although somewhat larger than she remembered. Her first view of the village had been colored by having lived near a proper town, in a three-story house, no matter how run-down, and from having passed through the state capital on her way east.

Annie counted five men down near the waterfront,

two women working in a garden, and a girl about her own age pegging sheets onto a line.

The girl looked the most approachable. "Good morning," she greeted, sawing on the reins the way she'd seen old Charlie do when he halted the wagon in front of the church.

The girl smiled. She was plump and pretty, though she was missing two teeth. "You're Eli's Annie, I reckon," she said shyly.

Annie introduced herself and said she supposed Mr. Gray must have mentioned her name, and the girl, whose name was Dulsie Scarborough, said that Mr. Jackariah had mentioned her, and she'd heard old Eli speak of her, too, and that everyone recognized Eli's mule, Jacob.

"I thought you was little, though. Shame yer paw had to leave out on the same boat you come in on. Seen him whack old Jacob on the stern and jump aboard the mail boat not long after you and Mr. Jackariah had rode off."

"Papa's gone somewhere?"

"Jest over 'cross the sound. He goes now and again, but he don't never stay long. I'd be right proud if you was to come and stay with me and my folks till Eli gets back." The girl had hardly taken her eyes off Annie's gown. By now Annie thought she must have counted the stitches in the seams.

"That's kind of you, but I'd better stay out there and look after things until Papa gets back. Which reminds me—Mr. Gray mentioned a Mr. Mingo and said if I ever needed help, he'd be the one to ask. Do you suppose you could give me his direction?"

Dulsie nodded toward two men standing under an enormous live oak tree. She grinned, her hazel eyes twinkling. "Yonder he stands." Giggling, she picked up another sheet and flopped it across the line. Annie took a deep breath and wriggled her behind in an effort to get the mule—Jacob?—moving in the right direction. She didn't dare dismount for fear she might never get up again.

So intent had she been on keeping Jacob from helping himself to the Scarboroughs' garden, she had barely spared a glance to the two men.

Now she did. "Oh, no. . . ." she whispered as embarrassment stained her face scarlet. Not those two again. Not the same pair who had been—

The pair she had accused of—

"Jacob, get your face out of those collard greens and turn yourself around," she muttered.

There was nothing for it but to apologize and get on with her business. If one of them was indeed her father's hired hand, then it was just possible she'd been mistaken about their intentions.

In fact, she thought with a sinking feeling as she approached the dark-skinned pair, she was quite certain of it. Cleaned up, they didn't look all that scary, even the one with the scars.

It was the other one who struck her as the more frightening of the two. She had thought his eyes cold? They were blistering! She saw him glance at her hair, which she hadn't taken time to brush and pin up again, and then his gaze dropped to her knees, which were showing between her petticoat and her mended stockings. Her wretched skirt had not been designed for straddling a blasted mule, and it kept creeping up!

She jerked it down again. "Which one of you is Mr. Mingo?" she demanded in her most imperious voice . . . which wasn't really all that imperious.

Each man nodded toward the other. She was put in mind of a pair of guilt-ridden youngsters, each attempting to put the blame for the missing cakes on the other. Irritated beyond bearing, she said, "Well, whichever one of you is telling the truth, would the other one please come with me? Mr. Gray said if I needed any help before Papa got home I was to ask for a Mr. Mingo, and I do. Need help, that is."

They stared at her as if she were speaking gibberish. She knew for a fact that at least one of the pair spoke the King's English every bit as well as she did. Hadn't he called her Eli's daughter?

Angry, embarrassed, and impatient, she twitched in her saddle. Jacob took it as a signal to turn back to the Scarboroughs' collard patch, and she was forced to tug at the reins and wriggle her bottom to get him headed in the right direction again.

Once she did, she said firmly, "Please! Papa's cows are fighting, and I can't make them stop. One big bully is trying to kill another cow by locking horns with him and then jumping up onto his back and kicking him in the shoulders."

When there was still no response, she raked her fingers through her hair and muttered a wicked word under her breath.

At least she thought it was wicked. Every time little Becky said it, she'd had her mouth washed out with soap.

"Listen here to me—I need help! Those cows are misbehaving, and if someone doesn't stop them, they'll kill one another!"

"Jacob likes licorice." It was the scarred man who spoke, yet her gaze kept returning to the one with gray eyes.

"Jacob likes licorice? What has that to do with anything? Didn't you hear me? I just told you, two of Papa's cows are trying to kill each other, and Papa's not there to make them stop, and they refuse to obey me. Won't you please do something?"

"They be in heat," the scarred man replied.

Annie stared at him blankly. "In heat? Well, of course they're in heat. Who isn't? It must surely be the warmest September in living memory. Please, won't you just come with me?"

"The bull mounts the cow, woman!"

Totally mystified, Annie felt like weeping out of sheer frustration. Wasn't anyone willing to help her? If this was all the aid she could expect from the man who was supposed to be her father's hired hand, she might as well resign herself to seeing that poor little cow pounded into a bloody and broken pulp.

"They mate, woman, they mate!" The man shouted, and then they both began to laugh.

Annie felt the heat rise right up to the top of her

scalp. Her mouth fell open and then clamped shut again and she flapped the reins until Jacob got the message and started moving.

While she sat there, her face burning fit to blister, the miserable old licorice-loving lump dawdled across the clearing, heading home.

This time when he headed toward the glade, Annie didn't even attempt to stop him. Perhaps if she got lost for a week or so, matters would resolve themselves without her help. Papa would come home, and the cows would stop fighting, and that mocking, gray-eyed devil would strangle on his own wickedness, and—

"Oh, balderdash," she muttered as the sound of laughter followed her into the steamy green shadows.

Chapter 3

"Now you'll have to go chasing off after Eli's spawn, leaving me to fish the net alone," said T'maho, his amusement fading. The two men stood watching as the mouse-gray mule headed off into the glade, the small, ginger-haired woman bouncing like a sack of grain on his back.

"I see no need to hurry. By now the bull has done his business and will be grazing peacefully. The woman does not understand that some matters are best left unattended. When we finish here, I'll go see that she does not get hurt trying to interfere. It'll take Jacob that long to find his way home."

"The woman is a fool," T'maho muttered.

"I doubt that she's a fool, only ignorant."

"Ignorant and useless, like all her kind."

Mingo studied his friend and wondered, not for the first time, how long it would take for T'maho to forgive himself for being half white. "Come, my friend, have you not forgiven the woman for trying to protect her father's property? Is your pride so tender?

It occurred to him that it might be better to send

T'maho to instruct the woman. Living as he did among friends, Mingo sometimes forgot the effect his face could have on strangers. The O'Neal woman was skittish enough without being frightened further.

T'maho leaned against the trunk of the gnarled old tree, his pale eyes hooded as he stared after the redheaded woman. Then, abruptly, he straightened, glared over his shoulder, and said, "Are we going to finish fishing the net, or are we going to stand around gossiping all day? In the old days, a man would have brought in his fish and his woman would have them gutted, scaled, and smoking by now."

Mingo smiled, his scarred features twisting grotesquely. "Talk is easier on the back than fishing a net, my friend. But if you'd rather go back to the old ways and spear each fish with a sharpened stick . . ."

"If I decide to go back to the old ways, it will be to peel your lice-ridden skin from your miserable body," T'maho threatened with a rare chuckle as they took up the large basket between them and headed out to the nearest of their three nets, the only one that could be fished without a boat.

"Once we pick the net, I'll head north and see to the woman. Perhaps this time she will not bar the door against me."

"And perhaps she will. I told you, the woman is a fool."

"Hmmm," muttered the shorter of the two men, his dark hazel eyes gleaming with amusement as he considered his friend's unyielding prejudice. T'maho had learned many lessons in his young life, but he could not seem to learn to bend with the wind. "The oak tree is no weaker for being shaped by the prevailing winds," Mingo observed with seeming casualness.

T'maho pointed to a giant dead tree that had been overtaken by the encroaching waters of the sound. "Nor is that cedar less dead for surrendering to the alien element."

Mingo scooped up a blue crab swimming upon the surface of the water, grinned at the wildly snapping red claws, and then carefully returned the creature to the water and watched him swim away. "Perhaps you're right, my friend. And perhaps not."

They had waded some distance from shore when a small figure raced down to the edge of the water and called after them, "T'maho! Etawak says she needs you to come *now*!"

Ignoring the summons, T'maho continued to wade, the water barely up to the edge of his loincloth. Etawak, the old woman who had raised his young half-sister, Saketa, and who had taken the youth T'maho into her lodge when his father had rejected him, was always making demands. Ignored, she was prone to utter dire predictions, none of which, to his knowledge, had ever come true.

It was Mingo who called back, "We'll come as soon as this net is emptied, Saketa."

"Etawak says *now*!" the small, calico-clad girl shouted.

"She says Etawak says now," Mingo repeated dryly to his friend.

"That old woman is *laucaumo*," T'maho muttered.

"Crazy or not, she knows how to make you dance to her tune."

T'maho glared at him. "I dance to no woman's tune."

Mingo only grinned and continued to wade through the shallow water.

Most villagers called Etawak crazy. The few Hattorask who still spoke the old tongue called her *laucaumo*, but in truth, she was no more than a lonely old widow who pretended to a wisdom she did not, perhaps, possess—a woman who cured yaupon tea, brewed strong acorn beer, and mixed potions in exchange for her needs.

A woman who had outlived her own children and taken in those of a young woman called Little Feet when that woman had died. Saketa had come to live with Etawak as a babe, T'maho as a boy of thirteen summers. At the age of sixteen he had moved into his own lodge, but he still looked after the old woman and his half-sister, Saketa.

"T'maho! You'd better come back here. Right *now!*"

Mingo glanced over his shoulder, his gaze dwelling longingly on the beautiful, dark-eyed girl standing ankle deep in the water's edge. "Your little sister grows demanding."

"All women are demanding," T'maho said dryly.

But Mingo had loved his friend's small sister since the day he had found her huddled in the mud under a tussock of water reeds, weeping because her skin was dark, her hair and eyes black like those of her mother's people instead of pale like her English seaman father, who, like T'maho's father, had remained on the island only long enough to get a child on Little Feet.

Through the years he had helped his friend T'maho look after the child, which was no small task, for Saketa was as wild as the wind. Willful, mischievous, and endearing, she had grown from an irritating child into an irritating young woman. And Mingo loved her still, no matter that she had humiliated him before the entire village.

"T'maho! Are you coming?" she screamed now.

"Tell Etawak I'll look in on her when I've finished fishing my nets," T'maho called back. He hated raising his voice. It reminded him of a certain yellow-haired woman who had once complained, when he'd gone whooping through his father's house after some boyish triumph, that he had the manners of a wild Indian.

"She needs to make a potion," Saketa screeched from the shore. "She needs you to trap her an otter! A *male* otter!"

Mingo grinned and began untangling a garfish from the gill net strung between shoals. "A male otter, hmm? Looks like we're going to have another little mouth to feed in the village."

T'maho shook his head, amusement overcoming his impatience. Everyone knew of old Etawak's potions and spells, not a one of which, in recent memory, had proved effective. The bone of an otter's penis, when ground and mixed with ashes of witch hazel and the ground seeds of the purple fox berry, after suitable incantations chanted on the dark of the moon, was supposed to return the tide of a woman's courses.

Idly, he wondered which of the village women had slipped away to Etawak's lodge under the guise of trading for yaupon tea and asked to be rid of an unwanted burden.

By the time she had been on the island three days, Annie had learned precisely how ill-equipped she was for even the most basic of household chores. True, she could make bobbin lace as delicate as a cobweb, and her stitches were so fine they were all but invisible. But her bright dreams of polished floors and Turkish rugs, of gleaming china on a mahogany sideboard and a little desk of her own where she could help her father with his clerical work—surely there would be clerical work, even in the cattle business—those dreams had died the day she had set foot on this windswept, fly-ridden desert island!

She was so hungry her belly button was knocking on her backbone. Little Becky, who had the most irreverent tongue of any five-year-old she had ever known, used to say that. At the thought of the precious, outrageous little scamp, Annie felt her chin tremble. She missed Becky. She missed them all, even Mrs. Biddlecomb, who was not always the easiest woman in the world to get along with.

But most of all, she missed having two good meals a day set before her, and her with nothing more to do than see that all hands were reasonably clean and all heads suitably bowed by the time Mrs. B. got around to asking the blessing.

Now, not only did she have no one to cook her own

food, she had no food to cook. And no money to buy it, even if she knew where the nearest market was. And even if she'd had food and someone to show her how to cook it, there was that wretched fireplace! Either the thing refused to burn, or if it burned, it refused to draw, filling the room with smoke. And if it did draw, it blazed up fit to burn Jerusalem.

If her father had a pantry, she had yet to discover it. She had dumped the crock of rotten fish out the door, and then gagged on the lingering stench that no amount of sand heaped on top of the mess seemed to quell.

Which left only cornmeal. She'd eaten it boiled, and she'd tried it parched. She had even tried to make bread, but evidently she lacked the proper ingredients. The stuff had come out burned black on the bottom and gummy in the middle.

And if that weren't enough, there was the everlasting sand and the flies and mosquitoes. The water barrel was filled with wigglers, and she was so sick of the smell of all those wretched cows and rotten fish that she could have wept.

Not that it would have done a speck of good. At least she was finally here after all these years, ready to make a home for Papa.

The first thing she was going to have him teach her was how to get eggs from a chicken and milk from a cow. She had named the chicken Queenie in hopes of flattering her into offering up her eggs, but after following the wretched bird for two days, all she had found was a mouse, a spider, a lovely pink-speckled seashell, and a mess on her shoe soles that'd had to be scoured off with sand, soap, and water and then left in the sun to dry.

As for milking a cow, the big ugly creatures either ran from her or lowered their horns and mooed, neither of which was especially encouraging. Although to be perfectly fair—which Annie always tried to be—even if one of them had offered her clotted cream in a china bowl, she wouldn't have had the least notion of how to go about collecting it.

Having learned her sums backward and forward, learned to read and write by copying every proverb known to man at least a hundred times—after reading every book of the Bible, including the ones she wasn't supposed to read, and the books on the top shelf of the library, which were supposed to be out of reach of young, innocent minds—Annie had considered herself extremely well educated.

Ha! If Mrs. B. had been any sort of a teacher at all she would have seen to it that each student was rotated through every single chore instead of being set to whichever task they seemed most suited for and kept at it for the rest of their lives.

Pamona Giles could play the pianoforte, never mind that the thing was miserably out of tune. Year after year she had spent her days giving the other girls lessons in music and voice. Her sewing was a disgrace, and she was as big a disaster in the kitchen as Annie was.

Annie couldn't play a tune if her life depended on it, but she'd made enough bobbin lace to reach from here to China, and hemmed enough ruffles to flounce every petticoat in the state of North Carolina. She had lost count of all the detachable collars, mobcaps, and chemises she had cut, tucked, and stitched, but she was quite certain she had embroidered enough bluebirds and roses to stock the Garden of Eden.

Fat lot of good it had done her! Acres and acres of cows right outside her door, and she couldn't even draw herself a cup of milk.

But worst of all, she was lonely. She had never lived alone before. Papa should have been back by now, even if he had sailed to the mainland. She'd had two invitations to go and stay in the village, but it seemed disloyal to simply close the door and walk away.

Still, she was tempted. She missed having someone to talk to, having lived in a noisy, cheerful, all-female household practically all her life. It was the thought of those two men and their wicked laughter following her as she'd ridden away from the village that kept her from going back.

One of them—the scarred one—had ridden up just before dark. She had watched from a window while he fed Jacob and rode out among the herd, but when he had knocked on her door, an irrational fear had kept her from answering right away. While she'd still been gathering her courage to let him in, he had ridden off again.

Just as well. Instead of coming when she had begged him to, he had come in his own sweet time. Annie had quite enough on her plate without having to deal with any such mulish creature. Jacob was bad enough.

If it had been the other one . . .

No matter. One was as bad as the other. At least now that the villagers knew she was here, perhaps someone would come to visit her. Dulsie Scarborough had seemed fascinated by her gown. Perhaps she would ride out one day and bring along a few friends, and they could all sit around and talk about fashions and sewing, and Annie could serve them—

Yes, well . . .

But no matter what, not if she ended up talking to herself like old Miss Hopsapple—not if she starved to death and sand covered her body and cactus grew on her grave—she would never ask for help from Mr. Mingo or his horrible friend!

Having taught herself to make a sort of gruel that was almost palatable by boiling cornmeal with a bit of salt, Annie was stirring a potful of the mixture when she saw a figure on horseback emerge from the glade, heading her way.

Her first thought was of her father. Tossing her spoon aside, she ran to the doorway. "Papa!" she cried, waving wildly as she climbed outside onto the stump.

But the closer the rider came, the more her face fell. It wasn't Papa. Not wearing a blue calico skirt and a white ruffled blouse tied around with a yellow sash. It wasn't even Dulsie Scarborough, not with all that long, glossy black hair.

Still, it was company, and after a week of talking to animals, who continued to ignore her, Annie was grateful for any relief.

Standing outside the doorway, she smoothed her hair

with the palms of her hands, wishing she had taken more time with her grooming. Her hair had always been inclined to curl, but lately it had become wildly unmanageable. Having lost most of her hairpins the day she had come upon those two wicked devils out behind the shed, she had taken to tying it back with a scrap from her patch-basket.

"Good morning," she called out. Her visitor was a young girl, pretty as a glass button. It was obvious that she was an Indian, and Annie wondered if Mr. Mingo had sent her. She'd seen him among the herd several times, but he'd made no further effort to approach the house. "Won't you come in where it's cool and have a glass of water?"

"I came to see Jackson Snell." Lifting her head, the girl scanned the horizon out over the sound, as if expecting to see him come walking in across the water.

"Mr. Snell?" Annie seemed to recall Mr. Jackariah saying a Mr. Snell was Papa's business partner. "He isn't here. My father could probably tell you where you might find him, but Papa's not here, either."

The dark, pretty face took on a petulant cast. "Old Eli's gone on the mail boat, everybody knows that. I don't want him; I want Mr. Snell."

It seemed to Annie that everyone knew a lot of things they had been slow to tell her about, but that was neither here nor there. She'd been in such a rush to get away that day in the village, she hadn't even remembered to ask where he'd gone and when he was due back.

Inviting her guest inside, she remembered that her

father's business partner also happened to be a justice of the peace. Perhaps the poor child—for she was scarcely more than that—was in some sort of trouble. "I'm afraid I'm no officer of the court," she said with a rueful smile. "However, I've been told I'm a very good listener. If there's anything I can do, you have only to ask."

Without even stopping to think, Annie slipped into her old habit of drawing out troubled children in order to soothe away their fears. Many of the children who came to Mrs. Biddlecomb's establishment were troubled in some way, most either frightened or grieving. This child, however, seemed more agitated than sad or frightened.

However, she obviously needed someone, and Annie was here. It was good to be needed again, to feel as if there was still *something* in the world she was capable of accomplishing, even if it was only providing a comfortable shoulder and a sympathetic ear.

Saketa studied the red-haired woman, taking in every detail of the yellow striped gown with the ribbon trim and the embroidered muslin apron. Her hair was curly. Saketa had always longed for curls, but her own hair hung straight as a bulrush.

Who was she? Did she come from the town where Jackson lived? Was she his special friend, too?

Jealousy lit a fuse that began to smolder. Perhaps he liked cat-green eyes and hair the color of iron rust better than he liked shiny black hair and skin the color of old ivory. Saketa sniffed and told herself that any woman, even old Etawak, would have looked pretty wearing such a fine gown, with her hair all curled around her face.

But jealousy faded as she remembered why she was here. She had been so certain Jack would be here. She needed him, *now*! Once she found him and told him about the baby, he would take her away to live in his house that had a floor made of polished rock, and mirrors in every room, and she would wear silks and lace and drink chocolate from a thin cup with flowers painted on the sides, brought to her every morning by a servant who would call her "ma'am." He had as good as promised her all that, hadn't he?

Caught up in her dream, Saketa graciously accepted a mug of water, then spoiled the effect by nervously gulping it down so fast she hiccuped.

"Would you care for more?" Annie inquired, holding the jug of rainwater she had strained and covered with a handkerchief.

"Yes, please."

Saketa told herself she must be very clever. This was not just another childish game. She simply had to find Jack before T'maho caught up with her! His sloop hadn't been at the harbor, and she'd hoped he had anchored off Eli's place and come ashore. Instead, all she'd found was this silly woman, who was no good to her at all!

Restlessly, she stood up and began to prowl, peering through first one window and then another. At any moment now her brother would burst into the clearing, following her tracks, she just knew he would! T'maho could track a bird through the air.

What she didn't know was how he could have found out about the baby so quickly. Etawak must have told him. He could never have guessed on his own, for Saketa herself had only just found out and it was *her* belly the baby was sleeping in!

But T'maho knew; why else would he be chasing her through the glade with that *look* on his face? It was sheer luck that she had seen him before he'd seen her.

Why now, of all times, should he turn suspicious? She'd been on her very best behavior for weeks, ever since the day Jack had told her that he loved her and wanted to marry her.

Well—not precisely in those words, but ever since he had taught her how to be a woman, he'd been telling her how beautiful she was, and how he carried a picture of her in his heart each time he sailed from the island, and how she must promise to keep their special friendship a secret so that T'maho wouldn't find out and try to keep them apart by making her marry one of his Indian friends. T'maho's hatred of the white man was well known.

So she had kept their secret, and they had gone on meeting away from prying eyes whenever Jack came out to the island, and in between times, Saketa had been very, very good.

Perhaps too good. Old Etawak had grown suspicious. Then, when Saketa's courses had stopped and she'd asked Etawak how that could be, the old woman had given her such a look! She'd forced her to drink some foul potion that had made her break out in a rash all over, but her courses hadn't come again, and then

Etawak had demanded to know which wicked man had been poking about under her skirts to make a baby.

Saketa had been so stunned it was all she could do to deny it. Fortunately, she was a skilled liar, for she'd had much practice. She had told Etawak that her courses had dried up because of a dream she'd had about a big snake chasing her up a tree in the glade. Everyone knew that dreaming about snakes could cause the bowels to lock up, so why shouldn't it cause a woman's courses to dry up?

But the minute she could escape she had hurried down to the dock to see if Jack's sloop was in sight, and when it wasn't there, she had come to Eli's, because she'd hoped Jack had brought the old man home and would still be here, anchored off the reef the way he sometimes did when the harbor was full of lumber barges.

She simply had to find him and tell him about the baby so that he could take her away before T'maho caught up with her! Because if her brother found her first, there wouldn't *be* any wedding! T'maho almost never lost his temper, but she knew him well. She would rather face six lightning bolts and a tote sack full of wildcats than tell him she had taken a white man as her lover.

"If there's anything I can do—?" The red-haired woman sat with her feet held primly together, her hands folded neatly in her lap.

Silly fool! What would she say if Saketa told her the truth? Swoon away like a scared possum?

However, an idea was beginning to take shape in her

mind. Dropping onto a chair, Saketa sighed dramatically. The woman might not be a match for T'maho, but if she could only hold him here long enough, Saketa could get away and hide until Jack could come for her.

Several minutes had passed without a word being spoken. Annie had heard the overdone sigh and recognized it as not untypical of adolescent girls. She guessed her young guest's age as being no more than fifteen—perhaps a year younger.

Clearing her throat, she tried once again to draw the girl out. "You look as if something is troubling you. Perhaps it would help to talk about it?"

An expression of cunning flashed across the girl's face, but it was followed so swiftly by a look of fear that Annie thought she must have imagined it. "It . . . it's my husband," the girl said hesitantly.

"You're married?" The child must be older than she appeared. "Is your husband in some sort of trouble? Do you need Justice Snell to advise you?"

"Oh, no, it's not that!" Saketa jumped to her feet and began pacing again, her eyes darting nervously to the window. "He—he beats me, you see. I'm afraid he'll hurt our baby."

Annie's jaw fell. "Your husband beats you and your child? How could any man possibly do such a wicked thing?"

But she knew. It could only be Strong Drink. Oh, she had heard many a pitiful tale from some of the poor orphans whose nightmares she had soothed away.

Strong Drink always searched out and exacerbated a man's weakness, be it laziness, gambling, or cruelty.

"Oh, no—I mean, I don't have a child yet. I—I'm carrying a baby inside my stomach," Saketa said earnestly, knowing all about such things now, thanks to Etawak's explanation just this morning when she'd come upon her losing her breakfast.

"Well, I never! Surely you have family who can—"

"Oh, you mustn't blame my husband. It's all my fault." Improvising wildly, Saketa blinked and actually managed to squeeze out a tear. "It's just that I feel so awful in the morning I can't do my chores, and so—so he beats me, and then I feel even worse, and so I ran away, only he's following me, and when he finds me, I'm afraid he'll do something awful just to punish me." Her voice dropped to a dramatic whisper.

Annie leaped to her feet, quivering with righteous indignation. "Over my dead body will that wicked man lay one finger on you! Now you listen here to me— what did you say your name was?"

"Saketa," the girl whispered.

"And I'm Annie. Now, you listen here, Saketa, no man is going to hurt you while I have the strength to prevent it. You're to stay right here for as long as you need to, and if any man comes sniffing around my door, he'll get more than he bargained for, that I can promise you!" Jutting her small, pointed chin, Annie braced herself to do battle.

No wonder the poor child was trying to find a justice of the peace!

Well, Mr. Snell might not be here to protect her—

and knowing the way the law worked, there would be scant protection from that quarter for any woman, much less an Indian—but Annie O'Neal was here, and protect her she would!

Hurrying the tearful girl into the bedroom, she urged her to lie down and try to rest. "We'll think of some way to bring him around to the side of righteousness."

If stern words were not enough, Papa's musket should do the trick. "I'm sure there must be a grain of common decency buried in the man somewhere, else you'd never have married him," she said, more for reassurance than because she believed it. "The first thing I'll do is appeal to his better nature."

Saketa cast her a sidelong look, squeezed out another tear, and crawled onto the lumpy mattress, which was spread on a plank platform without so much as a rail for a head or a foot. The thing smelled of fish, but then, everything hereabouts smelled of fish—at least what didn't smell of cow dung.

She would like to see the red-haired woman face a man like T'maho when he was on a rolling, boiling temper. Not all her pretty manners nor her pretty gowns would help her then. If there was one thing her brother hated more than a white man, it was a white woman.

Saketa told herself that she would soon have far prettier gowns—and certainly a far finer house. Even Etawak had a finer house!

With a murmur of reassurance, Annie slipped away. She placed her father's old musket beside the door and took up a position where she could watch through the window. She hadn't long to wait before a lone rider emerged from the glade.

He seemed to be in no particular hurry. Annie felt her gown grow damp with perspiration as, with a growing sense of horror, she watched him ride closer. Merciful saints in heaven, it was that same bold-eyed savage who had attacked her out behind the shed! The one who had laughed at her that day in the village.

With a feeling of fear mixed with dismay, she braced herself once again to do battle. "Well, sir, you might be Saketa's husband," she muttered, "but if you think you're going to lay one hand on that child in anger while Annie O'Neal is here to stop you, you'll soon learn the error of your ways!" Staggering under the weight of the heavy, brass-barreled weapon, she took up her position at the door.

T'maho spied Saketa's pony standing patiently outside the door of Eli's lodge. Did that limb of Satan think the scrawny ginger-hair would protect her? That one could not even protect herself.

Slipping off Maroke's back, he slapped Saketa's pony on the rump, sending her galloping off toward home. He still hadn't gotten over the shock of learning that his baby sister had lain with a man. At the time he had trapped the male otter old Etawak had asked for, he'd thought nothing of it other than a fleeting regret that an animal must be sacrificed in such a way. He'd known full well what it was to be used for. Everyone in the village knew Etawak's secret recipes, if not her incantations.

Only when the old woman had told him a few days later that it was time to find his sister a husband had he begun to wonder why Saketa had been behaving so well lately. She had avoided him whenever she could, and been entirely too sweet and agreeable when she couldn't. Which meant she was up to something.

Then, when he'd gone to check on Saketa this morning, the old woman had practically put it into words, saying that while she didn't know who had done it, she was damned well certain of what had been done!

Immediately, T'maho had set out to find his sister and learn from her own lips who had dishonored her. Whoever the wretch was, if T'maho had to crack heads to achieve it, he vowed to see them wed before anyone could say that Saketa was no better than her own mother had been.

But his heart ached, for he loved the child. She was all the family he had in the world—at least, all he cared to claim.

So he had trailed her here. Now, surveying the house, T'maho saw a movement in the doorway. A wisp of skirt showed momentarily against the weathered wood. Keeping his head lowered, he pretended not to notice.

Eli's daughter. Did she think a barred door and shuttered windows would keep him out?

Not this time. Not when he knew his sister was inside.

With a ferral smile, he leaped up onto the stump and grabbed the doorframe to catapult himself inside, only to feel something cold and hard against his belly.

"Not one step farther, you miserable worm of a man!"

T'maho fought briefly for balance, staring down in surprise at the tarnished brass barrel pressed against his bare flesh. If he weren't so concerned for his sister, he might even have laughed. The woman could barely lift the thing, much less aim it. He wondered if she knew the kind of load Eli used to scare wild dogs away from his cattle.

He wondered if the piece was even primed and loaded.

Not that he particularly cared to find out.

"I have come for Saketa," he said calmly. "Put away your weapon, woman."

"I'll put away nothing! Don't you dare set foot in this house!"

What could he do after that but step inside? Was it only the combination of wild ginger hair and blazing green eyes that challenged him in a way that made his blood race?

Or was it the memory of those few moments when she had lain beneath him, her belly soft beneath his swelling manhood, her small breasts thrusting against his naked chest?

The woman was a fool, T'maho told himself. She stepped back and the barrel wavered, but still she did not drop her guard. Seeing the faint blue shadows under her thin, pale skin, T'maho reminded himself of all the reasons why he despised such women.

In a silent battle of wills, they glared at one another

while the gun barrel slowly sank under its own weight until it was pointing directly toward his groin.

"Will you send Saketa out, or must I take her by force?" He stood perfectly still, waiting for her arms to tire and the barrel to drop farther before he made his next move. He would sooner risk a kneecap than the part of him now threatened. "You will not shoot me, woman. Put away the weapon."

Annie took one small step back and prayed that Saketa had used the time to hide herself under the bed. Grunting, she clutched the walnut stock tighter, causing the barrel to wave wildly. "I've never shot a man in cold blood," she warned, "yet. But if you don't get back on that horse and go back where you came from right this very minute, I cannot be responsible for your safety."

The devil stood his ground. The gray eyes that had come as such a surprise to her narrowed suddenly in his angular face. Muscles flexed subtly under his tea-colored skin—of which there was entirely too much visible for Annie's comfort.

Didn't the man possess a shirt?

"Shoo! Just go home! Saketa is safe where you can't hurt her!"

Without warning, T'maho struck. With one hand, he grabbed the gun barrel to shove it aside, but instead of releasing it and stepping back as any sensible woman would have done, the small ginger-hair dropped the heavy stock and swung her fist at his head.

Left ear ringing, he stared down at her, too shocked to be angry. Almost amused, in fact. He was close enough to see her lips trembling, to read the fear in her wide eyes. Close enough to smell the heat of her small body, which had the same effect on him now that it had the first time she had attacked him.

"Ahone!" he muttered in disgust, shoving her from him. He had more important things to do than let himself be distracted by one of her kind.

The room could not have concealed a small dog. T'maho's eyes flew immediately to the closed door on the far side. Without a word, he strode past her and flung it open. "Saketa!" he roared.

The woman was right behind him. "There's no one here, as you can plainly see!"

Slipping under the savage's arm, Annie planted herself in front of him, barring the way into the bedroom. If the poor child had crawled into her trunk and lowered the lid, she might suffocate if Annie didn't get rid of this blasted, bloody heathen quickly enough.

"Saketa!" he barked, glaring past her as if she weren't even there. "You defy me at your own risk!"

"Don't you dare threaten a guest in my house!" Flattening her hands against the rock-hard chest, Annie shoved hard, leaning her weight to the task. Without even looking over her shoulder into the room beyond, she cried, "Saketa, you stay right where you are! He can't make you go against your will!"

As if she were no more than a fly to be waved away, the man clamped his hands around her waist, lifted her off the floor, and swung her aside, not releasing her immediately.

Annie gasped. "Take your hands off me this instant, you—you bloody barbarian!"

Eyes gleaming palely, he continued to hold her, his hard fingers biting into her waist right through gown, chemise, bandette, and all. And then, abruptly, he released her and turned away. "Saketa! I'm tired of your foolish games!" he warned, stepping into the small room.

Annie shoved past him, looking around frantically. "Don't you worry, Saketa, he'll not take you away as long as I'm here to protect you," she cried.

Only there was no one there to protect.

Chapter 4

The room was empty, the only sign of occupancy a pair of small, ruffled pantaloons drying before the open window. The narrow bed was neatly spread, the coverlet—which consisted of a single panel of shabby brocade drapery—smooth and flat. Annie's three summer gowns, four aprons, and good black hat hung from pegs on the far wall, and in the corner stood her closed trunk with the sewing basket sitting squarely on top. Which meant that Saketa could not possibly be hiding inside.

Annie breathed a sigh of relief that the girl had managed to escape, but had to admit that she was somewhat disappointed. Company would have been nice. Now, knowing the tragic circumstances, she would worry herself sick until she was sure the poor child was safe.

Stealing a quick glance at the haughty profile, she found it all too possible to believe that this man would beat his wife. Hadn't she herself suffered his ungentle touch? No wonder the poor girl had run away from him. Those silver-gray eyes alone were cold enough to freeze Hades!

All of which made it difficult to understand the odd
sense of disappointment that crept over her.

Annie watched his gaze sweep the room slowly and
then return. Realizing just what had captured his attention, she felt the sudden heat rise to stain her cheeks.
Pride alone kept her from dashing past him to snatch
up her undergarment and hide it from sight.

T'maho looked out the window and then swore silently. He had missed her by mere minutes. Evidently,
thinking to outwit him, she had slipped out the window
at the back of the house even as he'd ridden up to the
front, knowing that her tracks would be easily covered
by the small herd that grazed near the house. For all he
knew, she had whistled up her pony and was racing
home, knowing that Etawak would protect her from the
worst of his wrath.

Neatly done, little sister, he saluted in reluctant admi-
ration, wondering what wicked tale she had told the
ginger-hair to make her stand guard like a bear with
one cub.

A sultry breeze stirred the dainty garment drying in
the sun on the windowsill, and unbidden, the image of
a pair of pale, slender limbs entangled in layers of
white ruffles intruded on his thoughts. This was not
the first time T'maho had seen such a garment, nor had
all of them been hanging out to dry. It was the first
time, however, that he had seen a pair of drawers so
delicate they could be drawn through a single mesh of
a gill net.

The wonder was that Saketa had not stolen the

thing, along with those dresses on the wall, he thought with wry amusement. The scamp had been stealing gowns from under the noses of the village women the very first time he had laid eyes on her nearly eleven years ago.

But it was not on Saketa that his thoughts dwelt as he strode silently through Eli's house, leaving the ginger-haired woman gaping after him.

Weak, foolish creature, he thought as he swung himself onto the bare back of his mare and turned southward. He could have broken her musket over his knee had he wanted to.

He could have broken *her* over his knee!

He compared her to the kind of woman he most despised. Spoiled, demanding, using woman's tears to get her way, as his father's woman had done all those years ago. Pulling her skirts aside to avoid brushing against him, as his father's woman had also done. No doubt expecting him to leap upon her at any moment and take her scalp.

Visualizing that wild red hair and the small, determined chin she had thrust forward as if that alone would protect her, T'maho was reluctantly forced to admit that the ginger-hair had done none of those things. Instead, she had come to his sister's defense, a thing few women of her kind would have done. Three days ago she had attacked him with a length of fencing to protect her father's property. Today, alone and obviously terrified, she had challenged him with a gun that was so heavy she could scarcely hold it.

Slowly, he shook his head in amazement. The wonder was that she hadn't blown a hole in the roof.

Or in him.

T'maho had known many women, both in his own village and in the lower villages on the island. He liked women. Women liked him. More than one yellow-haired, blue-eyed female had let her gaze drift over him in a certain way, telling him without words that should he follow her into the glade, she would slow her steps.

He ignored them. There were enough young widows of his own kind on the island, even though over many generations, the blood of his people had been thinned by being mingled with that of paleskins until few even remembered the old ways. They forgot the old tongue, wore white men's clothes and hard-soled shoes, and married without regard to their heritage. Saketa was among the worst in that respect.

He alone in the village insisted on living his life in the old way, at least as far as was practical. He had built his lodge in the old place, south of the village. When the time came for him to find a wife, she would be of his mother's people.

He had wanted the same for Saketa. On his last hunting trip to the big swamp country, he had met a fine young man of the Corree people. The boy was young, only a year older than Saketa. In a few years, he would have made her a fine husband, but if she was no longer a maiden, that would not be possible.

There was still John Tallhorse, however. His grandmother had been Scottish, but it didn't show. With three children and no woman, his wife having died in childbirth two years ago, John might be willing to make the match. He was fairly sober. He had a good boat, a straight back, and a level temper. He even possessed most of his teeth.

"Ahhh, Saketa," T'maho whispered against the pain in his heart, "where are you, you wicked *neckaun*? What have you done this time?"

The anger that had sent him flying after her had given way to a growing unease. Sensing his mood, the mare, called Maroke for the color of her hide, which was as red as the heart of a cedar, broke into a gallop.

He would find her. Knowing him as well as she did, Saketa would hide until she thought his anger had been consumed by worry, and then she would show herself. Another of her childish games, and she played it cleverly, he was forced to admit. With two such teachers as Mingo and himself, she had learned all the ways a cunning animal could elude the hunter.

Once her brother had ridden off, Saketa considered circling back and climbing in through the window again. The woman who called herself Annie had been kind. Kind, but extremely silly. She had believed every word Saketa had told her.

She could also have told the foolish creature that no musket would keep T'maho from going where he wished to go.

But at least it had held him off long enough for her to escape. If only he hadn't run off her pony, she would have been halfway to Cape Creek by now!

Mingling with the herd, she ran swiftly to the other

side of the dunes, where the sea would wash away her tracks. Then, allowing T'maho time to reach the village, she cut over into the glade.

Once deep into the cool shadowy place where dense stands of palmetto gave way unexpectedly to blackwater ponds, where bird calls echoed eerily in the green darkness of bay trees and live oaks, holly and ironwood, where gray beards and thick vines trailed from every bough, she could elude the cleverest tracker.

Saketa had often followed T'maho and Mingo when they had come to the glade to hunt. She had often played here as a child. Later, when she became a woman, she had come here to play another game—a game that Jack had taught her.

"Where are you, Jack?" she whispered.

From nearby, a gray and yellow bird mocked her words.

Hadn't he promised to return before the full moon? But the full moon had already come and gone.

She called him Jack in her heart, although he preferred to be called Mr. Snell. Especially when he made love to her.

How long before his sloop, the *Black Opal,* would return? Once they had even made love in the cabin, with the water lapping against the hull, causing it to bump gently against the dock. It had been unbearably exciting, right in the heart of the village with people all around outside, talking, working—never even suspecting what was happening only a few feet away.

Was that when they had made the baby?

There was still so much she didn't know about

woman-things. When Saketa had begun her courses, Etawak had mumbled something about moons and tides, but Saketa had barely listened. Any fool knew about the tides. One had only to look around to know that when the moon ruled from its throne high overhead, it tried to drag the tide up with it, pulling it ruthlessly away from the shore, but when the moon grew weary and lay on the horizon to rest, the clever tide slipped away like a runaway child, to play on the sandy beaches.

What did all that have to do with a woman's monthly pain and swelling and bleeding? And what did all *that* have to do with making babies?

Perhaps they had made their baby right here beside Long Green Pond, she mused. It had been here in their secret bower that Jack had first made her remove all her clothes and stand before him while he prodded her with his whip to turn this way and that, admiring her newly swelled breasts and her bit of private hair.

A frown clouded Saketa's smooth face as she recalled how he had hurt her that day. Perhaps it was making the baby that had hurt.

Or they could have made the baby the day Etawak had ridden down to Cape Woods with two casks of acorn beer to trade for salt beef. Saketa had stayed home to look at the pictures in an old copy of the *Elizabeth City and Eastern North Carolina Star and Intelligencer* that Dulcie had given her.

She had been trying to twist up her hair to look like one of the ladies pictured there when Jack had come to the house. He had made her remove all her clothes, even though Etawak could have returned at any moment, which had made it doubly exciting, and then he had forced her to kneel before him and—

And to do those other things. She had asked afterward if that was what wives did for their husbands, and he had only laughed and told her to wait and see.

She was still waiting, only now she could wait no longer, for if Etawak was right—and this time Saketa thought she just might be—then they had made a baby.

Etawak had sat her down and named every man in the village, demanding to know which one had lifted her skirts and planted his seed in her belly. Saketa had known better than to tell her, knowing she would tell T'maho, and T'maho would get that awful *quiet* look that made her think he was hurting inside.

Quickly she'd made up a story about promising to help Dulsie with her garden, and then she'd raced out to see if Jack's boat had come in so she could tell him he must hurry up and offer for her. No less than a fine bull and six cows, at the very least. Or maybe eight. She was worth it.

Besides, he had so very many.

But the only boats in harbor besides the village fishing boats had been two lumber barges and a battered old freighter out of Norfolk. No sign at all of the *Black Opal*.

Crawling deeper into the shadows, Saketa twisted a wisp of hair around her finger. She wanted to go home, but she didn't dare—not yet. That was the first place T'maho would look for her, and judging from the look on his face when he'd come charging into Eli's house, his anger hadn't even begun to cool down. Maybe Mingo would help her. He'd never been able to deny her anything she asked.

Releasing the twist of hair, she sighed, lifted her skirt, and idly scratched her knee. Poor Mingo. He still loved her in spite of the way she had shamed him. She didn't deserve his friendship, but she desperately needed it—at least until Jack could make his offer and take her to live in his fine big house in New Bern.

She shivered. It was beginning to grow dark. The air had turned much cooler. In the distance, she felt, rather than heard, the rumble of thunder. She would almost rather take her chances with T'maho than stay out all night in a storm. If she refused to speak, what could he do besides yell at her and call her wicked and willful? He'd done that plenty of times before. It didn't actually hurt . . . although she never liked it.

This time, though, he might do something more. He might be angry enough to make her marry the oldest, ugliest man in the entire village before Jack could come for her. In that case, she might just as well have taken Mingo when he had offered for her.

As if any woman could possibly want Mingo when she could have a fine gentleman like Jack.

Not that Mingo was really old, she supposed, but he was so ugly that as a child she had run and hid whenever he'd looked at her. Of course, that had been years ago. She hadn't run from him in years. He was her brother's best friend, after all—the second best fisherman in the entire village, next to T'maho, the second best tracker and the second best hunter in the whole world. Or maybe even the best.

She sighed. Poor Mingo. He deserved to find a woman who would love him for the goodness of his heart so that he wouldn't have to grow old all alone. But what woman would ever be able to see past his scars?

Curling up in a small knot, Saketa wrapped her arms around her body and rocked back and forth, wishing she could go home to her supper. Wishing Jack would hurry. It was almost too dark now to see across the pond, and she didn't much like the darkness.

How many times when she had cried in the night had T'maho told her that the dark couldn't hurt her?

But spirits roamed in the darkness. Everyone knew that. And there were snakes as big around as a man's arm, and they came out to hunt at night, and when they bit you, it hurt, and you turned black and swelled up and died.

She didn't want to swell up and die. Not now, just when her life was truly about to begin. She was only fifteen and a half years old. She didn't want to die until she was an old, old, woman—maybe even thirty years old.

Jack would come for her. He had promised. After what they had done together the last time, which made her blush even to think about it, he wouldn't be able to stay away. And when he didn't find her in the village he would know where to look, for they often met here by the Long Green Pond where the moss hung so thick a body could barely see through it. It was one of their secret places.

Nearby in the village harbor, a small, swift, black-hulled sloop glided silently up to the wharf. Having arranged for the transaction of his "business" with that meddling old fool O'Neal, Jackson Snell had raced northward to Roanoke Island and allowed himself to be seen talking to several prominent citizens, pretending to have just come down from Virginia.

Not that the deed could ever be traced back to him. He had made certain of that before he had set it into motion. Even so, a wise man left nothing to chance. The ownership of the herd was no problem—the old fool had never even questioned the fact that Snell took care of all registrations and bills of sale. Not that there were any. And now, as the surviving partner, the land would be his, as well. All he would need to do was file his claim and then hire someone to do O'Neal's work.

The Indian Mingo, perhaps. God knows, the wretch was ugly enough to scare off anyone who came around asking questions.

Not that anyone would. Snell had taken his time and covered his tracks well. Now all he had to do was wait for word of poor Eli's tragic accident to spread. He would be suitably shocked, of course. A touch of grief would not be amiss, for the two men had been partners for a goodly number of years.

And while he waited, he could pass a few pleasant hours with the bitch Saketa.

Snell had a way with women. At the age of thirty-nine years he prided himself that he looked ten years younger. He was even more handsome now than he had been as a youth—at least the damned spots had finally faded—but it was his high position and the aura of success he cultivated that drew women to him like flies to the honeypot.

Besides which, he knew how to deal with women. Catch them young, train them well, and treat them liked dogs. The bitches adored it. They practically panted to be mastered.

Carefully appraising his reflection in the shaving mirror, he arranged his pale, thinning hair to make it appear thicker, adjusted the hang of his broadcloth coat, and made to go ashore, already hot with anticipation. He had been too busy these past few weeks arranging for O'Neal's demise to seek out a woman.

Then, too, he had to admit that Saketa had temporarily spoiled him for the pasty-faced bawds at the Hens and Cockerel. Somewhat to his surprise—for he had played up to the girl out of sheer boredom at first—she had turned out to be quite the juiciest little morsel he had tasted in many a day.

But then, he'd always had a taste for wild meat. Venison. Elk. The dark flesh of the wild goose.

His little island bitch was amusing and quick to learn. She worshiped the ground he walked on. Such abject adoration grew tiresome after a while; still, she would serve well enough whenever he had business on the island. If she grew too demanding, he would simply take her with him and arrange to sell her at the Hens and Cockerel.

* * *

By nightfall, T'maho was more than uneasy. Etawak had not seen Saketa since early morning. For once, he was convinced the old woman's twisted tongue had spoken the truth, for she was too worried to lie.

With Mingo's aid, they had searched all the places she might have hidden. The glade—although there were too many places where one could hide and never be found. The shore—Mingo had ridden south while T'maho had ridden north, each covering the seashore first and then doubling back along the soundside, exploring the banks of each marshy creek that fingered in from the sound.

In the village and the scattering of lodges to the south, Etawak had asked if anyone had seen the girl that day. Saketa had many friends among both peoples. Dulsie Scarborough had seen her ride past, but she hadn't stopped. Aggora Hooper remembered seeing her ride north toward the glade, but Etawak had taken no comfort from that, for Saketa's pony had long since come home without her.

Under the long boughs of the oldest graveyard live oak, Etawak considered the secret she had shared with no one—although she thought T'maho must have guessed when she insisted it was time he found his sister a husband, for she was growing to resemble poor Little Feet more with each passing day.

Etawak had known for weeks. She had given her the potion, but something must have gone wrong with the incantation. It had failed.

Had she forgotten an important ingredient? Or had she mixed up her words? Was it *apome* or *apooke*? One word meant "thigh," the other, "tobacco." That could have made a difference. Perhaps she would do better to cast all her spells in the white man's language from now on, for the old language had fallen into such disuse that she sometimes grew confused.

But the bones spoke a silent language all their own, and she had cast them again and again—the leg of a loon, the pinion of a white brant, and the neck bone from a swamp turtle.

No meaning had revealed itself. No name, no pointing finger.

John Tallhorse? Saketa would never have lifted her skirt for such a longface. Still, he would make a good enough husband, for he was industrious and fairly sober. And if the babe she carried was a boy, he would be of great help in a few years, for John's children were all female. But he could not have been the one, so there was no use in searching for her there now.

The youngest Outlaw boy? He had looked at her more than once with a gleam in his eye. Etawak hoped it had not been that one, for T'maho would never let her marry him. He had no use for any white since his father had deserted him in favor of a white woman.

There was always Mingo. . . .

Mingo could never have fathered her babe. He had offered for her when she was little more than a child. Dressed up in a new pair of trousers and a new shirt, with a pair of hard, crippling shoes on his feet, he had ridden through the village to find her and make his offering in the old way, leading a string of fine mares and a beautiful stallion.

Before the entire village, Saketa had rejected him. She had laughed at him. Some of the villagers had laughed, as well, although not all. When he was little more than a child, Mingo had nearly lost his life saving a crippled old woman who had stupidly set her own lodge on fire. To this day he bore the scars. Everyone, Indian and white alike, respected Mingo. He would make any woman a good husband, but Etawak doubted if even T'maho could induce him to offer for Saketa again.

Yet if not Mingo, then who? Who was both strong enough to control the wayward girl and gentle enough not to break her spirit? Who in this small village was wicked enough to steal a young girl's honor and then leave her unprotected?

The same thing had happened to Little Feet. But Little Feet had been weak and foolish. Married at thirteen to an old man, widowed at fourteen, she had been dead at twenty-four. Between the widowing and the dying, she had been far too easily won over by a few sweet words. Both Saketa and T'maho were proof of that.

Poor Little Feet. Her heart had been good, but her head had been weak. Etawak comforted herself with the thought that whatever else she was, Saketa was not weak. Willful, mischievous—maddening more often than not—but never weak.

Humming tunelessly around the stem of her blackened pipe, Etawak tried once more to concentrate. She had always set great store on her ability to read character, but for the life of her she could think of no man who would so shame an innocent young girl, no matter that the girl herself had been born out of wedlock. The villagers were hard, but decent. They adhered to their own code of justice.

It must have been one of the bargemen who traveled back and forth, hauling oak limbs to make ships' knees, robbing the island of its forest. They were a wicked-looking lot. She should have warned the girl not to go near the harbor when the barges were in.

Etawak stared thoughtfully out over the silvering water, her squat body rocking gently to and fro. After a while, she began to hum, and then *"Ampkone, ampkone,"* she intoned solemnly.

No, no! That was the word for "frying pan," not the name of the Great Spirit. Distracted with worry, suffering from aching knees and stiffening fingers, she absently scratched her nose, thought for a moment, and tried again. "Swiftly, child, like the tern, to my lodge you must return."

Then, rising awkwardly, she waddled off toward her own lodge, wondering if this spell would be any more effective than the last. Or the one before that.

Faugh! She might as well turn Methodist!

T'maho thought perhaps his friend had not understood his words, Mingo stood for so long staring out the door of his tidy, rush-roofed lodge. A faded blue shirt stretched across his broad shoulders as he flexed his powerful muscles, fists clenched at his sides. They had searched for two days and nights. At first, T'maho had told his friend only that Saketa had run away from home in a fit of childish pique.

Knowing Saketa, Mingo had not questioned his word.

But now, after so much time had passed, T'maho had been compelled to share his full burden with the man who had patiently drawn an angry young half-breed into a bond of friendship so long ago.

"Did Saketa say this to you herself?" Mingo demanded harshly. He swung around, sunlight highlighting with cruel clarity the corrugations on his broad face. "Did she say the name of the man who did this wickedness to her?"

"Etawak as good as told me. I have not seen Saketa since then. Remember the day I trapped the otter? Etawak wanted only the one part. Which means—"

"It could have been meant for anyone."

T'maho shook his head slowly. "I know that potion. I know what it's meant to do and how it's made. It contains the purple fox berries. Since Saketa was this big"—he indicated with his hand a height of three feet—"every time she eats fox berries she scratches for days. They make her itch."

"She itched after you gave Etawak the otter?"

"She itched."

"And you think it's because—"

"I think it's because her courses had ceased, and Etawak gave her the potion, knowing that an itch can be scratched, but an unwanted child cannot be so easily dismissed."

"How do you know the thing didn't work?"

"Did you ever know one of Etawak's potions to work?"

A sad smile twisted Mingo's features. "I know at least one that did not." Once, a long time ago, the old woman had mixed up a gruesome salve of goose gall, mullet gizzard, and eagle dung, which she promised would remove his scars before the new moon. Instead, his face had swollen up and seeped pus for a week. He had burned with fever and heaved until his gut ached. It was T'maho who had found him thus, who had scrubbed the foul paste from his skin and forced him to drink water until he had flushed the poisons from his body.

"There was time enough if it was going to work. If it had, Etawak would not have told me to find Saketa a husband. Besides, why else would the girl run away? Does she think me a monster? Have I ever lifted a hand against her?"

He swore in a mixture of Hattorask and English, with a lack of control that was alien to his nature. "Damn *mattui kmoi*! Where the bloody hell can she be hiding? She knows I would never hurt her, no matter what wickedness she's done!"

"Easy, my friend, easy. Saketa is no fool. She knows your temper is like the dry shift. Little more than a hard wind that blows fiercely for a few moments and then dies away."

T'maho cocked an eyebrow. He'd rather thought his anger was more effective than that, but at the moment he was too concerned over to Saketa to respond to the insult.

"We'll find her." Mingo shrugged his massive shoulders. "Where can she go? She cannot swim to the mainland. No boat is missing. Her pony still grazes in Etawak's garden patch."

"She went first to Eli's place," T'maho muttered, his thoughts veering, not for the first time, to Eli's ginger-haired daughter. "Why? She didn't even know the woman."

"You don't think O'Neal—?"

T'maho laughed harshly. "God, no! The imp fancies herself mightily for her white blood, but she would never settle for an old relic like O'Neal!"

"He's a decent man," Mingo said quietly.

"For a white man," T'maho agreed.

"We'll find her. I'll try the Cape Woods again."

T'maho nodded. Both men thought of Etawak with her casting bones and her tray of sand, set out for the chickens to scratch a message in. After two days, the old grandmother was no closer to discovering the truth than they were.

"I'll ride north again," T'maho said, forcing back the fear that was beginning to burn in his brain and in his belly. "She went that way once before. She might have gone back. After the rain, tracking will be better."

Annie was scraping out the burned remains of yet another meal when she happened to glance southward toward the cool green shadows of the glade. Scattered in all directions, her father's herd grazed contentedly on

the wild beach grasses. She had almost grown accustomed to the scent of sweaty hides and fresh dung,
now that the lingering aroma of rotten fish was not
quite so prevalent.

She had to admit that here in the flatlands, where a
body could see from horizon to horizon with no hills or
tall forests to block the view, the sky was spectacular.
Today's sunset was truly beautiful, with layers of scarlet
and rose and gold faithfully reflected in the calm waters beneath.

Suddenly a movement caught her eye and she stiffened. Someone was coming. Silhouetted against the
glare was a single horse carrying a man who . . .

A man who was holding something—or someone?—in
his arms.

The burned pan clattered to the ground as she jumped
down off the stump. Someone was hurt. Her father?

"Oh, please, God, not Papa!"

Chapter 5

T'maho's worst fears had been confirmed. Saketa had been attacked. He had found her near the northern edge of the glade, so badly beaten she barely clung to life. From her stumbling tracks and the trail of dark blood it was obvious to him that instead of trying to reach the village, she had been trying to make her way back to the ginger-hair when she had collapsed.

She was wiser than he had thought, this irritating, enchanting, maddening little sister whom he loved with all his aching heart. Even mortally wounded, she had known enough not to go home, where the devil who had done this wicked thing to her could easily seek her out and finish what he had begun.

Encased in an icy, unnatural calm, T'maho was scarcely aware of the pain in his own heart. Unaware of the tears that dulled his vision, he rode steadily onward, carefully holding his burden away from his body so as to spare her even the gentle rocking motion of the mare. "He will pay, little sister," T'maho whispered. "Slowly and painfully, until he begs for a knife to pierce his black heart, he will pay." A tear broke through his dense lashes and trailed downward to splash on Saketa's bloody scalp.

She whimpered. "Hush now, little cricket," he told her. "Soon you will lie on a soft bed, with nothing to do but close your eyes and sleep. When you wake up, the pain will not be so bad."

It would be worse. It would be far worse before it ever began to get better—if she even survived.

If Etawak was right and Saketa had been with child, he suspected the child was now lost. He spared a moment of grief for the innocent life, for a child could not be blamed for the sin of its father.

But his greatest concern was Saketa. She needed a woman's help. She needed a physician, but there was none on the Banks, and it would take at least a week to find one willing to make the journey and return with him. In a week's time, Saketa could be—

It would have to be the ginger-hair. Perhaps Saketa had known more about the woman than he had taken the time to learn. Why else would she have gone there? Why would she have tried to return when she lacked the strength even to cry out?

Despite his personal bitterness, T'maho was forced to admit that the white man's medicine might be better than any of Etawak's potions. With the best intentions in the world, the old woman would probably have poisoned her with some vile potion concocted of bird droppings, fish entrails, and fermented animal parts.

Acting on instinct, he had turned northward, but it occurred to him now that he might have taken her to any one of the village women. Not one of them, he reluctantly admitted, would have turned her away. In that respect they were different, these island people, from the whites living in the mainland towns, with their fine houses and their fine clothes and their fine white manners.

But they would have talked. Once they discovered that Saketa had been with child, they would remember Little Feet and whisper among themselves that the acorn did not fall far from the tree. For all her waywardness, he would permit no one to disparage his little sister.

Holding Maroke to a smooth, swift canter, T'maho had almost reached Eli's house when the woman appeared on the stump outside the door. He watched as, arms outstretched, she leaped down and came running to meet him, bleating like a demented sheep. Baa baa baa!

He nearly turned back then. Everything in him rebelled at having to ask for help from such a woman. But just then, Saketa whimpered. One hand, the nails torn and bleeding, lifted to touch her throat, which was swollen and black with bruises. "We're nearly there, little cricket. Shhhh now, do not try to speak. T'maho will take care of you."

From the stump outside the door, Annie had recognized the rider right away by the arrogant tilt of his head. One would have thought he was President Jackson himself from the way he sat a horse.

She wondered why he was coming back. He had searched her house once. He knew very well there was no one there but herself. Even Papa was still gone.

And then, squinting against the blinding sunset, she saw what he was carrying. Dangling limbs, either mud-stained or bloodstained.

Oh, dear God, no! He was bringing Papa home!

Leaping down from the stump, she ran to meet him, heedless of the cactus, sandspurs and cow patties that dotted the hot sand. "Papa, Papa, Papa!" she cried.

And then she slowed her steps. That wasn't Papa who was being brought home in the arms of the savage. Not that limp, bloody form barely covered with a few fluttering shreds of blue calico and filthy white muslin.

Oh, merciful saints, it was Saketa! The wicked devil had found the poor child and murdered her, and now he was coming after the woman who had tried to protect her!

Walking his mare, he kept on coming, arms outstretched before him with that pathetic . . . *thing* . . . lying across them. Not daring to take her eyes from his terrible, beautiful face, Annie began backing away. When she tripped over a clump of dried grass and nearly fell, she spun around and fled toward the house.

Papa's musket! Where had she put it? Dear Lord, was it even loaded? She hadn't the slightest notion of how to tell, much less how to load it if it wasn't.

He was mad, quite mad, and he was dangerous, and he was coming after her!

Leaping up onto the stump, she scrambled through the open door and slammed it behind her. There was no lock, not so much as a bar. Thinking quickly, she unlaced one shoe, slipped it off, and jammed it under the crack underneath. It wouldn't stop him, but it might slow his progress long enough for her to hide.

Frantically, she looked for a place, but of course there was none. She could go out the back window and crawl under the house, but he would find her easily. He had found poor Saketa, hadn't he?

Where, *where*? Except for a handful of scrawny bushes that had been chewed ragged, there wasn't a single place to hide. Not a hill, not a rock, not a tree.

The privy? It was right out in the open. She could never reach it without being seen. The shed? Jacob and Queenie would kick up such a ruckus he would know immediately that someone was hiding there. The rain barrel? She would drown. It was full, and she lacked the strength to overturn it, and anyway, what was the use? He would only see the spilled water and look inside and find her.

But *why*? Did he hate her so much for hiding Saketa, however briefly? As if anyone with a speck of common decency in her heart could have turned that poor child away.

The door was three planks wide with heavy oak battens. Crouched behind the table, Annie eyed it warily. Her belly churning with fear, she expected at any moment to see it go flying off the hinges. The heel of her black kid high-top, the only pair of shoes she owned, and those nearly five years old and too small, looked so ridiculously inadequate for such a task that she nearly wept.

When the door didn't immediately collapse, she gathered her nerve, darted across the room, and peered through the window. Her heart jumped in her throat. She jerked her head back and flattened herself against the wall. He was standing just outside the door on the stump, holding that poor child's body as if she were some kind of sacrificial offering to his wicked heathen gods.

Father in Heaven, if you can hear me, she mouthed silently, *I need a bit of advice.*

What she needed was a fortress! Complete with an army!

By the time she saw the door tremble, Annie had armed herself with the kitchen knife. Clutching the bone handle tightly with both hands, she eyed the musket in the corner, but it was too late now for second thoughts. Green eyes widening in terror, she watched the worn heel of her boot scrape slowly across the floor.

And then he was in the room, Saketa's poor broken body dangling limply across his arms. Gathering her small store of courage, Annie stepped away from the wall, the knife held like a prayer book before her. "I'm warning you . . . just turn around now and leave quietly," she squeaked in a voice as thin as whey. "Don't make me have to hurt you."

Dear Lord, if only she were six feet tall and bold as

brass instead of five feet tall and a shivering, craven coward!

The cold-eyed devil regarded her as if she were the one who was demented, not he. "You will help her."

Tears of fear and fury burned her eyes as Annie stared down at the limp, bloody form in his arms. "Help her? There's nothing anyone can do for her now, except perhaps to bury her."

"She lives. Help her."

Annie leaned cautiously closer. Was Saketa truly alive? If so, it was no less than a miracle. There was dried blood at the edge of her hair, more congealed on her limbs. Her poor face was barely recognizable, and her throat— The cruel monster had wrung her neck!

"Oh, child, what has he done to you?" she whispered, watching as Saketa struggled to draw a shallow breath.

"You know who did this?"

Startled by the intensity of his voice, Annie stepped back. If she admitted knowing, would he kill her, too? Eyeing him warily, she shook her head. "Oh, no—but perhaps if you took her to the village?"

He stepped forward. Annie took another step back. "Doesn't she have a mother or a sister? Surely there's someone—"

"You will do what must be done," he said in a cold, flat voice that sent shivers down her spine.

"I'm sorry, truly I am. I know how to look after children's ailments—scrapes and sprains, belly aches and spotty fevers. But this—" She stared at the all but unrecognizable figure in his arms, her heart wrung with sympathy. "I wouldn't even know how to begin," she finished helplessly.

"I will tell you what to do. You will do it."

Warily, she peered up at his stony face. He was watching her, his eyes as cold as a January rain. As they continued to regard one another, the knife fell from her nerveless fingers and clattered to the floor.

"All right, then." What choice did she have? "I'll do what I can. Just place her on the bed and leave."

She watched as he laid the girl on the bed and smoothed the torn and bloodied remnants of her ruined skirt over her limbs. With hands that Annie knew all too well to be hard and merciless, he carefully arranged her arms at her sides and drew up the spread. Pretending he cared.

Heathen, savage hypocrite!

Marching into the other room, Annie filled a basin with water strained from the pitcher on the table. She dropped in a sliver of soap and snatched a thin huck towel from those she had washed just that morning.

Returning to the bedroom, she glared at the broad bronze back of the man leaning over the bed. If she'd thought he was up to no good she would have crowned him with the basin, but his hands were at his sides.

Didn't he own a shirt? All she'd ever seen him wear was those indecent buckskin trousers and a pair of moccasins.

"You'll have to leave now."

He turned and regarded her silently, then left the

room, only to return with one of the chairs, which he positioned beside the bed. For her own sake as well as the girl's, Annie didn't push her luck. If either of them was to survive this ordeal, she would have to tread carefully.

While the man stood by, arms crossed over his shamefully naked chest, those soulless eyes of his following her every move, she settled down to her task. She was wringing out the cloth when she heard the low groan from the bed, and she nearly dropped it in her surprise. Offering up a brief, silent prayer, she quickly forgot her wicked watchdog and folded back the spread. The first thing she must do was to determine the extent of the damage without making it any worse. Which might not be possible.

At the first touch of the wet cloth, there was another almost inaudible sound from the bed.

"Cold water," the savage grunted.

"It's warm enough. The sun's been shining on the rain barrel all day."

"Get hot water."

"Then build a fire and fill the kettle! I can't do everything!" she snapped, dipping the cloth back into the basin again.

The water was already turning pink. The more dried blood she washed away, the more evident the bruising.

But it was the cuts that worried her most. Some were still oozing blood. The more she washed away, the more flowed, but without cleansing them, she had no way of finding out how deep they were.

The man left the room. She was dimly aware of his going, acutely aware of his return. He hovered over her so near she could actually feel his breath stirring her hair against her cheek.

"Would you please go away?" she cried.

"Wring the water from the towel."

Numbly, she did as he commanded, not daring to disobey. And then he took her hand, towel and all, and placed it over the wound that was bleeding most freely. He pressed down. His arm brushed against her shoulder, and Annie flinched.

"Hold it thusly. The bleeding will soon cease."

She held the towel against the wound. The man held his hand over hers, and Annie told herself it was only to increase the pressure. She drew in a deep, shuddering breath. *Wood smoke, leather, and some clean, spicy scent that reminded her of wet winter days in the woods around the school. Annie Stevens O'Neal, you're demented!*

"I need more water—this is cold!" It was also filthy.

He moved back, and she didn't even bother to see if he'd gone to do her bidding. It was enough that he'd left her room to breathe.

The man was obviously a dangerous lunatic. She heard the clang of copper against iron from the next room, which indicated that he was probably doing as she asked, but it would never do to forget for one moment his true nature.

The jagged wound on Saketa's shoulder, which had been bleeding rather freely, appeared to have stopped. The savage had been right about applying pressure. Annie could only pray that none of her many injuries would turn septic. Now that some of the mud, blood, and green slime had been washed away, the wounds on her face and neck could be more clearly appraised.

Her throat was wickedly bruised. Perhaps even crushed.

A chill crept over her as Annie remembered the feel of a certain hand on her own throat. Poor child—poor, dear child! No wonder she'd been so terrified she had climbed out the window and run away.

There was a wicked cut on her forehead that sliced all the way up into her scalp and a swelling at the back of her head. Annie cautiously parted the matted black hair. Had her skull been crushed by a blow from a heavy instrument—such as the handle of a large knife? Or had strangulation caused her to lose consciousness and fall?

While she was wondering about the cause and the treatment of the head wound, Saketa gave a little gasp that made Annie wince, imagining how painful it must be even to draw a single breath.

At least she still lived, praise be to God!

"There now, lamby pie, Annie will look after you, just you wait and see." Meaningless words of comfort. Why on earth hadn't she had the foresight to clean out the medicine chest before she'd left the school? It was entirely possible that the vultures that had stripped the place bare might have overlooked the contents of the medicine chest. But with so much to do so quickly before the new owners took possession of the house, it was a wonder she'd even remembered to pack her own trunk.

At any rate, it was too late now. She would just have to make do with what was on hand. Which was precisely nothing.

Annie felt a trickle of sweat between her breasts. He had evidently stirred up the fire again to heat more water. It didn't take much to heat the two small rooms. Pausing in her labors, she glanced over her shoulder. The man—what was his name?

She didn't even want to know. The wicked devil! Hell was too sweet a reward for any man who would so cruelly use any woman.

Annie sensed his presence before she saw him. He was standing just inside the door again, arms crossed over his chest, watching her every move as she inched back the spread and reluctantly sought the source of all the blood on Saketa's limbs. She was afraid it had something to do with the baby Saketa had mentioned, and the thought nearly paralyzed her with fear.

God help her if the poor girl died!

"You there—" she broke off impatiently. "What is your name, anyway?"

"Tatamaho."

"Humph! Well, Mr. Tomahawk, or whatever you call yourself, you'd have done better to take Saketa to any one of the women in the village. I'm sure they all know more than I do about ... about such things."

"They talk."

She sent him a nasty look over her shoulder. "I'll

just wager they do, and that wouldn't suit you at all, would it?"

"There is blood on her skirt."

"I see the blood on her skirt! I'll get to that next; I'm working my way down." Annie told herself she was only working methodically, from the head down. The truth was, she was terrified. She knew less than nothing about childbirth. Oh, she'd heard the usual whispers that were cut off whenever she'd entered a room. She'd heard the veiled hints about Eve's fall from grace and woman's lot in life and the wages of sin, which sounded vaguely biblical, but didn't make a whole lot of sense.

Besides, strictly speaking, this wasn't even childbirth.

Despite the occasional moan, Saketa showed no sign of regaining consciousness, which was a blessing under the circumstances. But if she died, Lord forbid, then the murdering savage would blame Annie instead of his own wickedness, in which case no kitchen knife or brass-barreled blunderbuss in the world was going to save her.

She was preparing to remove the shreds of skirt that clung to the mess on her upper limbs when he moved to stand behind her.

"You can't stay in here now!" she scolded.

"I will stay."

"You will not! Either you go or I go, but I'll not have you glaring at me every minute while I . . . with this poor girl . . ."

Evidently he took her meaning. Annie didn't even attempt to sort out her own feelings. Whether it was modesty or fear, she knew only that if she had to feel those cold gray eyes of his boring into her back one minute longer she would scream.

Without even turning around, she knew the exact moment he left. Then, carefully peeling away the shredded skirt that had stuck to the dried blood, she whispered, "There, now, lamby pie, Annie will just clean you up and we'll see what can be done about— ahhh, no!"

Along with everything else, she'd been whipped. She wasn't wearing a stitch of underwear, and the telltale stripes that crisscrossed her upper limbs reached all the way up past her waist. Oh, dear God, how could any animal be so cruel?

Blinking away the tears, Annie muttered a threatening prayer and began bathing Saketa's wounds as best she could. Twice she had to change waters, adding more from the kettle in the other room.

The kettle was full, the fire small and hot. There was no sign of Tomahawk, or whatever his heathen name was. She hoped he had walked right off the face of the earth and fallen into the deepest pit in hell!

Returning to the bedside, she saw a bright red stain of fresh blood on Saketa's legs. "Oh, no," she cried softly. Hurriedly setting the basin down on the chair, she grabbed up a corner of the brocaded spread and held it between the girl's thighs.

"Pressure," she muttered, holding, praying, tears seeping from her tired eyes. "Please, oh, please make it stop!"

He came in silently. It was too much to hope he

hadn't heard her. For once, she was almost glad he was there. "It started again, and I don't know how to stop it," she whispered, and then his hand was on hers, his other hand pressing against Saketa's belly, and Annie simply closed her eyes and prayed.

"No more," he said after what seemed an eternity.

"It's stopped?"

"The child is truly lost."

Slowly, Annie began to sag. He managed to catch her before she hit the floor. Lowering her to the chair, he stood over her, and she tried to tell herself he was the devil incarnate.

The child is truly lost, he'd said. It could not have been sadness she'd heard in his voice; she'd only imagined it.

She leaned her head back against the rough-planked wall and closed her eyes as the full weight of all that had happened since she'd left the school bore down on her.

She'd journeyed three hundred miles to this godforsaken land only to find her father gone. She'd battled cattle and hunger and relentless heat. And now here was poor Saketa and her vicious husband, and she didn't know how she was going to go on another moment.

Her empty stomach growled. She was so tired. She should be ashamed of herself for thinking of food when poor Saketa lay dying, for all she knew, but she was so tired and so hungry. . . .

Forcing her eyes open, Annie stood up and bent over the bed. At least the girl seemed in no immediate danger of bleeding to death. There was still that awful lump on the back of her skull, and there could well be internal injuries. There was no way of knowing how much blood she'd lost before he'd brought her here.

Outside, it had gradually grown dark. Tomahawk lit the oil lamp and brought it in, and while he stood silently in the background, Annie made herself sum up the extent of Saketa's injuries, most of which were entirely outside Annie's experience. Aside from the loss of the child she'd been carrying, Saketa suffered a possible concussion, a broken wrist, either a broken or a badly sprained ankle, an assortment of cuts and bruises, and a badly crushed throat.

No wonder the poor girl was still unconscious! Under the circumstances, it was a blessing. Lacking laudanum, Annie hadn't a single thing to give her for pain, not even willow bark.

However, she did know how to go about setting a simple fracture. It was not an uncommon injury in a household of children, even little girls, who were supposed to be somewhat more civilized than little boys. Using strips of the tough brocade from another panel of drapery and a flat wooden cooking spoon, she set about finishing the job, with Tomahawk's help, before Saketa could regain consciousness.

If she ever did.

The next day passed with little change. Annie watched uneasily for a sign of fever and bathed her patient frequently in cool water just to be safe.

The savage—his name, he had haughtily informed

her through clenched white teeth, was Tomato, not Tomahawk—continued to glare at her. She continued to ignore him.

At least she tried.

Surprisingly enough, he actually seemed to be fond of Saketa. Annie puzzled over it, but decided that she could not allow herself to lose sight of his true nature.

Not until the second day had passed, with no sign of his wanting to do further injury to the girl, did she allow her guard to drop, and that only because she was so very tired.

She had barely slept, much less eaten. Not that there was anything in the house to eat. She was heartily sick of cornmeal, parched, boiled, or in any of her unsuccessful attempts at making bread.

A bit of butter might have helped her to force it down, but she might as well have wished for the moon. Cows as far as the eye could see, but not a speck of butter, cream, or milk to be found.

Which was probably her fault, too. She couldn't milk, she couldn't churn, she couldn't cook—she couldn't even talk the wretched chicken into giving her one small egg.

Poor Papa. He'd thought she was away getting educated, and the truth was, she hadn't learned one thing that was of the slightest use to anyone. No wonder she sometimes had the impression that that wicked, naked devil was laughing at her, even though he never made a sound nor cracked a smile.

At least he left her alone. He still watched from outside, disappearing and reappearing in some mysterious routine all his own. It never occurred to Annie to ask where he went or what he did. Sometimes she watched him, though, whispering in his horse's nose. Not his ear, but his nose! He took care of Jacob, and she supposed he must have taken care of the cows if they needed caring for. The other one never came around anymore. Papa's precious Mr. Mingo.

When she'd caught the savage sniffing at the place where she had buried the rotten fish, he had told her in that top-lofty way of his that water had to be poured off each day and more salt added, else the fish would spoil.

Now he told her!

Watching him late one afternoon, with the sun gilding his half-naked body, setting warm lights to dancing on his thick, near-black hair, Annie wondered how so much wickedness could be hidden away in such a beautiful figure of a man. Was it possible for a man to be both good and evil?

She thought of young Tom Sizemore, the sexton who'd sometimes visited old Charlie. Tom was a handsome boy, but he paled in comparison to Saketa's wicked husband. Quite literally.

For breakfast the next day, Annie managed to force down a few spoonfuls of the tasteless cornmeal gruel, then scraped the rest of it out the door for Queenie. She was washing the bowl when Tomato—what a silly name for such a fierce man!—came right inside the house and laid a fish, still flapping, on her kitchen table. Without a word he crossed to the bedroom, looked through the door, nodded once, and left.

Annie stared after him, her poor belly growling in anticipation. Meat! Genuine food, after nearly a week of existing on cornmeal!

Assuring herself that her patient still slept quietly, and that the fever that tended to rise during the night was cooling, she stared down at the fish.

The fish stared back.

She touched him. He twitched his tail.

"Oh, dear . . ." Finally, she took a towel and laid it over his head, then whacked him as hard as she could between the eyes. Only when he fell limp did she commence the task of hacking him open and removing whatever looked as if it needed to come out. She *did* know enough to do that!

After tenderly placing the gutted fish in the bottom of the only pot big enough to hold it, which was the soup pot she had brought with her from the school, worn thin and showing signs of many a tinker's dam, she poked several sticks of wood in the fireplace and stirred up the coals, praying it would catch and she wouldn't have to start all over again. She still hadn't quite got the hang of fire building, though she was learning.

Through the window she could see Tomato rubbing the front of his horse with a handful of dry grass. It looked as if he might be talking to the beast, for his lips were moving, and from time to time, the animal flicked an ear.

Not for the first time, it occurred to Annie that if he

had treated his wife with half the kindness he showed his horse, none of them would be here now.

And you wouldn't be fixing to have yourself a fish supper. No, you'd be all alone, talking to yourself, fretting over Papa, chasing Queenie, shooing cows away from the house and wondering what else to do with all the hours in the long, lonely days.

She poured a bit of water into the pot because the fish looked more natural in water, then swung the pot over the fire. Once the water started to boil, she looked in on Saketa and bathed her face and neck with a cool cloth. Covered only with the thinnest panel of drapery, she seemed to have fallen into a more natural sleep. Her first deep unconsciousness had been worrisome. Annie still hadn't quite lost the fear that she might slip deeper and deeper under the surface, never to awaken.

Which would have been a tragedy. From the short time they had spent together before all this had happened, Annie had formed an impression of a girl who was vibrant and full of life—somewhat spoiled, perhaps, but good-hearted and loving, for all that.

What she needed now was nourishment if she was ever to regain her strength. Somehow, Annie told herself, she was going to have to get something down that poor swollen throat without strangling the child. Fish broth would do to start with. It would have been tastier with a potato or two and an onion—perhaps a rib of celery, or even a turnip. Some rich beef broth would be best of—

Suddenly alerted by an all-too-familiar smell, Annie

dropped her cloth and rushed back into the kitchen in time to see smoke billowing up from the open pot. "Oh, no! Not my fish!" she cried, grabbing the kettle and pouring in more water.

Perhaps it had only just boiled dry. A bit of crust on the bottom wouldn't hurt ... would it?

But just to be on the safe side, she swung the pot out to one side before she hurried to the open doorway, flapping her apron in front of her face to clear the stench.

Thank goodness there was no one about to witness her latest disaster. Annie couldn't have borne it if Tomato had been there to make sport of her. Not that he ever really laughed. Or even smiled.

How on earth had such a creature ever convinced that lively girl to marry him? He was such a cold, emotionless stick!

Well, she amended ... hardly emotionless. Anger was an emotion.

He remained a mystery. These past few days, she had seen no sign of the vicious side of his character, but she knew for a fact that it was there, just lying in wait for something to set it off. Like a beautiful, colorful poisonous snake, basking in the sun. Lovely to look at, curious to ponder, but deadly to touch.

As if she would even consider it.

To her everlasting shame, however, she could not deny the small thrill of excitement that stirred deep inside her when she remembered being so close to all that sleek, gleaming flesh.

Oh, my mercy, if this is what a diet of cornmeal and

water can do to a body, I'd better learn how to cook, and quickly!

To make matters even worse, she reminded herself that these wicked thoughts she was entertaining concerned another woman's husband.

About to turn away, she become aware of a low masculine voice. And there he was, walking right into the middle of a whole swarm of cows, while they ignored him as if he were one of their own kind.

It was said, wasn't it, that the devil had cloven hooves?

Stupid animals! All she had to do was set foot outside the door and they scattered like a flock of partridge. You'd think an army of butchers was coming at them, cleavers in hand. Yet there he stood, wearing a pair of trousers that was made of some poor animal's hide, petting that very same calf she had tried for days to approach, and the little wretch was lapping it up!

As if sensing her eyes on him, he turned, sunlight glinting off his splendid body. His hair was neatly braided. In that respect, he was better groomed than she was.

Unable to turn away, Annie could only stare and wonder. Did all men have shoulders so broad? A belly so flat and smooth? She knew for a fact that few men had such beautiful eyes. Or such a proud nose. Or a mouth that made a woman feel all jangly inside, as if—

"Pretty is as pretty does," she muttered, wrenching her eyes away. She had written *that* on her slate more times than she cared to remember, too! The man was a devil, and she'd best not forget it.

Still, he hadn't seemed quite so threatening just lately. He had brought her the fish. He kept the wood bin filled. He'd kept the fire banked so that the kettle was always warm, yet the room never grew overly heated. She never knew when it was he tended these things, for he was never there when she came out of the bedroom.

A little later, as she bathed Saketa's body with cool water to keep down the fever that always seemed to rise at night, Annie tried to make sense of it all. Here was all the evidence anyone would ever need of the man's cruelty. Yet day after day he stayed just outside, looking in on the sleeping girl whenever Annie slipped out to the privy or to hang out the wash. She knew he did. She'd seen him at it. One would almost think he was sorry for what he had done.

Even so, she suspected that if anything went wrong, he would be on her in a minute, his knife at her throat. It didn't make sense.

Sighing, she wrung out her cloth and draped it over the windowsill in the sunshine, then went into the kitchen to take up the fish, which didn't smell particularly appetizing.

The truth was that nothing had made any sense since she'd first set foot on this wretched island. Why should she expect things to change now?

Mrs. Biddlecomb's School for Indigent Girls, and the orderly, if spartan, existence of the past dozen years, seemed a world removed. Annie could only take each day as it came and pray that Saketa would heal quickly

Chapter 6

He moved silently, following the edge of the pond. All around him the early morning sun slanted through veils of Spanish moss that swayed gently from every bough, like a woman's hair flowing in the breeze. Songbirds chirped noisily in the green shadows, undisturbed by his presence. Overhead, a fish hawk voiced its high, thin cry, while from out over the water came the raucous cries of feeding gulls.

T'maho's moccasined feet moved unerringly on earth still damp with morning dew. Narrowing his eyes, he scanned the imperceptible trail, noting a fan of crushed bracken here, there a vine torn loose from its mooring.

Spoor on a twisted root in the edge of the pond marked the place where a muskrat had paused to look over its shoulder before moving on to the entrance of its den.

Farther on he came upon the castings of an owl that had recently feasted on an unfortunate mouse. The papery shed of a long, slender snake lay across the barely visible trail. It had been torn and scattered by the passing of more than one pair of feet.

T'maho had gone first to the place where he had come upon Saketa's all but lifeless body and then began casting for signs. Her struggle had left marks that brought a painful tightening and a fresh resolve to his heart as he plunged deeper and deeper into the steamy environment. Some two hundred feet farther, he came upon a place where a startled deer had veered from the trail. A bit farther, he had picked up a track made by a hard-soled shoe, which led deeper still into the shadowy depths of the junglelike grove.

Tracks were plentiful. The glade was used as a shortcut by all who traveled north or south. It was frequented by trappers and hunters, and by children playing hiding games. Women gathered wild grapes and persimmons near the edge of the swamp.

And then, near the far end of Long Green Pond, he found a smear of dried blood on the underside of a palmetto frond. The trail of footprints he had been following were smudged, as if something had been dragged across them.

Suddenly every nerve in his body began to tingle. It had happened not far away—he could sense it. No man could do to a woman what had been done to Saketa without leaving behind a trace.

That was all he asked. A trace. A sign. Some small clue that would lead him to the cursed animal who had used an innocent girl for his own pleasure and then wickedly betrayed her.

Of their own volition, T'maho's fingers curled inward. Death would be too good for such a man. Instead, smiling coldly, he wished the devil a long life of endless, unspeakable agony. A life in which each second of every hour would bring pleas for release. A life in which—

Suddenly the very atmosphere seemed to grow still. Silence echoed all around him as he stared at the scrap of white cloth caught in a twist of cat-claw briar. Following a faint trail toward a cavelike bower made of an ancient, uprooted tree draped with deep curtains of Spanish moss, T'maho felt his own blood run cold.

It had happened here. In this place. He could feel the evil in the hot, damp air rising off the black-water pond. All around, the bracken was crushed, not unlike the places where deer bedded down near freshwater ponds, only here there were no small, two-pronged footprints.

He reached for the scrap of white cloth and fingered it thoughtfully, noting the quality, the silkiness of the weave. It was linen. Of a fineness unseen on the island, it reminded him of the shirts his father had worn. He could recall even now how he had stroked the first such shirt his father had had made for him when he'd turned twelve years old.

Allowing his gaze to lose focus, T'maho opened his mind and sought a vision. A face. A name. Something that would give purpose to the murderous rage in his heart. When he noticed a small rusty stain on the threads at one end of the scrap of cloth, a pain so fierce it struck the breath from his lungs caught him unexpectedly.

Lifting his head, T'maho closed his eyes and vowed revenge.

* * *

Hooking the fish for the ginger-hair had reminded T'maho that there were yet other matters demanding his attention before he could continue his quest. His big boat was not yet ready to work, but he had nets to see to. Mingo had taken them in when it became clear that neither man would have time to fish them, but perhaps it was time to set them out again. The hunt was taking longer than either man had expected, and the women who cleaned and smoked their fish counted on the work.

He said nothing of his earlier findings. After arranging with Mingo to set out the small net, he returned briefly to his own home south of the village, where his mother's people had once lived. His house, which was a blend of old and new, consisted of one spacious room, but unlike the old-style dwellings, his floor was of sawn wood, as were his walls, which were covered on the outside by overlapping squares of bark to shed the hard winter rains.

His roof was of thatch, which was easily renewed. On all four sides, the generous openings took advantage of the summer winds, but could be closed against the cold winter winds. From skinned-pole rafters overhead hung a supply of pelts that covered the floor and walls during the coldest months, ensuring warmth and comfort.

There was little furniture. A sleeping mat. A chair made of poles and cowhide. A chest that held his clothing and a few mementos, such as a necklace strung with shell and bone beads that had belonged to his mother, and which Saketa had disdained in favor of one of colored glass.

His books were also in the chest, remnants of a life he had lived briefly a long time ago. One which he wanted to forget, yet knew he must remember, for it served constantly as a reminder of who he was.

T'maho had been five years old when he had first met his father. A shy and scholarly man, Benjamin Jensen Hamilton had come to the island six years earlier in search of some trace of the English settlers who had left nearby Roanoke Island near the end of the sixteenth century and were thought to have come to the island that had then been called Croatoan.

In the village of Kinnakeet, a few miles north of old Croatoan, he had met Little Feet, and his pursuit of knowledge had ended. At the close of the summer he had left. There had been no question of taking Little Feet with him, for she would never have been accepted.

From the earliest times, life on the fragile barrier islands had been focused solely on survival, which had depended on the joint efforts of all—Indian, English, plus whatever else the sea cast ashore. Regardless of his blood, a man was valued for his character and treated with respect—as well as a certain amount of suspicion—until he proved his mettle, one way or another.

Such was not always the case on the mainland. As naive as he was in many ways, this much Hamilton had known.

Years later, he had returned to resume his unfinished

studies only to discover that he had a son. Little Feet had called him Benjamin after his father, and wisely or not, Hamilton had insisted on taking the boy back to the mainland.

To the five-year-old Benjamin, it had seemed like the greatest adventure. For the next few years he had been rigidly schooled by a series of tutors, which included his father. He had lived in a fine house, learned the advantages of riding with a saddle as well as the disadvantages of wearing shoes, woolen trousers, and a fitted coat.

He had missed his mother sorely at first, but after a while he had learned to call Hamilton "Father." He had soaked up learning the way a sponge soaks up water, and in time, although he still missed his old home, he might have been happy enough had it not been for the woman, Bridget.

At the age of forty-one, Hamilton had suddenly fallen wildly, foolishly in love for the very first time. Her name was Bridget, and she was fair-haired and blue-eyed, the orphaned daughter of a prosperous planter who had perished, along with his wife and two sons, when a few drunken renegade Tuscaroras had burned their plantation.

Bridget, who'd been visiting a cousin at the time of the attack, had flatly refused to acknowledge the young half-breed. "I'm sorry, I do care for you, and I wanted us to make a life together," she'd said over and over, wringing her soft hands. "But I could never accept a—one of *those*—in my home. Not after . . ."

Tear-filled blue eyes had been hard to resist. Hamil-

ton had not even tried. When it came down to a matter
of choice, Hamilton had chosen the woman. He had
told Benjamin that it was time he got to know his
mother's people as a young man. He'd said that in time,
Bridget would learn to accept him, and the moment
she did, Hamilton would come for him.

She never had, and *he* never had. Nor would T'maho
have gone. Before he had even left the ship which had
brought him back to the island, he had rejected his father's world by rejecting his name. Waiting to go
ashore, he had studiously ignored the sad, apologetic
man who stood beside him at the rail. Hamilton had
pleaded for understanding. Ignoring him, Benjamin had
stared down at the water, watching a long, needle-
nosed fish swim just beneath the surface.

"Benjamin, listen to me, son . . ."

The fish had looked fierce. T'maho had learned later
that such was not the case. Oblivious to his father's
pleas, he had leaned over the rail and watched the fish.
Tuh—tuh—

What was it? He knew the word; it was on the tip of
his tongue.

He knew this place! Knew that great sweeping live
oak, with the boughs that dragged the ground. Knew
those dense woods to the north, and the raucous sound
of seagulls and crows, fish hawks and wild parrots. And
oh, the familiar aroma of tar and drying fish, salt marsh
and wood smoke . . .

"Tatamaho!" he had cried, remembering his mother's
word for the "garfish." "My name is not Benjamin, it is
Tatamaho!"

Swiftly now, T'maho closed the chest, taking only a clean pair of buckskins. He found it amusing to recall that among his father's people, bathing was done sometimes monthly, sometimes yearly—sometimes not at all.

Among the Hattorask, cleanliness was considered no more than common courtesy toward one's close associates. T'maho had found it to be both relaxing and stimulating, depending on the need and the season.

Annie swore ineptly. She had little notion of what the words meant, but sometimes it came down to swearing or breaking something, and she could ill afford the latter. Fortunately, she had learned more than proverbs, Bible verses, and Italian hemstitching at Mrs. Biddlecomb's School for Indigent Girls.

The fish was inedible. Burned on the outside, raw on the inside, full of bones and scales as big as her thumbnail. The broth had cooked away, leaving only bits of blackened fish flesh and other unidentifiable bits and pieces stuck to the sides of the pot.

Saketa, even though she had yet to open her eyes, had managed to swallow a few sips of watery gruel, which was all Annie could think of to offer her, but she needed something more nourishing.

Her cuts were healing nicely, the bruises beginning to fade except for those on her throat, which were the worst of all. Her fever came and went, but Annie didn't know what to do other than what she was doing, which was to keep Saketa cool when she grew feverish, keep her quiet when she grew restless, and try to get whatever possible nourishment down her whenever she seemed to rouse a bit.

Setting the pot aside, Annie closed her eyes momentarily. Merciful saints, but she was tired! The first night Saketa had been here, she hadn't slept at all, fearful that Tomato would slip inside and do something terrible. All the next day she had stood guard, stealing away only to dash out to the privy or to wash and hang out a few cloths.

Between forcing her patient to take a few sips of gruel and changing the padding that soaked up her body waste—thank goodness for those old draperies!—Annie had dozed the second and third nights, waking only when she was about to topple from the chair.

But even when she had finally dropped her guard enough to sleep on a pallet on the floor, she slept only fitfully. There was scarcely space enough for one, much less for two in the cramped room. Heaven only knew where Papa had intended her to sleep.

But then, if memory served, Papa had never been a particularly practical man.

Annie didn't know if Saketa's husband slept outside or went home at night. It was aggravating enough that he insisted on spying on her all during the day, as if he suspected her of goodness knows what wickedness.

However, she no longer feared him quite so much. One could grow accustomed to anything, she supposed—even to having a grim-faced male stalking in and out of her house. As for his attitude, which she had once fleetingly thought of as proud, it was no more than sheer, bloody arrogance. That much she *did* know!

Which made it all the more puzzling that with every day that passed, she found it more and more difficult to reconcile the savage who had beaten his young wife senseless—the man responsible for the death of his own unborn child—with the silent, watchful stranger who provided her with food, water, and firewood while keeping a constant vigil over his sleeping wife.

The shameful truth was that more than once she had been in danger of forgetting just who and what he was.

T'maho, bringing with him a wooden spoon to replace the one the ginger-hair had used to set Saketa's arm, had arrived in time to see her scrape the ruins of yet another meal out the door for the rooster and whatever other animals cared to risk it.

The woman was unbelievably stupid. Even Saketa, spoiled from childhood by everyone, including himself, knew enough to pluck a goose or scale and gut a fish before cooking it. Years ago he had taught her how to spear a crab with a sharpened stick, then, using the meat as a lure, to draw a small fish into her cupped hands, and then use the small fish to catch a larger fish, all of which could be done without wading any deeper than her knees.

It was Etawak who had showed her how to prepare her catch with the leaves of the bay tree and juice from the sour berries of the red sumac. By the age of ten, Saketa could do all that and more.

At least when she wasn't busy stealing gowns from the wash lines of the village women and pretending to be some fancy lady from the city. T'maho would never forget the first time he had ever laid eyes on the little minx. An angry and hurting youth of thirteen, he had just arrived back on the island after what had seemed a lifetime away, and was trying to find his bearings when a small, dusky whirlwind clutching a long calico skirt around her waist had cannoned into him, nearly knocking him overboard.

Right on her heels, two old women had come panting up, one of them obviously Indian, the other obviously not, both screeching at the child, who'd been clinging to his legs by then.

"Saketa, you give Miss Lina back her frock!"

"If you steal one more rag off'n my clothesline, you little devil, I'm going to tan your tail good, you just see if I don't!"

Ignoring both angry women, the child had turned a gap-toothed grin up at Benjamin, who only a moment before had become Tatamaho, and said, "What's that thing around your neck called?" He'd still been wearing a cravat, which he'd tugged loose at her reminder. "Are you going to live here now? I'm an imp of Satan, who're you?"

That had been his introduction to his little half-sister. In some ways Saketa had improved over the years, in some ways she had not, but at least she could fill a man's belly without poisoning him.

What could the ginger-hair do? Nothing! Like all her kind, she was used to having servants to wait on her. Left to her own devices, she was as helpless as a soft-shelled crab.

If not quite so defenseless, he thought with reluctant

amusement. O'Neal should have provided her with a smaller gun before leaving her alone. In weak and unskilled hands, that ancient musket of his might be downright dangerous!

The next day T'maho snared a marsh hen, plucked it, and emptied the cavity. This he took to the house and flung down onto the table. "Saketa needs meat."

Annie nearly jumped out of her skin. It had been two days since he had spoken a word to her. Now here he was, appearing out of the blue, spouting commands.

"I'm giving her water boiled with a bit of cornmeal. It's the best I can do, and besides, a body can't eat and sleep at the same time, not without strangling. I don't know how she can even swallow with that poor throat of hers." She regarded him accusingly.

"Cook the bird, grind the meat and bones to a paste, mix it with broth."

"Of course! Now, why didn't I think of that?" Even bearing gifts, the man was utterly maddening. "If it were that easy," she snapped, "I'd have been doing it for days!"

If it were that easy, she wouldn't be seeing spots before her own eyes from a lack of sleep and a lack of decent food, but she refused to give him the satisfaction of knowing that she was reeling in her tracks. Stalking across to the fireplace, she began heaping up lengths of firewood, only to have him reach past her and remove all but two small splits of oak and one of pine.

His naked arm raked her shoulder, and she felt as if she'd been branded with a hot iron. Even his scent affected her. Wood smoke, leather, and horse—and something dark and exciting that made her feel as if she were starved for air. He smelled clean—probably cleaner than she did.

"To burn," he muttered, "fire must breathe."

And so must she, but at the moment she was having trouble managing even that simple function. It had to be fear that set her pulse to racing whenever he came too close.

He was standing too close now—so close she could see her own reflection in the dark pupils of his strangely pale eyes. Annie struggled against his silent intimidation. All her life, first as a child at home and then as a perpetual student in a rigidly ordered orphanage-cum-academy, she'd been told not only what to do, but also how and when to do it. A whimsical fate had chosen to plop her down haphazardly first in one set of circumstances, then in another, leaving her to make the best of it.

And make the best she had, but she was now an adult, answerable, until Papa came home, only to God and her own conscience. And if this hatchet-faced heathen with his naked skin and his nasty disposition thought he could frighten her into dancing to his tune, then perhaps it was time he learned the test of her mettle.

She glared at him.

He glared right back.

Annie told herself he was deliberately trying to frighten her by thinning his lips and jutting his chin and making the dark pupils of his eyes expand so that they covered the gray irises.

Well, she flat-out refused to be intimidated!

But how could gray eyes turn black—and then gray again?

Momentarily distracted, she forgot the marsh hen, forgot the recalcitrant fireplace—forgot for one single moment that the man staring down at her was not only married, but was of a totally alien culture.

Alien, indeed! She'd be lucky not to wake up one morning with his knife at her throat.

Plucked, the marsh hen was no bigger than her fist. Boiling, it looked greasy, the skin an unappetizing shade of gray, and it smelled strongly of fish and mud. But by the time Annie decided that it had boiled long enough, she was past caring. It was food, and she was starved. Poor Saketa wouldn't care how it tasted, either. Nourishment was nourishment, and that wicked devil was right—the child had to have something more than cornmeal if she was ever to regain her strength.

"Grind the meat and bone and mix it with the broth," she repeated under her breath. Sliding a trencher next to the pot in readiness, she jabbed at the carcass with the point of her knife, intending to lift it out, cut it into small pieces, and then pound it with whatever tool she could find to do the job. There weren't even any rocks in this forsaken place!

The unsavory-looking carcass bobbed and rolled over in its steaming broth. She jabbed it again, and again it rolled over, its bony back floating to the top of the greasy, grayish liquid. Annie muttered all the foul words she could think of with only the sketchiest knowledge of what they meant.

"Hold still, you bloody, pox-ridden whore!" She stabbed again, and her target struck the side of the pot, splashing hot broth over her arm and hand. Clutching her wrist, she jumped back, and her elbow struck the handle of the pot and tipped it over, spilling the contents out onto the floor. "Oh, no! Oh—hell, damn, spit!" she cried as tears sprang to her eyes.

He was beside her in an instant. Annie, bent over with pain, her scalded hand clamped between her knees, didn't hear him come in, wasn't even aware of his presence until he freed her hand, frowned at the angry red blemish, and led her by the wrist to the table.

"Stop that! Don't touch me!" The pain was excruciating enough without the salt from his sweaty palm making it worse, but when she tried to pull away, he only tightened his grip.

"Be still, foolish woman, or I'll cut off your arm and feed it to the turtles."

Annie gasped, but before she could recover from the threat, he had smeared her forearm and hand with the cooling grease that clung to the sides of the pot, then dipped the towel into the pitcher of water and wrapped it around the injured parts.

Swallowing hard, she lifted her eyes to his, dazed, but aware that the pain was already lessening. "I could have done that," she said when she could manage to speak. She had treated more than one burn in her years of looking after any number of younger charges. Seldom had anyone had cause to look after her. It felt . . . strange. "Thank you," she added grudgingly, and was amazed to see the corners of his mouth twitch.

"There's still enough broth left in the pot for Saketa. It'll serve well enough."

Even in her distracted condition, she noticed that he'd dropped the stiffness that sometimes caused his words to come out all hard and separate, like bits of gravel. Was he aware that sometimes he spoke English as comfortably as she did, while at other times he spoke so stiffly his words sounded almost foreign? It was as if he used the language to stress the difference between them.

But then, as she watched him collect what remained of the ruined supper, her empty stomach growled and she forgot about the riddle of the man called Tomato.

He skinned the bird and cut off a portion of breast, which would have fit quite well into a teaspoon. Annie's eyes widened as he handed it to her.

"But Saketa needs—" she murmured.

"Eat. I will see to Saketa's needs."

And eat she did, stuffing down the tiny, rank-tasting morsel and licking her greasy fingers. When she stared longingly at the small mound of meat he had cut off and begun to grind into a paste, he smiled. He actually smiled at her!

The next day T'maho snared a squirrel and a rabbit, then skinned and cooked them both over an outdoor fire. The delicate aroma drifted toward the house on the light southwest breeze. When the meat had cooled sufficiently, he slid them off the spit, put back the squirrel for himself, and took the rabbit to the house.

The woman had barely waited for him to turn his back before she had pounced on the meat like a starving dog. Thinking of her own poor efforts, his conscience stirred uncomfortably. She was helpless, as were most of her kind. Yet she tried. Grudgingly, he gave her credit for that much.

He had finished the net with Mingo at first light, and taken a fish to Etawak, who depended on him for meat. For nearly a week he had not had time to do more than meet quickly with Mingo in the edge of the glade and pass on what news there was. He'd had all he could do to keep Etawak from rushing to the side of her precious chick.

Mingo was even worse. "Has she spoken yet?" he'd asked just that morning.

"Not yet. She drinks, but it may be a while before she can speak. Her throat was badly crushed."

Mingo's massive fists clenched slowly at his sides. A pulse throbbed angrily against the ruined skin of his face as he fought for control of his emotions. "I've asked about strangers in the village last week. Snell's boat was in. There was a fishing smack up from Core Sound, put in the night of the storm. The usual lumber barges, but no one remembers seeing any strangers wandering around. The smack and the barges sailed as soon as they loaded up."

"No one remembers. That doesn't mean anything."

"It means only that no one remembers. Patience, my friend. She lives. She's safe. The worst is over."

But patience didn't come easy to either man. Both waited impatiently for some sign that the Saketa they had known and loved had returned to her poor, shattered body.

At first light on the sixth day after Saketa had been found, T'maho planked two fish and cooked them before hot coals. Saving the small croaker for himself, he took the sea trout to the ginger-hair, intending to tell her to mash it and force it between Saketa's lips, then stroke her throat gently until she swallowed.

Annie met him at the door. "She's awake," she exclaimed, her face radiant.

For one long moment, T'maho could only stare at the glowing green eyes gazing up at him from a pale, smiling face—at the cloud of spun copper that escaped a scrap of ribbon to spill in wild disarray over her slender shoulders. Instead of one of the paneled gowns she usually wore under her apron, she was wearing a filmy white garment that reminded him of the nightshirt he had worn in that other life, only hers had small flowers stitched about the neck, and the cloth was worn so thin he could see the pink glow of her flesh where it touched her small breasts.

"Did you hear me, Tomato? Saketa's—"

With a muttered word, T'maho shoved the fish into her hands and pushed past her so quickly she nearly dropped it on the floor. Hurrying to the bedroom on his heels, Annie tossed the hot, succulent food on the table, all thought of her hunger gone.

Oddly enough, it never even occurred to her that To-mato might harm Saketa in any way.

He was kneeling beside the bed. "Saketa, open your eyes," she heard him say. He rubbed her tan, fragile wrist. "The ginger-hair tells me you are awake now. Open your eyes, Saketa. No more games, little *cuvfmc*."

When there was no response, he turned to glare accusingly at Annie, who hovered over his shoulder.

"Well, she *was* awake!" Annie protested. "I didn't just dream it. I dropped my hairbrush, and when I went to pick it up, she opened her eyes and looked right at me!"

"She still sleeps."

Interpreting his words as an accusation that she was lying, Annie huffed up like a pigeon. She twisted her hands and then winced when the tender skin on her right arm pulled painfully. "She did *so* open her eyes! They're brown with little squiggles of green in them."

His look was disdainful, to say the least, as he held Saketa's small hand in his own much larger one. Annie reminded herself that it was this same man who had provided her with food—or tried to. It was this same man who had tended her own injury so quickly that there was no sign of blistering.

But, oh, mercy, he was arrogant!

"What was that thing you called her? It didn't sound very nice."

He regarded her in silence for so long, she wondered if he had heard her. "I called her *cuvfmc*. She is my sister. I called her that."

Annie blinked. His sister! Was this another of his

wretched games? She knew very well who he was! Saketa had told her . . . hadn't she? "Are you sure you're not her husband?"

It was T'maho's turn to blink. The look of amazement on his face could not have been feigned. "Saketa's husband? What man in his right mind would wed such a wicked little *neckaun*. Saketa is my half-sister, ginger-hair. We shared a mother."

They shared a mother. He was her brother, not her husband. Which meant he was not the man who had beaten her and then brought her here because he was ashamed to have it known in the village what he had done.

She opened her mouth and closed it again. And then, lifting her chin, she said, "My name is not ginger-hair, it's Annie. Or rather, Miss O'Neal."

For one crazy moment she thought he was about to stand and bow to her, which was just one more indication that too much salt air could cause the brain to mildew.

Instead, he indicated the woman on the bed. "Saketa," he said.

"I know that, for goodness' sake! And you're Tomato."

This time there was no mistaking the unholy glee in those chameleon eyes. "I am *Tatamaho*," he proclaimed gravely. "I am not a vegetable."

He most certainly was no vegetable! "Whatever you say," she snapped.

"What is my name?"

"Well, for goodness' sake, have you forgotten it already?"

"I have forgotten nothing. You say it."

"All right, all right—your name is ... Tatamato?" There was no way she could pronounce it as he did, with all those funny little puffs of air.

"Tah-tah-ma-*ho!*"

"Yes. All right! You're Tah-tah-ma-*ho!* And I'm delighted to make your acquaintance, and now if you'll be so kind as to step aside, I'll see if I can get Saketa to take a bit of mashed fish."

He looked even more disdainful, if that was possible. "From now on, I will cook. You will care for Saketa."

She thrust out her chin and her chest, and crossed her arms. "From now on, you can go to bloody blue blazes, for all I care, and I'll look after Saketa because I want to look after her, not because you tell me to do it! Is that clear?"

His eyes lit up with a look of amusement, and Annie realized for the first time that she was wearing only her nightshift. She'd been so excited, she hadn't even waited to get decently dressed.

Clasping her shoulders, she lifted her crossed arms even higher. Red-faced, she said, "I'll thank you very much to leave, Mr. Tah-tah-ma-*ho!* When Saketa wakes up again, you may be sure I'll call you."

T'maho left, carrying in his mind the image of a small, green-eyed woman who wore her anger like a hardened battle shield. Had no one ever taught her that a wise wren does not attack the eagle?

As for Saketa, he had seen for himself that she improved daily. He had seen the color begin to return to her cheeks as her bruises changed from black and purple to yellow and green. But seeing her lying there so small, so still, made him realize how very vulnerable a woman could be.

Perhaps he should have taught her to fight instead of teaching her how to lure a fish into her hand. He should have taught her to scream her head off if any man so much as laid a hand on her.

Growing up as she had in a small village, where all knew one another, she had never had cause to learn distrust. He had failed to teach her caution—and she had paid a bitter price.

And then he thought of Annie, with her pale skin and her ginger-colored hair and her fancy, flowered gowns and her complete lack of any skill at all as far as he could see. She was the kind of woman he had learned at an early age to despise.

Yet she had risked her life to protect a stranger, one who was not even of her own people. She had given up her bed, hard and miserable though it was, and he had watched day after day as she looked after his sister, bathing her, feeding her, changing her bedding, washing her rags and drying them, only to have it all to do over again.

Alone beside the calm waters of the sound that evening, T'maho fingered a scrap of stained linen and stared out toward the mainland. For some reason, his mind had been even more restless than usual that day. It occurred to him to wonder if his father was still alive. If he had married his Bridget and given her sons who bore his name. If he ever thought of the son he had taken into his home for a little while and then turned away.

Lying on her hard pallet that night, Annie thought about the strange ways the Lord had of going about His business. He had given Saketa and her husband, whoever the wicked man was, a baby, only to take back the unborn child.

Was it because He thought Saketa still had lessons to learn before He could trust her with a child?

That was obviously true of the husband.

Why give them the child in the first place? To Annie's way of thinking, it was an extremely poor way of going about matters, but then, who was she to question His ways?

She sighed. There was so much she didn't know, but how was a body to learn when most of the things she wanted to know fell under the heading of "Things a Lady Never Spoke Of"?

According to Mrs. B., that included how to deal with female complaints by taking to one's bed with a dose of medicinal whiskey and a hot brick; how to deal with wind in the bowel when one was forced to go about in society; and a few vague warnings about the dangers of walking in cabbage patches with persons of the opposite persuasion. Particularly in the moonlight, which evidently exacerbated the dangers.

Now that it was too late, Annie wished she'd insisted on knowing about the relationship between women, babies, cabbages, and husbands.

Because there most definitely was one. Too many

times she'd heard the girls whispering and giggling far into the night, and when she'd asked what they were giggling about, they only giggled harder and called her a teacher's snitch, which she was most certainly not.

But she was almost sure there was some relationship. And somehow, it had something to do with the strange, itchy feelings that came over her whenever Tah-tah-ma-*ho!* accidentally touched her.

He was Saketa's brother, she mused—not her husband. Just why that should have mattered so very much, Annie could not have said.

She only knew it did.

Chapter 7

Daily, Saketa seemed to regain strength. True, her fever rose as each day waned, and Annie awoke often in the night to sponge her off, but during the daylight hours she grew more and more alert. Once she even smiled. She drank whatever nourishing broth Annie spooned into her mouth, usually grimacing as she swallowed. Annie didn't know if it was from the taste or the pain of her injured throat.

But she never spoke.

Tah-tah-ma-*ho!* was a constant presence, if not in the house, then on the land. He had taken over completely the provision and preparation of food, although he disdained the use of her kitchen. Annie wondered if he even knew how to cook on anything other than a fire pit dug into the sand.

She suspected he might be afraid of being invited to join them for a meal and being embarrassed by his unpolished table manners.

Which made Saketa all the more of a puzzle. The pair might be brother and sister, but Saketa had been wearing a nicely made calico skirt and muslin blouse the first time Annie had seen her, while she had yet to see Tah-tah-ma-*ho!* in anything save those loin-hugging buckskin inexpressibles, or worse still, a flap of hide no bigger than a child's apron that barely covered his privities.

The first time she had seen him thusly clad, he'd come wading up out of the sound, carrying a string of fish. The garment had clung to him in such a way that she couldn't help but stare, and then, when he'd caught her staring, she had blushed fiery red.

One of the worst disadvantages of having red hair was the thin skin that went with it. A woman couldn't even keep her most private thoughts secret!

There were so many things Annie found puzzling about her two uninvited guests. Saketa spoke English as well as did Annie, yet Tah-tah-ma-*ho!* spoke more often than not as if he begrudged every syllable. The two of them together put her in mind of a panther she had once seen in the wild compared to the school's old mouser. Both animals had more or less the same features, the same coloration, and the same general conformation as far as appendages and appurtenances were concerned, yet if approached, one would purr and rub against your ankles while the other would not hesitate to rend you limb from limb.

Setting aside the questions that continued to mount up in her mind, Annie handed Saketa her supper, which was a bowl of roasted squirrel that had been cut into small pieces. Saketa had graduated to solid food now. "Tah-tah-ma-*ho!* is a wonderful cook. I wonder if he could make a molasses pudding."

Saketa mouthed the word *Tah-tah-ma-ho!* and shook her head.

"He can't?"

Saketa shook her head even more.

"Don't tell me he doesn't like molasses pudding. Everyone likes molasses pudding. Our old cook at the place where I lived before I came here made it with ginger and currents, and we always had it with a dollop of clotted cream."

With a look of disgust, the younger girl closed her eyes and pushed the bowl away, and Annie tried not to be discouraged. This was the first time since she'd been brought here that Saketa had even tried to communicate. At least it was a fair indication that her mind was unharmed.

If she'd had the molasses, and if Queenie would have parted with a single egg, she might have tried her own hand at making the girl a pudding. It couldn't be much different from making bread.

Of course, she had yet to master bread.

Tah-tah-ma-*ho!* probably knew how to make a perfectly acceptable bread. He was just too stubborn to do it. Roasting game over an open fire was one thing, but stepping into a kitchen to mix up a batter was something else again.

"Men," she grumbled aloud, taking up the skirt she was refitting for Saketa to replace the one that had been ruined.

Saketa's lips twitched, but she didn't open her eyes.

"I don't know if it's a man thing or a pride thing," Annie went on, "but I've yet to see a man do anything he can get a woman to do for him."

Which was so unfair she had the grace to blush. "Here, you'd better wake up and eat a bit more of this squirrel. Tomorrow I'm thinking of propping you up so you can see out the window for a spell. Maybe you can find out where that blessed chicken lays her eggs, for she'll not allow me anywhere near her nest."

Sometimes for hours at a stretch now, T'maho left the two women alone. He had ridden to the northernmost villages seeking word of any strangers on the island. No one had seen anything. Daily, he met with Mingo, who brought news from the village as well as the results of his own ongoing search. Neither man was any closer to solving the mystery.

"He wore fine linen. That's all I know. But until I find the *macherew* and bring him to justice, Saketa must remain hidden in O'Neal's lodge. She would not be safe with Etawak."

"I know, my friend. I've ridden as far south as Hatteras and had word from Ocracoke. It's not easy to ask questions without revealing too much. People are uneasy. They sense something is amiss. I told Etawak to put out word that Saketa was visiting up on the Currituck Banks, but I don't think anyone believed her."

"Why would anyone believe a woman who once told a man his wife was carrying a son, only to have her give birth to twin daughters three weeks later?"

Mingo chuckled. T'maho smiled grimly. Etawak's false prophesies were legendary.

"Saketa still won't talk," T'maho said quietly.

"Her throat—"

"Her throat is healing. She eats. She's gaining strength, I'm sure of it. Yet whenever I ask her who hurt her, she closes her eyes and pretends to sleep."

"Perhaps she doesn't know. Sometimes when a body has been badly injured, the mind plays games to help deal with the pain."

"She knows." T'maho knew his sister. Saketa was hiding something. He knew her stubbornness, as well. She would talk when she was ready to talk and not before. So be it. He was a patient man. "Let the devil dog walk today unhindered. Tomorrow he will look over his shoulder to find death staring him in the face."

"Saketa has already glimpsed the face of death. You and I, my friend, must see that it does not happen again."

For the sake of secrecy, the two men had sworn Etawak to silence, although Mingo had nearly had to use force the first few days to prevent her from rushing to the side of the injured girl. Mingo had put out the word that T'maho was looking after Eli's daughter in his stead. Some had glanced at his scars and looked away quickly, understanding how it was with strangers seeing him for the first time.

In the hour before daylight, while most of the village still slept, they met at their net, for it was expected of them, but they took care to speak in undertones. Voices traveled far on water.

"The child she carried," Mingo said now. "It is truly lost?"

T'maho nodded abruptly, then turned his attention to the task, at hand. Mingo was silent, and T'maho allowed him his moment of privacy. If the babe had survived, then Saketa would still be in need of a husband. She might have seen fit to accept Mingo's suit, even though she had once spurned him.

"Etawak ages daily. She grieves."

"Etawak," T'maho replied dryly, "has lived a turtle's years."

"Still she worries. I told her what you said, that Saketa is awake, that she eats well, that Eli's daughter tends her with great kindness, but she only mumbles her spells and fingers those bones she carries in the bag around her neck."

T'maho's bark of soft laughter held little amusement. "Perhaps it was Etawak's bones and spells that kept the ginger-hair from poisoning herself and Saketa. Her cooking is so bad, I've taken to doing it myself. She doesn't know enough to scale a fish before putting it into the pot. She calls Eli's rooster by a woman's name and searches daily for eggs."

"You didn't tell her?"

T'maho shrugged. "She didn't ask."

Mingo's distorted features stretched into a smile. His dark hazel eyes sparkled with amusement. "I'm beginning to see now why you spurned all those fancy tutors your father hired to teach you. Truly, what the white man calls education must not be so wonderful, after all."

It was a subject they seldom spoke of, T'maho's early years in his father's house. The tutors who had taught him for years. The books that even now rested in a chest in one corner of his lodge, and which sometimes, when the weather closed in and his mind grew restless, he took out and read again.

Mingo had long since learned the risks attached to reminding his friend that he was half white and only half Hattorask. Still, he sometimes found it amusing to court danger.

Hanging the wash over the line Tah-tah-ma-*ho!* had tied between the corner of the house and the shed roof, Annie was forced to admit that men had their uses, despite what Mrs. B. had claimed right up until the night she had run off with one of the scoundrels.

Now, if only he could find some way to keep those hellborn cattle from walking under the line and carrying off her laundry on their wicked horns, she would be satisfied.

How on earth, she wondered, had her father ever managed to dry his clothing?

And then she wondered if he had ever bothered to wash it.

Dear Lord, where *was* Papa? It had been more than two weeks. The mail boat had come and gone at least once since then, for she had recognized the sails when they'd passed by out in the channel, heading into the harbor.

Lately she had gone for hours without once thinking about Papa or wondering where he was and why he didn't come home. Which was only natural, she supposed, considering the fact that she had never really known him. Not as an adult.

Oh, she had a few dim memories of a small, cozy room filled with pipe smoke—memories of clinging to a man's strong hands while she walked up his legs and flipped over like a circus acrobat. *"Skin-the-cat, Papa—I want to skin-the-cat!"*

She could even hear her mother's voice chiding them both, although she could no longer picture her face. She seemed to remember that the house they lived in had belonged to Gramma and Grampa Stevens, her mother's parents, but she wasn't even certain of that. It had all happened so very long ago.

From inside the house came a scuffling sound indicating that Saketa was trying to get out of bed. Glancing around quickly to see if Tah-tah-ma-*ho!* was nearby, which she did now without even thinking, Annie pegged the last bit of laundry to the line and hurried inside.

"Where do you think you're going, young woman?"

Saketa looked up guiltily. She had hobbled across the room to fetch the sewing basket, which seemed to fascinate her to no end.

"That ankle of yours is almost well, but you're still not strong enough to be prancing around."

At Saketa's impish grin, Annie felt almost as if she were back at school, trying to keep up with the antics of the younger girls, who always seemed to have energy left over for mischief no matter how many hours they worked at lessons and chores.

Shaking her head as if she were an old crone rather than only a few years older than Saketa, Annie opened the trunk and burrowed under the layers of carefully mended clothing, which consisted of two shawls, two plain woolen gowns—both gray—and one elegant garment cut down from an old satin sacque Mrs. B. had grown too plump to wear. Annie had never worn it, for it was far too fine for everyday, and not quite right for church meetings.

"Ah, here it is," she pronounced, bobbing out again with the gold-colored sacque in her hands. Saketa would need something more to wear than the gingham skirt Annie had been adjusting for her. "I do believe this color would look lovely on you, Saketa."

Satin was wildly unsuitable for such a primitive place, but what young girl wouldn't love owning such a pretty gown? she thought indulgently. And if the other women of the village should happen to see it and admire the style and the elegant embroidery that covered all the stains and the seams that had been let out too many times and then taken in again—if they should happen to ask where they could find something as elegant, Annie would be glad to advise them.

Caught woolgathering, she stood up and shook out the deep yellow satin. "I do believe if we take it in just here to fit your waist and fill in the bosom with a strip cut off this lawn kerchief . . . hmmm. I could embroider it in gold and brown. A butterfly design would be lovely—or would you prefer flowers?"

Saketa's indrawn breath sounded painful, but her face was so rapt that Annie wished she had thought of it sooner. If she were ever to fully recover, the poor child needed something more to look forward to than an ongoing life of drudgery and brutality.

She only hoped Tah-tah-ma-*ho!* had caught that wicked husband of hers and banished him from the island forever.

"Here . . . try holding it just so with your left hand." She placed the refolded garment in Saketa's lap, secured it with her injured arm, and handed her a pair of small shears. "Let's see if you can take out the stitches with your right hand. Then we can fit it on you and I'll baste it up again."

After showing Saketa how to nip the threads without cutting the fabric, and promising to return in a few moments to see how she was going on, Annie stepped outside again to empty her wash water and see if Tah-tah-ma-*ho!* had—

And see nothing of the sort! What did she care where he went? Or how long he stayed away? And anyway, the man was purely irritating, the way he continually popped up like a jack-in-the-box when she least expected him.

She was just reaching for the wash pot when a brown and white cow rounded the back corner at a lope. The creature was obviously just as startled as Annie was. Waving her apron, Annie yelled and tried to shoo it away from her clothesline, but it was too late. One short, wicked horn caught the hem of her spare shift, the fine muslin blowing in the wind, and the beast went wild.

"Stop that! You come back here with my—" Waving

her arms, she raced after him. She had only two decent shifts to her name, and the one she was wearing had been worn so thin in the seat that it would no longer even support a patch.

The cow disappeared around the corner of the shed, the delicate shift streaming out behind its massive head like a white banner. Annie rounded the corner right behind the flying hooves, only to rebound off a solid wall of flesh.

T'maho grabbed the woman before she could fall. Caught off balance, he leaned against the building and held her tightly against him, stunned by the impact of her negligible weight and reminded all over again of the disastrous effect she invariably had on him whenever they happened to touch.

Righting himself slowly, he continued to hold her, even as he told himself she was the very kind of woman he had always disdained.

So why did his body react to the slightest touch of her, even the scent of her, as if it had a mind of its own?

In that first moment of contact, when her hands had flown up to brace against his bare chest, he had glanced down, half expecting to see their imprint branded on his skin.

Swearing under his breath, T'maho called on the great *Ahone* for patience. The woman's hair, never tidy, had once again escaped confinement. Smelling of soap and sunshine, it tickled his chin in a peculiar way that reverberated in his loins.

"Oh!" she gasped as color rushed to stain her cheeks.

T'maho stared down at her parted mouth and found himself wanting to cover it with his own. Grudgingly, he admitted to himself that she was not entirely unappealing. For a paleskin. For a scrawny, foolish, ignorant paleskin woman from some town across the sound.

A wicked impulse overtook him. "Were you looking for me, Annie?"

"I most certainly was not! I was chasing that . . . that wicked cow!"

Not by so much as the flicker of an eyelash did he reveal it, yet Annie gained the impression that he was secretly laughing at her. It was not the first time she'd been the object of laughter. Her wild red hair and thin freckled skin, not to mention her prickly pride and quick Irish temper, had made her a natural target in the early years at school until she had earned the respect of the others.

This man had laughed at her before. She hadn't liked it then, nor did she like it now. Unfortunately, he wasn't as easy to deal with as a group of whispering, snickering schoolgirls.

Twisting herself free, she stepped back, planted her hands on her hips, and tapped one foot silently in the soft sand. "I'll thank you not to delay me any longer, sir. I have business with that filthy, thieving animal who just stole my . . . my garment."

"The bull, you mean."

"Bull, cow, what's the difference?"

This time she was certain he was laughing at her! He pulled something white and frilly from behind his back. "Were you looking for this?"

Annie stared at the limp scrap of white lawn he held out to her. In his dark, square-palmed hand, it looked embarrassingly intimate. "How did you . . . ?"

"Grabbed it when he ran past."

She snatched it from him, rolled it into a small ball, and hid it behind her back, pointedly avoiding his gaze. "Thank you, Tah-tah-ma-*ho!* It was a—a dangerous thing to do, I'm sure."

"Extremely dangerous." His face was devoid of expression, but his eyes were dancing gleefully.

"Yes. Well, then . . . I'd better rinse it out again. One never knows . . ."

"One never does," he repeated gravely, and cheeks flaming, Annie spun away, only to be grabbed and spun right around again.

"My name is T'maho."

"That's what I—"

"Not Tah-tah-ma-*ho!*"

Flabbergasted, Annie stood there, one arm held in his forceful grip, and stared into his clear eyes until she felt her senses begin to reel. And then she jerked her arm away. "Well, for mercy's sake, I wish you would make up your mind!"

Before she could escape, he caught her head between his hands, tilting her face up to his. "Say my name," he commanded, his voice a soft threat.

"T-tah—"

That was as far as she got before his warm breath whispered over her face, fogging her brain, causing her lips to swell and soften, her eyelids to grow heavy, and her heart to pound like a drum.

Annie had been kissed before. She had known her share of sticky, childish smacks, usually smeared across her cheek at bedtime, but never in a million years could she have imagined the effect of the deliberate placing of one mouth upon another.

She certainly could never have imagined the feeling that had her clinging to the only solid thing within reach to keep from falling into the sun and drowning, the thing within reach being T'maho.

His lips were neither dry nor wet. They were firm, yet oddly soft. While he moved them slowly over her own, she clutched his arm with one hand, her wadded shift with the other, and stared wide-eyed at his left ear and the thick dark braid that hung over his shoulder.

Something broke the seal of her lips. Something small and wet and hot. Something that was stealthily invading her person!

Wave after wave of sensation swept over her, and Annie shut her eyes tightly. She was hot—she was cold—she was trembling. Somewhere a finger kept plucking on a single note, over and over again, only the note was reverberating not in her ears, but inside her body, down low, near the base of her belly.

Instead of hearing it, she was actually *feeling* it!

"Oh, my mercy," she whispered when at last he lifted his head from hers. "Oh, my mercy," she breathed as he blistered her with a furious glare, then wheeled away and left her standing there, limp as the damp garment she held in her trembling hand.

* * *

That evening, it was back to grunts and silence. T'maho brought in two roasted rabbits, flung them on the table, looked in at Saketa, and left again, all without a word to Annie.

She might as well have been invisible. In a house no bigger than a respectable chicken coop, with only two rooms and not a single place to hide, even if she'd wished to hide, he managed to overlook her as if she weren't even there.

Head high, Annie went about boiling the parched leaves he had brought her just that morning, hoping they wouldn't poison her. Tea, he had said—although it didn't look like any tea she'd ever seen.

Saketa was improving rapidly, but she still couldn't speak. Or wouldn't. She no longer seemed frightened, only weak. Annie wondered if she could have wiped the entire dreadful episode right out of her mind. Having heard of such things happening after some great tragedy, she'd set it down to the Lord's way of comforting folks who'd been burdened with more than they could carry.

At least her wrist seemed to be mending neatly. The swelling at the back of her head had gone down, and her foot was no longer swollen. Her bruises were no more than yellowish shadows on her tea-colored face, although the scars of some of the deeper cuts would remain for a good time to come.

As for Tah-tah-ma-*ho!* or T'maho, or whatever he chose to call himself, he continued to avoid her when he could, and to speak in that odd, stiff way of his when he couldn't. Annie knew for a fact that he could speak the King's English as well as she could.

Maddening man. Irritating, aggravating, provoking creature!

Unable to stop thinking about that extraordinary kiss that had happened between them, Annie wished more than ever that she had paid closer attention to Mrs. B.'s brief session on Behavior Becoming a Young Gentlewoman of Marriageable Age, which was offered to each girl at the age of sixteen when she prepared to leave the school for marriage or work.

As Annie had stayed on as an unpaid assistant, she had never actually heard it in its entirety, but over the years she'd heard bits and pieces. She knew, for instance, that it included such practical matters as avoiding bodily contact and avoiding any mention of bodily functions and body parts above the ankle and below the ears.

She did recall that when a young woman was overcome by palpitations and a feeling of restless agitation in the presence of a member of the opposite gender, one sure remedy was carpet-beating.

Unfortunately, Annie didn't possess a single carpet.

It was just after dawn when the *Black Opal* tied up at the dock in Kinnakeet. The two Portuguese crewmen, neither of whom spoke English, silently went about their business on deck, while in the main cabin below, Jackson Snell adjusted his silk cravat, fastened his short, double-breasted jacket, and reached for his beaver hat. He always dressed to suit his position as a man of the law—although it never seemed to impress the native Bankers, he thought disdainfully. They were a rough lot, interbreeding with Indians and whatever flotsam washed ashore without a single thought as to lineage.

This trip across, he had brought along his new Polish cape in case the weather should turn cool enough to wear it. It was more important than ever that these heathens be reminded of the dignity of his office, in case word had already reached them of O'Neal's demise.

Running his fingers under his pomaded hair, he lifted it enough to give the impression of fullness and settled his hat carefully on his head. For the desired effect, he wore it level, not cocked at a fashionable angle.

"Brilliant! Snell, my dear sir, you should have gone on the stage," he murmured to his reflection in the brass-bound shaving mirror.

And if anyone should mention the girl—although there was no reason why they should, for few knew he had even met her—he would have to be prepared to show the proper degree of astonishment.

Pity, he mused. He would miss the sport. But then, it was probably just as well. All women turned into shrews once they thought they had their hooks in a man's pocketbook.

For the next few weeks, it might be a good idea to take his pleasure at the Hens and Cockerel instead of looking about for a fresh young wench on the island to take Saketa's place. At least he would know from the start how much it was going to cost him.

The first person Snell saw when he disembarked was a grim old specimen who looked as if he'd as soon skewer a man as pass the time of day with him. He recognized him as one of the elders of the village, one whose word held weight.

If anyone had heard about O'Neal's accident, this man would know.

There was a small group of men standing beside an overturned boat, examining the bottom. A few more were mending a net hung from a line stretched between oak trees. He watched silently for several minutes, wondering how best to discover what they knew.

Gradually, it came to him that there was something peculiar in the atmosphere. The air was too still . . . as if there were a storm in the offing.

Or perhaps a death in the community.

It had to be O'Neal. The news had spread, as he'd thought it would, either by mail boat or some of the loggers who regularly came and went.

Possibly they had even found the girl's body by now, although he'd taken care to roll her into the deep end of the pond. Two deaths coming so close together in such a small village might cause speculation, but there was no possible way they could be connected.

"Here, you—Gray!" he called peremptorily.

A grizzled old fisherman turned to regard him with that disconcerting steadiness so common among the Bankers. He had never felt entirely comfortable there, but then, what civilized man would? There wasn't even a decent public house on the island.

"Has something untoward occurred?" he asked with

a suitable note of concern. "I do hope there's no sickness about. Measles over on the mainland, I'm afraid."

"No more sickness than ordinary."

The net menders ignored him, as did four of the five old relics gathered around the boat. Jackariah Gray continued to study him as if he were some overripe trifle that had washed up on the shore instead of a prominent officer of the court who had been coming and going on the Outer Banks with fair regularity for more than ten years.

Damn their inbred suspiciousness. Didn't the fools know that he now *owned* a good part of their cursed island?

They'd find out soon enough.

Snell felt a film of sweat break out on his brow. He wished now he had left off his woolen undershirt. It was the latest thing, but worn with a linen blouse, a brocaded waistcoat, a silk tie, and a coat, it was a bit much for this unseasonal heat.

He cleared his throat again. "I don't suppose you've seen O'Neal around here this morning? I was to meet him about a new shipment."

There—there's your cue, you stupid fools!

"Ain't back yet."

"Back?"

"Left out to go to Tar Landin' near 'bout three weeks ago come next Tuesday. Or was it Wednesday? Izzer, what day was it we set out them—"

"He's gone, then?" Snell broke in. *Of course he's gone, you fools!* "I've been up in Virginia. I supposed we just managed to miss each other. Pity."

He waited. And sweated. After a while, when no one seemed inclined to comment further, he said, "I suppose I might as well ride north and see if everything's all right. As long as I've come this far."

"Daughter's been lookin' after things, I reckon."

"Your daughter, sir? Is she a particular friend of Mr. O'Neal?"

The man sent him a scathing look. "*Eli's* daughter. I've not seen much of her, but she knows to come fetch Mingo if she needs help."

Chapter 8

Eli's daughter! The old bastard had claimed he had no family! Snell distinctly remembered the day they had first met. At the time, he'd been searching through the records for a parcel of unclaimed land somewhere on one of the strings of barrier islands to use in a project he had recently undertaken. O'Neal had been attempting to track down the location of a land grant he'd inherited from some long-dead relative or another. After a brief discussion, Snell had led the man to a nearby tavern and bought him a meal and a bottle.

Two bottles, in fact. And a pipe. Once the proper climate had been established, he'd set about trying to talk the ignorant old fool into parting with his inheritance.

"Fifty dollars, sight unseen."

"You're a generous man, Justice Snell, but—"

"Oh, please . . . Mr. Snell will do. My office is merely that—an office, hardly a title. One hundred."

"I'll say this, sir—it's tempting. I've not got much in this world, and that's a fact, but I been thinking I'd like to take a look at what me pappy left behind when he passed on to his reward. Figger it's the least I can do, seein's how I parted company with the old gent when I run off at the age o' sixteen and married me sweet Matilda."

Snell remembered ordering another bottle of rum about then and wondering if the man had a hollow leg. "Ah, I see ... family property. Then it's only natural you'd want to save it for your sons. I'm sure a gentleman such as yourself wouldn't blink an eye at all the expense and the work involved in establishing your claim."

Eli emptied his tankard and slid it toward the bottle. "Sons? As to that, sir, the Lord never saw fit to bless me with no son. Truth is, Tildie died a while back and I never got over missin' her. Took to drinkin', and it like to got the best of me."

That much Snell could easily believe.

"Then I took me this notion to search out a piece o' land old King Charlie give me great-grandpap. Heard tell it was out on some island. Never laid eyes on the place, meself."

"My condolences on the loss of your wife, sir. Drink up, drink up—the evening is young yet."

And drink they had. Snell recalled being delighted that the old sot had no one left to nose around into his affairs. He also recalled being horrified at the notion of any man being so stupid as to tie himself down to any woman at the tender age of sixteen.

Unless she happened to be sufficiently wealthy, and the old soak had shown no signs of wealth. Probably drank it all up.

Snell had attempted to talk him into selling out, but drunk or not, the old devil had been wily as a fox. In the end, they had struck a deal that had turned out even better in the long run.

With his own reputation as an officer of the court to guard, Snell had been carefully laying the groundwork for some time. It had all begun a few months earlier when a small band of cattle thieves had been brought before him. As it happened, he'd been alone at the time. The sheriff had left almost immediately to see to a ruckus in the tavern, during which he'd had the misfortune to get himself killed. Which meant that no one knew about the thieves he had just brought in.

Snell could have seen them all hanged, and that would have been the end of it. Instead, he had chosen to use them, always with the threat of a hangman's noose dangling over their heads. It had been profitable for all concerned.

Of course, he had been in no doubt the scoundrels had been cheating him right from the first. In their place, he would have done no less. But as long as he got the lion's share of the takings, with an out-of-the-way place to hold them until he could turn a good profit, he was satisfied.

The trouble was, he had just discovered that the land he'd been using had recently been sold, and the new owner was making plans to move his own herd in.

Which was where O'Neal and his land grant had come into the picture. The Banks were a natural corral. There were few people living in the small villages scattered up and down the narrow, isolated islands, and those who did were a closemouthed lot who kept their own counsel.

In the end, it had worked out better than he had ever dared dream. With O'Neal to oversee the day-to-day business and his small band of hangman's bait doing what they did best, he had, over the years, accumulated a valuable herd with little or no effort on his own part.

From time to time, to keep the machinery well oiled, he sold off small portions, splitting the take three ways, with the rogues going shares on their third. Naturally, he deducted an appropriate amount for his "expenses" first. The fools had never even questioned him.

Once the price of beef climbed high enough, thanks to the ever-increasing population and the decreasing supply of cattle, which was due in part to the constant pilferage, he had planned to sell out and then see that O'Neal met with an accident, which would leave himself as the sole owner of several hundred acres of potentially valuable land in an out-of-the-way location. He'd had in mind several possible ventures, as the place was convenient to more than one large port and far removed from prying eyes.

But then O'Neal had started asking awkward questions. It seemed that when he'd gone to arrange for the last load to be barged across the sound, the whole county had been buzzing about how bold the cattle rustlers were growing, to the point where it hardly paid a man to try to raise his own beef, much less beef for market. Snell had been forced to push ahead his plans instead of waiting for more favorable market conditions when the old fool had started poking his nose in where he had no business prying.

And now to find out he had a daughter!

Standing on the wharf beside the *Black Opal* while he waited for his horse to be brought around, Snell stroked his jaw and thought furiously. A child could be dealt with, but if the brat was old enough to look after Eli's interests, she might be old enough to contest any claim on her father's property. Snell knew he had covered his tracks sufficiently as far as the records were concerned. A bill of sale could be forged, as well as a registration, if one had access to the proper channels.

Still, Eli had asked questions. It might be awkward if someone else turned up and began asking similar questions. If some encroaching little courthouse snitch started checking, the dates of several recently reported thefts might coincide a bit too closely with the dates of his own acquisitions.

Careless, that. Not damning, but dueced awkward. Especially if the old sot had spilled his suspicions to his daughter.

Snell had no way of knowing. That being the case, there was only one possible course of action open to him at this point. Eli's daughter would have to disappear, too. Fortunately, the island abounded with deep, black-water ponds in well-hidden places.

He waited impatiently for the boy to return with the gelding he always hired when he was on the island. The arrangement was that anytime Snell's sails were sighted, the horse was to be at the dock, saddled and ready.

He pulled out his timepiece, glared at it, and snapped it shut. Time obviously meant nothing to these ignorant people!

Across the clearing from the harbor, a woman stepped outside and called quietly to a child who had been drawing a hopscotch pattern in the sandy road. Without a single protest, the child went inside. It occurred to Snell that there were no other women in sight, no children larking about under the trees. Only the fishermen and two youths spreading a freshly tarred net over the drying rack.

Abruptly, he tossed his cigar to the ground and crushed it underfoot, aware of an odd prickling feeling at the back of his neck that had nothing to do with unseasonable heat.

Could O'Neal or his daughter have spread word of his suspicions around the village? He'd detected no sign of anything untoward, but perhaps while he waited for his horse to be delivered, he'd best find out just what he was up against before he took the next step.

Forcing a jovial smile, he tugged at his cravat and sauntered over to the group of old men. "Fishing been good this fall?" he inquired, trying to look as if he gave a tippler's damn.

"Tol'able," nodded an old gray beard, without looking up. He'd been examining his knife. With cool deliberation, he tested the blade with his thumb.

Another man glanced his way, spat a stream of tobacco juice, and looked away again.

Snell felt his collar wilt. In the humid heat, the scratches on his cheek, nearly healed by now, began to itch. "Not much to do around here, I suppose. No newspapers. No way of knowing what's going on in the rest of the world."

Silence. God, it was like pulling hen's teeth! Clenching his fists in his pockets, Snell pretended to study the sky. He stared down at his gleaming boots. A light breeze carried a few words from the group of men mending net over across the way, and he strained to hear what was said.

"Old Etawak, she put out the word the girl was up to Currituck. Meself, I don't believe it," said a bent old man with knotted fingers as he nimbly wove his wooden needle down and around to the right, then over and under again.

"Wife says she heard she was took real bad off."

"Reck'n it must be a fearsome fever, the way they're a-keepin' the poor girl hid out. I told Achsah to keep the younguns in the house."

"Sickness?" Snell stepped down off the wharf and moved closer. "Did I hear someone say there's sickness about? Don't tell me the measles have come all the way out to the Banks."

One of the two youths who had been spreading the tarred nets out to dry on a pole rack wiped a pair of filthy hands on the seat of a pair of equally filthy pants and swaggered over to join the men. "Truth is, don't nobody know for sure, Judge Snell, but they're a-sayin' Saketa, she's been took real bad off, only nobody can't find her and nobody ain't sayin' what's wrong with her. Me, I bet she's all broke out and swole up and thrashin' around somethin' fierce, like Jim Henry done when he took the itch." The boy's blue eyes, round as marbles, glistened with innocent excitement. "Jim Henry's ma had to tie his hands to the bedposts to keep him from—"

"Hush your mouth, boy," one of the men growled, but Snell had heard more than enough.

He actually felt the color blanch from his face. God, was it possible? Could the little pagan still be alive?

Without a word, he tossed a copper to the boy who had just brought his gelding around. Acutely conscious of the barely healed streaks running down his left cheek and under his collar, he mounted and quickly set off for Etawak's lodge.

Half a dozen pairs of eyes bored into his back, right through four layers of clothing. Ignoring them, he ruthlessly applied his whip.

How the devil could everything have gone so wrong? He could have sworn the little bitch was dead when he'd rolled her into the pond!

She couldn't have said anything yet, else he'd never have left the docks alive. Which meant he still had time to find her and silence her before she talked!

God almighty, his heart was galloping like a runaway horse! He should have known better than to get mixed up with one of these clannish Bankers! Red, white, or royal blue, they were all alike when it came to protecting their own.

Damn. He *knew* better than to mix business with pleasure! If only the silly little twit hadn't had this certain way of walking—this certain way of cutting her big brown eyes at him and flicking her skirt, flashing those shapely ankles of hers! It had heated his blood to boiling quicker than anything had in years.

Etawak's lodge stood somewhat apart from the others, the yard littered with tea-making paraphernalia that included a large trough, a pile of smoke-blackened ballast stones, and several wooden casks. Unlike the old-style lodges, Etawak's place was sided with cypress, even though the roof was of thatched rush.

The old woman met him at the door, a tobacco-stained pipe clamped between her few remaining teeth, her broad, squatty figure planted squarely in his way. "Want tea?" she grunted.

Snell didn't make the mistake of thinking she was inviting him to partake. Forcing himself to be civil, he informed her that he had not come to buy her yaupon tea, nor did he want any of her acorn beer. What he did want was to see her granddaughter.

"Saketa not here."

"Perhaps you'd be so kind as to tell me where she is?"

"*Nowanus.*"

"Where?"

"*Accommac.*"

"Godamighty, woman, can't you speak English?"

Panic began to nibble away at the edges of his mind. He had to find the little bitch before she recovered enough to blab the entire tale to anyone who would listen! A well-placed pillow should do the trick quickly and with no fuss. If the old squaw tried to make trouble, it should be easy enough to lay the blame at her door.

Yes, yes . . . that was it, he thought frantically. He

had walked in and seen Etawak holding a pillow over the girl's face, but he'd been too late to save her. Heartbreaking. The old woman must have cracked under the strain of her guilty conscience. To have beaten the poor child so severely! Probably been beating her for years.

Of course. And who would take the word of a crazy old squaw over a respected justice of the peace?

Sweeping the old bawd aside, he strode into the room where Saketa slept. He knew it well, having once plowed the little bitch in her own bed.

The room was empty. Panic began to curdle in the pit of his stomach. He had to find her before it was too late!

"Where is she? Where are you hiding her?" he demanded, returning to find the old woman sharpening the blade of a hatchet on a flattened ballast stone.

He was still waiting for a reply, desperately fighting to control his rising alarm, when he became aware of an odd sound—something between the purr of a cat and the hiss of a snake.

After a nervous glance over his shoulder, he looked back to discover that the old witch was humming. *Humming!* And smiling! And not once did she even glance his way. He might as well not have been there.

Etawak blew a stream of smoke through the gap in her teeth. Snell swallowed convulsively and curled his sweaty palms into fists. Forcing himself to be patient, he repeated the question. And then repeated it again and again until he was practically shouting.

The demented old fool ignored him. She continued to grind her blade, continued to smile, continued to make that maddening sound, never once even looking up, damn her pox-ridden hide!

Snell tugged at the ruins of his silk cravat. He had to get out of there before he murdered her with her own hatchet, which would only complicate a situation that was rapidly threatening to come unraveled.

In a quiet rage, he slammed out of the cramped lodge and leaped into the saddle, ruthlessly kicking the gelding in the sides and then jerking the bit when the beast threatened to unseat him.

Damned stubborn heathens, every last one of them! They spoke the King's English well enough when they wanted something, but just let the shoe be on the other foot and they clammed up tighter than a virgin's snatch!

And there was still Eli's daughter to be dealt with.

He galloped away, oblivious to the old woman who stood in the clearing, staring after him with a thoughtful look on her wrinkled face.

Annie, pleased with having for once managed to cook a decent pan of bread—at least she hadn't burned the bottom and it wasn't still squishy in the middle—went to the door to see if T'maho had returned. For no real reason, it was important to her that he know she wasn't a total incompetent.

He had set out this morning to check on the northern edge of the property, where he'd said a large part of the herd had gathered in a grassy area near a series of brackish ponds. It seemed to Annie that he constantly patrolled the area, almost as if expecting a pack of wild dogs to attack her father's cows.

There was no sign of his horse. The mare usually stayed close to the shed with the mule in the heat of the day, taking advantage of the shade. Out in the sound, several head of cattle stood hip deep in the water, tails lazily swishing away the flies, and Annie was reminded of the day she had seen the pair mating and gone running to T'maho and Mingo for help.

Small wonder he thought her a fool.

Saketa, who had been feverish again during the night, was still sleeping. Annie wasn't really worried. Her fever came and went, usually rising in the evening, falling again come morning. Children tended to react the same way. Without really understanding it, Annie took it as a natural part of healing.

Turning to go inside, she became aware of someone approaching from the south. Pausing, she waited, squinting against the brassy glare of the sun. At first she thought it might be her father's hired man. Mingo hadn't been around since that first week, as far as she knew. She supposed he and T'maho had worked out the duties between them, and really, there wasn't all that much to do besides feeding Jacob and seeing that the cows didn't get into trouble.

As he came closer she could see that it wasn't anyone she knew. Certainly it wasn't T'maho, because he'd ridden north. Besides, by now she could recognize him as far away as she could see him, just from the way he sat his horse. Back straight, shoulders level, head tilted back ever so slightly, so that he always appeared to be looking down his nose at her.

As the visitor came close enough to see, Annie thought briefly of her father, who'd been gone nearly three weeks now. Whoever he was, she knew instinctively that this man wasn't her papa. Not unless Papa had changed beyond all recognition. He was riding a big yellow horse and as he came closer she could see that he was blond, fairly tall, and quite fashionably dressed.

Which certainly did not describe the Papa she remembered.

"Miss O'Neal?" He hailed her from some distance away.

Annie waited until he came to a halt beside the stump. The fleeting thought occurred that she wished T'maho were nearby. Not that she really needed a savage to help her deal with a man who was obviously a gentleman. "I'm Annie O'Neal. Were you looking for my father?"

"I'm Jackson Snell. I take it you're Eli's daughter?"

"Oh, Mr. Snell! I'm sorry, but I'm afraid Papa's away on business."

His eyes seemed to roam over her in a way that was slightly disconcerting. She thought he seemed rather surprised, which was probably only her imagination. And of course, he'd been expecting to find her father at home.

Hesitating only a moment, she invited him inside. She'd never been one to make snap judgments, but there was something about the man that didn't set quite right, even if he was her father's business partner. Telling herself she was being foolish, she went out of her way to be gracious. "Would you care for a cool cup of yaupon tea? I've some left over from this morning."

She was startled to see a shudder of distaste pass over his face. The native brew wasn't to everyone's taste, but Annie had found it surprisingly pleasant. It was certainly better than no tea at all.

Jackson Snell declined the offer of refreshment, and she seated herself, indicating for him to take the best chair, the one with the back. "I, um . . . my, it's warm today, isn't it? I assumed my father had gone to meet with you, Mr. Snell. I hope you haven't crisscrossed each other somewhere along the way."

Snell opened his mouth and closed it again, and Annie stared at his lower lip, which was unusually full and wet. T'maho's lips were thinner, but nicely curved. They looked moist, but never red and wet.

He was saying something. Distracted, she'd missed the first part. "—expect he's away on another buying trip up to Virginia. The shame is that he had to leave you here all alone."

Without a thought, Annie said, "Oh, but I'm not alone, I assure you."

She watched, fascinated as his pale brows arched inquiringly, as if inviting her to explain. For reasons she didn't even try to understand, she chose not to. She wished he would go.

"Not alone?" His glance at the mean surroundings made his opinion patently clear. "You have a husband, perhaps?"

"I have a—um, a friend visiting. With her brother. And of course, there's always Mr. Mingo. He's usually around somewhere." He wasn't, of course, but Mr. Snell didn't have to know that.

"Then it's just as well I came along when I did. These Indians—you know how they are. A sorry bunch, even your father's man. Not to be trusted. Perhaps I'd better just stay on until—"

"My friends," Annie said hastily. "I mean, there's really no room for more than the three of us, and Papa will be back most any day now, Mr. Snell, but I do appreciate your concern."

Why on earth did she feel so vulnerable? She had never been overly impressionable—at least, not until quite recently.

Jackson Snell thought frantically. The stupid woman! She had no right to be here at all!

Instinct warned him not to inform her of her father's "accident"—not until he could plan several steps ahead. There had already been too many surprises, and Snell didn't care for surprises. Not unless they were of his own making.

Was she staring at the scars on his cheek? They were nearly healed, but in certain lights a faint redness was still visible. Fortunately, it was too dark inside to see the marks where the little whore had scratched him.

Suddenly he was sweating again. God, he hated it when things didn't go according to plan! Twelve years—twelve long years, and now, suddenly, everything was coming apart!

He still had Saketa to find and deal with, which was

unfortunate, because much to his surprise, the O'Neal filly showed a good deal of promise. He'd always favored redheads. Their skin was so incredibly thin. Wondering idly how deep a mark his whip might leave on her buttocks, he found himself growing excited at the thought of having her at his mercy both physically and financially.

Such fine, long hair . . . endless possibilities there. He could even use it as a restraint. Of course, it might hurt her a bit.

He smiled. "Are you quite sure you don't need me to stay on until your father returns, Miss O'Neal?"

"Thank you. I'm quite sure. My—my friends look after everything."

Well, Miss Prunes and Prisms, Snell mused with malicious anticipation, *your friends won't be around to protect you forever. We'll just see how prim and proper you are when we're alone together in this godforsaken wilderness. Do you like it rough? I promise you, my dear, I'll have you on your knees begging for it before I even lift my whip.*

Breathing heavily, Snell crossed his legs and blotted his sweating forehead with a damp linen handkerchief. He forced himself to think of what must be done first. Before he could afford to enjoy himself with the delectable Miss O'Neal, he had to find Saketa. The little bitch must be silenced permanently before she could make trouble for him.

Real trouble. A bit of irregularity in the paperwork he could handle. He'd had years of practice in covering his tracks.

But not this other. Never before had he been forced to involve himself directly in the . . . dispersal of extraneous personnel.

Of course, there had been that whore up in Virginia. But that had been an accident. A bit too much enthusiasm on his part, coupled with an unexpected reluctance on hers.

After watching him ride away, Annie hurriedly poured herself a basin of water. For reasons she didn't even attempt to understand, she felt compelled to wash herself thoroughly.

Freshly bathed, her hair dampened and momentarily constrained in a neatly coiled braid, she glanced proudly at the pan of bread cooling on the table and then slipped into the bedroom to see if Saketa was awake. She wanted to share the triumph of having finally succeeded in baking a decent pan of bread.

She needed, too, to wipe away the oddly unpleasant feeling that had come over her in Mr. Snell's presence. The man had a way of looking at her with those watery blue eyes of his that made her feel almost unclean. Her imagination was certainly serving her a turn today.

"Saketa? Are you . . ."

She glanced first at the bed, then at the corner where the chamber pot was kept behind a hastily improvised curtain. Last of all, she took in the open window. She had purposely shut it to keep any stray breeze from blowing directly on her patient. Not to mention keeping that dratted chicken from roosting on the sill.

"Saketa," she whispered, but she knew. Without knowing how or why, she knew the girl was gone.

Chapter 9

Under cover of the dozen or so head of cattle that grazed on the beach grass behind the shed, Saketa staggered toward a grove of stunted juniper and yaupon that grew on the low ridge, praying Jack would not emerge from the house before she could hide herself. It was the first time she had been out of bed for longer than it took to use the chamber pot, and she was shocked to discover how very unsteady she was.

Her head ached, but only dully, and her ankle no longer throbbed like a rotten tooth. Weakness was a problem. She was as dizzy as if she'd spent the day sampling Etawak's acorn beer.

But it was her voice that worried her the most. She could almost speak again. A few more days and she would be able to make herself understood.

And once she did, T'maho would demand to know who had put a baby in her belly and who had beaten her, and when she told him—which she would have to do because he always knew when she was not telling the truth—he would murder Jack, and then men would come and take him away and hang him, because no In-

dian could get away with murdering a justice of the
peace who lived in a big house and knew everyone in
the whole world of any importance. They would hang
him. She couldn't bear for that to happen, because she
loved her brother better than anyone. Better than she
had ever loved Jack.

Curled up on the warm sand, she considered what to
do next. There'd been no time to think once she'd
heard that familiar voice in the next room. Sick with
fear, she had been expecting Annie to lead him into the
bedroom at any moment.

For the first time, Saketa began to understand her
brother's deep-seated mistrust of all whites. It had
never occurred to her before, but she had been rejected
just as surely as T'maho had. However, her father had
never taken her into his home and reared her as white,
only to turn her out again when he grew tired of her.

But he had rejected her, even so, by leaving before
she was even born and never coming back to claim her.

Of course, her mother had left her, too. According to
Etawak, Little Feet had died a week after Saketa had
been born. Still, she hadn't left deliberately, the way
her father had.

Strange, how quickly trust could be destroyed.
Saketa had always trusted everyone. She had never before been given a reason not to trust. She knew everyone in the village. They all knew her. Even the old
women who had shouted at her for stealing their
clothes off the lines when she was small and wanted to
play dress-up had given her sweets when she'd played
with their children. Dulsie's mother had showed her

how to make a mud doll with a round shell for a face and sticks for arms and legs, and even given her an old kerchief to dress it in.

Saketa had trusted Annie because she'd had no choice. But now . . .

Perhaps it was better not to trust at all.

Jack had claimed to love her. If he hadn't actually said the words, he'd as good as said he would marry her that day when she'd asked him if what they had just done together was what wives and husbands did, and he'd told her to wait and see.

So she had waited. And then he had tried to kill her!

Holding her knees, Saketa rocked back and forth, weeping silently. If a few squeaks and wheezes escaped, the sound was lost in the roar of the nearby surf.

Again and again she heard Annie call her name, sounding truly concerned, but she didn't dare risk answering. For all she knew, Annie might have already told Jack where she was, and he was just waiting to hurt her again.

She had to get away from here quickly, before he could return. Somehow, she had to think of a place to hide herself where he would never think of looking for her. It would take strength—possibly more strength than she possessed—but what choice did she have?

Saketa mopped her eyes. She blew her nose noisily on her skirt. Resolutely, she struggled to her feet, praying that by now Jack would have left. She made her way cautiously to the shed and peered around the corner.

And came face-to-face with a startled Mingo.

By the time T'maho rode in from the north, the western sky had turned the color of tarnished brass. By then, Annie was nearly frantic. If she'd been more of a hand with animals, she would have ridden Jacob to the village to see if Saketa had gone there, but the blasted mule had taken one of his touchy spells. The minute she'd opened the gate, he'd gone charging out, braying his head off. She'd barely managed to catch him, and even now that he was back in the shed, he was far too skittish to approach, which Annie put down to the weather. It had been trying to storm all day, which always seemed to make the animals edgy.

To make matters even worse, if that was possible, she had managed to walk under the rafter where Queenie roosted, and now her boots were ruined again.

Exercising her small store of profanity, she was wiping the sole off on a patch of dry grass when she glanced up and there he was, sitting up on that sleek red horse of his, looking down his nose at her.

"Where the devil have you been all day?" she demanded.

"North."

"North. Well, that's just fine and dandy! It may interest you to know that Saketa crawled out the bedroom window and ran away again, without even so much as a by-your-leave!"

If she'd thought to get his attention, she surely suc-

ceeded. Never had she seen a face change so swiftly.
His nostrils flared. She could have sworn his cheek-
bones flattened out, and his lips, which on rare occa-
sions would twitch at the corners when he was amused
and didn't want her to know he was amused, thinned
out into a flat, forbidding line.

"How long?" he demanded.

"Since she left? An hour—perhaps a little longer. I'm
not exactly sure just when—"

Before she was done speaking, he was gone. He slid
down off his mare, and while Annie stood gaping at his
back, he raced off toward the house.

She took off after him and had just managed to
scramble up onto the stump when he emerged from
the door again, nearly knocking her off her feet.

"Well, for mercy's sake! You might watch where
you're—"

Ignoring her, he stalked off around the house,
searching the ground, peering underneath as if he half
expected to see the poor girl hiding behind one of the
underpinning poles.

Too worried to be truly angry, Annie plodded right
behind him. When he stopped suddenly, she slammed
into his back. Catching her by the shoulders, he said in
that soft, deadly voice she had almost forgotten, "Someone has been here."

Shaken, Annie couldn't think for a moment. She
stared at his mouth, now so grim and forbidding, trying
not to think about that other time . . . the time when
he . . .

"Who was it?"

She blinked. "Oh. You must mean Mr. Snell. He came looking for Papa."

His eyes moved over her face as if he would read the very thoughts in her head. Then, apparently satisfied, he nodded. "Go inside. Stay. Do nothing."

"But I—"

"Woman, go!"

Totally flummoxed, Annie went. She'd had just about all she could take of men for one day. The creatures had never played any great part in her life except for the fact that one of the species had put her in a school for orphans and then gone off and left her there for the next dozen or so years, while another had been responsible, if only indirectly, for her eventual release.

Now, just as she was beginning to grow accustomed to having one of the blessed things around, he went and turned on her like a rabid animal!

Feeling ill-used, she stood at the window and watched while he prowled around outside, searching the ground. He studied the place where horse tracks mingled with cow tracks, but he lingered longest behind the house, studying the place just underneath the bedroom window. He was moving toward the ridge behind the shed when he stopped suddenly and reversed his path.

Annie snorted. Imagine any man tracking his own sister the way he might track a wild animal!

She was still busy coming to terms with a mixture of indignation, anxiety, and something not so easily definable, when she heard him whistle. Obediently, the rust-colored mare trotted right up to him, just as sweet as you please.

Arrogant, maddening man! Obviously, he expected all females to do his bidding without question. The wonder was that he and Saketa had shared even one parent. Saketa had dressed in calico and muslin. Annie had yet to see T'maho in anything other than buckskin.

Saketa loved the smell of French-milled soap, and admired the silk brocade and dimity and faded chintz of Annie's gowns, while her brother smelled of wood smoke and outdoors, and seemed to despise everything she stood for.

That is, when he wasn't kissing her senseless.

Annie had no way of knowing whether or not a half-brother and -sister would be different in all respects, or as alike as two peas from the same pod. For as long as she could remember, all she'd ever had by way of family was Papa, and she could hardly even recall what he looked like.

Questions with no answers. All she had found on this desolate, far-flung speck of land was one question after another, and not a single answer. "And I'm getting hell-damn tired of it!" she snapped.

Sometime later, unable to settle, Annie paced from room to room, pausing now and again to glance out a window. Dusk had come early, not because it was particularly late, but because of the dark clouds that completely covered most of the sky.

Suppertime came and went. Eventually she made herself a pot of bitter, dark green tea and drank it, breaking off a chunk of bread to go with it. Her beautiful bread. She'd forgotten to salt it, but it was still her best effort yet. Hardly soggy at all.

Maddening man! Hell-damn heathen! Where *was* he? Why didn't he come and tell her what was going on? Why had Saketa run away again, without a word of warning?

If Annie had been inclined to be sensitive—which she wasn't—she might have gotten her feelings hurt. She'd thought they were friends, she and Saketa, even though there were walls of silence between them that had yet to be broached.

T'maho had to have found her by now. Where could a body hide on an island so small one could stand in the middle and see both sides, if not quite both ends?

Outside, the wind picked up, whistling around the corners and through the cracks in the walls. The eerie sound only served to emphasize the emptiness of the two small rooms.

The emptiness of her whole life, Annie thought in a rare mood of self-pity.

Saketa had T'maho. They doubtless had other family, as well. Most of the children at Mrs. B.'s had had someone somewhere, even if it wasn't convenient for them to be together.

Just as she had Papa. Only Papa wasn't here, and she didn't know where he was or when he would be back, and quite suddenly she felt as if she were the only person alive on the entire island.

Which was downright foolish. There was a whole village full of people a few miles away. There was Mr. Gray and his wife, Rachael, and his ox, Paris France.

There was Dulsie Scarborough. There was Mr. Mingo and T'maho and Saketa . . .

Annie sighed. Because she had to do something to keep from thinking about how very lonely she was, she decided to wash her hair. The simple task had always had a comforting effect on her, perhaps because it was one of the few things she could recall her mother doing for her as a child. Washing, brushing, braiding, fussing . . .

Mama, Mama, I got soap in my eyes!

Hush, Anna—here's a rag; hold it over your face. Sheep's wool! Honestly, it snarls up worse than sheep's wool!

She filled the basin from the kettle, added cool water from the pitcher, and used a sliver of French milled soap, bought with her hard-earned sewing money. She had shared it with Saketa, who had loved the delicate scent.

By the time she was done with that, her gown was so wet she peeled it off, tossed it aside, and then proceeded to bathe herself from head to toe, scrubbing her skin ruthlessly all the way up and all the way down under the modest cover of her chemise.

Mrs. B. had sternly warned all her girls of the dangers that lurked in nakedness. And while those dangers had never been specifically described, Annie had never been one to court disaster.

It was there in the kitchen, with her hair dripping all over her damp chemise, that T'maho found her. He came in silence, as always, unannounced. He hadn't meant to startle her. Hesitant, he stared at the vision before him, unable to speak, unable to leave.

Pink flesh glowed through white muslin worn thin as gossamer. Her shoulders were even paler than her face. Pale as the alabaster urn he remembered seeing on a mantel in his father's house. It was all he could do not to touch her, to see if she was as cool as alabaster or as warm as his restless dreams.

How could such a woman affect him the way she did? On a day when it was so hot a man could hardly breathe, she wore a cage strapped tightly about her waist. Her hair was the color of his horse. Her skin was so thin he could see the veins at her temples. He knew any number of dark-haired women with rich, golden skin, who were far more beautiful, and had sense enough not to wear so many clothes.

Swallowing hard, he lowered his gaze to her feet.

Small, naked white feet with pink soles and pink toes, with ankles so delicate he could have ringed them with thumb and forefinger.

He was losing his mind!

"Annie," he said gruffly. The sound of his voice tore at the silence, startling her.

Annie spun about. "T'maho! I didn't hear you come in!"

The earth tilted as she stood frozen, staring. In the wavering light of a single candle, she felt her heart begin to pound. Forgotten was all her loneliness. Forgotten, all her anxieties.

He had come back!

Then, suddenly struck by the realization of her own state of undress, she snatched her apron from the peg on the wall and held it before her. "For mercy's sake, have the decency to turn your back!"

Without comment, he turned away. Annie scooped up the soiled gown she had tossed aside and dragged it on over her wet chemise. Belated concern for Saketa calmed her sufficiently to do up enough buttons and tapes to hold herself together.

"There, now—you can turn around again. Did you find Saketa?"

"I found her." T'maho kept his eyes properly downcast, and Annie had no way of knowing he was staring at the small pink toes that peeped from under the bedraggled hem of her everyday dimity.

Acutely aware of the tapes still undone and buttons yet to be fastened, she adopted an air of calm dignity. "Well, as you're back, I assume she's well. Did she say why she left?"

Lightning lit up the night for an instant. A moment later, a blast of thunder rattled the pot on the hearth.

"She is safe."

Which wasn't precisely what she had asked, but it would have to do, she supposed. If there was one thing she had learned about men in general and T'maho in particular, it was that they did what they pleased, when they pleased, and devil take the hindmost.

Annie had lit a single candle, one of her father's fast-diminishing hoard. The tiny circle of yellow light seemed to add a suffocating degree of intimacy to the small room. With fumbling fingers, she hastily tied on her rumpled apron, needing what scant protection it offered.

Protection against what, she couldn't have said, having finally been convinced that T'maho would never deliberately hurt her.

Not that he was without fault. Proud he certainly was—not to mention stubborn and abrasive. But in spite of her first impression, when he'd been wielding a knife against one of her father's calves and she'd had cause to believe he was about to choke the breath right out of her body—and later, when she'd thought he had done those terrible things to Saketa—she knew he was not a cruel man.

Suddenly the room exploded in cold brilliance. An instant later, thunder slammed against the earth. Annie flinched. Swallowing her nervousness, she said, "Are you quite sure she doesn't need me to come look after her?"

"She is safe."

"Well, of course she's safe, else you'd never have left her. That's not what I—"

Before she could finish, rain struck in a solid, wind-driven wall. The candle flickered and went out. Annie dived for the open door and managed to get it shut while T'maho moved unerringly through the darkness from window to window, pulling in and barring the shutters.

The darkness was thick and smothering.

"Papa keeps a store of friction matches in a tin on the shelf," she said breathlessly, feeling her way across the room. "Not the square tin, but the one on the end."

Tracing her way around the table, she reached out, only to encounter a wall of sleek wet flesh. Startled, she jumped back, striking a chair, which toppled noisily.

A pair of hands closed over her shoulders and she found herself set aside. "Woman, be still," T'maho growled.

"The lucifers are in the—"

"I know where they are kept."

"Yes, but—"

"Quiet!"

"I will not be quiet. This is my—"

He drew her against him. He was wet. "Quiet," he whispered, and this time it was not an order, it was sheer enticement.

It never occurred to her to be frightened, which was almost frightening in itself. She was all alone with a man who, while he might have become a part of her daily life, was nevertheless a stranger. The strangest kind of a stranger.

So why did it feel as if she had finally come home?

The match went unstruck, the candle unlit. T'maho's hands moved over her face, and all she could think of was how good it was to be held in those arms, to breathe the essence of healthy male flesh and rain.

At the warm touch of his breath on her face, she closed her eyes and lifted her face to his. Just as lightning struck again, the last remnant of reason she possessed flickered out like a candle in the wind.

Oh, how she had hungered for this! He was like an addiction—once having tasted his lips, she could never get enough. No wonder Mrs. B. had warned all her girls against the dangers of allowing one's person to be touched by a man!

His arms held her tightly against his lean, hard length so that she could feel the ragged movement of his breath as he lifted his mouth from hers to trail his lips down her throat, to the curve of her shoulder.

A thousand butterflies took flight inside her, and she gasped.

Her bosom tingled. It ached in the strangest way— not painfully at all, but pleasurably. Pressed tightly to his chest, she felt as if there were pebbles between her breast and his, and the pebbles demanded attention.

And then he attended them.

Oh, my mercy!

It was like an itch that needed scratching, yet scratching only made it worse, so she pushed herself against his hands, and he stroked her and she could actually feel herself growing fuller, heavier.

His mouth found hers again. Sweetly, insistently, he explored her with his tongue. It was the strangest sensation she had ever experienced, yet she wanted it to go on and on forever . . .

Only she lacked the strength to stand!

"Oh, my mercy," she breathed when at last he lifted his lips from hers. Her hands, which by then were clinging to his granite-hard forearms, slipped on his wet skin, causing her fingers to brush against his naked sides. Never in her entire life, until she had come to this place, had she seen a man's naked chest.

Or even thought about such a thing!

This man flaunted his nakedness as though it were

the most natural thing in the world. He lived in the wild, hunted for his food, and cooked it over a pit in the ground. They had one thing in common, and that was Saketa, and now that she was gone, they lacked even that.

So why, when he stepped away, did she feel as if an integral part of her own body had been removed?

There was a scratching noise. She smelled the strong fumes of sulfur and blinked as yellow light pushed back the darkness. For a small eternity they stared at one another.

It never happened, Annie told herself. She'd only imagined it. T'maho would no more dream of touching her that way, in that particular place, then she would dream of allowing it.

"Yes, well . . ." She cleared her throat. "I expect Saketa was tired of my poor efforts at cooking," she said lamely, studying the floor, the ceiling, the smoke-blackened hearth.

He said nothing. Neither of them mentioned the fact that T'maho had taken over most of the cooking himself. Outside, the rain continued to drum relentlessly.

"I do believe the storm is moving on," she declared in a voice as brittle as spun sugar.

Thunder continued to rumble. The storm was far from over, and they both knew it. Annie wasn't sure it would ever be over. "I expect you're eager to get back home, in case Saketa worries about your being out in all this rain." She wrapped her arms around herself, shivering in the fresh, cool air that blew through the cracks in the wall.

"Go, please, just go," she said with a sigh of resignation. "Tomorrow, I'll be quite myself again— commonsensical as a cabbage."

T'maho nodded. She wished he would say something. He was probably just as embarrassed as she was, which made it even worse. "T'maho, you mustn't think—that is, I'm sure it was just the storm. Why, even Jacob was not himself today." She laughed, but it was a pathetic effort. "Now I know why people put up all those newfangled lightning rods to capture the dangerous energy in the atmosphere."

T'maho scowled. Oh, dear, now he was going to go all stiff and polite again, the way he invariably did when he wanted to point out their differences.

As if she needed reminding. In a desperate attempt to relieve the tension that sizzled between them, she said, "Did I tell you how skittish Jacob was when I tried to saddle him? He actually kicked the gate open and ran off."

"Licorice would have calmed him quickly enough."

"Yes, well . . . I managed to get him back in without bribing him, and anyway, if Papa had any licorice, the ants will have eaten it by now."

Words. Meaningless words. Annie told herself that what had happened between them could not possibly have taken place. All her life she'd been taught the proper behavior of a young lady. There was nothing the least bit proper in what they had done, and the worst of it was that she had wanted to go on doing it!

T'maho looked as if he wanted to speak, yet he remained silent.

"I expect you'd better go. It's probably going to drizzle all night, and I'm sure you need to—that is, you probably want to—"

Babbling. She was babbling like a two-year-old, and making about as much sense. If he'd suddenly asked her her name, she doubted if she could have told him.

And then, with a look that made her toes curl on the damp, gritty floor, he walked out.

Annie had felt abandoned when her father had left her at Mrs. Biddlecomb's school. She'd felt abandoned all over again when she'd opened the japanned tin on the shelf and come across her own unread letters.

It was nothing to what she felt now.

"She is sleeping now," Mingo said quietly. He had watched T'maho ride in and stepped outside so that they could speak in privacy. The two men had been friends since the day a thirteen-year-old youth named Benjamin had come ashore, angry and bitter and spoiling for a fight.

It had been Mingo, two years older and a decade wiser, who had dragged the young warrior off to cleanse his wounds after he had tackled three bigger boys who had waited for the mail boat to sail, and his father with it, and then told him just what his mother had been before she had died.

"Has she spoken yet? Has she said what frightened her into running away?" T'maho asked now.

The older man shook his head. "She either cannot or will not speak. We cannot force her."

"Damn all, Mingo, when there's a rabid animal on

the loose, a wise man doesn't wait for it to attack a second time, he goes after it!"

"We don't know that he's still on the island. Even so, he will not touch her a second time. She will be well guarded."

"I know, I know."

"Patience, my friend. Hunting by day and guarding by night is hard work. What you need is sleep."

The look T'maho gave him would have blistered paint. Raking his hand through the thick black hair he wore neatly braided, he swore, using a mixture of tongues. Having lived on the mainland for so many years, he had picked up the common trade language called Mobilian, which was mostly Chocktaw with touches of several other tongues. "I forgot to ask Annie if anything had happened that might have caused Saketa to take fright."

"Annie?"

"Eli's daughter. The ginger-hair."

"Ahhh . . . *that* Annie."

T'maho sent his friend another scathing look. He was in no mood for Mingo's notion of a joke. "Has Etawak been a problem?"

"She came twice, once to bring clothes, again to bring one of her potions, which she said was for the healing of womanly parts."

"A potion! You didn't leave her alone with Saketa, did you?"

"I told her Saketa was sleeping and that I'd see that she got the potion as soon as she awoke."

It had been difficult enough to keep the old woman

from revealing Saketa's hiding place when she was miles away, separated from the village by the glade. Now that Saketa was back in the village again it might not be possible. "She left with no trouble? Did anyone see her?"

"No one saw her come. No one saw her go. She left with no trouble, but not until she had knelt on my best shirt to toss her bones and mumble some foolishness about moon tides and maiden skins."

"Laucaumo tumpfeis!"

"Which means?" prompted Mingo with a grin. Unlike T'maho, he had never tried to hold on to the old tongue, much less learn new words.

"Which means she's a crazy old woman, and you're a lazy, worthless *kahaunqoc.*" T'maho, tired and worried though he was, chuckled softly.

"I won't even ask what that is."

"Better to live in ignorance."

Mingo grinned.

T'maho, the fleeting amusement gone as if it had never been, stared unseeing at the neat compound his friend had constructed on a ridge in the edge of an oak grove. "I will speak to Etawak and make certain she stays away. Saketa will be safe only so long as no one knows where she is."

"She'll remain safe here, my friend," Mingo said simply, and T'maho knew that it was so. Wisely or not, Mingo loved Saketa more than any man should love any woman. No harm would come to her while she was in his keeping. "But will you?"

But will you. The gently mocking words followed

T'maho as he rode off through the woods toward his own lodge, which stood some distance apart from all others.

That night for the first time in a long time, he opened the chest and removed an oilskin-covered parcel. There were seven of them, all told. Books his father had given him. Books bought at great expense. Books T'maho had first come to love when his father had read to him before an open fire crackling on a tiled hearth.

He could still recall the feeling of excitement that had come over him when he realized that it was possible to live many lives through the magic of the written word. It was that same fascination that had made him study hard, hungry for knowledge of people who lived in far distant places, people who sailed vast seas in search of new lands, who found strange animals and strange customs and told strange tales of even older civilizations.

Even after he had renounced all his father stood for, T'maho had found it impossible to forget the spells cast by such stories. After a while, when he had grown comfortable once more among his mother's people, he had wanted to share the stories. Mingo had listened politely, but he had not heard the magic. Etawak had called them a wicked spell cast by a white man and warned that if he insisted on dwelling on such things, his brain would soon be as soft as a dead trout left three days in the net.

Saketa had been far too impatient to learn to read, although T'maho had offered to teach her. To please him, she would listen for a little while when she was younger, but her fidgeting would soon make him impatient so that he would send her back out to play.

Once he had become a man, with a man's responsibilities, he seldom found time to read for pleasure. However, now and then when he was troubled, he found that reading was a good way of removing his mind from a problem so that he could view it from another place.

T'maho was troubled. There was the problem of Saketa. There was the problem of Annie. Both women must be guarded until the island was once again a safe place for a woman to move freely.

But most troublesome of all was the problem of his own body and the way it responded to the ginger-hair. The smell of her skin, the sight of her naked feet, watching her small hands at even the simplest of tasks—any one of those could suddenly fill his mind with a kind of craziness that had never before afflicted him.

The last thing he needed now was distraction.

At times, T'maho envied his friend. Mingo had accepted life as it was instead of growing bitter trying to make it into something it could never be. He had accepted white men's ways, wearing their clothes as comfortably as though he'd been swaddled in rags instead of buckskin and moss—sharing their work, eating their food, laughing at their jokes. If it were not for his face and the fact that he had long since given his heart to Saketa, he would have no doubt married one of their women by now.

And been none the worse for it, T'maho was forced to admit. At least, as long as he remained on the island. Life on the Banks was unlike life on the mainland. He had never recognized the difference as a child, but he had soon learned the reality of those differences in his father's home, among those people. He had returned to the island determined never to forget the lessons he had learned there.

Once—he must have been about nine years old at the time, with a penchant for asking unanswerable questions—he had asked his tutor about the people who had lived in this land before the coming of the English, before the Spanish, who had brought the first people from Africa to the eastern shores, and even before the coming of his own people.

He had never received an answer. Perhaps there were no answers. Perhaps he would do better to simply accept the fact that he was neither the one thing nor the other, but a part of two worlds, each of which was only a remnant of other worlds, long forgotten.

Carefully, T'maho wrapped the seven volumes in translucent oilskin and laid them back in the cedar chest in the bed of dried wax myrtle leaves that Etawak swore would keep them safe from all predators for at least a hundred years.

A hundred years from now, who would read his books? Who would wonder about the man who had stored them so carefully, enthralled with the glimpses they gave of other worlds—curious about those worlds even as he told himself he despised them?

In a hundred years, who would know or care that on

this day in the white man's year of eighteen hundred and thirty, one gray-eyed Hattorask fisherman had kissed a small red-haired woman not of his people— had touched her woman's flesh, and had enjoyed the event so greatly that even hours later he was tempted to spill his own seed, something he had not done since he was fifteen.

Chapter 10

Desperate, Snell had finally ended his search just before dark and returned to the *Opal* barely in time to escape the storm. There he'd finished off a bottle of bourbon, then opened another to soothe his nerves, soon falling into a heavy sleep. He woke up drenched in sweat, sun streaming in through the porthole, and pounded on the bulkhead.

A few minutes later, Inacio brought him a pot of strong black coffee, then disappeared to rejoin his worthless shipmate.

Useless pair of pirates! He'd have thrown them overboard long before now, but there were certain advantages to having a crew that spoke little or no English.

Somewhat revived, Snell changed his rumpled clothing and rode off toward the old woman's lodge, determined to discover the truth for himself.

Dammit, she couldn't have survived! Even after he'd beaten her senseless, he had strangled her for good measure. She had been dead when he'd shoved her into the water—or all but dead.

If by some miracle she had managed to survive, she had to be in the old woman's care. He had searched there before, but the wily old bitch had no doubt hidden her in one of her stinking tea-curing casks!

She was not with the Scarborough girl, nor was she with her brother. He had waited until he'd seen T'maho ride off, and then searched the place himself, careful to leave no trace behind.

Some fifty feet away from the old woman's cluttered compound, he dismounted, tied the gelding, and crouched down behind a stand of palmettos, swatting mosquitoes and swearing under his breath.

How could everything have turned sour so fast? He had planned it all so carefully, down to the smallest detail. He had invested years in this venture and now everything was threatening to fall apart!

It had all started with Saketa, the little bitch! None of this would have happened if she hadn't come whining to him in the first place, expecting him to marry her!

If she hadn't gone and gotten herself with child!

As if that weren't enough, he still had O'Neal's girl to deal with once this other business was finished.

However, he was rather looking forward to dealing with such a tender little piece. He had always had a weakness for redheads. Temper and timidity . . .

Snell wiped his mouth with a crumpled handkerchief and swore. Everything was piling on him, and he didn't like to be rushed. If he'd known the old bastard had a daughter, he could have planned it all out ahead of time.

If O'Neal had a will—!

Think, Jackson, think. Knowledge is power.

He was the only one who knew that O'Neal was dead—except for the simpleton who had held him under until he was good and dead while Snell watched to see that it was done properly. And even if the fool talked, who would believe him?

Which meant that if the old sot had left a will, there was plenty of time to find and destroy it. Then he could use his influence to convince the county officials to grant him property rights over the daughter, who was only a woman, after all.

Snell tugged at his cravat and then tore it off. He stuffed it in the pocket of his coat, then wondered why he'd even bothered to wear the bloody thing. Even the heathen Indians knew better than to smother themselves in so many layers of clothing they broke out in a rash!

He had left off his undershirt, and now his shirt stuck to his skin wherever it touched. This damned heat! Not a breath of air to be found anywhere. One would have thought last night's hard rain would have cooled things off. Instead, it had created steam.

As if that weren't bad enough, he'd heard Gil and Inacio talking last night about a tropical storm headed up from the Caribbean. If it weren't for two bloody, stupid females, he'd have already been on his way north to sell his herd and collect his money before the wretched things drowned.

He swore and scratched, and slapped another mosquito. From his vantage point behind the palmetto thicket he watched the old witch come and go about her business. Now and then she glanced over toward where he was hiding, but she couldn't have seen him. Probably half blind from drinking her own filthy brew.

He'd give it another half hour, and if the old bawd didn't give herself away, he would go back and search the glade again. Just to be sure. Still, he supposed even Saketa wasn't dumb enough to go back to the place where he'd left her for dead.

Snell took out a fresh linen handkerchief and blotted his face. To think she'd actually been waiting for him there, in what she'd referred to as "Our Place." Waiting beside that stinking mud hole, behind all that smothering Spanish moss, to tell him her wonderful news.

At least now she knew what he thought of her news.

Dammit, she was supposed to have died! Her body should have sunk in the mud and stayed there until there was nothing left but a few bones! Where *was* she? No one could simply disappear into thin air!

Removing his coat, Snell fanned his damp face with his beaver hat and raked a hand through his pomaded hair, leaving it standing on end, with more than one small insect caught in its sticky strands.

God, he almost wished it would rain again! Not yet midday, and already the air was hot as the hinges of hell.

His stomach rebelled against the harsh black coffee. His head protested the abuse of the night before. He prided himself that he never drank immoderately. A man in his position could ill afford the indulgence—especially now, with so much at stake. It was crucial that he keep his wits about him.

But God, this infernal heat!

Lowering himself stiffly to the ground, he ignored the dampness that seeped through the seat of his fine buff trousers, and tried to formulate a plan. Gradually, the cacophony of bird song seemed to grow more distant as his mind began ticking over his options with the exaggerated precision of a wag-tailed clock.

Why hadn't he taken care of the O'Neal woman while he'd had the chance? It could have been that his unconscious mind had held him back from making a reckless move. Two women turning up missing on the heels of O'Neal's death might have raised awkward questions.

But then, no one yet knew about O'Neal.

Very well, then. Perhaps before the news spread, he would take his pleasure with the redhead, and if there was anything left when he was done, he would arrange her disappearance. Surely he could come up with some clever means of disguising the deed.

A drowning, perhaps? If there was a hurricane on the way up the coast, what could be more reasonable than a drowning?

However, once the news of Eli's death got out, someone might remark on the coincidence of a father and daughter both drowning in separate accidents within weeks of each other.

Besides, if her body was marked, as it undoubtedly would be . . .

He couldn't afford the speculation.

Still, storms had been known to cause stampedes. Even a small electrical storm, such as the one that had pounded the island for a few hours last night. If the girl's poor, broken body happened to be found a few days hence, why, then, who would wonder at a few additional marks? And with that task accomplished, he could concentrate on finding out the truth about Saketa and dealing with her once and for all if she still lived.

Slapping a mosquito that persisted in trying to explore his ear, Snell swore under his breath and slipped away to where he'd left his horse. With so much to accomplish, he couldn't afford to waste another moment. Even if Saketa was here, the old squaw was not about to let him come near her hiding place.

Despite the sweltering heat and the relentless pounding of his head, Snell prided himself that his mind was working with unusual clarity. He assured himself that Saketa could not possibly have survived, and if she had, she could not possibly have talked. Else he'd never have been allowed to set foot on the island.

Of course, even if she'd managed to drag herself out of the pond, it was entirely possible that her wits had been permanently addled when he'd cracked her on the back of her head with the butt of his whip.

Back and forth his thoughts went, back and forth.

He could hear the ticking of a clock, see the pendulum swinging, back and forth, back and forth . . .

Dragging himself up onto the restless gelding, he kicked the beast in the flanks. Stupid, vicious animal! Someone was smoking fish. Someone was *always* smoking fish! In the still air, the rank smoke hung like a pall, turning his stomach. Making him feel as if he were being buried alive. His collar was too tight. He was sweating from every pore in his body, beginning to feel sick in his belly.

Easy, Jackie boy, easy. You can't afford to panic now. Control your emotions and you control the situation.

Even as a small boy living in a household ruled by a despotic father, Jackson Snell had been driven to seek control in the only way he could. A skinny, undersized youth, he had quickly learned the advantage of developing his mind.

Knowledge was power. Knowledge that was not common knowledge was power multiplied a hundredfold if one waited until just the right opportunity to use it.

At an early age, Snell had developed the ability to gain hidden knowledge, and thus the sweetest kind of power of all. Even his own father, who'd been a well-connected appellate court judge, had learned to fear him before he'd died.

Choked on a chicken bone. Or so it had been said.

Think, Snell, think! Just because a few small parts of your plan have shifted, that doesn't mean you have to discard the whole and start over.

Knowledge. Snell knew O'Neal was dead. No one

else on the island did, including the daughter. Which meant that she would have no reason to look for a will or ask awkward questions about his estate.

Still, it would be best to act quickly.

His mind fanned out from there. He would tell her about Eli, and then he could take either one of two options. He could use her and then wring her scrawny neck and dump her body where it would be trampled beyond all recognition . . .

Or he could marry her so that he could use her at will. And so that whatever property she inherited would legally become his, with no questions asked.

Knowledge. What a powerful tool! If the common man had any notion of what power lay in the hands of those with a rudimentary knowledge of the law and a basic understanding of people, every law school in the nation would be overrun.

Saketa's foot ached. Leaning out the window, she arranged her face in what she knew to be her most fetching expression and waited for Mingo to look around at her.

When he didn't, she clapped her hands together. *Why do I have to stay here?* she mimed petulantly.

"Where would you go?"

Oh, how she wished she could talk. Once she truly got her voice back, she would tell him a thing or two! *Anywhere but here!* She formed the words with exaggerated care, feeling more than a little foolish. *I could go stay with Dulsie. At least then I'd have someone to talk to.*

His expression made her draw back inside the window, so angry she wanted to throw something at him.

The big, stubborn ox! He didn't have to make her feel like such a baby—she was a woman, not a child! It was time he started treating her like a woman!

Mingo finished splicing a mooring line that had parted during the recent thunderstorm. Unless he misread the signs, he would soon need every line he could lay his hands on. The next storm would not be so gentle. Even now T'maho was bringing in their nets. The big boat would be anchored out in deeper water away from the shore, a staysail set so that she would ride with the wind. The smaller boat had been dragged up onto high ground and secured. Later on that day, T'maho would see to old Etawak's lodge, storing her precious brewing and curing casks and her chopping trough so they wouldn't wash away in the high tides that always accompanied such a storm.

From the oceanside came a loud report that sounded like cannon fire as another comber cracked against the shore. They came more frequently now, the big ones, coursing over thousands of miles of open sea. Two days at the very outside, he estimated. By morning, the horizon would be filled with small clouds scurrying away from the storm's center. Next the rain would begin, warm and deceptively gentle.

But it was a storm of another kind that was brewing in the village, one that was far more unsettling than the storm that was even now blowing up from the Caribbean. Violence, although not unheard of, was rare on the Banks. Saketa's mysterious disappearance had left the entire village uneasy.

Now yet another rumor was spreading. Eli had been gone far too long with no word. The old man had lived alone, but he had been a part of the community, nevertheless; two or three times a year he had butchered a steer, parceling the meat out among the villagers, who grew heartily sick of fish and fowl, in exchange for food from their gardens and bread from the women's ovens. It was not like him to stay away so long.

Mingo was uneasy. He had sensed the same uneasiness in T'maho. Someone would have to go and fetch Eli's daughter back to the village until the storm passed. It would be better if she stayed close until something was heard from the old man. Or at least until Saketa's attacker was caught and taken away.

He made a mental note to mention it the next time T'maho came by. There was no room in his own house with Saketa there, but the woman would be made welcome in any home in the village.

Finished with the line, he coiled it neatly and hung it on the side of his net shed, then took down another. Saketa poked her head out the window again. This time she held up a basin and sponge and mouthed more words.

She wanted a bath, Mingo interpreted.

"Then bathe," he said.

Scowling, she ducked away and returned a moment later with the kettle. "You want a hot bath? Then heat water."

Pretending to pout, she pointed to her wrist, which he happened to know was nearly healed. "You are too ill to build up the fire? Then perhaps you'd best go back to bed."

I hate you! She threw the sponge at him.

He grinned and ducked. He had known her for too many years to be put off by her ways. The girl was young yet. She was spoiled, which was not entirely her own fault. Both he and T'maho could take some of the blame. After what she'd been through, he didn't regret a moment of it. He would willingly have devoted the rest of his life to making her happy if she would allow it, for spoiled or not, her heart was as true and steady as the North Star.

One day she would give herself to a man—had already done so, to his great sorrow. From the depths of his soul, Mingo envied that man.

Saketa clapped her hands imperiously. *I hate you,* she mouthed again.

"I know you do, little sparrow. I have always known that."

Mingo took down another line and tested it between his two hands, causing his muscles to bunch under the coarse white muslin of his shirt. He could feel her scowling at him, and he turned deliberately so that the watery sunlight fell across his scarred face.

Little sparrow with a broken wing, today I hold you in my hand, but one day soon you'll fly away. I will watch you go, and you will never even look back. Never know all that is in my heart.

* * *

Annie woke up feeling that something was amiss. The air was too still. Queenie hadn't flown up to the kitchen window to announce the rising of the sun. Even the gulls feeding out over the shallows were silent.

It was going to be another sweltering day. Mercy, it had been hot every day she had been here, but today was going to be even worse! The sun had barely even cleared the horizon and already the air was suffocating. Puffy little clouds were just skittering across the horizon, no doubt heading north to a cooler clime.

Tiredly, for she hadn't slept at all well even though she was back in her father's bed now, Annie dragged herself through her morning chores. A handful of cornmeal for Queenie. A forkful of sweet grass for Jacob, who had been meekly awaiting his morning feed outside the shed this morning.

She was learning.

As for the cows, the only ones in sight were bunched up near the ridge except for one small calf that had waded out in the sound to cool off and escape the yellow-eyed flies.

Annie was tempted to do without her tea rather than heat up the house with a fire. But then, like as not, she'd just go through the rest of the day with that unsettled feeling she always had when her mornings didn't start in an orderly fashion.

The truth was, she already felt unsettled. Not to mention uneasy, as though she'd gone to bed the night before and left some important task unfinished.

With a fleeting thought to the man who had, until recently, kept her fire in order and her wood box full, she uncovered the banked coals, added two splits of pine, filled the kettle, and swung the wrought-iron arm over the flames just as the wood caught up.

Then she unwrapped the bread she had baked the day before—had it been only yesterday?—cracked the hard, flat loaf on the edge of the table, and broke off a chunk for breakfast.

She had just finished rinsing out her teacup when Jackson Snell arrived. He hailed her from a distance, which was probably a good thing, for as edgy as she was feeling, she might have greeted him with her father's musket.

"Miss O'Neal! Have I come to call too early?"

"No, sir, I've long been up and about." She waited for him to dismount, noting as he did that he looked as if he'd slept no better than she had.

"This weather is rather distressful, isn't it?" she asked with a forced smile. She hadn't been drilled all her life in common courtesy just to forget it now. "May I offer you something to drink?"

Snell dismounted, looking as if he hadn't bothered to freshen himself since the last time she'd seen him. Not that it would have done much good when it was hot enough to melt a candle without even lighting the wick. "Thank you kindly, Miss O'Neal, but I'm afraid I've come on a sad mission. Are your, um . . . friends still visiting?"

Just in time, Annie remembered what she had told the man. "No—that is, yes, but they're not here at the moment." Was it her imagination, or was that a gleam of satisfaction that flared briefly in his pale blue eyes?

She was almost too distracted to wonder. Something must have happened to Saketa. "Please," she whispered. "You say you have news?" *Please, God, not Saketa and not Papa!*

The justice of the peace removed his hat, fanned his face with it, and then placed it reverently over his chest. "My dear young lady, I'm afraid I come as the bearer of sad tidings."

Annie felt for the doorframe behind her and gripped the rough wood. *Please, God!*

"I'm sadly afraid your dear father, my good friend Eli, has—"

"Papa!"

"—has met with an accident."

"An accident?" Annie jumped down off the stump and grabbed the velvet lapels of his double-breasted clawhammer coat. "Tell me what happened! Is Papa badly hurt? Is he here? You must take me to him immediately!"

He removed her clutching fingers from his coat and smoothed the stand-up collar. "Please, let us go inside, my dear. Perhaps I could pour you a glass of something restorative?"

"No—yes—" Annie pressed her hands to her cheeks. Suddenly she felt cold. "But where is Papa now?"

Snell urged her inside, where she shook her head distractedly at his offer of brandy if she had it, water if she didn't. By the time he had finished imparting the sad news, he prided himself that he was once more back in control.

Of the options available to him, marriage, he decided, would be the simplest and the least likely to give rise to speculation. The sooner it took place, the better. Rubbing his hands in anticipation, he stared at her small mouth. The lower lip, while not overly full, was nicely ripe. And while that hideous rag she was wearing buttoned all the way up to her stubborn little chin didn't exactly hint at a passionate nature, with a redhead, one could never be sure. She was a virgin, of course. He liked virgins. Innocence went hand in hand with fearfulness, and fear could be wildly exhilarating.

She sat perfectly still, staring as if she were dazed. Snell cleared his throat. "I understand the departed was laid to rest on a lovely knoll overlooking the Alligator River. Naturally, my dear, I intend to take you there so that you may pay your last respects."

She continued to stare into space, her face utterly blank, her eyes wide without so much as a single tear. It would not be long before he saw her tears—saw a river of tears. "Of course, if you'd rather, I'm sure arrangements could be made to have his remains moved to—"

"No, no—that is, are you absolutely sure it was Papa?"

Tremors began to course visibly down her small frame and Snell smiled in satisfaction. How sweetly things fell into place when nothing was left to chance. "I'm afraid there was no doubt, my dear Miss—may I call you Annie? Certain documents were found on your father's, er—person. They, um . . . included a letter addressed to me, saying he hoped I would take care of his darling daughter."

"I don't even know what he looks like anymore." Her lower lip trembled and the tip of her nose grew pink.

Snell shifted position on the backless chair and crossed his legs to hide his growing excitement. "Well, now, as to that, my dear, you do understand that after the remains have been in the water for any length of time, especially this time of year, that—"

Slowly, she began to slither to the floor. He leaped up just in time to catch her under her arms, supporting her negligible weight. Excellent, excellent! Now all he had to do was introduce the idea of marriage while she was in this weakened state—call it a marriage of convenience. She didn't have to know whose convenience was being served.

Annie regained consciousness almost immediately, and then the tears came in earnest. She wept noisily, pouring out all the grief, longing, and loneliness that had been locked up inside her for so long. There was no sofa, no chair large enough for two. Rather than soil the knees of his trousers by kneeling on a bare wood floor, Snell continued to hold her in his arms. "Oh, my dear, sweet Annie, you can't know how sorry I am. I promise you that I'll take the very best care of you. Your father wanted it that way, you know."

Annie fumbled for a kerchief and blew her nose, her

own mind too full of regret to pay much attention to the words being spoken.

"We shall be married at once, of course—a small, private affair in light of the, uh . . . sad circumstances. I'll just take a few moments now and go through your dear father's papers to be sure we leave nothing of importance behind, and then we can sail on the tide and be married as quickly as possible." He patted her carelessly on the shoulder, his gaze avidly searching out anyplace where papers might be kept. "There, there, my dear, don't cry so. Come, let's go begin packing for our journey."

He was just leading a tearful Annie into the bedroom, one arm around her waist, her head pressed against his shoulder, when T'maho appeared suddenly in the doorway and froze, as if he'd been stunned by lightning.

Then, with one swift movement, he was across the room, prying Annie from the other man's arms. "What is he doing here?" he demanded fiercely.

Snell seemed to swell up visibly. His face turned dangerously red. "By God, I'll see you hanged for this! When a filthy savage can barge into a decent woman's home and threaten her—"

Ignoring him, T'maho turned to Annie. "Annie? Has he hurt you?"

"Mind your own business, damn you!" Snell shouted.

T'maho turned on him with a look of icy stillness. "Annie is my business."

"Not anymore, she isn't! I promised Eli I'd take care

of her if anything ever happened to him, and I intend to do just that! Now move aside and allow my future bride to pack her belongings so that I can take her away from this wretched, godforsaken place!"

Numbly, as though she hadn't heard a word of the angry exchange, Annie moved closer to T'maho. Staring up at him through tangled, tear-drenched lashes, she said, "T'maho, is Saketa all right? Has she found her voice yet?" And then she simply leaned against him. "Oh, T'maho," she wailed softly, "Papa's dead!"

Chapter 11

Annie?" T'maho held her and stared over her head at the dapper justice of the peace. Annie and this sniveling dog?

"Now, see here—" Snell sputtered.

T'maho's arms tightened painfully around her and Annie stirred and pushed herself away. Seeming to grow in stature before his very eyes, she drew in a deep breath and said again, "T'maho, Papa's dead. Mr. Snell just brought the news. I think . . . I believe . . . if you don't mind, I need to be alone."

"You wish me to go?"

Looking from one man to the other, she nodded. "Please. I—I need time to think."

Snell tried to interrupt, but she held up her hand. "Truly—while I'm honored by your proposal, Mr. Snell, I couldn't possibly—that is, I can't think of anything now except . . ." She swallowed hard. Her small chin wobbled and her back stiffened. "If you please?"

T'maho left first, his head high, his back rigid with displeasure. Watching him leap onto Maroke's back and ride off, Annie wanted nothing more than to call him back and hide in his arms forever.

But that would solve nothing.

Papa . . . oh, Papa. She wept silently.

"Did I hear you mention someone named Saketa?"

Sighing, Annie turned away from the door in time to see Snell loosening his crumpled collar. In this heat, she wondered distractedly why he didn't strip down to the essentials like any man with a grain of common sense. Like T'maho.

"Yes, she's my—that is, she was staying with me until recently. Mr. Snell, while I'm conscious of the great honor you do me, I must ask you to—"

"The girl—I understood she was ill. A fever of some sort?"

"No. That is, she was ill, but her fever—" Annie broke off, tears threatening once more. "Please," she whispered. "Could we speak again tomorrow, perhaps? I . . . I'm afraid I must ask you to leave."

To his credit, Jackson Snell didn't argue. Indeed, Annie thought much later, he seemed almost anxious to go, promising to return on the morrow and finish their discussion.

T'maho galloped into the wind, carrying with him the scent of her in his nostrils, the feel of her on his hands.

Annie and Jackson Snell? His future bride? Something inside him exploded. The fragments drifted down on the air and settled heavily all around him.

There had never been a time since he had come to know her that the hours had hung about them like ripe, sun-warmed grapes on a vine, just waiting to be picked and enjoyed at their leisure. Yet, there had been moments ... Only now, when even those were snatched away, did he realize how he had come to prize each one.

Annie and Jackson Snell. He should have known. They were both of the same background. Snell had been O'Neal's partner. What could be more natural than an arrangement between those two?

He was furious at himself for having ever dared dream—

He had *not* dreamed, he had only lusted! She had come into his arms willingly enough—he had not imagined her response, unpracticed though it was.

Annie and Jackson Snell. *Boketawgh attomoy!*

T'maho rode as if the devil were on his heels, rode hard to escape the vision of Snell's pale, stubby-fingered hands touching Annie's body, combing through the living fire of her hair. He was more than halfway to the glade before he realized that he was being followed. Recognizing the big yellow gelding, he swore, more from bitterness than anger.

Did the fool think he needed T'maho's permission to pay court to O'Neal's daughter?

The woman was nothing to him.

Perhaps Snell was riding out to hire Jackariah's ox-cart to haul Annie's belongings to the *Black Opal*. Now that O'Neal was dead, his daughter would have no reason to remain on the island. What other reason could she possibly have? he asked himself bitterly.

O'Neal was dead. She had said so. Snell had no

business leaving her alone in her grief, even for so short a time. T'maho told himself that if she'd been his woman—his to comfort, his to hold—he would never have left her in tears.

Unbidden, he saw again those drowning eyes, that small, pink-tipped nose. Heard again the anguish in her voice when she'd cried out, "Oh, T'maho, Papa's dead!"

And then he thought about what else she had said. Was it only his imagination, or had Snell grown strangely still when Annie had blurted out Saketa's name?

But how could that be? Saketa was nothing to him. As far as T'maho knew, Snell had never even met his sister. The man came and did his business and left.

But now that T'maho thought about it, the *Black Opal* had been tied up at the docks for the past few days. Had Annie told him about the attempt on Saketa's life? If so, in his capacity as justice of the peace, he might feel the need to inquire—might even feel the need to offer his aid in bringing the scoundrel to earth.

A grim smile touched T'maho's lips. Snell could keep his white man's law, with its convoluted twists and turns, designed to thwart justice more often than not. The law of the Hattorask was both swift and efficient.

In all probability the man was not following him at all, only returning to the village by the shortest route. There was one way of finding out, T'maho told himself, a grim smile lighting his eyes.

Abruptly, he veered from the trail toward a deer run that cut into the glade some distance to the west.

A furlong behind him, Snell turned his gelding westward.

Deliberately, T'maho slowed Maroke to a walk.

Easing his pace, Snell maintained the distance between them, and T'maho's eyes narrowed. The man followed, yet he did not approach when given the chance?

Strange . . .

T'maho had never spoken more than a dozen words to Jackson Snell. If he disliked the man, it was on principle, because he disliked what Snell stood for, not for any personal reason. Yet every atavistic sense he possessed now whispered a warning.

Recalling the tableau that had presented itself in Eli's house, he sorted over the pieces, one by one.

"Is Saketa all right? Has she found her voice yet?"

Snell had grown still at her words. Had his face actually grown even paler, or had it always been that yellowish, pasty color?

And what about those faint red marks on the side of his face that disappeared under his collar?

T'maho's body tensed, causing the mare to shy. Without thinking, he laid a hand on her withers, telling himself it could not be true. Just because he despised a man, that didn't make the man a villain. Snell had been known to the villagers for years.

Yet something was setting T'maho's nerves on edge. Something more than seeing Annie in another man's arms. On the day Saketa had escaped from Annie's house, he had found the tracks of a large horse outside. He knew the tracks of Mingo's workhorse and the gelding he rode when he wanted to show off. He knew Jacob's tracks, and those of Saketa's pony.

Snell's borrowed gelding?

If the man was following now with the hope that T'maho would lead him to Saketa, there could be two possible reasons. Either he wished to question her, or he wished to silence her.

If he wished to question her, T'maho reasoned, he would have no cause to hang back. If, on the other hand, he wished to silence her, there could be but one reason.

Despite the sultry heat, T'maho felt a chill rake down his flanks. Touching the steel blade that was never far from his side, he eased Maroke into a smooth canter, forcing himself not to look over his shoulder.

He would allow the quarry to stalk the hunter. If in doing so the scoundrel came to believe that he was the hunter instead of the hunted, he would quickly learn to his sorrow that he was no match for Tatamaho of the Hattorask.

An honorable hunter does not kill without cause. Where is your proof? The words crept into his mind unbidden, and he scowled. He needed no proof! Manito, the great unseen, had planted the seed of truth in all men. A wise man had only to heed his inner voice.

And then, as if he were a lost youth trying desperately to learn all there was to learn so that he could please his father and fit into a world that was not his own, T'maho heard another voice. His tutor's voice, echoing in the schoolroom on the third floor of the Hamilton residence on River Street. "A man is deemed to be innocent until proved guilty. That, young Benjamin, is the cornerstone of our system of laws. Suspicion without evidence is not enough to convict any man."

Under a hazy sun, the bay mare picked her way daintily along the narrow deer run while T'maho struggled to throw off the burden of knowledge of the white man's law. In the end it was caution and not fairness that won out.

He could wait. He would lead the black-hearted devil deep into the glade and leave him to wallow in his own sour sweat for a few hours. With a storm in the offing, the man would not dare sail even if he found his way free.

Then he would go to Saketa and discover the truth, and this time her stubbornness would not help her. This time he had a name to put before her. He had only to watch her eyes as he spoke Snell's name and he would know, for over the years he had learned to judge the amount of truth in her words by the degree of guilt in her eyes.

It took little more than a quarter of an hour to lead the fool deeply into a tangle of jungle growth so dense that it would be days before he could find his way out. Leaving him there to blunder around in swamps and cat-claw briars, T'maho swiftly cut across the deer run, across three muskrat slides, skirting Burnt Stump Pond and Palmetto Swamp and jumping Cecil's Creek, where he met up with the main glade trail again.

But then, instead of turning south toward the village

as he had intended, he abruptly wheeled his mare to the right and headed north.

Eli was dead. In his unexpected rage over seeing Annie in Snell's arms, T'maho had not considered her condition. The old man was dead, leaving his daughter helpless before the coming storm. Helpless and at the mercy of any scoundrel who happened upon her.

In all good conscience, T'maho knew he could not leave her there alone. He would take her to the village—to Scarborough, or Gray, or even to Etawak.

After that he would be free to go first to Saketa and then, if his suspicions proved correct, to Snell.

Recognizing the lone rider in the distance, Annie turned away from the window, her heart leaping about like a caged canary. She blew her nose and dried the last of her tears. By the time she heard Jacob's bray and Maroke's answering whicker, she had recovered a good part of her composure.

Papa was dead. Only now did she dare admit that for days she had felt in her bones that something was wrong. "Oh, Papa, Papa, how could you go and get yourself drowned, just when everything was going to be so wonderful?"

In truth, she had hardly known him, for the older she'd grown and the more she had learned of reading and writing, the more unsatisfactory his rare letters had become. Like a child's squiggly bread-and-butter notes: "How are you? I am well. The wether holds fine. Two cavs was borned the day before yestiddy. Your father, Elias Jos. O'Neal."

Hardly enlightening, and yet she'd never stopped loving him—at least, loving the man she remembered dimly from her childhood. But it was not of her father that Annie was thinking as she wandered to the doorway and watched the approaching horseman silhouetted against the calm, silvered surface of the Pamlico Sound.

Was T'maho still angry with her? It was surely not the first time, yet this time was different. To her everlasting shame, though she had sent him away, his going had left her feeling even more bereft than the news of her father's death.

Which was purely nonsense. They were friends, no more. He was the brother of a girl she had cared for. He had befriended her on Saketa's account and for no other reason. So he had kissed her once or twice. He had meant nothing—it had simply happened, and besides—

"Well, just besides, that's all," she muttered. Sniffing one last time, she watched Maroke twitch her ears at Jacob, watched T'maho slide off the mare and stalk toward the house without once taking those cool, gray eyes from her face.

"Did you forget something, sir?" she asked when he came within range. She vowed to be polite if it killed her. Not for the world would she let him know how she longed to hurl herself into his arms and pour out all her sorrows and fears.

She had asked him about Saketa and where she was and how she was, and for the first time it occurred to her that he hadn't even answered.

But then Jackson Snell had been there, and she'd just learned about Papa, and nothing had made sense. Snell had left soon after T'maho had ridden off, and since then, Annie had done little but weep and stare at the only thing she had left of her father—the house he had built.

She stood in the doorway, steeling herself against weakening. T'maho leaped up onto the stump, and she stepped back, wishing she weren't so aware of the familiar musky, smoky scent of his body. "I told you, I wish to be left alone," she said firmly. Stealing a glance at his face, she saw that his silvery eyes had gone the color of pewter, which meant he was angry.

"I don't trust Snell. Stay away from him."

Annie's mouth fell open. Well! If she had expected anything at all—and she certainly had not—it would be a word of sympathy, or at the very least, some news of Saketa. Lifting her chin, she said with a dignity all out of proportion to her circumstances, "Mr. Snell was my father's business partner. What's more, he's a gentleman, and he happens to be a justice of the peace."

"You cannot stay here alone."

"I most certainly can and will!" she declared. Had she needed something to put starch in her backbone, she could have found nothing better than such an ultimatum.

"There will be a storm."

"Pooey on your storm!"

The corner of his mouth twitched, and Annie forced herself to concede the man his due. It was quite true that from the very first time she had laid eyes on him, he had by turns terrified, humiliated, and infuriated her, and turned her knees to jelly. He had also looked after her as well as he had his own sister. She might have starved by now; yet he had not only brought her food, but prepared it, as well.

Reluctantly, she admitted that she probably owed him an apology.

But then, he owed her one, too, and neither was likely to be forthcoming. "Yes, well . . ." she reminded herself, " 'Prudent, cautious self-control is wisdom's root.' "

T'maho stared at her as if she'd lost her wits. "Wisdom's what?"

"It's something a man named Pope once wrote. I did it in cross-stitch. Perhaps we'd both do well to heed his words."

"Pope's Second Moral Essay. I know. I had only to memorize the phrase." Catching himself with a scowl, T'maho said, "Damn all, Annie, a storm is on the way! You cannot stay here alone."

He knew Pope? He couldn't. Indians didn't read philosophy . . . did they? "I told you, T'maho, I'm perfectly capable of looking after myself. It stormed last night, if you'll recall, and I came through unscathed."

Mercy, she had to go and remind him of *that*!

T'maho lifted his eyes heavenward. Did the little fool think she was any match for the kind of storms that regularly swept the island, carrying off all that wasn't battened down and much that was?

"This time there will be higher tides and stronger wind than you have ever seen. Take whatever you wish to keep safe. Jacob will carry your baggage. Maroke will carry us both."

"I have no intention of—"

"I will not argue with you, woman."

"And I'll not leave my father's house!" Blasted tears, if they betrayed her now she would never forgive herself! It was simply that too much had happened too quickly. She was overwrought. "T'maho, Papa's dead, can't you understand? This is all I have left—his house, his cattle. If there's going to be a big storm, I can't just walk off and leave it all to be washed away."

T'maho opened his mouth to warn her about another kind of danger, but the words wouldn't come. In his heart, he knew Snell was guilty, but lacking evidence, he would not lower himself to blacken the man's reputation. Snell would keep. The man would not escape the island even if he should find his way out of the glade.

"Annie, the house will stand or fall whether you stay or go. There is nothing you can do here."

"But what about the cows? What about Queenie?"

T'maho tried to recall the exercise in patience he used to have to perform whenever he chafed at being trapped in the schoolroom when he wished to be outdoors running in the woods. *Five, ten, fifteen, twenty—* "If I can catch that damned rooster, you can take him with you, but the herd will have to fend for itself. A few head will drown. Most will come through safely. There's nothing—"

"What rooster?"

"The one you call Queenie! Now will you please go

pack your belongings so that I can get you stowed away before the creeks rise any higher?"

Never had anyone gotten under his skin the way this woman did! The most irritating thing about her was that he could not be in her presence for more than a few minutes before he found himself reverting to his early years.

Thinking white.

Even sounding white!

Annie quivered with indignation as T'maho towered over her, glowering in self-defense. "You might have had the courtesy to tell me Queenie was a rooster before I wasted all that time trying to find her—his nest."

Lifting his eyes to see the smoke-darkened ceiling, he spread his hands helplessly. "Annie, if you wish to take anything at all with you, go tie it into a bundle that will fit on Jacob's back. I'll lift your trunk onto the bed so that when the tide comes inside, what's in it won't be ruined." If there was anything left standing when the waters went down again.

"But I told you—"

"And I told you, woman!" T'maho roared. He hadn't lost his temper in more years than he could remember. Grabbing her by the shoulders, he turned her toward the bedroom and gave her a shove that was not altogether gentle. Annie caught herself before she could stumble. She cast him a blistering look.

It was then that they heard the sounds of distress coming clearly through the open window.

It was a calf, and the thing was obviously in trouble.

"You stay here and prepare to leave," he told her. "I'll see what's afoot."

But Annie wasn't about to leave one of her papa's precious calves to the mercy of a man who had told her flat out that some of them would be lost to the storm. It wasn't storming yet, it was only raining—hardly more than a heavy, blowing mist.

And from the sound of it, that poor baby was in grave danger.

"Wait for me!" she cried, holding her skirt and leaping off the stump. Shoving her hair back from her face, she ran toward the edge of the water and squinted through the fine rain. Some distance out from the shore, she could see a small black and white calf. It appeared to be struggling, as if its foot was caught in a trap.

T'maho waded swiftly through the thigh-deep water, trailing a wake behind his buckskin-clad limbs. "What happened?" Annie called after him. "Did something bite him?"

"Mud!" Slowing, he approached the frantic animal cautiously. "Dammit, Annie, go back to the house! There's nothing you can do here!"

Disregarding the damage to her one good pair of shoes, Annie waded out ankle deep and then halted uncertainly. Why was T'maho yelling at her? It wasn't her fault the poor creature had gotten himself stuck in the mud. It wasn't her fault another storm was coming. She certainly hadn't asked him to come back and look after her!

She was on the point of telling him so when a tremendous commotion took place. The calf floundered, splashed, and bawled piteously.

T'maho splashed, swore, and fell back.

From somewhere behind her on the shore, a large black and white cow came charging down from the ridge, bellowing insistently. Annie barely got out of the way in time. The calf came bounding frantically ashore, and she lunged to catch it, but it rolled its eyes and dashed right past her.

"Oh, fine! Now you worry," Annie called after the delinquent mother. On the point of turning away, she glanced out to where T'maho was bent over, his face nearly touching the water. He seemed to be contorted into an awkward position, but when she called out to him, he only shook his head and groaned.

"T'maho, what's wrong? Are you stuck in the mud?"

He turned his back to her, his head still lowered, both arms extending under the surface of the water.

Suddenly Annie was alarmed. Something was wrong. "T'maho! Answer me! Are you hurt?"

She thought the words he flung back must be profanity in another tongue. They had that feeling about them. "If you're not stuck in the mud, then tell me what's wrong! Did you cut yourself on a sharp shell? Is that it?"

No response. His shoulders bowed, he seemed to be swaying rhythmically, submerged up to his armpits while the rain came down harder than ever. Already soaked clean through, Annie took matters into her own hands. Hiking her skirts up about her hips, she waded out, shoes and all, fearful of what she would find. Dear

Lord, if anything happened to T'maho, what could she do? She couldn't bear it if he was hurt!

Nearing where he still knelt in the shallow water, she slowed. He was mumbling.

No, he was groaning.

Or was he cursing?

He seemed to be on his knees, clutching his hands before him under the water. Perhaps the calf had trod on his fingers. "T'maho? Please tell me what's wrong."

The look he turned on her then was pure savage. His eyes were red-rimmed from salt, his lips a thin, harsh line, and there was a streak of black mud across one cheek. "Leave—me—alone!"

Stunned at the harshness of his tone, Annie scrambled backward and nearly fell. "But you're hurt," she said, regaining her courage along with her balance. "I can tell that much, for mercy's sake, so you might as well not play brave soldier. Just tell me where you hurt and we'll go back to the house and I'll bind it up for you."

And then he began to laugh. It occurred to Annie fleetingly that she had never heard him laugh before.

Nor was it a sound she cared to hear again. There was certainly little amusement in it.

He got to his feet. He was swaying slightly, still bent over at the waist, and she waded forward and moved in beside him, positioning herself under his arm so that he could lean on her if he wished to. "Come along, now. No matter how many fingers were stepped on, it won't do you a speck of good to stay out here in all this rain and catch your death of cold."

Grimacing at the absurdity of the situation, T'maho allowed himself to be helped ashore, half led and half supported. The sickening agony in his groin was somewhat diminished. It had been a glancing blow, which was fortunate. Even so, the small, sharp-edged hoof could have inflicted lethal damage to that part of him which was most supremely sensitive.

"There, now, let me see," Annie cajoled as they reached high ground. Hands on her hips, she looked him over. "Which hand was it?"

He shook his head.

"Well, was it your foot? One of your, uh . . . limbs?"

Still aching, torn between anger and amusement, he said, "Not my limb, woman—my root."

Annie stepped closer, her sodden gown clinging to her body, and bent forward as if expecting to see taproots sprouting through the knees of his wet buckskins. "Your what?"

The wind picked up suddenly, blowing a sheet of rain in his face. Nearby, the calf bawled again, and quite suddenly T'maho had had all he could take in one day. Snatching her upright, he yelled into her face, "My root, woman! That part that makes me a man! It hurts like the bowels of hell, and if you ask one more stupid question, I'll lift your scalp and use it to bind up my wound!"

Annie was inexperienced; she was not stupid. In a face that was unnaturally white, her cheeks suddenly blazed like hot coals. Tearing herself from his grasp, she lifted her ruined skirts and marched awkwardly, head held high, through the wet sand. Scrambling up onto the stump, she hurled herself into the house, her heart pounding like a marching parade.

What on earth had happened to the T'maho she had come to know and—

Well, to know, at least.

How could she have forgotten those early days, when she had believed him capable of doing all sorts of wickedness? Perhaps her instincts had not been so far off course, after all. What did she know of men? Particularly men of T'maho's stamp?

Peering around the door, she saw him coming toward her in that odd, lurching walk. Suddenly Annie had taken quite all she could. From the day she had set foot on this hell-damned island, everything had gone wrong! All in the world she wanted at this moment was to be left alone to try to sort it all out.

And if the wind wanted to blow her away and the tide wanted to wash her out to sea—well, just let them try it!

By the time T'maho approached the house, Annie was shaking, but quite firm in her decision. This had been Papa's house. It was now hers, and here she would remain, until *she* decided to leave.

T'maho leaped up onto the stump, and she reached for the only available security. Her father's old musket. She would never dream of using the thing even if she knew how, but at least it would lend authority to her words.

"Don't you come one step closer," she warned through the cracked door. She saw him staring in her direction, saw one hand clasping his privities under those wet, clinging buckskins. Dear God, he wouldn't!

T'maho didn't much care for the feeling of being in the wrong, but pride would not allow him to shirk his duty. He owed her an apology. The woman had only tried to help. Was it his fault she had no more knowledge of men than she had of chickens? Or cattle?

He would apologize, although it went against the grain, and then he would see to removing her to the village so that he could forget her and get on with more important matters.

"All right, woman, you—"

"Go away."

"Hear me out, for I've little patience left!"

"I've heard all I want to hear from you, so please leave me alone."

"Dammit, woman!"

Just as he lunged, the world exploded over his head. He felt a gust of wind and a light peppering, like blowing sand, against his scalp as he fell backward off the stump.

Chapter 12

Annie sailed out the doorway, barely grazing the stump, and landed on her hands and knees in the wet sand beside the prone figure. Against the wail of the wind and the muted drone of rain, she began to voice a litany of protest. "Oh, no, no, no—oh, please, God, no!"

He was dead. She had killed him. In a flash, all his unexpected kindnesses, the small intimacies, and the rare moments of shared understanding came rushing back, and she moaned. He was dead and it was all her fault, and now she would never again be stricken by the sweet paralysis of being held and kissed by such a man. Never share the laughter that was not quite laughter, but only a sparkling of the eyes.

She had murdered him, and the shameful selfishness of her reaction never even occurred to her. Hesitantly, she reached out and touched the hard wet silk of his shoulder. He was still warm. She searched the ground around his dark tangle of hair for a sign of seeping blood.

"Oh, please ..." she whispered brokenly. "I didn't

mean to do it. T'maho, I would never hurt you, please, please believe me!"

The man lay facedown. Hesitantly, she touched his back. Merciful heaven, she had killed him.

The thought of what his face—his beautiful, gray-eyed face—must look like now brought a fresh round of tears, and Annie, sick with regret, with the horror of what she had done, swayed forward on her knees. Her face settled onto the small of his back. With one hand braced on the sand, the other curved of its own accord over the hard swell of his buttocks, she wept and gulped apologies and then wept some more.

"Oh, p-p-poor Saketa!" she choked. Her tears, mingling with the rain, mingling with the salt water of the Pamlico, trickled down the valley of his spine to disappear under the edge of his sodden buckskins. "How can I ever t-tell her I've murdered her brother when she's already been through s-so m-m-much?" She sniffled and wiped her nose on his cold, leather-clad behind. "I never truly disliked you, T'maho, I didn't. Not even when I thought you the one—and even then, once I came to know you, you were so—and I— Oh, T'maho, wake up, please—*please*, wake up!" The squeaky thread of sound was barely audible above the rising roar of the nearby surf. Clutching a fistful of slick, wet buckskin, Annie wailed afresh. "T'maho, please don't be dead! I don't think I can stand it if you're dead, too!"

But T'maho was not yet quite dead. In fact, he was no more than stunned by the impact of the explosion; the powder had clearly remained dry enough, but the rice Eli had used instead of rock salt, which would have melted, had long since softened in the constant humidity.

True, his head throbbed alarmingly, but the ache in his nether regions was fast being replaced by a rousing interest. If the woman didn't quit stroking his ass with her chin and muttering those tantalizing phrases, she was going to see just how quickly the dead could rise again.

With a noisy sob, she crawled around to kneel at his shoulders. Cupping him under the arms, she began to tug. Curious to discover her intent, T'maho remained a dead weight. "Come—*on!*" she grunted. "I can't let your poor—beautiful body—lie out here in the—rain a—moment longer! You'll catch your—*death!*" The words were punctuated by grunts, pants, and tugs that threatened to remove his shoulder bone from its socket, and then she burst into fresh wails.

For someone so small, she was surprisingly strong. One would have thought she'd been moving bodies all her life. T'maho would willingly have made her task easier, but he had fallen in a nest of sandspurs. The pesky things were everywhere. Each slight movement brought fresh pain, and that was the very least of his worries.

"Oh, mercy, I'll just have to go find Mingo," she cried, falling back on her rump. Awkwardly, she stood, her ridiculous, ruined shoes with their pointed toes and tiny heels nearly touching his shoulders. Without stopping to think, T'maho snaked out a hand and caught her by the ankle, toppling her onto her backside again.

Before she could react, he rolled over and knelt astride her thighs, his hands braced on either side of her terrified face.

"Oh! But you're not dead!" she gasped.

Rain was pounding down steadily now. The wind had taken on an unpleasant whining note as it flattened the beach grass and whipped at the scraggly shrubbery. Evidently, his weather sense was not quite so perfect as he had thought. He had misjudged the timing of the storm by several hours.

He had misjudged more than that, T'maho thought with wry amusement, not the least of which was this small, prickly woman. "Since I awoke this day I have ridden miles on a fool's errand. I have been cursed, I have been kicked, I have been shot at. I have at least a dozen sandspurs digging into my carcass at this moment, and next, you'll probably offer to feed me, which will finally put an end to my miserable existence."

"Feed you?" Annie repeated numbly, still dazed at finding him alive. Feeding him was the last thing on her mind. To save her life, she could not have said what the first thing was—she only knew that never had she felt quite so vulnerable, not even when she'd thought she was sharing her house with a murderer and his intended victim. "I'm s-s-so sorry," she whispered.

Despite the surface coolness of his skin, the warmth of the man reached out to envelope her. She breathed deeply, savoring the scent of him, which had moved her in the strangest way right from the very first.

With one finger, T'maho traced the rim of narrow lace that edged the scoop neck of her ruined gown, and she shivered, her eyes never once leaving his. All around them, the early stages of the hurricane raged—the surf had already breached the dunes. Yet neither was aware of the storm. Only of another storm, one even more compelling. A storm that swept them into its vortex and held them captive there.

Without another word, T'maho leap to his feet and swung Annie up in his arms. "The tide is rising too swiftly," he muttered.

Annie's breath was coming too swiftly. Her head was reeling. He really had no business carrying her—he had been injured—yet she felt weak as rainwater. If he'd set her on her feet, she would have likely collapsed.

She was burningly aware of every place where he touched her—his arm under her knees, his other arm at her back, her shoulder against his, and her cheek tucked into the curve of his neck.

She drew in a deep, shuddering breath, which only made it worse. The very scent of his skin had become a part of her being, yet it still wasn't enough—it only made her hungry to know more of him.

Frantically, Annie rifled her memory for something that would account for the phenomenon. Mrs. Biddlecomb had said that under certain circumstances, boys and girls—that is, men and women—that is, the male and female of a species . . .

Oh, dear!

T'maho leaped up onto the stump and thrust Annie through the door. Before she had quite recovered herself, he said tersely, "Close the shutters!"

"Where are you going? You can't leave now. You're hurt!"

But he was already gone. Dazed, Annie wandered through the two rooms, reaching out to pull in the crude shutters and drop the bars into place. Rain dripped steadily through various leaks in the roof. Wind whistled around the corners and through the cracks.

Out in the shed, Jacob brayed piteously, and for a single moment, Annie almost forgot T'maho in her worry over her father's livestock. Some would survive, some would be lost, he'd said. There was nothing she could do about it. She offered a brief, distracted prayer for the calves, even for the miserable little devil who had stuck itself in the mud and then attacked its rescuer.

Where was T'maho? Had he truly left her here alone? She'd told him to go, but somehow, she hadn't really expected him to take her at her word.

Oh, she didn't know what she expected! Didn't even know what she wanted!

Oh, yes, she did. She wanted T'maho. She might not know precisely what that wanting implied, but she did know that the world would not start turning again until he came through that doorway.

And then the world began turning again.

"I thought you'd gone home," she said breathlessly.

"Too late. Foolish woman, you delayed us too long, and now the tide covers too much of the land."

For some reason, his words hurt her feelings. Annie blamed the storm for her increased sensitivity. She had never been a sensitive blossom, folding her petals at the least sign of conflict, but there was a limit to what even the strongest soul could bear.

She stood, shoulders slumped, in the preternatural darkness. Seeing the spirit leach out of her, T'maho knew a moment of regret for his part in her troubles. He had brought Saketa to her, thus weaving her into their lives as surely as his namesake, the garfish, could weave itself into a gill net.

Snell was another matter. He spared a moment of thought for the man he had lured deep into the glade. Guilty or not, his fine feathers would be ruined by the rain. He would be frightened, perhaps, but there was high ground nearby. There were trees to climb. Unless he panicked and stumbled into one of the deeper ponds, he would not drown.

What was it the white men had said about witches some two hundred years ago? If they were guilty, they would float. If they were innocent, they would drown.

A look of wry amusement touched his face and was as quickly gone.

Peering through a crack in the shutters, Annie stared at the wild, gray world outside. "I should have brought in more firewood before it started to rain."

Without a word, T'maho turned and left. Shortly after that, splits of pine and oak began to appear in the doorway, three and four at a time. They were wet on two sides, dry otherwise, from being stacked just so. As T'maho shoved them through the doorway, Annie carried them across the kitchen and stacked them, wet side out, near the fireplace, praying she could stir up the banked coals left over from morning.

A sense of urgency quickly replaced her earlier uncertainty, and when the wood ceased appearing, she set about putting containers under the worst of the leaks. Outside, T'maho was leading Jacob and Maroke into the deepest shelter of the shed, and she prayed the thing would not blow down. The wind was incredibly noisy. There was no sign at all of Queenie, poor thing. She—he—it had probably blown away by now.

Last of all, T'maho filled the pitcher and kettle from the rain barrel, which was already overflowing. Annie waited to see what needed doing next. She had experienced electrical storms and snowstorms, and once a whirlwind had twisted off several trees and lifted the roof off an outbuilding at the school, but this kind of storm was entirely outside her experience. Already the water had risen to within a few yards of the house, covering the very ground where T'maho had fallen only a short while ago.

How high would it come? Would the ocean waves soon be breaking against the walls? Could any building stand against such a force?

Oddly enough, Annie realized she was not frightened. Curious, perhaps—even exhilarated in an odd sort of way. The tension that sizzled in the air, making her skin prickle whenever T'maho came into the room, she set down to the storm because she had to set it down to something, and the alternative was simply unthinkable.

At last, when there was no more that could be done, he came and stood before her. She had lit a candle, one of the stinking tallow ones, and now she stared up at him like a bird in thrall to a blacksnake. Waiting for the inevitable.

Slowly, his eyes never once leaving her face, T'maho slid the long knife from the leather loop at his waist. He lifted it so that the candlelight glittered on the freshly sharpened edge, and mesmerized, Annie stood before him, her lips slightly parted, her heart fluttering so she could hardly breathe.

"Sandspurs," he muttered, his voice a soft growl that raised gooseflesh along her flanks.

He gathered up a handful of hair, wet now, tangled by the wind, and curling wildly about her face. While she stared at him, seeing the small red places where rice had peppered his forehead, the mud that still clung to one eyebrow and the thicket of short black lashes that surrounded those startlingly pale eyes, T'maho carefully cut a cluster of sandspurs from her hair and another from the hem of her apron. She hadn't even known they were there.

He picked several of the pesky things from his buckskins, two from his own hair, and then slid the knife back in its loop.

And then he began to smooth her hair back from her face, pausing to stroke a damp curl over his forefinger, while Annie, as though the hair were not her own, gazed down at his hand.

It had never before occurred to her that hands could be so different. Four fingers. A thumb. Hands were hands. Yet she had particularly noticed that Snell's fingers were thick and pudgy, his bulbous thumbs oddly

repellent. By contrast, T'maho's hands were beautifully
formed, his palms square, his fingers long and straight.

When those strong, beautifully formed hands clasped
the sides of her head and tilted it back, she accepted it
as the most natural thing in the world.

There was a sense of inevitability about what followed. She lifted her lips to his with an eagerness it
never occurred to her to deny. Soft, warm, moist, and
trembling, she pressed her mouth to his. He touched
her only there—his hands on the sides of her face, his
mouth firm against her own—yet she could feel the
heat of his body reaching out to envelope her. The
spicy scent of wood smoke and musk, of rain and salt
water and mud, mingled with the sharp scent of the
tallow candle into an ambience that was both soothing
and exhilarating, both rare and familiar.

And then his hands left her face. His arms closed
around her, and with a groan that touched the very
depths of her soul, he crushed her against his hard
length. Twisting his face against hers, he forced her lips
apart, sacrificing the sweetness of her untutored ac-
ceptance for the even greater sweetness of her passion.

Annie felt a hard ridge pressing against her belly.
The handle of his knife? Then it moved, but before she
could wonder at that, she began to wonder at the
strange sensations that raced through her own body,
settling in those private parts that no lady ever thought
about, much less referred to aloud. How could she?
Such parts didn't even have a name.

Low in her belly and lower still, she felt dizzy.

Her knees felt dizzy.

But dizziness was an affliction of the brain . . .
wasn't it?

Something hot and wet and slick slipped between
her parted lips. She had felt it before, but this time, instead of merely teasing her lips, it began to thrust
deeply into her mouth. She clutched his naked shoulders, her eyes widening in the near darkness.

He lifted his head imperceptibly. "Shhhh, do not be
afraid, little ginger. Let me taste you. Know that I
would never hurt you."

And then he did it to her again.

Dazed, Annie sucked experimentally on his tongue
and found it above all things pleasing. She heard him
gasp, felt that strange poking thing against her skirt,
and twisted her hips in an effort to relieve the odd tension that was rapidly gathering there.

"T'maho, something's wrong with me. I don't understand—"

"Nothing is wrong with you, sweet ginger-hair." He
sighed. Reluctantly lifting his face, he tucked the top of
her head under his chin and stared, unseeing, at the
guttering candle. His swollen man-flesh still ached
from his earlier injury, but he ached even more with
the need to bury himself in this woman and ride her
until they both collapsed with pleasure.

She didn't understand. God help him, he understood
only too well. If she were anyone else, he would not
stop now, for he knew as well as he knew his own
name that at this moment, she was his for the taking.
He wanted her as he had never before wanted any

woman, and it was that knowledge that made him uneasy.

When this storm was over, he told himself, the tide would return to its own place and he would return to his. And when the mail boat came again, she would return to her own kind.

In all honor, T'maho knew he could not send her away without that small bit of skin a woman needed if she were ever to find herself a decent husband.

And God knows, he thought with painful amusement, this small, difficult female needed a husband if she were to survive. Alone, she was as helpless as an unfledged nestling.

Reluctantly, he put her from him. His breathing was harsh. He could feel her puzzlement as clearly as if she had spoken it aloud. They would be trapped here together for hours—perhaps, if the storm continued on its present course, for days, for even when the tide receded, the beaches could be treacherous with beds of quicksand where none had been before.

But the danger of stumbling onto a patch of quicksand was nothing compared to the danger of remaining here with this woman, with his body so throbbingly alive that not even the weight of his heavy wet buckskins could cool his ardor.

Turning away abruptly, he cocked his head to study the pitch of the howling wind. "It changes. The eye is passing to the west of us. Open the leaward window to relieve the pressure."

He only wished his own pressure could be so easily relieved, but with the storm whipping up the waters of the sound in its northward journey, the tide would not soon recede. He would simply have to find some way to keep his hands and his mind occupied and off the woman.

Annie, puzzled and somewhat hurt by T'maho's sudden aloofness, fumbled on the shelf for another candle, lighting it from the first, and wishing she had oil to spare for the lamp. She needed to see more clearly. She needed to be able to breathe.

What she really needed was to understand this man and the terrible, wonderful thing that was happening to her. But as an hour passed, and then another, she was no closer to understanding.

By the time darkness fell, it was plain to Mingo that the storm had picked up forward speed and would not wait until tomorrow. Since T'maho had not returned to the village, he made one last trip to Etawak's lodge to be certain the old woman was secure. It would be like her to decide to petition the storm gods on Saketa's behalf.

If he thought it would do any good, Mingo would have offered up a few petitions on his own behalf. Sharing his small lodge with Saketa these past few days was enough to drive a sane man to distraction. The more maddening she grew, the more he loved her, and if that didn't prove that the fire that had ruined his face had destroyed his brain, then nothing would.

Returning, he circled his own neat grounds and made one final check. He had thrown an old net over his roof and staked it down. He would not lose too many rushes. The small boat he and T'maho used to fish the middle nets was lashed securely between two trees and weighted with ballast stones. It would survive unless a tree fell on it. His laying geese were safely impounded. He would have freed them to weather the storm in the wild, but the foolish things were so fat with his corn they would probably sink like a fleet of rocks.

Lingering a moment, he gazed regretfully at his garden patch. Likely the tide would never reach this high, but it would not recover this season.

So be it. He would plant again. After the storm, the villagers would pool their resources and survive in the same way they always had.

Before he even reached the door, he heard her swearing. The voice was rusty with disuse, but there was no mistaking it. Besides, no one could swear quite like Saketa. She had learned at an early age from him and T'maho, who had been young and foolish enough to consider it a great jest. Pausing just inside the door, he regarded her silently.

A pair of guilt-stricken eyes, glistening like polished jet, stared back at him. Saketa cleared her throat and affected a look of great pain.

Slowly, Mingo shook his head. "No, no, little sparrow, that won't do. I heard you speak."

"Oh, but I didn't—I was only coughing," she said hurriedly. And then, realizing that she had spoken again, giving herself away, she bit her lip in confusion and fell back on her oldest trick. One that had never failed her.

She began to cry.

Mingo crossed his arms and remained where he was. After a few minutes of loud, pitiful sobs, she lowered her arms just enough to peer over the top with one dry eye.

"Are you going to tell me now who hurt you, or are you going to do without your supper?" No matter how she clutched her throat and pretended great agony, her appetite had never failed her. Mingo was a fair cook, and Etawak had kept them both supplied with sweets, which were Saketa's particular weakness.

She shook her head, keeping her face hidden.

Leaning against the wall, Mingo crossed one leg over the other and waited. After several minutes had passed, he said, "Sleep, then. I believe I'll have my own supper before the worst of the storm hits. Likely I'll be too busy then to eat." Setting out one tin plate, one crockery mug, and a bowl of cold stewed fish with potatoes and onions, he ignored her renewed sobs. "Etawak's honey cakes will go stale if I don't eat them. Perhaps she'll make more in a week or so, once she's recovered from the storm."

A fresh burst of wails assaulted his ears, these sounding more genuine. "I c-can't," came a muffled voice.

Mingo scarcely glanced at the figure huddled on a fur-covered platform on the far side of the room, which was his own bed. He bit into one of Etawak's cornmeal and honey cakes. "Mmmm, the old woman can't cast spells any better than a fish can cast a net, but she can make damned fine cakes."

"Mingo, don't eat them all. I *can't* tell you!"

"Can't or won't?"

"Can't." A loud sniffle was barely audible over the whistling wind and the driving rain. "I—I'm ashamed."

"Ashamed?"

"Afraid, then!"

"Afraid?" he repeated calmly, knowing better than anyone how to deal with this small, contrary female.

And then suddenly she launched herself across the room and commenced pummeling him with her fists, scattering crockery and cakes across the once immaculate floor. "Damn you, Mingo, why won't you leave me alone?"

His arms closed around her then, and he drew her onto his lap, his heart aching, breaking, swelling with the love that had only grown stronger over the years in spite of a complete lack of encouragement.

"Oh, Mingo, I've been such a fool! I thought he loved me—he said we would be married, and I . . ." she choked on tears and Mingo's face twisted with pain. He had known, of course, that there had been someone. Some bastard had gotten her with child, his precious little sparrow.

He would know his name. He would kill the miserable dog slowly and painfully, and then he would take her away to a place where she could make a fresh beginning. He would buy her the kind of husband she wanted—someone handsome, someone kind—a man who would see her for the beauty of her spirit as well as the beauty of her face.

He could sell his share of the boat and nets. He had

spent the winter season tying a new gill net. He could sell the small herd of horses she had disdained when, in the old way, he had so proudly offered for her when she was little more than a child.

"No, little sparrow," he said sadly. "If there's a fool among us, I am that fool. Tell me his name now, and I make you this promise—it will go no further than this house. Once I have dealt with the dog, I will take you away from here and buy your happiness if it takes the rest of my life. This I promise you, Saketa. But you must tell me, for as long as such an animal walks this earth, you will not be safe."

Chapter 13

Calmly, methodically, T'maho set the meal crock, the salt box, and a rusty coffee grinder on the table, and the firewood on top of those. The floor was some four feet off the ground, the hearth three bricks higher than that. There was a chance the water might not rise much higher than it was now. He stacked Annie's trunk and the chairs on top of the bed, and then turned to the gowns that hung on the wall, their dangling hems already threatened by the rising water.

Annie watched as he lifted them down as carefully as if they were costly creations from the finest dressmaker instead of a patchwork of old draperies, bedclothes, and Mrs. Biddlecomb's castoffs. While she stood paralyzed, he folded them and placed them atop the trunk.

With each fresh gust, the house moved and groaned. Water boiled through the cracks and the knotholes in the floor, forced its way through dozens of holes in the roof as, one after another, the shingles blew away.

Annie feared that at any moment they would be launched out to sea. She stared at her night shift hanging limply on its peg, and couldn't have moved if her life depended on it. T'maho sloshed across the floor and lifted it down. He stared at the flimsy bit of embroidered lawn, then raised his eyes to hers, and her knees threatened to fold under her slight weight.

It was the wind, she told herself—the constant screaming wind that was driving her frantic, not the sight of her intimate garment held in his strong, hard hands.

As he waded back and forth, preparing against the storm, Annie fought to subdue her panic, and then wondered if even panic wasn't preferable to the wicked thoughts that kept filtering into her brain. Unwilling to allow him from her sight, she slogged after him and watched from the doorway as he opened and closed first one window and then another, testing the wind, testing the depth of the rising tide.

For all the communication between them, they might have been strangers. They were more than that, of course. Not lovers, certainly, for they were too different. But something . . .

Friends?

Yes, most certainly friends, she decided, turning away from the thought of love and gentleness and tenderness, and the spark that seemed to ignite between them whenever they happened to touch.

Love?

No, certainly not love. Annie knew about love. She had read all about it in the books she had discovered on a high shelf in Mrs. B's sitting room, and it had sounded wonderful, only not quite real. Besides, in the few volumes she had read, there were no instructions about how to go about doing it. Loving, that is. Or even how to recognize it if it happened to occur spontaneously.

She sighed. It was the wind. The weather in this place was entirely too intimate. One needed hills and trees and thick walls and glass windows, and lots of people around for distraction.

She cut him a sidelong look, wondering if he thought of her as just something to be secured from the storm. Another bit of furniture to be stacked and forgotten.

Was he planning to lift her onto the table, too? she wondered. Or the bed? And then she wondered why that thought should send blood rushing to her face.

Moving restlessly across to the northeast window, she tried to peer through the crack in the shutter. "Do you suppose the shed is still standing? I can't see a thing."

He said nothing. Nor did he look at her.

"Poor Jacob and Maroke," she said nervously. "I hope they know how to swim if worse comes to worst."

"They know how to swim."

"And Queenie . . ."

He shrugged. Or perhaps he spoke and she couldn't hear him above the noise. It sounded as if the ocean were trying to push through the walls. Rain splish-splashed monotonously through the roof onto the steadily deepening tide inside the house, yet even with all that, an unnatural silence seemed to stretch out between them.

Annie longed to break it, but couldn't think of a single intelligent thing to say. She considered screaming, but knew she could never bring herself to do it. She thought about how it would feel to throw something. She had once made a ball for the younger children, using scraps of cloth and string wrapped tightly and soaked in water for weight.

She had no ball, but if something didn't happen soon to break the tension, she just might try her arm with one of her father's two china mugs. It should provide a nice, satisfying crash.

Earlier, T'maho had made a mark on the wall with a bit of charcoal. From time to time, he lowered the candle to examine the mark. Twice he made another mark, higher each time than before, but the last time he had nodded in satisfaction, set the candle back on the table, and returned to this vigil at the one opened window.

It was the back bedroom window now. Earlier, it had been the side window, and before that, the one at the end of the kitchen. Evidently, the wind couldn't make up its mind which way to blow.

Annie knew the feeling. She herself felt as skittery as a water spider. It was all she could do to stand quietly while the cold, dark waters rose about her ankles, and not give in to hysteria.

"The tide is beginning to fall," T'maho said. He didn't bother to turn away from the window, and she stared at his dark shape against the darker night. His shoulders filled the space between the window frames. His hair, which had long since come loose from his neat braids, hung like a curtain of black silk, making her wonder how it would feel to run her fingers through it.

Hair was hair, she told herself sternly. His, though it was black as pitch with only the slightest warm cast in the sunlight, would feel no different from anyone else's hair!

Annie expelled the breath she had unconsciously held too long. "Then it's all over?"

He turned toward her then, his pale eyes gleaming oddly in the flickering candlelight. "The storm has moved on. The rest will take time. Do you wish me to go?"

"No!" *Don't you dare leave me,* she wanted to say, but that was absurd. Abruptly she slogged into the bedroom, snatched a chair off the bed, brought it back to the kitchen, and plopped it down with a splash. Seating herself primly, she smoothed her skirt and arranged it just so, never mind that it was a sodden ruin and the bottom four inches dangled into the black water that still swirled about her feet.

"I meant to say, you're certainly welcome to stay until it grows light. Morning can't be all that far off, can it? Mercy, it seems as if we've been shut up in here for days!" *Keep talking! Talk about the weather. Talk about Papa's cows. Keep talking, and perhaps he'll forget what happened earlier.*

Not that he showed any sign of remembering.

Her teeth began to chatter, more from nerves than from the damp chill that had crept into the room. She peered up at him. "T'maho, you said there was quicksand. Surely you wouldn't risk Maroke while there's still danger?"

"There are ways of going safely."

And going, she thought, was probably a good deal safer than staying. The air felt positively explosive. She could sense his eyes moving over her as if he were actually touching her with his hands. Crossing her arms, she clasped her shoulders and tried to think of some way of keeping him there without actually begging. She had too much pride to beg, and she suspected he had even more than she did. Not long ago she had thought him the most arrogant creature of all time.

Which he was. But oh, he was so much more than that! "I suppose you're anxious to get back to Saketa. You never did say where she was."

"She is with Mingo. She is safe."

"Is anyone ever really safe? Sometimes I feel as if my whole life has been lived inside an eggshell. Now that the shell's been broke, I'm not sure I know—that is, I'm afraid I . . ."

Embarrassed at having spoken her thoughts aloud, she cleared her throat, touched her hair, and rearranged her skirt, grateful for the shadows that hid her red face. "Well, never mind all that. But about Saketa—I'd be glad to have her back again. Truly, it would be nice to have someone to keep me company until I decide—"

"No."

"No?" Pride, anger, and desolation warred inside her. She chose to go with pride. "I assure you, T'maho, she would come to no harm here. I've learned now to cook—well, after a fashion. My bread is really quite passable and I've been thinking of trying my hand at something more ambitious. It can't be all that difficult. You do it well enough."

That had sounded rather condescending. She hadn't intended it that way. Peering through the gloom, she tried to see if he looked offended, but there was no change in his expression.

No change in his attitude, either. "Saketa will remain where she is."

Head high, Annie told herself her feelings were not hurt, and if they were, it was no more than she deserved. "I thought I might go into the village as soon as this is over and see if I can arrange to buy supplies. Meat. Vegetables. A chunk of sugar and perhaps some real tea. I do have money, you know." She had exactly two dollars and thirteen pennies, and enough knowledge of household accounting to know that it would not go far.

"Saketa will remain where she is," he said flatly, and that, Annie told herself, was that.

Tears threatened to spill over, and she pinched herself on the arm. *It's only the storm,* she told herself. She had already learned to her sorrow that violent storms could have a treacherous effect on one's emotions.

Mrs. Biddlecomb had warned all her girls of the dangers inherent in allowing one's emotions to get out of hand. To that end she'd had all her charges fitted with a stiff corset once they began sprouting bosoms and getting weepy once a month. There was nothing like a good, rigid zona, according to Mrs. B., to remind a woman that under even the most trying of circumstances, one must never lower one's standards, for the entire weight of civilization rested on the shoulders of the world's women. Men, according to Mrs. B., if left to their own devices, would still be living in caves and wearing animal skins.

T'maho wore animal skins. For all she knew, he lived in a cave. And in the unremitting heat, with no one to know or care how she went on, Annie had daringly left off wearing her stays.

Which probably explained all these peculiar urges that had afflicted her with increasing frequency just lately.

Stiffening her posture against the battered old straight chair as the tide slowly receded about her feet, she sighed. T'maho, his lithe form as still as a lizard on a rock, stood beside the window.

Splish-splash-splat. Drip-drap. She thought of her father's gun, lying out there somewhere under tons of rushing water. She thought about Queenie and the calves. About all her father's cattle. They were probably terrified, poor things—those that hadn't drowned. And there wasn't one single thing she could do about it, corset or no corset. One would think that, having been schooled for twelve years, one would be capable of dealing with almost anything that came along, but for all her fancy stitchery and the proverbs she had painstakingly copied, committed to memory, and then been forced to cross-stitch on canvas, Annie had never felt more useless in her life.

Something brushed past her ankle and she shifted

her foot. Whatever it was—a floating towel or a wooden spoon, perhaps—it seemed to have caught on her boot laces. Leaning forward, she peered at the murky, candlelit surface of the water.

And then she threw back her head, squinched her eyes shut and screamed.

T'maho was beside her in an instant. Jabbing a finger toward the horror that was twining around her limb, she lapsed into a series of whimpered pleas. "Get it off! Get it away from me, oh, please get it off!"

Swiftly, he slid his knife free. Using the side of his blade, he eased the snake away from her feet until he could grab it behind the head. In sheer, stark horror, Annie saw the writhing body wrap itself around his forearm as T'maho waded to the window and flung it away, then leaned as far outside as he could, bracing himself on the sill. Guarding, she prayed, to see that it didn't try to return.

Oh, merciful saints in heaven, she was going to be sick!

At the window, T'maho breathed deeply of the warm, wet air. God, he *couldn't* be sick now! Not in front of Annie! No one except for Mingo knew of his irrational fear of snakes—even the most harmless of them. He should have outgrown it years ago, but he hadn't. Knowing the fear was groundless did nothing at all to help him deal with it.

"I'm sorry I screamed." Annie's small voice broke through the nightmare memory of two small boys digging into a warm mud bank and uncovering a nest of young cottonmouth moccasins. One of those boys had dared the other to poke a stick into the squirming mass the way they sometimes did when one of them uncovered an anthill, waiting until the last moment to fling the stick away and run.

But before the dare could be acted upon, the writhing, glistening knot of young snakes had swarmed about the legs of the oldest boy, and he fell screaming in agony while his terrified playmate kicked away the excited reptiles and tried to drag his friend to safety.

It was too late. The snakes were everywhere. For years afterward, he kept seeing them. They invaded the house he lived in, the bed he slept in. They invaded his dreams until the boy named Benjamin was afraid to close his eyes.

The other boy had not been so fortunate. Swollen horribly, his skin blackened by poison, he had died before the day ended.

"T'maho, are you all right?"

With one last gulp of air, he drew his head and shoulders back inside the window and forced down the nausea that threatened. Her hand was on his arm, as if she sensed his distress. T'maho was ashamed of his weakness, embarrassed that he had allowed it to show. Scowling, he muttered, "Many creatures are displaced by the water. They are as frightened of you as you are of them."

"I doubt that, but thank you for trying to make me feel less cowardly. If that wretched snake knew how terrified I was, he'd be out there right now laughing his head off."

T'maho managed to smile, and Annie felt a relief all

out of proportion to the small act. He crossed to the fireplace and raked away the rain-dampened ashes to find a live coal, then added a stick of pine. "The wind has dropped. Even if the chimney has been damaged, there's small danger of fire with the roof so wet."

Grateful for something physical to do, Annie began restacking the firewood on the table. Just why, she could not have said. It was simply a need to do something physical—anything!

The pine caught, and T'maho wedged in a piece of oak, then swung the kettle over the flame. As he stepped back, his foot came down on hers, and they both jumped. Once again, the air felt brittle enough to shatter.

"Tea!" she exclaimed breathlessly, fumbling in the near darkness for the tea canister. T'maho took down two cups, the flowered one she had brought with her and another that had belonged to her father. He shifted her chair closer to the fire, and she stepped back to avoid touching him again, then turned toward the bedroom to bring in the third chair.

"Here, you must be tired," she said. "You've been pacing all night long. Is this what one usually does during a storm of this kind?" There, that was nicely done, she thought proudly. Social chitchat was like oil on troubled waters. All those boring monthly tea parties in Mrs. B's parlor had not been wasted, after all.

T'maho stood stiffly behind the chair, his arms crossed over his chest. Annie stood beside her own. Cautiously, she slid it six inches farther away, then seated herself, arranged her skirts, and crossed her own

arms. Only then did T'maho take his seat. Looking anywhere and everywhere but at each other, they sat in silence while the fire caught up, the copper kettle ticking
as the water began to heat. After a while, a whisper of
steam rose from its battered spout, and leaping to her
feet, Annie reached for the handle just as T'maho did.
Their hands touched, and sparks ran right up to her
bosom. Guiltily, both jumped back.

"You'll burn your hand. Annie, I—"

"My apron—T'maho, you mustn't think that I—"

"What?" T'maho prompted. "What were you going to
say?"

"No, you first."

The first gray light of morning was beginning to
creep across the muddy floor as they stared at one another. Somewhere in the back of her mind, Annie realized that the wind was no longer blowing. The rain
must have slacked off, too, for she could hear the
ragged sound of T'maho's breathing quite clearly.

"*Ahone,*" he muttered suddenly, and then he said
something that sounded almost like "cow-waiver."

"I beg your pardon?" she whispered.

"The word *caw-wai-vuh* means a be— That is, it re-
fers to a piece of furniture. That is, I was thinking that
soon the tide will be gone, and the room may be put to
rights."

The word meant "bed." From the first time he had
seen her standing beside O'Neal's ugly bed, his treacherous mind had pictured her lying there as he knelt
over her. Since then he had pictured her lying unclad
atop the sandhills, in the glade, in the shed among the

mounds of sweet grass heaped in one corner—he had
even pictured them mounted together on Maroke, moving to the rhythm set by the galloping mare.

Truly, he had sunk beneath contempt. His mind had
been poisoned by too many years of bitterness and too
many of Etawak's nasty potions. Filled with self-
derision, T'maho told himself he should leave now, before he committed the most grievous mistake of his
worthless life.

Resolved to leave her and send Mingo back to set
her house to rights again, he stood just as Annie stood.
She looked up, and in that one unguarded moment, every good intention fled.

As he swept her into his arms, Annie wondered dazedly how long a body could live without air. Her heart
was racketing around in her chest and she had clean
forgotten to breathe, and now her knees were threatening to give out on her again.

She thought she whispered something and prayed he
had not heard it. Being back in his arms was like coming back to a home she had never even known. As if
the storm had never happened. As if the calf had never
gotten stuck in the mud and she had never taken her
father's gun to him. . . .

T'maho lowered his head just as she lifted hers. This
time there was no gentle beginning. This time the em-
bers burst into flames the instant his mouth covered
hers. In the moment before her entire body melted like
a tallow candle set too near the fire, he swept her up
into his arms and carried her into the bedroom.

And then he stood there, staring at the trunk and the

stacks of clothing he had placed upon the bed, out of reach of the tide.

He swore. Annie sighed and turned her face to inhale the intoxicating fragrance of his skin. She knew what was going to happen. He was going to lay her on the bed, and then he was going to do something to her that they both wanted, only she didn't quite know what it was. She was beginning to suspect, however, that it had little to do with cabbage patches and carpet beating, and everything to do with satisfying this heavy, sweet hunger that pervaded her body whenever he touched her. Whenever he looked at her. Whenever she even thought about him.

T'maho lowered her to her feet. He reached for the trunk, and then turned back and said in a voice that was almost unrecognizable, "I can leave now if you wish, Annie."

She clutched his arms. "No, please don't go!"

"If I stay, you know what will happen."

"I know, and I want it, truly, I do." Whatever "it" was, she wanted it, had wanted it almost from the first time she had laid eyes on this tall, gray-eyed savage, when she had knocked him down with a fence paling, and he had fallen on top of her, pressing her down into the hot sand while he stared into the very depths of her soul.

At least it felt that way now, she told herself, forgetting all those weeks of fear and doubt and uncertainty. "That is, if you do," she whispered.

For an answer, he swung the trunk down off the bed, carried her neatly folded clothing and laid it carefully on top, and then lifted her and placed her almost reverently in the middle of the narrow mattress.

Like flowers on an altar, she thought bemusedly as he lowered himself to his knees on the floor beside her.

He touched her hair. He touched the cool damp skin at her temple. Then he leaned over and placed his lips on that sensitive place where her neck met her shoulder, and she shuddered and gasped as lightning streaked through her body, stabbing repeatedly at those private places that she had never even known the names of.

And then all thought of flowers and altars fled as her senses went wild.

His breath sweet on her face, his hands warm on her body, he felt for the fastenings of her gown, fumbling with tapes and buttons until she slid her hands under his and completed the task. When there was only her chemise between his hands and her flesh, he laid his warm palms over her breasts and lightning struck again. Annie's eyes widened in the faint gray light of dawn as she felt the tips of her breasts tighten.

Was this normal?

It was delicious, but was it natural?

"Touch me," he commanded softly, and he lifted her hands to his shoulders and left them there to stay or stray.

They strayed. Curious, Annie explored the breadth of his shoulders. Muscle, sinew, and bone. Smooth as satin, hard as granite. She trailed her fingertips experimentally across his broad chest, feeling the subtle flexing of muscles she was quite certain she didn't even possess.

And then she forgot those as her roving fingers discovered the tufts of hair underneath his arms. "I thought Indians were born with no hair," she said.

"Most people are born with no hair," he replied, laughter and something else running like a deep current beneath his voice. "Some never change, others do."

"Do you shave the hair from your face?"

"Yes."

"Do you—"

"Do I what, sweet Annie?"

But she couldn't ask that. He had no beard, like those on the trappers who came into Hillsborough to trade their pelts for supplies. His chest was smooth, and his arms. But what about . . .

Shifting restlessly, Annie was reminded by the lightest pressure of T'maho's hand on her belly of where else a body might wear hair. Hers was red. She had looked at it once years ago, amazed and not a little frightened that it had sprouted there at all.

Was all private hair red, or was his black, to match the hair on his head? It was too dark to see the tufts under his arms clearly, but she rather thought they showed a tinge of red.

"What strange thoughts chase those shadows across your face, Annie O'Neal?"

"No thoughts! That is, I'm not thinking anything," she said hastily. "Truly I'm not!"

And then, horror of horrors, she yawned.

T'maho swore softly. Reluctantly, he stood and pulled

the spread over her half-clad body. Annie reached for his hand and held him there. "Please, T'maho, don't go! I'm sorry—it's just that I've been awake for days, what with one thing and another."

"Do not apologize. I think perhaps your body is wiser than mine. Mine thinks only of the moment. Yours thinks of the future."

"Bodies don't think. T'maho, don't leave, please. What if a snake should crawl through the window?"

"Call out. I will be just beyond the door."

She sat up, clasping the loose neck of her thin chemise to her breast. "But I don't want you beyond the door, I want you here. With me! There's room, honestly. I can scrunch up against the wall. I don't take up much room, and I don't snore, and the cover is wide enough for two, I know it is."

Thus it was that T'maho, son of a long line of the Hattorask, who had been known among all the Algonquin for their honor, their daring, their ability to bear great hardship in silence, for their keen minds as well as the comely features of their women and the fine, tall, strong bodies of their men, did surrender to the enemy like a cringing *tumpfeis*, an old woman.

Annie rolled over to face the wall. T'maho slipped into bed behind her, first removing his buckskins, which would take many days and much soaking in fresh water before they could be dried sufficiently for comfort.

A single layer of cloth was between them, a sufficient barrier, he told himself. Nevertheless, he hugged the edge of the miserable, sea-grass-filled pad, vowing to have Etawak make her a decent bed, one filled with the springy gray moss that hung from the trees in the glade. Once the red mites crawled out, it made a fine mattress, one he greatly preferred over the soft feather-filled tickings in his father's house.

After a few gasps and gulps, Annie's breathing settled into a soft purr. She slept. T'maho had never felt further from sleep in his life. Her warmth reached out to him. The scent of her in his nostrils made his flesh leap eagerly, which brought pictures to his mind that no amount of effort could dispel.

Cautiously, he slid one foot closer until he felt the answering warmth of her small soles. In her sleep, she settled her foot on top of his and left it there, and T'maho stared into the darkness, wondering just when he had lost his wits.

Eventually, he, too, slept. All the days of watching over Saketa and searching for her assailant took their toll.

It could have been minutes later—it could have been hours. Cramped, Annie turned over onto her other side. T'maho came instantly awake. When her arm flung across his waist and then slipped down, the warmth of her knuckles brushing against his rigid man-flesh, he nearly wept.

Did she know? Was she taunting him deliberately?

In his heart, he knew she was not. Her breathing was too slow and regular.

His own was ragged, so raw it hurt. He would sooner

be kicked in the groin again than suffer this torture. It could hardly serve him worse.

Slowly, almost reluctantly, T'maho moved his hand down to where hers rested limply on his thigh. Carefully covering the back of her hand with his own, he moved it to that part of him that throbbed and thrust so eagerly, willing himself to do no more.

Closing his eyes, he breathed roughly through his open mouth for a moment, and then he made the greatest sacrifice in his life. For her sake—and for his own honor.

Chapter 14

Annie awoke to the pungent smell of mud, to a sky of startling loveliness, and to the disconcerting realization that she was alone. For a long time she lay there, reluctant to get up and face a new day. Could she have dreamed it all? The storm? Begging a man to sleep with her?

The snake?

She remembered dreaming about a snake—vestiges of the dream still clung to her mind.

But had she only dreamed T'maho's mouth exploring her own, his hands moving over her body?

Half afraid of what she might find, she glanced down at the bodice of her night shift. No scorched handprint. Under the thin lawn, her chest looked the same as always—not as generous as Mrs. B.'s, but not quite as flat as Cookie's.

No, she could not have dreamed it all. She wouldn't have known how to dream such things. Not the doings—and certainly not the feelings!

Stiffly, she sat and drew up her knees, curling her toes into the lumpy mattress. The narrow strip of sky

visible through the shutters might have been painted by
a fanciful artist. Yesterday the world had been drawn in
shades of gray. Today the sky could only be described
as heavenly—turquoise and flower-petal pink, with tiny
white clouds drifting past like blobs of meringue on a
bowl of blue custard pudding.

Unconvinced that she was not still dreaming, Annie
blinked to see if she would find herself back in her narrow bed on the third floor. She listened, half expecting
to hear the sound of babies grizzling for their morning
feed while the older girls squabbled over whose turn it
was to use the wash water first.

No grizzling. No squabbling. Only the ever-present
roar of the sea and the raucous laughing noise she had
come to identify with feeding gulls.

Flopping back onto her pillow, she sighed, wrinkled
her nose, and sniffed. What on earth? It was like nothing she had ever smelled before, not even after she'd
dumped out the crock of rotten fish.

Surely she wasn't dreaming that stench!

She swung her feet off the bed, felt the sticky ooze
between her toes, and cried, "My floors!" Shaken at
finding herself surrounded by utter chaos, Annie felt
the full weight of the previous twenty-four hours come
rushing back.

She groaned. Her cheeks flamed. Merciful saints in
heaven, no wonder T'maho had left without saying
good-bye! She must have embarrassed the poor man to
death!

Not that he had ever bothered with good-byes, she
thought, partly amused, partly dismayed. If Annie had

prided herself on her own independence—and she most certainly had—then T'maho could easily give her lessons.

So. He was gone again. And she was still here. Unaccountably depressed, she tried to call to mind some suitably inspirational passage. " 'When duty whispers low, Thou must/ Then youth replies, I can.' "

Taking a deep breath, she stood, lifted her chemise up above the slime, and set about surveying the damage.

The walls revealed a watermark several inches above the floor, as did her poor trunk. She only prayed the thing was waterproof. Her summer gowns were all neatly folded on top where T'maho had put them—at least those had been spared.

Her shoes were quite beyond redemption, but as they were the only ones she possessed, she put them on anyway over dry stockings and then shuddered at the clammy feel of the soaked kid leather. Squishing across the sticky floor, she threw open the shutters, allowing fresh air and sunshine to spill into the house. Cautiously, she peered out.

It was truly a beautiful day as long as one kept one's eyes above the horizon. The earth might lay in ruins, with the house in little better condition, but determined not to be discouraged, Annie told herself that at least the house was still standing. And so was she.

Gazing around at the muddy mess left on the floors and walls by the receding tide, she was glad T'maho had insisted on filling every available container with fresh water. Before she could even begin to scrub things clean, she would have to slosh away the slimy, stinking mud.

Which she did, using broom and pail. Before she was half done, she was forced to go outside to the rain barrel for more water, which meant wading through puddles and clambering over drifted mounds of dank-smelling sea grass that had washed up from the sound shore.

The privy was gone. Oh well . . . it had been listing, anyway.

Toes squelching unpleasantly inside her wet shoes, Annie picked her way through odd ends of lumber leaning drunkenly against the foundation of the house, bits of rope, a tangled length of net, a scrap of torn canvas sail, a bedraggled muslin mobcap, and one dead seagull. She thought of all the snakes that could be hiding under the debris and shuddered, but slogged grimly on to the barrel, which T'maho had lashed to the foundation of the house to keep it from floating away.

Thank heavens! With all the rain, it was full to over-flowing. On an impulse, she stuck her finger in and tasted it.

Salty! Merciful heavens, and she had used all the fresh water they had saved to wash away the mud! What was she supposed to drink?

Too late to cry over spilled milk, she reminded her-self. Milk . . . oh, how she would love a tall tumbler of cool, sweet milk!

Her stomach growled hungrily, and she told herself

that was what came from trying to take comfort from a
bunch of silly proverbs.

However, even proverbs were better than no comfort
at all.

The brackish water would do to scrub with, and the
first order of the day was to scour everything the stinking mud had touched. By then, perhaps, it would rain.
Hope springs eternal in the human breast, she thought
before she could stop herself, and then she snorted and
dipped in her pail.

By the time the sun was more or less directly overhead, the floors, the lower walls, and the legs of the
furniture had been scrubbed to her satisfaction. Lye
soap, she discovered, did not lather in salt water, but a
sufficient application of water and elbow grease did
the job well enough for the moment.

Oh, but she was hungry. Thirsty, too. In fact, the
more she dwelled on it, the thirstier she became. She
thought of Mr. Coleridge's tale of the Ancient Mariner,
which was not a part of Mrs. B.'s curriculum, but
which Annie had found in the old library and read,
nevertheless.

"Water, water, everywhere," she muttered, staring at
the empty kettle. "Oh, bloody whore damn spit!"

It was late afternoon when Mingo picked his way
through the storm wrack, mounted on what even Annie
recognized as an unusually handsome animal. Annie,
thinking at first glimpse that T'maho had returned, hid
her disappointment well. Mingo came bringing food, a
small keg of water, news of the village, and a message

of sympathy over her father's death. Either Snell or T'maho must have spread the word throughout the village.

"Your father was well liked, Miss Annie. His friends will miss him greatly. They send word that you will be welcome in their homes."

Annie tried and failed to swallow the lump that rose to her throat. At a time when some of them had probably lost everything they possessed, people she didn't even know offered help.

"That's truly kind. Please tell them I appreciate their offer, but I'm managing quite well," she said to the man who had known her father far better and far longer than she herself ever had.

Perhaps she should be offering him condolences. "Was there much damage in the village?"

"No more than usual in such a storm. Jackariah's roof blew off. Family's moved in with Miz Rachael's folks until we can get it mended. Miss Achsah's chickens took a whipping. Climbed up in a cedar tree, but it blew over." He studied the nearby shore, which had changed drastically in the past twelve hours, as though he were searching for something—or someone—and Annie waited politely for him to resume.

"No strangers wandering around hereabouts?" he asked.

Annie shook her head. "No. No one at all. Does it always stink like this after a storm?"

"Sometimes more. Wait three days."

"Then the smell will be gone?"

"Then it will be worse," he said, and Annie detected a hint of a grin on his somber face.

"I'm sorry about the chickens and the roof, but I suppose they can be replaced," she said, not wanting him to leave quite yet. She wasn't ready to be left all alone again, and although she hardly even knew this man, he had known her father. And he knew T'maho.

"About the damage in the village . . . is there anything I can do?"

He smiled, and it occurred to her that he must once have been a handsome man. "Roofs and chickens can be replaced. Two boats were holed and sunk when a bundle of net stakes came washing up the creek." He shrugged, still staring out at the water. "They can be floated and patched. Most gardens was ruined, but they can be planted again. Whole crop of acorns stripped off the trees, too. Old Etawak's already out searching the woods for what's left, for her beer." This time he did grin, twisting the scarred side of his face grotesquely, but for all that, Annie found him friendly and not nearly as frightening as she'd thought the first time she'd seen him.

He began walking his horse toward the shed and she followed, picking her way carefully over the piles of debris. "I see your shed took a lickin'," he said. The whole structure was leaning at a drunken slant, but surprisingly, it still held together.

Looping his reins around a lone fence post that was all that remained of the small paddock, Mingo set about feeding and watering Jacob while Annie looked around for some sign that Queenie had survived the storm.

She was trying to think of some way to ask about T'maho when half a dozen cows trotted up from the south, heads swinging as they scented the sweet grass.

Mingo tossed several pitchforks full of the damp grass onto the ground. "It'll spoil now that it's been wet. Might as well let 'em have it."

"I'm sure you know better than I. Mr. Mingo, perhaps you could—"

"I'll see about sending off for some feed to get you through the winter."

"Thank you. With Papa gone, I suppose they're my responsibility, though I must confess, I don't know the first thing about taking care of them."

"Don't have to. There's mast enough in the glade."

"Mast?"

"Browse."

"Oh . . . browse," she repeated, as if she had the least idea what he was talking about. "Yes, well . . . perhaps. But Mr. Mingo, could you tell me how I might go about finding someone to take them off my hands? I thought perhaps Mr. Snell might be interested in buying my father's half."

Mingo looked up sharply from his task. "Has he been back here?"

"He was here . . . let's see, was it yesterday or the day before? With the storm, I seem to have lost track of the days. He came to tell me about Papa, but then he seemed in a hurry to leave—something about getting his boat ready for the storm, I expect."

Mingo scowled at the pitchfork. Annie waited for him to say something about her idea of selling the herd. When he continued to stare at the pitchfork, she said impatiently, "Well? What do you think? Is it a good idea? Do you think he'd be interested in taking them off my hands?"

"Wait."

Puzzled, she waited. When he didn't say anything more, she shook her head and sighed. "Wait! That's all very well for you to say! You're not the one who has a yard full of cows scratching their itches on your corner posts, ripping your wash off the lines, and getting themselves stuck in the mud." Unbidden, all the irritations and frustrations she'd been holding back came pouring out. "What am I supposed to do, stay here alone and devote the rest of my life to these wretched animals? I'm a seamstress, Mr. Mingo, not a—a cow person."

He regarded her silently for so long that Annie wondered if there was something wrong with his hearing. It was late. She was tired and she was hungry, and her patience had stretched just about as far as it would stretch. Planting her fists on her hips, she tapped her foot on the squishy brown grass. "Just forget I mentioned it, but if you see Mr. Snell, you may tell him that Miss Annie O'Neal would like a word with him on a matter of mutual interest. Whether he cares to purchase Papa's half of the herd or not, I suppose he'll have something to say about the matter."

His eyes narrowed but he didn't refuse. Nor did he make any comment.

"Well, that's that, I suppose. Now, if you know of anyone in the village who needs a house—it's not much, but perhaps someone can use it—you may tell them I'll be leaving on the next boat out, just as soon as I can make the arrangements."

If he'd even heard her, he gave no indication. He looked off toward the house, his eyes narrowed, and then he went back to staring at his pitchfork.

Suddenly the last few strands of Annie's patience, never particularly strong and badly eroded just lately, snapped. "Forget I asked!"

"Miss Annie, you'd better come to the village with me."

"I'll go to the village when the mail boat comes in, and once I've spoken to Mr. Snell about the cows, I'll be—"

"I wouldn't do that."

"It seems you wouldn't do much of anything, sir! Well, some men are not so disobliging! Mr. Snell was my father's business partner. He even asked me to— Well, at any rate, I'm sure he'll take care of everything."

Mingo shook his head. "If you won't come with me, I'll send T'maho back for you."

Beware the fury of a patient man. Annie didn't remember who had spoken those words, but she couldn't have agreed more. "Mr. Mingo," she said very quietly. "I don't need to see T'maho, I need to see Mr. Snell. If you cannot do as I asked, then please do nothing at all. It happens that this has been a perfectly miserable day, one of the worst I have endured in a long, long time. So if you've done what you came to do, then you may leave with my blessing!" She swung around to leave, then turned back. Angry or not, a lifetime of training would not allow her to ignore his gifts, which he had set on the stump outside the door. "I thank you for the water you brought and whatever it is that's wrapped in that napkin."

"Saketa made bean bread."

"Saketa . . ."

Well, if Saketa was up to making bean bread, whatever that particular delicacy was, then Annie needn't worry about her any longer. With a brief nod of her head, she turned back toward the house in time to see a bedraggled Queenie, minus all but one tail feather, pecking away at the small bundle of food.

"Get away! Shoo! Scat!" Screaming threats, she ran, flapping her apron, and Mingo took that opportunity to fork out the rest of the ruined feed.

He was beginning to understand how the small ginger-hair had managed to entangle his friend in her net. It would be interesting to watch matters settle out between them.

T'maho had come by his house early that morning to see how they had fared. He'd asked to speak to Saketa, but having stayed up all night, she had been sleeping. He had gone on to Etawak's to put her place to rights again, then returned, saying he would stay until Saketa awoke, for he would speak to her.

The beach road, he had reported, was all but impassable, the soundside road no better. As for the trails through the glade, a few, T'maho had said, were above water. Most were not.

Mingo had asked about Eli's property, and T'maho had looked away. "It still stands," he'd said.

"And the woman?"

"Fares well enough."

Mingo had read more than was stated in those few words. "Then as long as you're here to keep watch, I'd best go see to the old man's herd." He'd half expected T'maho to offer to go for him, but he'd only suggested that he take along food and fresh water.

"Bring her in if she'll come with you. I don't want her out there alone, not once the trails are open again."

Perhaps, Mingo thought now as he finished pitching the damp grass out where the cows could get to it, he should have insisted. T'maho was right. The woman should not stay here alone. Not until all danger was passed, and if Mingo had his way, that would be the moment the glade trails were dry enough to traverse.

If by then T'maho had finally come to terms with his inner devils, the woman's future would no longer be in question.

As he rode past the house, Annie appeared in the doorway, licking crumbs from her lips like a child caught in the cookie crock. Food and fresh water had obviously taken the edge from her anger. "Thank you for feeding up, and thank you again for this . . . well, whatever it is, it's delicious! I never heard of putting beans in cornbread before."

"T'maho thought you might be hungry." He grinned as he watched her face turn almost as red as her hair. "I'll saddle Jacob for you if you'll ride in with me now.

The herd will fare well enough, but perhaps it's not such a good idea for you to stay out here alone. Any family in the village will be glad to take you in."

Her eyes snapped green fire, and he thought, *Oh, yes, my friend, this one will lead you a fine dance!*

"Mr. Mingo, I thank you for your offer, but I am perfectly capable of looking after myself. I'll leave when the mail boat comes in and not before."

"Do you know how to use Eli's gun?"

"Papa's gun was . . . um, lost in the storm."

He lifted his eyebrows at that—at least, the one eyebrow he still possessed. But he merely nodded, shrugged, and turned away.

Annie watched him out of sight, a vague feeling of unease settling in. Why had he asked about the gun? Snakes?

It must be snakes. Or rats. T'maho had mentioned something about creatures being displaced by the tide. Besides, what else was there to fear on an island so small that all the people knew one another? And if T'maho could be believed, most were connected by marriage, if not by blood.

But then she thought about Saketa. She glanced out over the bleak, ruined landscape, at the shadowy glade and the deceptively placid waters of Pamlico. Closing the door, she slid a chair against it and wished she had a heavy dresser. Lacking that, she lifted the meal crock up onto the chair, and then she added the kettle and two spoons to the stack.

At least she wouldn't be taken unaware.

* * *

The sun was high overhead when Mingo dismounted and turned his stallion, Raputtak, into the pen. He usually rode his workhorse, but now and then he enjoyed testing the old devil's mettle—as well as having his own mettle tested by the stallion's strength and contrariness. Raputtak was leader of the string of mares he had once offered for Saketa. He didn't know why he kept the old troublemaker around—perhaps to remind him of things best forgotten.

T'maho hailed him from nearby, where he had been unlashing the small boat, which had come through the storm in fine shape.

"You stayed long enough."

"Did a bit of hunting in the glade on the way back."

T'maho's eyes narrowed. "Supper?"

"Vermin."

"What luck?"

"None. Creeks still too swollen to go far off the trail. Water's still halfway up the big ridge."

T'maho coiled the lines and tossed them aside. "Got any particular reason to believe there's vermin in there that needs hunting down?"

"Got any reason to believe there's not?" Mingo came back.

T'maho's smile was no more than a twist at the corner of his mouth. His eyes remained guarded. "I thought I'd go in once the water goes down, maybe set a few traps for muskrat."

"This time of year?"

"I'm not setting for prime, I'm setting for meat."

"Since when did you take to eating swamp rat?"

They were both sparring around the subject that was foremost on both men's minds: Jackson Snell. After tackling Saketa on the subject, T'maho was all but certain of the man's guilt. And he alone knew where to find him.

Mingo might have guessed, but T'maho was not yet ready to discuss the matter. Snell was his. He intended to go in alone and bring him out as soon as the water went down sufficiently to leave the main trail.

"Did you see Annie?" he asked, not looking up from his task.

"I saw her." There was no mistaking the amusement in Mingo's tone. T'maho heard it, rightly surmised the source, and swore quietly. Too many things were coming to a head all at once. He needed time to sort out his thoughts. "Did you ask her to come to the village?"

"I asked."

"Well? What did she say?"

"What did you expect her to say?"

"Dammit, Mingo—!"

"That woman of yours could teach stubborn to a mule."

T'maho tensed, his fists knotted at his sides, but then he slacked off and began to chuckle. It was such a rare sound that Saketa, hearing it, came to the window, demanding to know who had said what, and why her brother was laughing.

Hiding his emotion at hearing her rusty voice again, Mingo said, "We spoke of you, ugly grasshopper. I told him you were grown so meek and obedient lately I thought your brain must have been afflicted by the fever."

Saketa threw a biscuit at his head. Mingo ducked, and T'maho caught it. Both men laughed, but then, sobering, turned to stare northward. Toward the glade, where T'maho had left Snell two days before. Toward Annie's house, where he had left her only a few hours ago. There were many questions T'maho wanted to ask of his friend, yet he couldn't bring himself to speak.

Besides, he had a feeling that Mingo knew most of those unspoken questions, and more than a few of their answers, and was finding not a little amusement in the situation.

There was much to be done in the village after the storm. T'maho found it impossible to get away as quickly as he had planned. As the day wore on, he grew more and more agitated.

She was out there all alone.

He helped the younger men drag two damaged boats up onto the shore and roll them over for drying and patching. He went up a tree to bring down Miz Achsah's old coon cat, and suffered a few scratches for his troubles.

If Snell did manage to find his way out of the glade, he could just as easily go north as south.

T'maho sweated. He swore. He grew so distracted that Mingo had to yell to get his attention when the two of them headed out in the skiff to bring in the big boat from where she'd been anchored out in the channel.

More than once he tried to get away, but there was always one more task that needed doing. No sooner was a house lifted back onto its supports than someone needed help in righting an overturned shed. Or a boat that had been cast up onto her beamside.

Or rounding up a penful of hogs that had escaped when a tree had uprooted, tearing down their fence.

Wading out into the sound after that particular undertaking to cleanse himself of the stench and the mud, he muttered, "Dammit, Mingo, I have other things that need to be done!"

Mingo shrugged. "Then go. The tide is still too high for vermin to range so far north. Your woman will be safe."

T'maho uttered a curse. Annie was not his woman. But the thought of what could happen to her if Snell happened to find his way out of the glade was enough to send him off at a lope to where he had left his mare, with Mingo grinning after him.

Even riding hell-bent for leather, it was well past dark when he reached the small, isolated shack. By that time, fear and an overwrought imagination had worked him into a fever of concern.

No gleam of light was visible from any of the windows.

She was probably sleeping.

But God, what if Snell had come back? What if she had angered him in some way? What if she had agreed to go off with him and was even now aboard the *Black Opal*, at the mercy of a ruthless devil who would cruelly use her and then discard her—or worse?

Swearing softly, he slid off Maroke's back and dropped the reins, haunted by the chilling thought that had sent him racing off through the darkness. Just because he had not been able to find Snell did not mean that Snell had been unable to find his way out. Even a blind mule sometimes stumbled across a trail if he wandered long enough.

Too much time had passed since he had led Snell into the glade and left him there. He had not planned on being delayed so long, but the storm had come up faster than anyone had expected.

He had gone to warn Annie of the storm. He had stayed far longer than he had planned to stay, and what had happened there had left him badly shaken. He needed time to sort out his feelings.

Then there had been Saketa to deal with. That, too, had taken longer than he had expected. Now every minute was a living agony. He should not have left Annie here unprotected. He should have taken her, forcefully if necessary, into the village and given her into the keeping of one of the village women until this thing with Snell was settled.

Leaping up onto the stump, he tried the door and swore softly when it refused to budge. Exerting more force, he felt it begin to give.

And then all hell broke loose. There was the clatter of something falling, a crash and then the sound of something heavy rolling away.

Annie sprang out of bed and snatched up the knife she had placed under her pillow. Someone was trying to break into her house!

Who? And dear Lord, why? There was nothing here worth stealing!

Blinking off the numbing effects of a nightmare, she considered crawling out the window, but dismissed it. She'd sooner face most anything than take her chances in the dark, amid all that debris. She had seen three more snakes that afternoon, and no matter what T'maho had said, they couldn't be any more frightened of her than she had been of them.

"Annie? Are you in there?"

Oh, merciful heavens! "T'maho, what are you doing here at this time of night?"

She hurried to let him in, forgetting the knife in her hand, forgetting everything except that T'maho was back.

The door moved, sliding something heavy across the gritty floor. Her barricade!

The crock had fallen, and she knelt and collected the kettle and then felt for the two spoons. "Wait a minute," she panted.

But he didn't wait. The door swung inward, sliding over the fingers of her left hand, and she cried out. He was on his knees instantly, holding her, rocking her, clutching her head so that her face was pressed to his throat and she could barely breathe.

"T'maho, I can't—"

"You're all right! He didn't come!"

"Who? Oh. Mingo. He came, but he left hours ago. T'maho, let me put the knife down before one of us gets cut."

In the stifling darkness—she had closed all the shutters, feeling oddly threatened after Mingo's veiled warning—Annie laid the big kitchen knife on the floor and gave herself up to the glorious comfort of being held. At this moment, her world began and ended with the feel of T'maho's powerful arms holding her as if he could never let her go.

Only now did she allow herself to admit how very disappointed she had been when she'd woken up in her bed alone that morning. And when he hadn't come back all day, what else could she think but that he regretted what they had done—what they had so nearly done . . .

Whatever it was.

Leading her by the hand, T'maho crossed the room and felt for a candle. A moment later, light flared. Annie stared at the streak of what looked like blood on his throat.

"You're hurt," she whispered. Touching the place, her finger came away wet. "I didn't mean to cut you."

But then he grabbed both her hands, and she saw that it was her own blood, where the bottom of the door had raked over her fingers, scraping off the skin. Only then did she feel the fierce burning pain.

"Ah, *ne-toppe,* let me wash it clean," he murmured, and then there was the business of finding something to spread over it. "Plantain," he said. "Not mullet gizzards. Not a decoction of spider venom. Not mink dung."

She nodded as if she understood every word he said and agreed with it all. He could have plunged her hand in boiling oil for all she knew or cared. He was here. He had come back.

The plantain, T'maho told her, would have to wait until morning. Meanwhile, she needed tea, and he found the kettle where it had rolled into a corner, built up the fire, and set about boiling the last of the fresh water. Annie watched, just as if she were accustomed to being visited in the middle of the night by shirtless men wearing low-waisted buckskins and knee-high moccasins.

T'maho dumped in a double handful of the parched green leaves, his hand unsteady, his mind seething with fear and relief and a need so powerful it all but destroyed his ability to think clearly. All but forgotten was the fact that his world and Annie's were far apart. Forgotten, too, were all the many reasons why he had sworn never to acknowledge his father's blood.

"I'm sorry I hurt you," he said quietly. "I should have called out before I tried the door, but I was afraid—"

Annie laid a finger over his lips. "It doesn't signify." It was nothing compared to the hurt she had felt when she'd woken up and found him gone. Or the ache that had intensified during the long hours of the day when he hadn't returned. "I barred the door because of the snakes. I was afraid one might crawl inside. Then, too, something Mr. Mingo said . . ."

"What did Mingo say?"

T'maho righted the chair and seated himself, drawing Annie down onto his lap. So that he could tend her injured fingers, he told himself, breathing in the warm, clean scent of her hair. The whole house smelled of lye soap, and so did Annie. On her, it smelled sweeter than the wild yellow flowers that grew on vines at the edge of the glade.

She squirmed, and momentarily he lost his train of thought. "What did Mingo tell you?" he repeated.

"Ummm . . . nothing, really. It was just that I thought he was warning me against . . . well, I'm not sure. But I thought it wouldn't hurt to close the shutters."

"And barricade the door so that a snake trying to crawl under it would be crushed before he could search out the egg basket."

Her lips twitched. "That reminds me—Queenie came back. She—that is, he—lost some tail feathers, but otherwise he seems to have fared well enough."

But T'maho wasn't interested in roosters. Or snakes. Or even the fear that had brought him racing back through the darkness before the moon had even lifted above the trees, galloping through several inches of standing water on the trail.

She was safe. She was in his arms where he could see that no harm came to her. Reasonable or not, he wanted this woman as he had wanted no other woman—wanted her in ways that he could not begin to understand.

Most of all, he wanted her now, with an urgency that could no longer be denied. Cupping her bandaged hand in his, he placed it on his shoulder and lifted her chin with his thumb. "Annie," he whispered, "do you know what I wish to do?"

Candlelight glinted from her hair, shone right through her clear green eyes. With a look so brave and direct it left him feeling weak, she nodded. "I think so, T'maho."

"Do you wish it, too?"

She nodded again, slowly. "I do if you do."

Groaning, he gathered her up and stood, one arm under her knees, the other under her shoulder. Leaving the safe haven of the lighted kitchen behind, he strode into the dark bedroom and kicked the door shut behind him.

Chapter 15

This time there was no turning back. Compelled by a force more powerful than any hurricane, one he did not even try to understand, T'maho lowered Annie to her feet beside the bed and slipped her loose night shift from her shoulders. As it slithered to the floor, he caught his breath. Reaching past her, he opened the shutters on the window, allowing the light of the low-riding moon reflected from the nearby waters to spill into the room and halo her hair, gild the delicate curves of her body.

"Do not hide," he whispered hoarsely when she attempted to cover herself with arms and hands.

He reached out and gently removed her clumsily bandaged left hand from her small bosom. Bringing it up to his lips, he brushed a kiss on her palm, and then gently nipped the tip of one finger. Her hands were small and shapely, but not nearly so smooth and soft as they had been when she had first arrived.

Had he thought of her as frivolous and foolish, a useless ornament of society, a woman like the one his father had married? She was so much more than that.

She was strong and kind and gentle. She had taken in Saketa without a question, and cared for her as tenderly as any mother had ever cared for a child.

She was brave. Had she not attacked him when she'd thought he was murdering her father's calves?

He had called her scrawny. He had called her pale as the belly of a dead fish. Could any man call the new moon too thin, too pale?

Careful, a small voice whispered. *Deep waters flow here—strong currents that can sweep a man to his doom before he can find his footing.*

Ignoring the inner warning, T'maho drew her into his arms. She came without hesitation. If she had ever feared him, she no longer did, he thought, his heart swelling with a joy that held more of wonder than of lust.

She was trembling. His own hands were none too steady. The warm scent of lye soap and wood smoke and desire eddied around them, nearly bringing him to his knees. Burying his face in her hair, he willed his loins to patience and told himself that they would both be pleased by this night's work.

T'maho knew he was experienced enough to bring a woman to pleasure. He prided himself that he was a generous lover, for he had been taught well as a young man by a widow who had been married long enough to know what she wanted from a man.

But, he reminded himself, this was no widow, this was Annie. Innocent, vulnerable Annie, not one of the many experienced women who, over the years, had taught him the art of love.

And then: *Vulnerable?* he thought. The woman who had knocked him off his feet with a blast from her father's gun? The woman who had attacked him with a length of fencing and threatened him with a kitchen knife? The Annie he had come to know was as bold as any warrior. If she wanted him gone, she would not hesitate to send him packing.

And if there were certain flaws in his reasoning, he did not allow himself to search them out.

Besides, T'maho told himself as his hands moved up over a pair of delicate shoulders, down over a pair of surprisingly well-rounded hips, it was not as though he had come here with the deliberate intention of bedding her. If he did so now, it was only because they both wanted it.

He had ridden north again only to assure himself that she was safe, telling himself that tonight he would sleep just outside her door, and tomorrow he would take her to Etawak or one of the other villagers, where she would be safe until she decided to go back to her own people.

All this he told himself as his hands cupped her and lifted her against him. Her small, proud breasts brushed against his bare chest, and he felt the hard tips brand him like living fire. His breath came in ragged gasps, and he closed his eyes against the raw, compelling hunger that urged him to ride her until he was sated, then wake and take her again and again until he finally returned to his senses.

Conscience and desire warred within his virile young body.

"T'maho, what's wrong?" Annie whispered.

He shook his head. With unsteady hands, he fumbled at the tie of his buckskins and pulled free of their soft confinement. Then, closing his mind to all but the fierce need that drove him so relentlessly, he lifted her, laid her on the bed, and moved to follow her there.

One knee on the mattress, he reminded himself once more that this was no eager young widow, nor one of those women known to all unmarried men, who traded their favors for food or trinkets.

This was Annie. Annie, who had never known a man. Annie, who could not even tell a rooster from a hen, a cow from a bull. His little ginger-hair. So small, he thought fleetingly as he steeled himself not to leap on her like a rutting stag. So full of fire, yet so delicate that he must guard against hurting her—

He must . . .

With a groan, he collapsed, allowing her to bear his full weight for only an instant before he took her in his arms and rolled over with her onto his side. Finding her mouth, he covered it with his own, forcing her lips apart while her silken limbs moved restlessly against his.

Reluctantly, he broke away from the kiss. "Annie, listen to me," he said urgently, prodded once more by a conscience that refused to be dismissed. "Do you have any idea what it is I'm about to do to you?"

She lifted her head and he could see her eyes glowing in the moonlight, even though he could not see the color. With a soft groan, he leaned over and drew the tiny lobe of her left ear between his lips. He suckled, and then whispered, "Annie? Did you hear me?" –

Dazed by what was happening inside her body, Annie shook her head. How was it possible that having her ear licked could make her feel as if she were being licked somewhere else? She told herself she was not afraid, because whatever it was that T'maho wanted to do to her, he would never hurt her. He was the gentlest of men. Except perhaps when he was angry. Or impatient. Or—

But he would never willingly hurt her, he had proved it over and over, and besides, what he was doing to her now was delicious beyond anything, and she wanted more of it.

"Annie, are you sure?"

"Oh, yes," she said with a sigh, and his arms tightened around her. Her head was on his shoulder, and she felt as if she were surrounded by him. All over. Inside and out, which didn't even make sense.

And then his mouth came down on hers again, barely brushing her lips, and he felt warm and moist, soft, yet firm. And oh, so sweet she wanted to lick him, too! When the very tip of his tongue probed for entrance, she parted her lips and he entered her. Hesitantly, she began to suckle. In that same moment she felt something hard and hot leap against her belly, and startled, she bit down on his tongue.

T'maho jerked back his head. *"Mettowe boketawgh!"*

She gasped. "I'm sorry! I didn't mean to bite you, but—but T'maho, there's something down there that keeps moving."

He closed his eyes and groaned.

Her fingers gripped his arm. "T'maho, you don't think a snake could have crawled into bed with us, do you?"

He managed a laugh that sounded more pained than amused. "If it is a serpent, it is one that will never hurt you, that I promise. Here . . ." He took her hand and guided it. "You have only to touch him on the head and he will be your slave forever."

Cautiously, Annie allowed her hand to be guided to the thing that insisted on shoving itself against her belly. It felt warm, not cold. It felt smooth. And hard. And it was most definitely alive, for it leaped even as she touched it.

But the most startling discovery of all was that it was firmly attached to T'maho himself. Daringly, Annie allowed one finger to stray along its length, and then she jerked her hand away. "T'maho, did you know you have private hair, too?" She was shocked, yet oddly relieved to find that she was not the only one so afflicted.

He laughed, but the sound was strained. "Have you never before seen a man's body?"

Wordlessly, she shook her head.

"Not even that of a boy?"

"The school took in only girls. We had only women working there, except in the barnyard."

He sighed, almost as if in pain. She felt his hand move down between them. His fingers brushed against her secret place, and she drew back, tightening her thighs against the alien intrusion. "T'maho, you mustn't—"

"Oh, yes—I think I must," he whispered unevenly. She could almost hear the beat of his heart in the sound of his voice.

And then he found her, and she moaned. She whimpered. She felt a peculiar wetness between her limbs, and she could have died from embarrassment, but oh, it felt so—

So very . . . *"T'maho, what are you doing?"*

His mouth brushed slowly back and forth over her own, then moved down over her jaw to her throat. When he reached that sensitive place at the base of her neck, she jerked her shoulder. Chills cascaded down her body. She felt his touch on her breasts and she could hardly breathe, and when his mouth followed where his hand had been, she no longer even tried.

Out of a clear sky, lighting stabbed through her body again and again, sparkling all the way down to the pit of her belly. As if his fingertips were matches, fire blazed up wherever he stroked her—she tried to tell him this, but he kept stroking and stroking, and reaching out to explore the unexplored, and—

Oh, sweet merciful heavens, something was happening to her! Her limbs fell apart and her hips began to heave, and she whimpered, "Please—oh, please, T'maho—*do* something! I think I might be dying!"

He moved over her then, blocking out the silvery moonlight with his shoulders. His hair, unbound, brushed her face, and she drew in a deep, shuddering breath, wildly excited by the spicy, musky scent of him, and then he pressed her limbs even farther apart.

"Annie, don't be frightened—"

"I'm not frightened, it's just that—oh! T'maho, it—"

Something large and blunt began to probe, to push against her. It hurt. Something inside her burned. It felt as if she were being pried apart . . . and yet, she felt her hips lift closer, and she couldn't seem to help herself, and then the burning stopped, and something else commenced, and she—

"Oh, wait—something's happening! I feel—I feel—"

Panting, clutching, she hung on as he moved inside her, touching parts of her she could not even name, much less explain. Rainbows of color began to pulsate inside her, coming closer, closer—and then he began to move faster still, and she was moving, too, and then something exploded, and she came apart, shrieking again and again as she fell. "Don't leave me out here, T'maho, don't let go of me! Catch me, oh, please hold on to me!"

As the thunder of his heart finally slowed, T'maho continued to hold her even though she slept. Much later, when the moon had crossed over, leaving only a shadowy darkness behind, he slipped out of bed, stirred up the fire, and heated water. Bringing in the basin, he washed her sleeping body, tenderly wiping his seed and her maiden's blood from her slender thighs.

Once more in his right mind, he could not believe he had done this thing. Not to Annie—to a woman of her kind. To old Eli's daughter.

How would she find a husband now? Even if she found a man willing to marry her, he would not value her as she should be valued. If he told others that his bride had not come to him untouched, then they would look at her knowingly and whisper among themselves the way the villagers had whispered about Little Feet.

Would she leave here? Where could she go? Who would look after her?

Yet if she chose to remain on the island, how would he feel, facing her day after day when he had taken her innocence, knowing even as he did so that it must end there?

Annie stirred in her sleep, and T'maho grew still, one hand on her small foot. A foot, he reminded himself forcefully, that women of her kind insisted on forcing into a ridiculous shoe, the way they forced their bodies into stiff, uncomfortable garments and miserable stays.

T'maho told himself that she was no different from the woman his father had married. She could never fit into his world, even if he wished her to, nor could he fit into hers. He had tried it once. His father's rigid world had fit him no better than the stiff, oak-soled boots he'd been forced to wear.

Suddenly his heart grew still within his body. What if there was a child? A son, like the son his own father had sired onto a woman he had used solely for his own pleasure?

What then? Could he leave his son to be raised by a woman, as his own father had done to him?

Or would he keep the boy with him when she went away? And perhaps after a while, when his business prospered and he took a wife from among his own people, would she refuse to accept his son, who would be more white than Indian? Would she ask him to find the child's mother and give her back her son?

No man knew better than T'maho that a child of two worlds belonged wholly to neither. Clenching the washcloth tightly in his fist, he cursed himself for a fool and willed his seed to fall on fallow ground.

Then, sensing that he was being watched, he looked down to find Annie gazing up at him. He would have thought it impossible for a man of his years and experience to color like an untried maiden, yet the heat in his face was unmistakable.

"I have bathed you," he said gruffly.

She closed her eyes and turned away. "You shouldn't have done that. It's unseemly."

With a shrug, he rose and took the basin away to empty it out the door. He shouldn't have done any of the things he had done, but it was too late now for regrets. To his shame, T'maho knew that he would have taken her more than once had he not fallen into such a deep sleep. It had been weeks since he had slept the night through. That he had done so now was due only to the complete satisfaction his body had known, which did little to lessen his guilt.

It might be well, he told himself, to begin looking around for a woman of his own kind. When a man's lust overruled his brain to such an extent, it was time to take a wife.

"Come, get dressed, and I will take you into the village now," he said, avoiding her eyes as he spoke.

"To your house?" Annie bobbed up, clutching the bedcover up over her breasts.

Had he once thought her pale? She glowed all over. Red hair, pink face, enormous green eyes. "That would not be wise. I will take you to one of the village women, where you'll be safe until—"

"Until we can be married? Oh, T'maho, how long? I don't want to wait a minute longer than . . ."

She must have seen something in his face. Her voice trailed off, and he stalked off and busied himself at the fireplace, refilling the kettle, setting out a cup. One cup, not two.

"You'll find a husband from among your own people. Annie—I will tell him, if you wish me to, that I took you against your will, and if he's a decent man, he will not . . . Annie?"

The glow was gone. It was as if the life had drained right out of her body. "You don't want me?" she whispered, and his fingers gripped the tin canister until the sides bent inward.

"You could never be happy here. You would grow old before your time. Life on the Banks is not the kind of life you're accustomed to. It is hard. Here there are no servants to cook for you, to take care of your clothes, to wait on you. You would—"

"Do you think I care for any of that?"

"You do not belong here, Annie."

She had followed him to the kitchen. Now she stood, trailing the panel of rose brocade, its color suddenly reflected in her cheeks in ragged patches. "I do *so* belong here! *You're* here! Wherever you are, that's where I belong, because I love you, T'maho!"

"You do not love me. It is only that I was the first man who—your first . . ."

"You don't want me, then?" Once more the color fled. She reminded him of a small candle, flickering bravely in the wind, one moment burning too brightly, extinguished the next.

He steeled himself against weakening. If his mother had been stronger—or his father . . . "Any man would want you, Annie."

"Then why don't you?"

He swore softly under his breath. "We would not suit!"

She seemed to swell before his eyes. Chest heaving, eyes snapping, she pointed to the door with one hand, holding the bedcover like a faded, rose-colored shield with the other. "Then get out of my house, because I don't want you, either. You're nothing but a . . . a coward!"

And because nothing would be solved by his staying, he went.

An hour later, Annie sat at the table, her cup of tea untouched. She had dressed, going through the motions as lifelessly as a cuckoo in a clock.

T'maho was gone.

She told herself she was glad. She told herself that what had happened meant nothing, changed nothing. T'maho was right. They would never have suited, not in a hundred years. He was one kind of person, she another. It was merely a fluke they had ever met at all. In

Hillsborough, such a thing would never even have happened.

She sipped the tea. It was cold and weak. She had come to enjoy the taste of the native yaupon tea. She would have to ask . . .

No. She'd do no such thing. By this time next week, she promised herself, she'd be sipping China tea, not some homemade weed.

Her mind kept straying back over the past few hours, and she finally gave in and allowed her thoughts full play. Might as well think it all out so that she could get on with the business of forgetting.

Forgetting! Merciful saints, she could hardly believe it had happened in the first place! He had seen parts of her body that she had never seen in her entire life! When she thought of what he had done to her—what they had done together—where he had put that *thing*—!

Closing her mind to the ache in her heart, which was far greater than the ache in her body, Annie told herself she would have to leave on the next boat, that was all there was for it. It wouldn't be easy. All she had in the world was two dollars and a few pennies, plus whatever small sum she could get for her father's cattle, if she could ever find a buyer.

It would have to be Mr. Snell. He certainly looked prosperous enough. From what she'd seen of the villagers, they lived close to the bone, providing for most of their own needs and bartering for the rest.

Barter wouldn't help her now. It took money to travel. It would take even more to see herself settled in

some decent community where there would be a demand for her skills.

Wistfully, she thought of the way Dulsie Scarborough
had admired her gown that day she had ridden Jacob
into the village. And the way Saketa had fingered the
fabric and admired the embroidering about the hem.
For a little while she'd dared to hope . . .

Well. Enough of that. She had too much pride to
stay on in a place where she was not wanted. She
would catch the mail boat as she had originally
planned, get off at the first town large enough to support a dressmaker and small enough not to have one,
and start all over again. It wouldn't be the first time.

But it had blessed well better be the last, for she
didn't think she could stand much more upheaval in
her life!

What she needed was a small shop, perhaps just a
room in her house—if the sale of the cattle brought
enough so that she could even afford a house. Which
brought her right around to Mr. Snell again. She would
have to find him herself, since no one seemed willing
to help her.

Her mind strayed back to the night before, and her
eyes grew softly unfocused. Had she *really* felt all those
things she thought she'd felt? Did other people know
about it? And if they did, why didn't everyone do it all
the time?

Forcing her unruly mind away from the past and
back to her plans for the future, Annie told herself that
she could make do with a combination of workroom

and living quarters until she got herself established, which shouldn't take all that long.

She could always return to Hillsborough. She knew the name of the shop that had bought and sold her work for the past half dozen or more years. She knew the town, even knew a few of the townspeople. By sight, at least. Mrs. B. had not encouraged her charges to go into town except for Sunday services, where they entered in stairstep order, filled two and a half pews, sat stiffly under stern orders not to fidget, and then filed out again in reverse order, all without speaking to a soul.

No, not Hillsborough. Recalling the miserable journey that had taken her three weeks and nearly all her savings, Annie knew she would do better to look for somewhere close by.

Starting today. Starting this very minute!

Abruptly she stood up, gasped, and grabbed the edge of the table. Mercy! She ached in places she didn't even know could ache! Which reminded her all too vividly of just how those particular aches had been acquired.

"Balderdash," she muttered. She'd do better to stop her foolish daydreaming and get busy, if she planned on setting her plans into motion before another day had passed. Which she most definitely did.

How could hands so hard and callused be so gentle? How could they possibly—

Stop it this very minute, Annie Stevens O'Neal! You can be sure he'll not waste time thinking about you.

T'maho had stated his feelings quite clearly. They would not suit.

The only trouble was, they *had* suited . . . suited so incredibly well in such a way that she was afraid she would never be able to forget. By the time the morning was half over, Annie had hung all her clothes out to air, fed Jacob, and filled his trough with the brackish water from the rain barrel, which he didn't seem to mind.

When Queenie came running to see who was being fed, she threw out the last of the cornmeal, which was getting webby, anyway. Dusting off her hands, she marched inside to begin packing her trunk.

She'd never even gotten around to unpacking it, not completely, she thought as tears brimmed her eyes. Ruthlessly she scrubbed them dry. What did that signify? Nothing had turned out the way she had expected it to. Papa was gone, the house she had so looked forward to was little better than a ruin, and T'maho—

Well, the less said about T'maho, the better. There were times when a body was better off staying busy, and it had nothing at all to do with idle hands and the devil.

T'maho spent the morning searching for Jackson Snell. Somewhat less concerned now with vengeance than he was with justice, he wanted only to get the task behind him, for he had other things on his mind.

Unfortunately, tidewater still swelled Cecil's Creek to twice its usual size, covering most of the surrounding trails. Leaving Maroke on the main trail, he made his way east, toward the place where he had left the man, nearly bogging down twice and breaking out in a cold sweat once when a water moccasin swam past right in front of him.

His mind turned back to Annie, and with grim ruthlessness he jerked it back to the present. He had done the right thing. She did not love him any more than he loved her.

Besides, he was not at all convinced that the thing called love was anything more than a clever device invented by women for their own ends. Women were foolishly emotional creatures.

Lifting wet curtains of moss, he peered under tangled vines, searching for some sign of the man he had fully expected to find cowering in terror after experiencing the full force of a hurricane alone in the wilderness. He searched in caves made by uprooted trees. Then, retracing his steps, he searched again.

Nothing. The man was gone.

T'maho swore, using fragments of every language he had ever been exposed to. "Snell!" he roared, his words echoing eerily though the green gloom of the storm-raked forest. "I'm coming after you, do you hear me? You'd best start praying now to whatever gods will claim your miserable remains!"

With water still standing several inches deep in the low ground, tracking was all but impossible over much of the glade. T'maho began casting out farther from Long Green Pond, climbing one ridge after another, searching for some sign of a trail through thickets of yaupon so dense a boar hog couldn't penetrate them, over beds of tide-bent bracken and knife-sharp fans of palmetto.

He felt a powerful need to keep moving, as if by moving far enough and fast enough, he might outrun his thoughts.

Four hours later, T'maho admitted defeat. It did not come easy, for he prided himself on his ability as a tracker. This time, however, he was forced to admit that his quarry had escaped. Broken trees fell over many of the trails, making movement all the more difficult. The only trail he had picked up after hours of searching was that of a pair of trappers.

T'maho knew which men trapped this section of the glade. From the freshness of the tracks, they had checked their traps early that very morning. From the depth of the same tracks, they had gone out more heavily burdened than they had come in. They would not be taking furs this early in the season. Possibly venison, if their womenfolk had tired of fish and fowl and turtle.

At any rate, they had taken something of considerable weight.

Maybe they had found Snell. Or he had found them. After all this time, the bastard had probably been suffering so from fright and exposure, they'd been forced to carry him out.

Feeling no guilt at all at having marooned the man, T'maho began to run back toward where he'd left Maroke, moving silently and swiftly over the littered forest bed.

Mingo had suspected Snell, too. He had all but

admitted to having searched earlier. Although he would not leave Saketa unguarded to search again, he would have arranged to see that the *Black Opal* did not leave the harbor, if it took every boat in the village to blocade the channel.

Riding swiftly toward the village, T'maho thought of Annie as he had left her. So proud, so angry . . . so hurt. She did not yet understand. He would have to convince her.

But first he would have to convince himself, for the farther south he had ridden, the more he had known it could not end there.

T'maho told himself that he would see justice done—if the trappers had not found Snell, then he would take Saketa to Etawak and he and Mingo would search every swamp and ridge, every swale and creek, until they found the man and brought him in.

And then he would be free to turn his mind to another, more important matter.

Chapter 16

Saketa stood beside the window and preened before the small mirror Mingo had given her just that morning as a reward for staying hidden for a few more days, until her assailant could be captured, brought in, and shipped across the sound for trial.

She had begged for a looking glass of her own ever since she'd seen the one Dulsie had gotten for her birthday.

For days she had been wondering if she would have to go to court, too. She had always wanted to go to the mainland, to see what a real town looked like, but T'maho would never allow it. He said towns there were wicked places, and there was nothing there worth having.

But if she was forced to go, he could hardly object. Besides, who else could tell a judge all the wicked things Jack had done to her?

Well . . . perhaps not *all* of them. She would be too ashamed.

Gathering her hair in one hand, she wadded it into a knot and turned her head this way and that, picturing herself in a courtroom filled with handsome men wearing wigs, and envious women wearing gowns that were beautiful, but not as beautiful as the gown Annie had promised to give her. It even had lace at the neckline.

She was all but done with hiding. T'maho had wormed the truth from her, without her ever having to say a word. And she was glad it was finally over. Now, or at least just as soon as T'maho brought Jack in and sent him off to be punished, she would be able to go back to Eli's house and fetch the gown and the skirt Annie had given her. She'd been so frightened she had left them behind when Jack had showed up that day just before the storm, but they were hers. Annie had promised to give them to her, and Annie would never go back on a promise.

Saketa wished she could be more like Annie O'Neal. Independent, with no one to tell her to do this, do that, and stop being childish!

Holding the mirror up to reflect her face, she tilted her head this way and that, wishing her skin were not so dark. She had tried lemon juice and green persimmons, and Etawak had mixed her a special paste that was supposed to turn her skin as pale as Dulsie's, but instead it had made her break out in spots.

" 'Keeta? What are you doing out of bed?"

Saketa jumped and hid the mirror behind her. Mingo was always taunting her about being vain, which she was not. But she could hardly help knowing that her eyes were well set, that her mouth was well shaped, and that, with a bit of stuffing in the front of her gown, her figure was every bit as good as Dulsie Scarborough's.

She knew, too, that Mingo still loved her, and sometimes she felt almost guilty when she daydreamed about marrying some tall, handsome man with yellow curls and soft hands, who wore a clawhammer coat and knee britches and shoes with silver buckles, like the gentleman pictured in the *Elizabeth City Star and Eastern North Carolina Intelligencer* that Dulsie had shown her last month.

She pointed to the bean bread, all neatly wrapped in corn shucks and ready to drop into the stew pot as soon as the meat was tender. She was proud of her cooking, which was better than Annie's.

"You do not have to work in my house."

Saketa's cheeks flushed. She had done it because she felt guilty, because the first chance she got, she intended to go back to Annie's after her clothes no matter what Mingo and T'maho said about keeping herself hidden away until it was safe to show herself in the village. "Even work is better than doing nothing," she said. She was so tired of having to stay inside with no one to visit with and nothing to do.

Mingo, seeing how forlorn she looked, stepped out of his sandy shoes and left them beside the door. He wore shoes instead of moccasins only because he knew Saketa admired them.

Which only proved what a fool he was. Hanging his leather vest on a peg, he crossed to the fire and lifted the lid on the cook pot. "Smells good."

She pointed to the string of onions. "Two onions,

three potatoes. And salt. It was a big flipper, Mingo, even with all the fat scraped off." She could cook well enough when she set her mind to it. There was nothing difficult about stewing turtle or fish or salt beef. It was simply boring.

Now, if she were cooking for a husband—for the man she loved—why, then, it would be different.

Dancing around, she teased Mingo with a flirtatious look, wishing he weren't in such a serious mood. She almost wished she had not let him know she had found her voice. Miming had been fun. Even a dull game was better than no game at all.

Instead of responding to her teasing look, Mingo turned away, causing her to wonder what she had done wrong. She didn't like it when he ignored her, even when she deliberately taunted him into losing his temper.

Sighing, she wandered across to the bed and flung herself down to mope. She was half tempted to force him to pay her attention, but if she made him truly angry, he might send her back to Etawak, and she'd rather stay here. Etawak's house smelled of acorn beer and dried frog skin and fish entrails.

Was he angry because he knew who her lover had been? She was almost sorry she had told him, but even if she hadn't, T'maho would have told him, because T'maho had guessed right off. He had said Jack's name, looking right at her, and even though she hadn't opened her mouth, she knew from that "quiet" look that came over him that he had guessed her secret.

But she couldn't bear for Mingo to know how

shamefully she had acted—what a fool she had been to believe all Jack's lies, which was a silly vanity on her part, for sooner or later the whole village would have to know. She didn't care about the others, not even Dulsie, who would probably insist on knowing every detail, but she hated for Mingo to know of her shame. When he was angry with her, it hurt, it truly did!

Ignoring her, he drew a stool up to the table and began grinding the stubby blade of his oyster knife. She waited for him to finish, then assumed a pouting expression. "You're a wretched old spoilsport!"

He nodded, frowning over an imagined nick in the blade. Stung, Saketa blinked several times in an effort to produce a few tears, which always brought him around. The tears refused to come, and she sighed heavily instead. Finally, pushed beyond her limited patience when he continued to ignore her, she cried, "You don't love me, anyway, no matter what Etawak says, and I certainly don't love you!"

"I know that, little sparrow. I have always known that," Mingo said quietly, and then she did cry.

Turning away, she hid her tears, staring blindly out the window while they ran freely down her cheeks.

At first the village seemed empty when T'maho rode out of the glade into the clearing. There was little wind, but the temperature had begun to drop despite the fact that the sun was still high in the sky.

He paused for a moment, his hand resting on Maroke's withers. He had thought to go straight to Mingo's lodge, but he needed to know. If the trappers had indeed brought Snell in, they would be down at the harbor. The big bent oak by the fish house was the gathering place for the village men. He would go there first.

As he walked the mare toward the harbor, T'maho's thoughts turned not toward Snell and the justice that would soon be meted out, but to Annie. He should not have left the way he had.

Yet, if he had stayed, what more could he have said? Some men lied and spoke of love at such times, and he did not love her. He admired her. She had more courage than most women he knew, in spite of her lamentable ignorance of even the most basic matters.

He liked her more than he had ever thought it possible to like a woman. But love her he did not. He had vowed long ago never to love any woman. Love made a man do foolish things. Wicked things. Love made a man betray his own flesh and blood. T'maho had learned early in life that what women called love was no more than greed and ambition.

No, he did not love Annie O'Neal any more than she loved him, in spite of what she thought now, but that had not kept him from taking her innocence. For that he owed her more than just his walk-away tracks.

He had acted without honor. As soon as this business with Snell was finished, he would write a letter to his father on Annie's behalf. Hamilton, if he was still alive, would be able to help her get established. For himself, T'maho would have died before asking a favor, but for Annie's sake, he would willingly humble himself.

But first he must take care of Jackson Snell. For Saketa's sake, and because no woman would ever be safe with such a one walking free. If it meant enlisting the aid of every man in the village, he would do so.

Long before he took the bend of the road that led down to the harbor, T'maho could hear the buzz of talk. He set the mare into a smooth canter, wondering if the discovery of a man who had ridden out a storm alone in the glade could be the cause of all the commotion. In spite of the rumors, no one yet knew of the wicked part Snell had played in Saketa's disappearance.

Dropping the reins, he slid to the ground and made his way through the circle of people gathered around some central point of interest.

And then he came to a dead halt. Sweat beaded his forehead. The last meal he had eaten, which had been too many hours before, threatened to return on him as he stared down at the body of Jackson Snell, his ruined finery covered with gore, pink scalp showing through his thinning hair, a hatchet protruding from between his shoulder blades.

A feeling of awful finality came over T'maho as he stared at that hatchet. He recognized it. The blade was no different than most hatchets, but the handle was as familiar to him as the knife at his side.

It was old Izzer Clark who spoke first. "I reckon we all know what's been done. Any man here know who done it?"

Several people edged back uneasily. There was a general shaking of heads and a murmur of denial. T'maho stood as if frozen in place.

God, he had wanted justice, not vengeance! At least, not this rough vengeance.

At least, not lately. His first hot rage having cooled, as it always did, he'd been left with a determination to see the man punished to the full extent of the law. He would have preferred the old Hattorask law, which was more direct, but he'd made up his mind to settle for a court-ordered hanging.

Still, he felt cheated. For Saketa's sake, he had wanted to be the one to bring him in. It was a matter of honor. If Snell happened to be injured in the process, T'maho would not have been overly concerned, but neither would he have struck from behind. That was an act of weakness, not of honor.

"Gawks amercy, he don't look near so fine now, do he?" murmured one old woman, peering from behind her uplifted apron.

"You say you found him thisaway near Little Oak Grove?"

One of the trappers, a set of empty traps still dangling from his shoulder, nodded. "First light. We was on our way in. Saw somethin' lyin' alongside the first ridge. I sent John James over to see what it was, and he commenced to hollerin' fit to wake the dead." He tipped his hat, a battered beaver with sweat-stained band. "No disrespect intended."

Jackariah Gray, as spokesman for the village elders, stepped forward and turned to survey the crowd. "Any of you recognize that there hatchet?"

It seemed to T'maho that all eyes turned to him. Surely there wasn't a single person who didn't recognize the hand-shaped persimmon wood haft. He had proudly marked it with his sign and used it since he was a boy, right up until he had himself a newer, heavier hatchet. Before he had given the old one away, he had sharpened the blade to a fine edge, but as the handle had still been sound, he had merely pounded the wedges in tighter.

The rock-hard wood was now shiny with age and use, but his sign was still visible—the same sign that marked his net floats and his few traps. The same sign he had painted so proudly on the stern of the boat he had recently bought with a view to hiring men to fish her for him, so that he could go into the business of trading smoked and salted fish across the sound for things the villagers could not provide for themselves.

Numbly, he stared now at the grisly sight.

"T'maho, I seem to recollect you was asking around about Snell jest before the storm," said Jackariah. "Don't suppose ye ever caught up to him, did ye?"

Silence fell over the crowd. All eyes turned on him, and T'maho straightened his shoulders. "I found the man. He followed me into the glade and I left him there. I did not kill him."

"Well, as to that, I reckon we'd best let the law decide, seein's how your hatchet come to be stuck in the man's back."

Separating from the crowd as naturally as cream rose to the top of the pan, the five village elders moved to stand before him. "I'm right sorry it come about this way, boy, but I reckon you'd best let us take you into keepin'. Marcus Aurelius is headed out across the sound come morning. Reckon he might's well fetch us a justice o' the peace out here to set things straight."

All eyes turned to the body that lay on the wharf at the center of the circle. Jackson Snell was their justice of the peace. Although no one much cared for the man, he had served the Banks these past dozen years in that capacity. Not that they'd ever had much need of his services. In Kinnakeet, as in all the other villages on the Banks, people tended to settle matters among themselves.

T'maho stared stoically ahead. There was only one way he could clear himself, and that would mean implicating someone else. He had given the hatchet away years ago. God alone knew how it had gotten where it was, but then, with half the village underwater, things had a tendency to get washed away, buried, and otherwise misplaced.

"They say death comes in threes," said a woman in baleful tones. "I heard tell Eli was gone, now Snell. Lordy, Lordy, I wonder who's next?"

News traveled fast in such a small community. Mingo had been shoring up the foundation of his house, which had been undermined slightly when the creek had overflowed, when young Cormick Barnes came by to bring him a water barrel that had washed up against the Barnes's net shed.

"This here one looks like your'n, Mingo. I still ain't found our'n. Reckon by now it's halfway across the sound."

Mingo straightened, his wide, powerful body wet

with sweat. "Thank you. It is mine, but if you have need of it, I have another."

"We got a spare, but thankee just the same."

Saketa, hearing the voice of the handsomest boy in the village, could not resist hanging out the window. She waved to get his attention, grinned, and then ducked away when Mingo turned on her, his face a stern mask.

"So this here's where Saketa's been hiding out, is it? They say she was took real sick, with spots and ever'thing."

"I do not have spots!" came a loud screech from inside the house.

"Saketa! Behave yourself!"

The boy looked at Mingo and then at the open window where Saketa remained just out of sight, curiosity alive on his smooth young face.

Stiffly, Mingo said, "If that's all, then I thank you for taking the trouble, Cormick."

But the boy wasn't done yet. "Reckon you've not heard the news. They brought Justice Snell in early this morning, deader'n a drownded rat, and T'maho, he's been took up for killing 'im. They're a-holdin' him aboard Snell's boat, since she's the only one that don't have no work to do. Them two Porteegee deckhands o' Snells, they done took off 'fore the storm hit, else they coulda done it." He shook his head, causing his blond hair to slither over a pair of generous ears. "Ask me, that there hatchet o' T'maho's musta hurt somethin' awful. Busted clean through his backbone. You shoulda seen the blood! Ruint his coat all to pieces. Reckon he'll have to change clothes afore they lay him out to bury him."

But Mingo hadn't stayed to hear the end of the report. Yelling over his shoulder for Saketa to stay where she was, he ran to the pen, snatching Raputtak's reins off the fence as he passed.

Saketa was safe! The wall of fear that had held him imprisoned ever since she had come so close to dying began to crumble and fall away.

His little sparrow was safe. He would deal with her later. Right now, he had to pull T'maho's acorns from the fire. If there was one thing he knew about his friend, it was that T'maho could never have killed a man in cold blood, no matter how great the temptation.

Cormick walked backward for a few minutes, eager to get back to all the excitement, but almost as eager to see whether or not Saketa had spots. It wouldn't take long. He'd lay odds she'd be slipping out of that house before Mingo was even out of sight. If there was one person in the whole wide world that girl loved more than she loved herself, it was that brother of hers.

Annie had seen the familiar-looking sails offshore nearly an hour ago. They'd hung slack as a wet bedsheet, as the wind had been fitful all day. Of course, it might not even be the mail boat, but if it was, she couldn't take a chance on missing it. If Mr. Snell was not readily available, the sale of her cattle would simply have to wait.

Hastily, she dressed, put up her hair, and then hesitated over whether or not to wear her hat. Deciding that her standards of dress had fallen woefully short, to the detriment of her behavior, she jammed the thing on her head and rammed home two hatpins that had already rusted from the constant damp salt atmosphere.

She wore her stays, as well, lacing them up tight enough to suit even the highest stickler. Perhaps if she'd never taken to leaving them off in the first place, she would not be in the fix she was in now. Slovenly dress, according to Mrs. B., led to slovenly behavior, which led directly to the devil's domain.

But then, Mrs. B. had run off with a traveling man—stays, gloves, ostrich-plumed turban, and all.

"That's as may be, there's no use in crying over spilt milk," Annie muttered. She had made a mistake, and that was that. Moping and wailing wouldn't change it. She had things to do and places to go, and the sooner she got started on her way, the better!

The cattle could take care of themselves until she could make other arrangements. She intended to be on that boat when it sailed out of Kinnakeet Harbor. As for her destination, the mail boat could decide that for her. Any town large enough to support a posting office would likely be large enough to support a seamstress.

Looking back on all that had happened in the short time since she had come to the Outer Banks so full of hope and excitement, Annie felt the tears threaten. If crying would have done a speck of good, she would have bawled her eyes out, but tears wouldn't bring back Papa. Tears wouldn't make T'maho love her.

According to the Bible, there was a time to weep and

a time to laugh. At the moment, neither seemed particularly appropriate.

"Poor Jacob," she murmured as she took down the bridle, which was somewhat the worse for having been buried under a ton of storm debris. "You miss Papa, too, don't you? Perhaps you'd like to go and live with Mr. Mingo. He seems a kind enough man."

As for that contrary old chicken, it could fend for itself.

Annie glanced toward the sound. The sails were still some distance out. She prayed the wind would lay long enough for her to reach the village and arrange for someone to ship her trunk to her once she was settled.

She prayed she wouldn't have to see T'maho before she sailed.

And then she changed her mind and prayed she would.

Which was just about as sensible as anything else she had done since she had first set foot on the island, she told herself, laughing a little in spite of her aching heart.

A few miles away in the village of Kinnakeet, the tide was dead low, causing the black-hulled sloop to ride well below the level of the wharf. Barely had the door closed behind him before T'maho began feeling trapped. He clutched the brass rim of the partially opened porthole and stared out at several pairs of legs that all but blocked his view of the proceedings. They still hadn't moved the body. What were they waiting for?

Who could have killed the bloody bastard?

More to the point at the moment, how long could he stay sane, locked into this suffocating box that reeked of bay rum and unwashed bodies? He had always had a problem with small enclosed places, which was why his lodge had windows on all four sides, and why his new boat was an open one, with only a canvas shelter against the weather.

Recognizing the elders by their footwear and trouser legs, which was all he could see from his particular vantage point, T'maho pressed his ear to the partly open porthole in an effort to hear what was being said.

The men spoke in undertones, as if conscious of his nearness and embarrassed by it. T'maho was embarrassed, too, but more than that, he was beginning to realize that he might be in more serious trouble than he'd first thought. Here on the island, he was known to be a man of honor.

But what if, instead of bringing another justice of the peace out here, they took him across the sound? No one on the mainland could speak for him. What chance would he have? An Indian, and not even from an important tribe. A Banker, at that. Bankers were widely thought to be uncivilized. On the mainland, it was even said that they deliberately lured ships onto the shoals, while the truth was that most of the village men, at one time or another, had risked their lives to save others.

But truth walked slowly while a lie flew on swift wings.

Ahone! As the full gravity of his plight began to sink

in, T'maho thought about his father. Was the man still alive? It had been years—twelve years, to be exact—since Hamilton had brought him out to the Banks and left him, not even waiting to learn that Little Feet, T'maho's mother, had died giving birth to a daughter.

What kind of a man would do that to his only son?

But perhaps T'maho was no longer his only son. By now he might have a dozen yellow-haired sons, all looking exactly like the woman he had chosen over his own flesh and blood.

He swore, slammed his fist into his open palm, and then turned back to the porthole. And there, not five feet away, stood Mingo's double-laced boots. T'maho recognized those boots. Mingo had bought them more than a year ago when he'd overheard Saketa admiring a pair of similar boots worn by a logger who'd come out to the island to oversee the harvesting of oak knees to be sold to a shipyard up north.

What the devil was Mingo doing here? He should be back at his lodge looking after Saketa! The danger was past—still, with T'maho gone, someone would have to look after both Saketa and Etawak.

And Annie, he thought with a growing feeling of loss. Someone would have to take care of Annie now—see her settled somewhere, or at least decently housed. Perhaps in his own lodge. He would tell Mingo that if he didn't come back, Mingo should give the house to Annie. And sell his new boat and give her the profit, and look after her, for she couldn't look after herself. She wouldn't know what to do, where to go.

What if another storm struck? What if lightning

caused the herd to stampede? That old shack of Eli's would be no protection at all!

Swearing silently as he thought of what he had done that he shouldn't, and all the things he had not done that he should have, T'maho rapped sharply on the glass. "Mingo, you damned old buffalo," he called out, "stop talking long enough to listen!"

With an impatient twist of the brass screw, he undogged the porthole, shoved it wide, and stuck his face in the opening, drawing in a lungful of air rich with the mingled scent of salt and iodine, dead fish and tarred nets.

Which was a damned sight more welcome than sweat and bay rum!

Just then there was a general shuffling of feet outside, and several voices were raised. Mingo's shoes were no longer visible. The next thing T'maho knew, footsteps were clattering overhead on the deck of the *Opal*. A broad grin broke across his face. Mingo had talked them into letting him go! God alone knew how, but he had done it!

The polished mahogany hatch opened. Mingo's big, booted feet, followed by two more pairs of boots, came down the narrow companionway ladder, and T'maho readied himself to leave the stuffy cabin. "It's about time, you old—"

"Sorry, Mingo," said Izzer Clark. "It don't seem right. T'maho shoulda said it was you that done it, but I reckon seein's how you two are such friends, he figgered to take it on himself."

T'maho's grin faded. "Mingo? Izzer? What's going on?"

"Mingo here, he says he done it, so I reckon you're free to go, T'maho."

T'maho swore. He grabbed the handle of his knife, which no one had thought to relieve him of. "Damn all, Mingo, you're lying! You no more killed that bastard than—" he'd started to say than he had, but in that case, Izzer and the others might have thought to look further. Sooner or later, someone would have remembered that it was not T'maho who had been using that particular hatchet for the past several years.

"Mingo didn't do it, Izzer. That's my hatchet and you know it. You saw my mark on the handle."

The two village elders looked from one man to the other. "I never knowed you to lie, son," said Jackariah.

"I do not lie," T'maho said flatly.

"On the other hand, I don't see no cause for a man to say he done a wickedness when he didn't. Reckon we'll just have to wait and let the court decide the straight of it. That set all right with you, Izzer?"

The other man stroked his jaw, studying first one and then the other with eyes that had gauged both the weather and his fellow man for more than seventy years. Finally he nodded. "I'll see to your womenfolk, T'maho. Both of ye better write out what ye want done with yer boats and nets and such-like, and whichever one of ye don't come back, I'll see that yer last wishes is carried out."

* * *

Some distance from the harbor, half hidden behind the weighty boughs of the big oak, Saketa clung to Cormick Barnes's hand until he winced from the pain of her grip. "They're taking Mingo down below," Saketa whispered hoarsely. "Oh, no—not Mingo, please!"

"Reckon he done it, then, not T'maho. T'maho, he's got a hot 'nuff temper, but I'd ha' never thought Mingo had it in him. Hard to tell about a man. Reck'n he's ugly enough, though."

Saketa flung the hand from her and turned to glare at the boy she had once considered the handsomest in the village. If it weren't for that stinky old asafetida bag his mother made him wear around his neck to ward off the influenza, she might even have considered marrying him in a few years.

"Mingo is not ugly! Just because his face got burned a long time ago, that doesn't mean he's ugly!"

Cormick shrugged and said nothing, which only irritated her more.

"I'm going to tell it that you were the one that put that dead cat down Miss Parthenia's chimney."

"Then I'll tell it that you stuff rags down the chest of your frocks."

"I do no such thing, Cormick Barnes!"

"Oh, yes, you do, too. I watched you wading in the creek one day last summer, and I saw that wad o' rags that floated out when you stepped in a muskrat hole and went under."

Saketa swung at him, but then she turned back to the *Black Opal*. Two men had just came back up on deck. Izzer Clark and Jackariah Gray. Once again she

Chapter 17

Annie left her trunk just inside the door, ready to be collected at a later date. After some consideration, she set her valise, her shawl, and her reticule on the stump where she could ride by, lean down, and scoop them up on her way past. Mounting Jacob required both her hands and her full attention. The first time she had tried it with her reticule in hand, it had swung on its strings and slapped the mule in the side, and he'd nearly kicked the gate down.

She was just slipping the bridle over Jacob's head for the third time—and this time correctly, she sincerely hoped—when Saketa came barreling up and slid off her pony just outside the shed. "Annie, you've got to come. *Now!*"

At the intrusion, Jacob shook his head, dislodging the bridle, which went sailing across the shed. "Saketa? Oh, my mercy, you can talk! But that's wonderful! I've been so worried—"

"Never mind that—come right *now!* T'maho needs you!"

"T'maho?" Annie had heard of blood running cold.

Hers did. She felt a chill settle over her that had nothing to do with the falling temperature. "Is he ill? Has he been hurt?"

Saketa collected the homemade bridle and grabbed Jacob by his short mane. Glaring into his small, wary eyes, she slipped the thing over his head, jerked the lark's knot into position, and handed Annie the looped end. "You need a saddle?"

"A saddle?" A ladder she might have accepted, but Annie couldn't even lift her father's saddle, much less figure out where all the various flaps and straps were supposed to go.

"Then come on! They're planning to leave just as soon as Marcus Aurelius's mama irons his shirt and mends his good coat. They're not even going to wait for Gil and Inacio to come back."

"Gil and Inacio?" Leaving? *Marcus Aurelius?*

"The Porteegees. Hurry!"

Of course. The Porteegees. Annie wondered if she could have fallen and struck her head without knowing it. Nothing Saketa was saying made sense.

But then, when, just lately, had anything made sense? "Saketa, would you please slow down? I was on my way to the landing to catch the mail boat. Exactly where is it you wish me to go?"

"To the landing. The mail boat's not in yet, but it can wait. I can speak for Mingo, but if I do that, I won't be able to speak for T'maho, so you'll have to save him."

While Saketa held the mule steady, Annie climbed to the third bar on the sagging gate and attempted to drag herself over onto Jacob's back. It was no easier this time than it had been the last time she'd tried it, but eventually she succeeded. Saketa swatted his dusty backside, and Annie grabbed handfuls of coarse, mouse-gray hair and struggled to regain her balance. If she fell off, she would be trampled to death, and then she wouldn't be able to save anyone.

"W-wait! My reticule," she cried weakly. "M-my v-valise!"

But Saketa had raced off ahead, leaving Annie to bounce along behind her, skirts blowing up over her knees. She clung to the reins with both white-knuckled hands while her hat, which had been anchored to her coiled braid with her last two hatpins, slipped farther westward with every bounce.

"Stop flapping your ears, Jacob, I'm not trying to tickle you!" Nevertheless, she tried to grip his sides with her limbs instead of her toes. "Saketa, slow down! Come back here this minute and tell me exactly what's happened! Has T'maho been badly hurt? Is he asking for me?"

"Not yet," the younger girl called over her shoulder.

"You mean he hasn't asked for me?"

"I mean he hasn't been hurt bad. Yet!" And then, mercifully, she slowed down enough for Annie and Jacob to catch up.

Annie shifted to a more secure position so that she would not bounce quite so much. Fortunately, there was a nice sag in the middle of Jacob's back. "What's happened to T'maho? Saketa, where am I going? What am I supposed to do when I get there?"

"You don't have to do anything," said Saketa. "When we get there, all you have to do is tell Mr. Izzer and Mr. Jackariah and the rest that T'maho spent last night with you."

Annie felt as if someone had given her a hard whack in the chest. "He *told you*?"

Twisting around, Saketa stared at her, dark eyes round as chestnuts. "You mean he *did*?"

"Saketa, would you please start at the beginning and tell me what's happened, and just what it is we're supposed to be saving your brother from?"

"Hanging."

Annie lost her concentration, Jacob changed his gait, and she nearly fell off again. "God in heaven—did you say *hanging*?"

"They're saying he murdered Jackson Snell. Right in the middle of the storm. John James said as to how a dead muskrat started out limp, and then he got stiff, and then he got limp again if you waited too long to skin him out, but if you waited *too* long—"

"Saketa!"

"Well, what he said was that when they found—"

"Saketa! I don't care about dead muskrats! Why would anyone say such a terrible thing about T'maho?"

"I was just trying to show how they—yes, well . . . Anyhow, they say it must've happened late last night, on account of he was all stiff when they found him this morning when they went in to set out their traps again now that the water's gone down some, and they say T'maho was asking about him, so when he rode off into the glade just before dark last night—"

"Saketa! Get to the point!"

"Yes, well—he didn't. Leastwise, I don't think he did, but even if he did, he deserved it, but I can't bear to see him dragged off to some awful place where he won't even be able to see outside, because T'maho purely hates to be shut in—or Mingo either, because they'll hang him and I'll never see him again, and even if he makes me mad as spit, I love him more than anyone in the whole world, and—"

Annie shook her head dazedly, further endangering her hat. Saketa had gotten her voice back, only what had happened to her wits?

"Saketa, slow down and start over," she ordered firmly. "Now, just who murdered whom, and who said T'maho did it? Who's holding him, and where does Mingo come into all this?"

By the time they arrived at the village, the capricious wind had shifted, driving whitecaps toward the shore. The air had grown distinctly brisk. Annie was shivering, but it had nothing to do with the temperature.

In her singularly disjointed way, Saketa had explained that Jackson Snell was the man who had beaten her, the man who had gotten her with child, and T'maho had found out about it, although she thought he'd already suspected the truth. Everyone seemed to know that both T'maho and Mingo had been searching for someone for days, even though no one was certain who it was they'd been searching for, or why.

"So when Snell was found with a hatchet in his back

just this morning, they said T'maho did it, and then Mingo came and said no, he did it, and now they're holding them both penned up on Jack's boat until Marcus Aurelius can take 'em across the sound to a judge."

"But why hold both of them?" Annie asked. Despite Saketa's twisted recital, she thought she finally had all the details; trying to piece them together was like working out the design of a patchwork quilt with both eyes shut.

"Well, if it had been just one, the old men would have settled it amongst them. Likely they'd have sent whichever one did it down the sound and told him never to come back again, and naturally, he wouldn't," Saketa said with such an artless look that Annie could only believe her. "It'd be fearsome awful, never being able to come back home. Only now they aren't sure which one did it, and they can't hardly punish them both, so they have to have an outsider to settle it for them. I s'pose the wreck commissioner could do it if he happened to be down here, but he's not been in months, not since that ship load of logwood come ashore near Trent Hills."

Annie shook her head, dazed. She had not had much experience with the law, but this seemed a strange way of dealing with such matters. However, her only concern was T'maho. "So they've both been accused of—of murder?"

Saketa shrugged. She was wearing scuffed shoes with no stockings, a faded blue India cloth skirt, and a plain muslin shirtwaist. The brisk breeze coming off the water did not seem to affect her at all. "Jack was killed sometime during the night. T'maho's mark is on the hatchet that's stuck in his back, only it's not his anymore, and then Mingo upped and told everybody he was the one that did it, and T'maho said Mingo did not, and Mingo said yes he did, and now neither one will back down."

It took a moment to digest, even at the second telling. And even then, Annie felt as if she must have missed some vital detail. Just because Saketa had regained the use of her voice, that didn't mean her train of thought was any easier to follow than it had been the first time Annie had met her.

Jackson Snell? A respected officer of the court? Her father's partner? Annie had felt an instinctive dislike of the man after the first few minutes in his presence. She found it almost impossible to believe that he and Saketa had—

But evidently they had.

Not for a moment did she doubt that if T'maho had learned the identity of the man who had done such a heinous thing to his sister, he would be capable of murdering the man.

But not with a blow to the back. Despite her first impression of him—that he was a cruel, bloodthirsty savage—Annie knew T'maho would never stoop to anything so cowardly. She had known him only a short time, but during that time she had come to know him better than she had ever known any man. And she knew as well as she knew her own name that he had more honor in his little finger than most men had in their entire body.

"So will you do it?"

"Will I . . . you mean tell them *that*? Well, of course I'll do it!" If T'maho had asked her to walk through fire for him, she would have lifted her skirts and waded in without question.

The crowd was still gathered, the discussion having shifted to who would sail Snell's *Black Opal* across the sound, because naturally Marcus Aurelius wanted to take his own boat; and whether or not they should try to round up Snell's crew; and whether the hatchet should be removed from the victim's body before he was shrouded and carried on board.

"Reck'n it be evidence," said Izzer Clark of the hatchet.

"Might be evidence, but it ain't fittin'," commented Jackariah.

It was someone else's opinion that the hatchet should be removed, wrapped separately, and laid alongside the body, and then, of course, came the question of who would do the deed.

No one volunteered.

Saketa slid off her pony, dropped the reins, and strode forward, leaving Annie to dismount the best way she could. Annie was thankful that no one was watching her less-than-graceful descent, as all eyes were on the dark-haired young girl who planted herself directly in front of the five elders.

"Mr. Izzer," said Saketa, her young voice ringing out

clearly in the sudden hush, "you might as well go fetch
Mingo back up on deck and turn him loose, because
whatever he told you he did, he didn't. Leastwise, he
didn't kill Jack Snell. And if you want to know how I
know he didn't, it's because Mingo was with me all
night long, from supper last night to when he woke up
this morning, and he didn't sneak out of bed and go off
to no glade to put a hatchet into Jack's back, because
I would've known if he so much as wiggled his big toe."
Her chin lifted to an imperious angle. She was the center of attention, and it was plain that she relished the
position. "Because we were *that* close!" She held up
two fingers pressed together. "So you just go fetch him
up out of there, right *now*!"

Aboard the nearby sloop, two men stood at the open
porthole, listening in stunned silence. "You were?"
asked T'maho.

"No." Mingo's face wore an expression of dazed disbelief . . . and of hope. But before either of them could
say more, Annie had pushed her way through the
throng to speak her piece, her cheeks flaming every bit
as brightly as her hair.

"You may release Mr. T'maho at the same time," she
said in a high, thin voice that rang with conviction for
all its lack of strength. "Because—well, for the same
reason."

All eyes swung back to Saketa, and Annie rushed to
explain. "No, he was with me! I mean T'maho was,
not—" Closing her eyes, she plunged to her doom.
"What I mean to say is that T'maho and I were together

all night long. In my bed. So you see, he couldn't have
. . . well, he just couldn't, that's all."

The west wind whistled mournfully through the rig-
ging of the dozen or so fishing boats moored around the
harbor. In the distance, the mail boat came about on
her final tack before heading into the home channel.
No one noticed. Shivering, Annie wrapped her arms
around her body. She could not have felt more exposed
had she'd peeled off every layer she wore, right down to
her stays and her much-mended stockings.

Face averted from the awful sight of Snell's body, his
once fine suit of clothing now ruined, she told herself
her own reputation didn't matter a hill of beans compared to T'maho's life. No one here in Kinnakeet knew
her anyway. Papa was gone. Her fall from grace couldn't
reflect on him. And once she was gone, her ruination
would soon be forgotten.

As would she.

Five old men moved closer together. Heads down,
they spoke in an undertone. Now and then a grizzled
head nodded. Occasionally one shook from side to side.
The process dragged out until Annie felt like screaming. She had expected someone to hurry below and release the two prisoners.

Instead, they talked. And talked. And talked!

Saketa pushed through the crowd to greet her
friend Dulsie Scarborough, and the two of them put
their heads together, whispering. Once or twice
Saketa nodded, smiling as if she were the heroine of
the hour.

As indeed, Annie supposed, she was.

Annie stood stiffly at attention. Never in all her years at Mrs. Biddlecomb's academy-cum-orphanage for indigent girls had she felt so isolated. So totally alone.

Miserably aware of the speculation in the eyes of several of the village women, she fingered the tassels that had once graced the back parlor draperies and now edged the bodice of her gown, while the five old men launched into a fresh discussion, this one concerning whether or not the two women should be put on board along with the prisoners and sent across the sound so that the court could get to the bottom of the whole unhappy business.

"They're evidence, jes' like that there hatchet," said Izzer Clark.

"They ain't evidence, Izzer, they're womenfolk, and a man don't just ship a woman off thataway."

"Think they're a-tellin' the truth?"

"Truth! That young'un wouldn't know the truth if it was to rise up and bite 'er on the chin."

"O'Neal's girl?"

"No, not O'Neal's girl. That there Saketa! Told me once her pa was a king in one o' them foreign countries, and he was a-comin' to fetch her home to live in some kindly of a castle just as soon as she give out the word."

Numbly, Annie heard it all. There followed a rash of tales, all bearing witness to Saketa's vivid, if unreliable, imagination, yet a certain fond tolerance underlaid their gruff voices.

Annie waited for her fate to be decided, shivering

silently. She wanted to scream at them to stop yammering and let everyone go!

"Yonder comes the mail boat," cried one of the children who had grown bored with all the talk and gone off to skip shells across the water.

"Seems to me we got us a murder that nobody done," said one of the elders. "Way I see it, we might's well let ever'body go home."

Yes! Annie cried silently. *Just let us all go home and set the clock back to yesterday!*

"Still and all, the man was a genu-wine justice o' the peace. It don't seem right not to hold nobody responsible."

"On the other hand," chimed in another voice, "that hatchet could've just flew up an' knocked him dead on account o' him bein' such a miserable, puffed-up son of a bitch. Me, I've knowed stranger things to happen."

"You mean it's open season on sons o' bitches? I got me this son-in-law up to Chic'macomico that's—"

"Stow it, Lonzo. We all know 'bout yer son-in-law. Now, me, I vote we turn 'em all loose, sew Snell up in some of 'is own canvas, an' dump him overboard out to Diamond Shoals. If there's ever any question comes of it, we say we don't know who done it," said Jackariah Gray, calling the informal hearing back to order. "Which," he reminded them piously, "is naught but the God's honest truth."

The chorus of agreement was just about to progress to a show of hands when Etawak waddled up and gazed down at the body from a pair of enigmatic black eyes buried deep in a bed of wrinkles. The old woman sniffed disdainfully. Then, with a surprisingly graceful sweep of an arm strengthened by years of chopping yaupon, she retrieved the murder weapon.

"My hatchet," she grunted, wiping the blade on a filthy apron. "I put 'im there. I take 'im home now."

While the entire village looked on in stunned silence, the old woman waddled off without a backward glance.

Dead silence ensued. Then chaos broke out once more until Jackariah beat on a barrel with an oar for silence. "Now, then. Reckon we all know old Etawak is crazy," he said in stentorian tones.

There was a murmur of agreement.

"Truth is, a body can't believe a word she says."

Several heads nodded in confirmation.

"Any one o' you folk ever knowed one o' her foretellin's to turn out true?"

The response was decidedly negative. When all else failed, most had appealed to Etawak at one time or another. She claimed to be able to cure everything from falling hair to impotence, and hope was a powerful force.

"As for Snell, reck'n we all know the man was a cattle thief. Maybe worse." The ready murmur of agreement took Annie by surprise. "I suspicion he had more to do with Eli's passin' than he let on, but what's done is done. I heard tell folks over across the sound was gittin' right riled up over all them cattle stealin's, so the way I see it, Snell would've got hisself killed sooner or later. Happen it was sooner."

Heads leaned together. Lips moved rapidly. Annie felt as if she had tumbled headlong into a nightmare. Stolen cattle? Mr. Snell? *Papa?*

"Way I see it, whoever planted that hatchet in Snell's back done us all a favor. First thing ye know, Snell, he'd've got hisself into trouble and brung it out here with him, and we'd be overrun with lawyers thicker'n rabbits in Trent Hills."

In a daze, Annie heard the concluding arguments of the informal trial for the murder of Justice of the Peace Jackson Snell. The woman called Etawak was generally agreed to be crazy, but as far as anyone knew, she was harmless as long as one stayed away from her potions. She had never been known to do anyone an injury.

At least, not on purpose.

She had taken in Little Feet's young'uns when they needed a home.

And she was, after all, a woman. A Banker. One of their own.

Besides, she did make outstanding acorn beer.

Before the furor had completely died down, two skiffs had been moved so that the mail boat could tie up in the place set aside for its use. Little boys scurried around her, catching lines, making them fast as the main was hauled down to lie in stiff gray folds over the boom.

Her eyes caught by an emerald green bonnet, Annie turned to stare at a fashionably dressed figure standing at the rail, gazing out over the crowd. What on earth was such a woman doing here? Who was she searching for?

Numbed by all that had taken place over the last hour, Annie watched as the woman summoned a member of the crew. After a few brief words, she handed him a coin and he hurried down the hastily placed plank and approached the group of elders.

A brief conference took place. All eyes swung from the woman to the elders and back again, but Annie had lost interest in the mysterious passenger. She was still waiting, painfully embarrassed, for T'maho to be set free.

"Hamilton?" Jackariah's voice rang out clearly, catching her attention again. "You say she's askin' after a man named Hamilton? Well, blessed saints, if that don't tear the rag off the bush."

The young crewman handed a crumpled letter to the village spokesman, tugged the brim of his cap, and jogged back on board the mail boat just as the two prisoners were led up on the deck of the small, elegant black sloop.

Off to one side, Jackariah Gray squinted at the letter and then spoke quietly to the other men, but Annie had eyes for only one man. Catching a glimpse of him through the crowd—of his bare chest, his stiff shoulders, the proud carriage of his head—she wished the ground would open up and swallow her. Pride alone held her bolted to the spot.

Had he heard? Did he know what she had confessed to before the entire village? If he did, would he think she was trying to compromise him?

She simply couldn't face him. She had to get away.

Torn between escape and finding the captain of the mail boat and asking him to hold a place for her until she could retrieve her things and get back, she was edging through the crowd when she caught sight of T'maho again. He was staring at the woman in green.

Curious, Annie followed his gaze. She was certainly worthy of attention, being strikingly beautiful in a slightly faded way. Along with everyone else in the crowd, Annie watched curiously as T'maho and the woman continued to stare at one another. Despite his proud carriage, he looked wretched, his hair unbound, his expression grim.

Her heart ached. He looked as if he hadn't slept in a week, and she wondered if, after all, he even knew she was here.

Or cared.

"Benjamin," the strange woman cried softly, and through a freak of the wind, her voice carried to where Annie stood at the edge of the wharf. "Oh, Benjamin, you're all grown up. Oh, my dear, Jensen would be so proud. You have his eyes—I never noticed that."

Slowly, Annie turned away. She didn't know who Benjamin was. She had never heard of a Jensen, and she most definitely did not want to know what business T'maho had with the woman with the silvery gold hair, who was dressed in green, mink-trimmed velvet under a scoop-brimmed emerald bonnet that cast her pale beauty in shadow.

Whoever she was, she far outshone a ginger-haired

woman wearing a gray secondhand gown that had been refurbished using a section of faded drapery.

Annie told herself she hadn't expected to be thanked for what she had done.

Or perhaps she had. . . .

Still, she had only told the truth, even if that truth did condemn her as a fallen woman before the eyes of the entire village.

Had T'maho seen her? Had he heard her? If so, would he think she was waiting to claim a reward for telling the truth?

Ironically, as it turned out, she might as well not even have spoken, for after the old Indian woman had reclaimed her hatchet, the two men would have been freed anyway.

Never again would she be able to face him, Annie told herself. Not after today. Fortunately, she would not need to.

Firmly holding back the tears that threatened to rise to the surface, Annie waited near the edge of the crowd for a chance to bespeak herself a place on the mail boat.

At this rate, it might be better to hurry off and fetch her belongings and try to get back before the boat sailed.

Oh, she couldn't think. She couldn't even see! The smell of smoking fish and tar vats was making her eyes water. . . .

Making up her mind suddenly, she turned and hurried to where she'd left the mule tied to a hitching post. Jacob, as if sensing her mood, allowed her to clamber up onto his back, offering no help, but no hindrance, either.

All in all, Annie decided, it had been the worst day of her entire life. She seemed to remember having had several of those lately, but today was the very worst of all. She had compromised herself beyond redemption to save the man she loved and then watched as that same man ignored her and turned to another woman. She had narrowly escaped being taken away as a witness in a murder case, only to discover that she was implicated, at least by association, in yet another crime. The cattle her father had promised would someday make them wealthy beyond all imagining had been stolen.

They would have to be returned. But how? To whom? And by whom? Annie hadn't the least notion of how to go about giving back stolen cows. She had hoped to sell her father's half of the herd for enough to see her established in her own business.

Jacob, from force of habit, began to plod toward the glade trail, and Annie let him go, even clucked at him in an effort to move him along a bit faster. She would have to hurry if she wanted to be back in time to board the mail boat before it sailed.

Everything else would simply have to wait until she had settled somewhere and had time to think things through.

At least there was a bright side. Swallowing the painful lump that had formed in her throat, she reminded herself that she no longer had to worry about her house being washed out to sea with the next tide. Let it go, with her blessing!

She would no longer have to worry about having to deal with wigglers in the rain barrel, or a flock of ornery cows that kicked would-be rescuers and stole the wash from her clothesline and scratched their assorted itches on the corner of her house, rattling the cups on the shelf.

She no longer had to wear holes in her heart wondering if T'maho was ever coming back. He obviously had better things to do with his time now.

So be it. The only thing she needed was for the mail boat to stay in place just long enough for her to collect her belongings and get back to the harbor. By then, she sincerely hoped, T'maho and his woman would have left so that she could board with some vestige of dignity.

Back at the harbor, T'maho had searched the crowd eagerly. He'd been released, found innocent of the charges against him. There had been no attempt to pretend that the informal hearing would have passed muster in any court of law in the land, but neither had there been any attempt to hold him.

Or Etawak, thank God. The old woman would never have survived captivity. He had hoped against hope that no one would remember that he'd given her his old hatchet, but in the end, it hadn't mattered.

One after another, the elders had nodded to the two men as they'd been led out of captivity. Mingo had nodded back. T'maho had been too busy scanning the crowd, looking for a certain head of ginger-colored hair.

Oblivious to the talk all around him, he had searched. Annie was small. Unless she stood on something, he would not be able to see her above the heads of the crowd. But, God, he needed to see her, to touch her. To hold her! Knowing her pride, he still could not quite believe that she had sacrificed her good name for him.

"I won't be needin' all my decoys this season, T'maho. If you want to set a few out in that there cove behind your place, you're welcome to help yourself," one man had said. It served as both apology and exoneration.

"Obliged," he'd replied absently, still searching for one particular figure.

Izzer's wife stepped forward, hands clasped underneath her voluminous apron. "I stewed up a big mess o' drum yestiddy. You're more'n welcome to come go home with us for supper. Mingo, you and Saketa come, too."

Grinning, Mingo politely declined. He'd just caught sight of his quarry. "Much obliged, Miz Parthenia, but I think Saketa made turtle stew." The gleam in his eye had little to do with food, however, and the old woman smiled and gazed after him as he hurried off toward the bent oak where Saketa was waiting.

Snell's body had been wrapped and laid out aboard the *Black Opal,* with one man left to stand guard as a measure of respect for his office, if not for the man himself. It had been decided that he would be buried at sea, and his sloop anchored at the place where his cattle were usually barged ashore, and left there for the time being.

Ignoring the woman who had called out to him—or rather to someone named Benjamin—T'maho made his way quickly through the crowd. He couldn't find Annie! He knew she was here! He wanted to ask after her, yet he hesitated. Not that anything he said now could possibly make a difference, for she had told the entire community that they'd been together all night, knowing full well what that implied. To a woman like Annie, reputation was everything, and she had traded her reputation for his life.

The meaning of such a gesture was only now sinking in.

"Benjamin . . . please?"

Reluctantly, T'maho turned his attention from his search for Annie to the woman standing at the rail of the battered old schooner that hauled mail and freight out to the Banks. Something inside him seemed to shrink as he heard in his mind that same woman's voice saying, "—*don't care, Jensen, I could never forget—filthy, heathen devils murdered my whole family—love you dearly, but either he goes or I go.*"

And he had gone. The filthy heathen devil had gone back where he belonged, and the woman had stayed on in the house on River Street.

"Benjamin?" she said now, her voice thin and unsteady. While T'maho stood there, painfully reliving the past, she came forward to greet him.

"Madam."

"I don't suppose you ever thought to see me again," she said hesitantly, pausing several feet from where he stood.

T'maho remained silent. Twisting her gloved hands, the woman glanced quickly at his eyes and then away again. She was old, he thought in amazement. Somehow, he had always thought of her as young, but she had not been young even then. Now she was an old woman, beautiful still in a pallid way, but her face was covered with fine lines and the hair that had once been bright gold was now well laced with silver.

"I know you've never forgiven me, Benjamin. . . . What I did was unforgivable, but I was so afraid of being alone. I don't suppose you can understand, but I needed your father so desperately."

Needed him so desperately that you could not even share him with a child? he wanted to ask, but didn't. It would serve no purpose after all these years.

"Won't you even speak to me, Benjamin?"

"I am called Tatamaho."

She smiled then, but it was a rather sad smile. "Your father told me you had given yourself some heath— some Indian name. He couldn't recall what it was, though."

They were standing on the wharf beside the mail boat. As the mail was called off and the freight set out, the crowd gradually drifted away, but not without curious looks toward the tall young half-breed and the elegantly dressed woman.

"Why have you come? Is my father dead? Do you wish something from me?"

She flinched as if he'd struck her, making T'maho feel like a cowardly dog. It was not in him to be deliberately cruel to any woman, even one he despised.

"Jensen is alive, but he's very ill. Will you hear what I have to say? For your father's sake, if not mine?"

Chapter 18

For perhaps the first time in her life, Saketa felt shy. She slapped her pony on the rump, sending him trotting toward Mingo's compound, and ran along behind him.

Were they all still whispering about her? Soon everyone in the village would know about her and Jack Snell.

Mingo already knew. He had said nothing, but she had seen the hurt in his eyes. Could he ever forgive her? That first night he had found her, after he'd taken her home with him, he had held her and comforted her, and when she'd cried, he had rocked her in his arms and said words she hadn't understood, but had liked hearing all the same.

When T'maho used the old language, he was usually swearing; Saketa wanted to believe Mingo had been saying something altogether different. But that had been before Mingo knew who her lover had been.

Perhaps he'd only felt sorry for her. A week ago—even yesterday—pity would have been enough. She would have thought of the best way to turn such feelings to her own advantage and used them, as she had always used them—teasing, flirting, playing at being angry when it suited her purposes.

But now she knew that was no longer enough. Sympathy wasn't what she wanted, not from Mingo. Nor even teasing. Her footsteps slowed. She sensed he was right behind her, but she didn't want him to see her looking back. Swishing her skirts, she picked up her pace again.

So did he. She was sure of it. She slowed, and he slowed, too. She knew it just as clearly as if she had eyes in the back of her head. When she could no longer stand the waiting, she whirled, shaking her finger scoldingly, all set to chastise him.

Only there was no one there.

"Mingo?" she called uncertainly. Her eyebrows lowered. "Mingo! You come out from behind that tree, I know you're there!"

Nothing. No teasing word, no taunting laughter. No Mingo.

Saketa's heart fell. Her lower lip quivered, and she covered it with her fingers to hold it steady. And there wasn't even anyone around to appreciate her distress.

Morosely, she turned and continued on her way, wondering if her enormous lie had given Mingo such a disgust of her that he had finally stopped loving her. Knowing that if he had, which was no more than she deserved, then she would never again be happy even if she lived to be an ancient old woman, as old even as Etawak.

Outside Mingo's neat, rush-roofed cypress house,

she paused, unsure of whether to go inside or to go back to Etawak's. Now that the danger had passed, there was no reason for her to stay with Mingo any longer.

She didn't want to go back to Etawak's lodge. It smelled bad. Oh, it was clean enough, for she saw to that herself, but all those musty old crocks and bundles of dried weeds that Etawak kept on hand for making her potions stunk to high heaven.

Mingo's house smelled clean, like smoke and lye soap and food, which was the way a house should smell. It was a good house, not all cramped and airless, like some. He had built his house and he had laid out the garden and built the horse pen, and a pound for his laying geese. Together, he and T'maho had built the boat they used to fish their small nets. Next, they planned on building a warehouse where they could store the fish they caught from T'maho's big boat after they were smoked or salted, until T'maho could take them across the sound to trade for coffee and sugar and cloth and tools and such.

Mingo could do anything, and do it better than most men. He had the kindest, most generous heart in the whole world, and she had laughed at him and taken his love as her due, offering him nothing at all in return.

What if he had finally grown tired of her? What if he brought some other woman into his house to cook his food and mend his clothes and sleep in his bed?

With one last glance over her shoulder, Saketa pushed the door open, her eyes dimmed by tears of self-pity and something more—something strangely unsettling. For perhaps the first time in her nearly sixteen years, she sensed that what was at stake was more important than anything that had ever happened to her. Including Jack and the loss of her baby, and the beating that had been meant to put an end to her life.

And then she yelped. "Mingo! You startled me!"

He had evidently cut through the woods, and now here he stood, arms crossed over his massive chest, looking familiar and dear and forbidding all at the same time. "I have packed your belongings. It is time for you to go back to Etawak's lodge."

Her face crumpled, but she refused to look away. If he read what she was feeling in her eyes and laughed at her, then it was no more than she deserved. "You want me to go?" she whispered.

He waited so long to reply, she was afraid he hadn't heard her.

And then she was afraid he had.

Something hot and powerful blazed in his eyes and was immediately damped down. "Do you wish to go?"

Wordlessly, she shook her head.

"Then stay."

She waited. It was not enough. "Why?" she whispered, not quite meeting his eyes.

"Why? Why did you lie about sleeping with me?"

At that, her head lifted proudly. "I did not lie! Well . . . not exactly. I did sleep in your bed. I like sleeping in your bed. Why shouldn't I say as much?"

"Perhaps I am tired of sleeping on the floor."

She shrugged, busying her fingers with the tassels

that hung from her braided leather sash. "The bed is big enough for two. Sleep where you wish."

Again, heat flared in Mingo's eyes. This time it was not damped down. "And if I wish to sleep with you?"

Having thoroughly tangled the fringe, Saketa's fingers began nervously to pleat the fabric of her skirt. "Do what you want to do, I don't care."

Mingo took a deep, steadying breath, hardly daring to trust what he was hearing. "I want only what will make you happy, little sparrow. You have always known that."

Hope lit Saketa's face, like the first warmth of the morning sun. She waited.

Mingo waited.

Saketa knew that it was up to her to make the first move. An honorable man, Mingo would never hold her to what she had said on the docks. It was not in him to hold any woman against her will.

Saketa did not intend to make the same mistake twice. She might not get another chance.

Suddenly she hurled herself into his arms and cried, "You! You make me happy!" She buried her radiant, tear-drenched face against his crumpled shirt. "Please don't send me away, Mingo. Don't ever, *ever* send me away!" Weeping, laughing, she clung to him and began kissing all she could reach of him, starting with his scars, moving on to his mouth.

A long time later, Saketa sighed in satisfaction and began all over again as Mingo, lying beside her, lay limp with blissful exhaustion. Turning to gather her into his arms, he winged a silent prayer to Ahone, plus any newer gods who might happen to be listening in. Wordlessly, he expressed his gratitude and pleaded for strength and patience to bear up under this wonderful new blessing they had finally deigned to bestow upon him.

It seemed to Annie as if hours had passed since she had ridden away from the scene of her disgrace, yet the sun was just now settling down onto the water. When she'd left, the captain had been calling off the mail, his voice ringing out over the noisy crowd that still lingered at the dock as if unwilling to have such an exciting day come to an end.

The captain had called out a letter for Germainy Hooper from her sister in Newport News, and then waited for a woman to come forth and claim the missive. Next came a parcel from a jobber in Elizabeth City for Captain I. W. Casey. Captain Casey, it seemed, had already left, and someone was sent to bring him back.

With any luck at all, Annie told herself, everyone in the village would get at least one letter today, and she'd have time enough to collect her things and get back before the mail boat set sail again.

"Move along, Jacob! For mercy's sake, don't dawdle so!"

As she neared the house, she eyed the assorted parcels she'd left on the stump, wondering how she was going to balance the bulky valise. She had crammed in a single change of clothing, her hairbrush, and her night shift, and that would have to do until she could send for her trunk.

As her gaze strayed to the tiny shack, perched up like a six-legged wading bird, she felt the strangest urge to shoo Jacob into the shed and stay a little while longer. She had left it shuttered and closed up against the weather, and it looked so forlorn that for a single moment, she felt like a traitor for leaving it behind. One could do worse than settle here on the Outer Banks.

But then, that would be impossible now. "Good-bye, Papa," she whispered. "I'm sorry we never got around to doing all the lovely things we'd planned to do."

That *Annie* had planned. She rather doubted that Eli had planned much at all that had to do with his daughter. He hadn't even bothered to read her letters, not after the first few, written when she'd scarcely been able to print out the alphabet. Postage was dear, and Mrs. B. had allowed them only two letters a year.

She sniffed and felt in her sleeve for a handkerchief before remembering that it was in her reticule. Taking advantage of her momentary distraction, Jacob plodded on toward the shed.

"Whoa! Back up!" She sawed at the reins, and he ignored her, his mouth being considerably tougher than her hands. Jiggling her bottom, she tried to urge him back to the stump so that she could lean down, scoop up her things, and be on her way, but Jacob had other ideas.

"Stubborn creature, you've already had your breakfast! It's not time yet for supper!"

Annie was clutching her hat to keep it from being scraped off by the low shed roof when she caught sight of a rider approaching from the south, followed by half a dozen riderless horses. Even against the glare of the late afternoon sun, she recognized the rider. There couldn't possibly be two people in the world who sat a horse with quite the same arrogant grace.

But why was T'maho leading a string of horses?

Unless they'd been stolen, and he thought that just because she kept a herd of stolen cattle, she might agree to keep them for him.

But no. Not T'maho.

Torn between a fierce desire to run and meet him and an equally fierce desire to run and hide, Annie slid off the mule's back, clutching the reins as she waited. Had he come to tell her about the woman in green? Or to thank her for what she had done?

Jacob tossed his head, the reins fell from her fingers, and still she stared, unable to take her eyes away from the magnificent man who was so much a part of this wild, beautiful place. His hair, still unbraided, blew like a curtain of black silk in the stiff offshore breeze.

Not a word was spoken. Annie's mouth was dry as a fresh-picked cotton boll as she watched him dismount and walk toward her, leading the magnificent horses. There was something different about him, but she couldn't think what it was—couldn't seem to think at all.

The tension was broken momentarily when Jacob and the biggest horse took a disliking to one another.

Jacob brayed. The horse, a black that gleamed red in the sunlight, pawed the earth and rolled his eyes.

T'maho turned and said something to the restless horse, and as if it had been charmed, the animal settled down, sweet as molasses candy.

Annie, her heart fluttering so fast it took her breath away, followed the small drama, wondering why he seemed so different.

And then it came to her. T'maho was wearing a shirt! Of fine linsey-woolsey in a muted shade of blue, it fit snug across his shoulders, as if he had done some growing since the shirt had been cut and stitched. The high collar was unbuttoned, the full sleeves turned back over his muscular forearms, his skin gleaming warmly in contrast.

It was the first time she had ever seen him fully dressed. He was beautiful! The color of the shirt made his eyes seem more blue than gray, and she thought, not for the first time, that she had never seen eyes so lovely.

But it wasn't the shirt that made him beautiful. To her shame, she admitted that he'd been every bit as beautiful wearing nothing at all.

Annie's face flamed, but pride would not allow her to look away. "Did you leave something here?" she asked. "I've closed the house, as you can see, but please feel free to go inside."

Ignoring her remarks, he stepped forward and held out the leads to the string of horses. He didn't smile. He didn't speak. Shirt or not, he had never looked more the haughty savage. Annie, every shard of her broken heart aching, stared back at him and at the six horses—five mares and a stallion. She tucked her hands behind her. If he thought she was going to take on another burden at this point in her life, he had radishes for brains!

"I don't need any horses, but thank you all the same."

Stepping back, T'maho dropped the leads and crossed his arms over his chest, threatening the shoulder seams of his shirt. The horses began grazing on the stubby, salt-burned beach grass. It occurred to Annie that if this was his way of repaying her for saving his life, she'd just as soon go unrewarded.

Not that she had actually saved it. In the end, her ruinous gesture had been unnecessary. He would have been set free in any case.

"T'maho, I assure you that I neither need nor want your thanks. I did only what any other person would have done, under the circumstances. I simply told the truth." She dropped her gaze, afraid if she looked at him one moment longer, she might lose all sense of dignity and throw herself into his arms. "Of course, at the time I had no way of knowing my testimony wouldn't be necessary."

His eyes flashed in the fast-fading light. Had she thought them more blue than gray? They were the color of a January sky just before the snow began to fall.

Annie shivered. She had probably already missed the boat, and now she would have to wait until the next one, which could take a week—maybe even longer.

She would die of shame long before that. "Please," she said in a voice held steady by dint of sheer will. "I can't keep your horses, you know I can't." Why was he so anxious to pay his debt, if that was what he was doing? So that he could go back to the woman in the green bonnet at the waterfront with a clear conscience?

Another thought, one that was even more painful, struck her then. Perhaps the horses were not meant as a payment for speaking up in his defense, but for . . . other services?

"You may as well take them and go. You owe me nothing, T'maho."

"It is the way of my people," he said. "My mother's people."

What a fool he had been, T'maho thought, believing he could remain true to his heritage by ignoring so large a part of himself. He was beginning to understand how a man could so love a woman that he lost sight of everything else. Jensen Hamilton had lost a son because he'd been obsessed by a woman.

His son had nearly lost the woman who meant more to him than anything else in the world because he'd been obsessed by his mixed heritage.

Soon he must go and make peace with his father. He had promised the woman, Bridget. It was time. Bitterness held too long ate into a man's belly like a rat chewing through a grain bin.

Jensen Hamilton was slowly dying, the woman had said. The greatest wish of his heart was to see his son once again. According to the woman, his father had grown old and sad, mourning the son he had lost. Now he was bedridden, unable to make the journey himself.

T'maho remembered his father's fine house—remembered the vast fields of corn, cotton, and to-bacco. Now the land lay fallow and neglected. According to the woman, Bridget, Jensen had always been more interested in books than in farming, and he was too ill to see that his overseer was a drunken fool who cheated him openly. Jensen needed his son, and his wife had come to ask forgiveness for them both.

So he would go, T'maho resolved. He knew little about crops, but he did know men. And he had come to know something of business.

But first he must speak his heart in a way that honored both parts of his heritage. In a way Annie could understand. He could not allow the same stiff-necked pride that had kept a son and father apart all these years to separate him from this woman.

She was watching him steadily, giving away nothing of her feelings. T'maho cleared his throat. He wished now he had taken the time to braid his hair. "Annie, I—that is, would you—"

He cleared his throat again, telling himself that in Annie's world, which was his father's world, he would first have settled the arrangements with old Eli and then gone before her on bended knee to speak pretty words.

But Eli was dead. By Snell's hand, or at least under Snell's direction, according to the letter from an officer of law in New Bern, that had come on the same boat that had brought his father's woman.

And now Annie needed him more than ever. He could not allow her to refuse him, for her good as well as his own. And if that meant bending his knee and saying pretty words, why, then he would do that.

Bracing himself, he flung his arms wide, causing his shirttail to slip free of his tight-fitting buckskins.

Annie, her eyes widening, her breath caught somewhere between the lump in her throat and the butterflies in her belly, marveled at how very handsome he was, in a way that was uniquely his own. A way that was essentially wild and free and wonderful.

"Among my mother's people," T'maho said, his voice deep and thrilling, "when a man wants a woman, he offers her cattle or horses. I want you. You refuse my horses? I will send them away." Clapping his hands, he sent the herd galloping across the sands. "Among my father's people, these things are done another way. You want pretty words? I will give you pretty words."

With a laugh that sounded suspiciously like a sob, Annie said, "You'll give me *what*?"

"Words. Pretty words and bent knees." Lifting one long, muscular limb, he flexed it at the knee and then lowered it again, bracing his moccasined feet apart. His face split in a broad grin.

"What on earth do you think you're—"

"Bent knee. Now the pretty words. Eldorado? The eldorado is a most beautiful fish that few men have ever seen, for he swims only in the deep water offshore. Honeysuckle? Smells sweet. What about sugarcane? And currants? Not pretty, but sweet. *Che-a-wanta*, which is the robin. Pretty. And the parakeet." He did not know his people's word for "parakeet." So many words had been lost over time, replaced by others more commonly known.

But then, words were meant to communicate. Perhaps, after all, it was best to use those words that were understood by all.

Slowly, Annie sat down on the stump, her green eyes glistening with amazement. *This* was the stern man who had once rationed his words as if they were grains of corn in a famine? This, the man who had scared her out of her wits on more than one occasion?

"Tell me, T'maho, what am I supposed to do with all these pretty words of yours?" she asked, a smile quivering on her lips in spite of her best effort to suppress it.

He sobered then. Stepping closer, he reached for her hand, and after only the briefest hesitation, she let him take it. "Take them into your heart," he said quietly. "Accept my words if you cannot accept my horses. They have the same meaning. They say that my days are dark without you, and that my heart weeps when you turn away. They say that my body aches for yours. They say that I want you to live in my lodge, to share my fire, my table, my bed. To bear my children and my name."

"Oh, T'maho," she whispered.

"My name is Benjamin," he corrected gently. Gathering her into his arms, he lifted her off the stump and walked with her across the barren stretch of land that led to the low dunes. There, gazing out at the ocean, which was still sullen from the recent storm, he said gravely, "I give you my sea, that belonged to all the people who lived before me. It is yours now, as well."

Turning back toward the calm waters of the Pamlico, he said, "I give you my fishing grounds. Those, too, are now yours."

Pointing overhead, to where the first few stars of the evening were beginning to twinkle, he said, "My heavens. My sky. They are yours now. My nets. My house. My boats. All I have is yours, Annie. All the love I have inside me—it is yours, if only you will accept it."

Annie wriggled free of his arms and stepped back. With a dignity that would have made Mrs. Biddlecomb proud, she said gravely, "I accept. I have nothing of value to give you, but my heart is yours. My world will always be your world, T'maho, for it's wherever you are."

A fire was lit in his eyes and echoed in her heart. "Benjamin," he whispered against her lips.

"Benjamin," she repeated dutifully.

But even as he claimed her mouth, Annie knew that in her heart, he would always be T'maho.